A TALENT for
TRICKERY

ALISSA JOHNSON

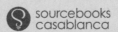

sourcebooks
casablanca

Published by Sourcebooks Casablanca, an imprint of Sourcebooks, Inc.
P.O. Box 4410, Naperville, Illinois 60567-4410
(630) 961-3900
Fax: (630) 961-2168
www.sourcebooks.com

Printed and bound in Canada
MBP 10 9 8 7 6 5 4 3 2 1

For Amelia, Henry, Jack, and Julia

One

1872

Owen Renderwell, the first Viscount Renderwell, marched up the front steps of Willowbend House with the determined stride of a man who was less enthusiastic about reaching his destination than he was reliant upon the power of momentum to see him there.

He stopped short of reaching for the knocker.

Behind him, Sir Samuel Brass shifted his mountainous frame and scratched thoughtfully at his full beard. "Reconsidering, are you?"

"No."

Brushing at the sleeves of his fashionable coat, Sir Gabriel Arkwright's equally fashionable face lit with a mocking grin. "I believe our fearless leader is now contemplating the fact that this is our last chance to turn back."

"It's too late to turn back," Samuel pointed out. "We're already here."

"We are not turning back."

"One can turn back after arrival," Gabriel countered. "It's called retreat."

"We are *not* turning back."

Owen didn't want to turn back. That was, perhaps, the most disconcerting aspect of his current predicament. A good part of him wanted to be here, in Norfolk, on the steps of this very country house. That part of him had, in fact, wanted to make the trip years ago and was as eager to knock on the door as the rest of him was reluctant.

It was an uncomfortable thing to simultaneously wish to press forward and step back, and Owen recognized his incongruent feelings as the same he'd experienced at age nine, when his sister Eliza had convinced him it would be great fun to hurl a stone at a wasp's nest. It was the delicious thrill that came from succumbing to the allure of a *very bad idea*.

Resolute, he grasped the knocker and brought it down for three quick raps. Then he stood back and waited to regret his decision.

A silver-haired woman with light eyes clouded by age opened the door. She looked between them with open suspicion. "Yes?"

"Lord Renderwell to see—"

"Oh." Instantly, her demeanor changed. She stepped back, allowing them entrance, and waved a maid forward to take their hats and coats. "Welcome, my lord. Welcome to Willowbend. You honor us."

It still amazed him how efficiently his title removed obstacles from his path. It had been a revelation when he'd inherited the barony at sixteen and had only become more pronounced since he'd received the viscountcy.

As a child, he'd known few advantages of being the son of a baron. His family of nine had resided in what was laughably referred to as genteel poverty, which was, as far as he'd been able to tell, really no different than your common variety poverty. One could not fill an empty belly with an obscure title.

But a smart man could use it to open doors like this one.

The housekeeper showed them into a small but well-appointed parlor, and for a few disorienting seconds, it seemed to Owen as if he had stepped into the past. He'd never been in this house, never seen it. But he knew this room. How many times had he walked across that counterfeit Axminster carpet, or lit one of the brass lamps, or smirked at the large, imposing oil portrait of William Walker hanging over the fireplace? How many times had he sat on the pale blue sofa or in one of the matching wing chairs?

"Someone has taken up sketching," Gabriel announced.

Owen turned to see him pick up a sketchbook from a monstrously oversized escritoire (featuring a large number of carved animal heads) that was shoved awkwardly into a far corner.

"Quite good, really," Gabriel said, and he held up a skilled rendering of a rearing horse.

And just like that, the illusion was broken. Owen couldn't say with any degree of certainty if one of the younger Walker children had been artistically inclined eight years ago. But he knew with absolute certainty that he had never seen that hideous desk.

"Miss Esther Bales is quite accomplished," the housekeeper said with pride. "Fond of horses, that one. Doesn't miss a single detail." Then she took a second look at the sketch and paled. Because it wasn't just a horse. It was a stallion. In all his intact glory. And Esther had, indeed, not missed a single detail.

With a speed that was nothing short of miraculous, she darted across the room and nipped the sketch out of Gabriel's hands. "That is… I do believe this is Mr. Bales's effort. I'll just…I'll see he finds it, shall I? And fetch Miss Bales. I shall fetch Miss Bales directly." She headed for the door, paused, and turned round again, this time with a small blush. "It is Miss Bales you wish to see, is it not? Miss Charlotte Bales?"

"It is," Owen confirmed. "Thank you, Mrs…"

"Oh. Lewis, my lord. I do beg your pardon. Mrs. Lewis."

"Thank you, Mrs. Lewis."

Owen waited for the housekeeper to curtsy and hurry out of the room. "Is distressing elderly women a new vice of yours?" he asked Gabriel. "Or one I've merely overlooked?"

Gabriel lacked the shame to hide his smile. "It wasn't intentional. I didn't notice the details; I was taken with the picture as a whole." He walked past the settee to inspect a door to an adjoining parlor. "Charlotte won't agree to see us, you know. We'll have to fetch her out."

"Perhaps." Owen hoped not. He couldn't imagine this going well, exactly, but with any luck, it wouldn't go so badly as to require brute force.

"She refused to see you the last time," Samuel reminded him.

"That was a long time ago."

"Think she's changed?" There was an unmistakable wisp of hopefulness in Gabriel's voice. He headed to the row of windows along the front wall and closed the two left cracked open. "Do you suppose any of the Walkers have changed?"

"It's Bales now, and I don't know."

"Peter will have," Samuel pointed out, unnecessarily. Peter had been no more than six when last they'd seen him.

Gabriel shook his head. "I still say he's the one we should be asking—"

"No." They'd agreed to keep the youngest Bales-formerly-Walker removed from the situation until they knew how informed the boy was of his family's past. Or rather, Owen had ordered his men to keep their mouths shut around the lad, and his men would obey.

"Please see we are not disturbed, Mrs. Lewis," a familiar voice sounded from the foyer.

Owen barely had time to register the pleasant tingle up the back of his neck before the parlor door opened and Charlotte strode into the room, exactly as she had the first time they'd met—with the grace, confidence, and bold defiance of a monarch whose claim to the throne came by virtue of having personally pried its original occupant off with a sword.

If pirates had a queen, he mused, she would enter a room like Miss Charlotte Walker-Bales.

Owen resisted the urge to shift his weight. Seeing her again felt like an unexpected shove. The sort one had a masculine obligation to pretend not to notice.

No easy task, that. Not when everything about her was just as he remembered—keen dark eyes in a heart-shaped face, thick black hair done up in a loose topknot.

She'd adopted the current fashion of narrow skirts and bustle, he noted, but he saw none of the flounces and frippery that were all the rage in London. No ruffled underskirts for Charlotte. No fringe or bows or buckles, nor dizzying, contrasting patterns that made a man's eyes cross. Just a simple gray gown with a small train and a single red ribbon woven through the top edge of a square-cut bodice. Elegant, severe, and alluring, all at once.

And there was that stubborn jaw and the mouth that turned up ever so slightly at the corners, lending the impression of a woman in possession of a wicked secret. Quite possibly *your* wicked secret.

There had been a time when he'd been captivated by that secretive mouth and spent more hours than he cared to admit looking for ways to turn that promise of a smile into the sparkling laugh he knew was hiding just beneath the surface. He couldn't imagine trying, let alone succeeding, in such an endeavor today. And so he kept his own voice polite but detached as he greeted her.

"Miss Bales."

The three men bowed in unison. In return she said, "Well," and looked at each of them separately. "You're still alive, I see."

"And you're still angry," he replied.

"How very observant of you. Eight years and not a thing has changed," she drawled. "I vow, I feel a young woman of two-and-twenty again."

Things *had* changed. Drastically, in his mind. They'd been friends once. But her father's death had shattered her world, and for that, it seemed she would never forgive him.

He wanted to tell her that it wasn't his fault, that Will Walker had brought about his own demise and they both knew it. Frankly, it was a miracle the old criminal had ever made it past thirty. But she appeared no more inclined to admit the truth today than she had all those years ago. The last time she'd agreed to see him was the day he'd brought the news of Will's murder. The next six or seven times he'd called on her, he'd been turned away at the front door, and the letters he'd written in the following weeks and months had been returned to him unopened.

In the face of her continued refusal to have anything to do with him, Owen had set aside his desire to make things right between them. He had tried to forget her and, for long stretches of time, he had failed.

"It is good to see you again, Charlotte."

"Is it?" She tossed the pen she'd been holding onto a small side table, where it clattered softly against the varnished wood. "What are you doing here? I presume this is not a social call?"

"No, I'm afraid not."

She walked around the sofa and took a seat without suggesting they do the same and without taking her eyes off him, even when she said, "Stop sniffing about like a blind hound, Mr. Arkwright. There are no eavesdroppers on my staff."

No, there wouldn't be—not in the Walker-Bales household.

Gabriel straightened from where he'd been leaning an ear against the door to the foyer. Scowling, he returned to his original position next to the window. "One can never be too careful."

"No, one cannot," she agreed. "It is the mark of a fool to trust overmuch."

Ignoring the implied barb, Owen stepped closer. "We've come because we need your help."

One finely arched brow lifted slightly. "You must be joking."

"To be more precise, we need your father's help."

"My father's?" She let out a small puff of breath that may have been a laugh. "At the risk of repeating myself… You *must* be joking."

"He kept journals. Detailed notes on specific encryptions employed by the various smugglers and gangs in and around London. Some of which he created himself."

"Yes, I know."

"Because you encrypted or deciphered a few of them for him." He wasn't sure why he was stating what everyone in the room already knew, except that it lent a businesslike—and therefore familiar and comfortable—air to an otherwise agonizing scene.

"And for you," she reminded him.

"Later, yes," he agreed. "Do you recognize this?" He pulled a letter from his pocket, unfolded it, and handed it to her.

She studied the long lines of letters and numbers. "No."

Damn it. He was certain the encryption was similar to work Will Walker had done in the past. "Pity. Nonetheless—" When he reached for the letter, she pulled her hand away and continued her inspection.

Interesting.

Gabriel stepped forward from the windows. "Certain you don't know it?"

She looked up. "Yes."

"Why should we believe you?"

"Still the thickest of the three, aren't you?" She glanced at Owen. "Why ever have you kept him around so long?"

Owen shrugged lightly. "He's a good shot."

"There is something in that, I suppose." She turned her focus back to Gabriel. "I cannot refuse to share that which I do not possess, Mr. Arkwright. And I would rather the pleasure of informing you I *will not* help than admit to the fact I *cannot* help. Yes?"

Rather than reply directly, Gabriel sent a smirk to Samuel. "This one hasn't changed."

Neither had Gabriel, Owen thought. He had always enjoyed needling the Walker sisters.

Owen took hold of the letter and slipped it free from Charlotte's fingers. He didn't want her needled right now—he wanted her cooperative. "She doesn't know it." Clearly, it had intrigued her, but that was another matter. "Do you still have your father's journals?"

"Perhaps. Somewhere." One shoulder hitched up. "What does it matter? He gave you every cipher on which he worked. Your men had access to everything."

Doubtful, he thought. *Highly* doubtful. "We hope there might have been something we overlooked. Perhaps a codebook or cipher he'd forgotten—"

"You mean something he kept hidden from you," she translated.

"It makes little difference to me, either way."

"He gave you everything we had," she said coolly. "Just as he promised."

Had the situation not been quite so tense, Owen might have laughed at that nonsense. Will Walker had not been a man to keep his promises, nor give away all his secrets. "We should like a look at them, all the same."

"Would you?" She leaned back against the sofa cushions. "Dead these eight years and still you want my father to do your job for you."

Samuel stepped forward, breaking his silence. "We're offering more than equitable pay for the journals—"

"I don't need your money, Mr. Brass." She held up a hand. "I do beg your pardon. It's Sir Samuel now, isn't it? And Sir Gabriel?"

"May we *see* the journals?" Owen asked, before the conversation could veer into his men's elevation to knighthood and the painful circumstances surrounding it.

For the first time since she'd walked into the room, Charlotte's lips curved into a true smile. "You haven't my father's chance in heaven, but do give him my love on your way to hell."

Owen folded the letter and tucked it away. "A woman has been murdered."

The smile disappeared and she stared at him a moment before looking to Samuel. "Is this true?"

Samuel nodded. "A Mrs. Popple."

Charlotte went very still. "Maggie Popple? The madam?"

"Yes."

Owen resisted the foolish urge to step forward

and take her hand. She didn't want his comfort. Nonetheless, he said, "I'm sorry."

She blinked and lifted her shoulder again. "She was my father's acquaintance. I scarcely knew her." She looked to Samuel once more. "The murderer sent the letter to you?"

For some reason, Owen found himself irritated that she would turn to Samuel now. "He left it with her," he answered and waited for Charlotte to face him again. "And three more just like it at the sites of burglaries in and around Belgravia."

"And how is it they came to be in your possession? It was my understanding you left the police. Private investigators now, aren't you? For the wealthy and well connected? How modern."

"You've kept informed," Gabriel said with a small smile.

"One does hear things."

"A former colleague requested our assistance," Owen told her. "Inspector Jeffries. Do you recall him?"

"Vaguely," she replied. "He gave you the letters?"

"They're copies. Tidier than the originals. But identical in every other way," he was quick to add. "Down to the length, width, and slant of every letter."

"Hmm. And does Inspector Jeffries know you've brought them here?"

"No." As far as most of Scotland Yard was concerned, the Walker children had emigrated to Boston immediately following the death of their father. Only Owen, his men, and the Crown knew the truth.

"I see." She stayed quiet for a while, drumming three fingers against the arm of the sofa in a pattern utterly familiar to Owen. The index finger twice, then the middle finger once, then the ring finger twice, and back to the middle finger for one tap, then the index finger twice again, and so on. He couldn't say why it pleased him to see she retained that odd little quirk.

"You may see the journals," she announced and stopped drumming.

Owen nodded, not particularly surprised by her decision. There had never been a question of whether or not she'd hand over her father's notes once she learned of the murder. The question had been—and continued to be—how painful would she make the process?

She rose from her seat and brushed a hand down the front of her gown. "Most of my father's belongings are stored away. It will take some time to find—"

"Time is of the essence," Gabriel cut in.

She gave him a withering glance. "You don't say."

"We can help," Owen offered.

"No."

"Be sensible, Lottie."

"Don't call me that."

He hadn't meant to. It had slipped out of its own accord. "Apologies. Charlotte—"

"Miss Bales."

Though that was reasonable and expected, it, too, irritated him. "Miss Bales, the quicker we look through the journals, the sooner we—"

"Those journals are hidden away for good reason. They're not to be gone through in the parlor in the middle of the day. And you cannot stay here at night, when they can safely be pulled out of hiding. Therefore, you cannot help me. There is an inn in the village. It's the… It's…" Charlotte trailed off with an uncharacteristic awkwardness as her eyes caught and focused on the window behind him.

Following her gaze, Owen spotted a small, blond woman and a black-haired young man climbing the front steps. They walked arm in arm, carrying what appeared to be a kite. "Peter and Esther?" He looked to Lottie, studying her face. "You weren't expecting them home yet."

She pinned him with a cold, hard stare. "You will follow my lead in this, or God help me, I will burn this house down with you and your precious journals inside."

"Understood."

There was just enough time for Gabriel and Samuel to nod in agreement and for Lottie to open the parlor door before Peter and Esther entered the foyer.

"Lottie!" Peter's young and decidedly robust voice rang clearly through the house even as he looked over and discovered the group in the parlor. "Oh. I beg your pardon."

Lottie greeted them both with a broad, cheerful smile. "Peter, Esther. You've returned early."

The boy held up his kite without looking at her. He was all eyes for the newcomers. "Broken, I'm afraid."

"A fortunate mishap, as it happens." She gestured them into the room. "You've arrived just in time to meet our guests. Lord Renderwell, Sir Samuel Brass, Sir Gabriel Arkwright, you remember my brother and sister, I presume?"

"Miss Esther. Mr. Bales—"

"What a delightful surprise to see you again,"

Esther chimed. Unlike her brother, who appeared bemused by the presence of strangers in his home, Esther merely seemed amused. Her eyes shone with the light of recognition and a spark of mischief that reminded Owen of her late father. "Simply *delightful*."

Peter shook his head lightly. "I'm sorry. We've met?"

"You were just a lad, Mr. Bales," Samuel offered. "No more than five, I'd wager."

"He was six," Lottie corrected and smiled at Peter. "These gentlemen were in business with Father."

"Were you? Truly?" Suddenly animated, Peter set the kite aside and grinned at his guests with unabashed excitement. "Oh, splendid. This is absolutely splendid. I've always wanted…" His gazed tracked past Samuel, then shot back again. "Er…that is, I should like to hear…" A line formed across his brow and he lifted a finger to point at Samuel. "I… Do you know… I *do* remember you. You once carried me up a staircase on your shoulders."

Samuel smiled, clearly pleased. "I did."

"Well"—Peter chuckled with a hint of good-natured embarrassment—"it is a pleasure to see you again under more dignified circumstances."

"You were sufficiently dignified for a boy of five," Samuel assured him.

"Six," Esther corrected cheerfully. "Pray tell, what has brought you all the way from London, gentlemen?"

Lottie waved the question away. "They've come for a bit of old paperwork, that's all."

Peter looked to Owen with a curious smile. "We could have sent papers."

Young perhaps, but quick and inquisitive, Owen

noted. "We are returning from a trip north and, I confess, we were eager for the opportunity to look in on the Bales children again. You were scarcely past knee-high last I saw you. And now you are in your third year of schooling with Mr. Derby in Poundswich, I believe?"

Peter looked to his sisters with surprise. They stared at Owen.

"I am," Peter confirmed after a moment.

"Performing well, I presume?"

The young man straightened, his face lit with pride. "I am, my lord. Quite well."

Samuel nodded approvingly. "Always were a bright lad."

"Thank you, sir."

"Yes, we're quite proud of Peter," Lottie agreed. "Gentlemen, I'm sure you will wish to secure a room at the inn before—"

"The inn?" Peter looked at her, aghast. "Rubbish. You'll stay here. We have plenty of room."

"Peter, I think—"

"The White Calf is a fine spot for a drink." He sent a quick, sheepish look at Lottie. "I'm told. But its accommodations are lacking. We haven't much call for lodgings in the village. The nearest railway station is nearly two hours by horseback." His cheeks bloomed pink. "But you'd know that, I imagine. Just come from there, have you?"

Lottie stepped forward. "I'm sure Lord Renderwell—"

"Would be happy to accept your generous invitation, Mr. Bales." Owen stepped forward as well.

"Thank you. You've raised a gracious young man, Miss Bales."

The smile she gave him was so sharp, Owen wondered it didn't draw blood. "His generosity is entirely of his own making, I assure you. Peter, would you be so kind as to inform Mrs. Lewis we are to have houseguests?"

"Of course. My pleasure."

And by the look of the ear-to-ear grin on his face, it genuinely was. Owen watched as Peter took his leave and was mildly surprised the boy didn't break into a skip.

"He is a fine boy, Lott—" he began when Peter was out of earshot.

"*Miss Bales*," Lottie hissed, spinning about to glare at him. She stepped forward again, and then again, until they were nearly nose to chin in the center of the room. "This was not part of the agreement, you rotter. You've no right, no *right*—"

"No, I haven't," he agreed. "But the alternative is the entire village of Wayton speculating as to why the Bales household could not, or would not, put up a visiting viscount for the night."

Before Lottie could answer, Esther shrugged and smiled. "I wouldn't mind a spot of gossip. It might liven—"

"You will take your dinner in your rooms tonight," Lottie interrupted. "And breakfast in your rooms tomorrow. You will make every effort to avoid Peter, and under no circumstances will you engage him in any discussion regarding this family. Are we agreed?" Her eyes narrowed. "Or shall I fetch a candle and a stack of hay?"

"We're agreed." They would play things her way, for now.

Samuel and Gabriel nodded.

"Good. Cross me"—she placed a small hand on his chest and shoved him back an inch—"and I will cram that hay down your lying throat before I set it ablaze. Understood?"

She didn't wait to see if he had, in fact, understood. She simply spun on her heel and strode out of the room, a blatantly amused Esther in tow.

Two

LOTTIE BALES WAS NOT A WOMAN PRONE TO VIOLENCE. In years past, she had been a woman prone to swindling and stealing, and, currently, she was a woman of some deceit, but never had she been moved to do a person bodily harm.

And yet, as she looked down on the activity in the front drive from Esther's bedroom window, she could not deny that it would a pleasure—a very great pleasure—to grab one or more of the various sharp objects to be found so conveniently on the desk next to her and rain them down upon Lord Renderwell's dark head.

Oh, it would be so easy.

He was right there, standing on the front terrace not ten feet out from the house. Just *standing there* as if he had every right to be on *her* front terrace, ordering *her* staff to put his belongings in *her* home.

As if he had every right to come crashing back into her world.

Pity he didn't feel the right to be a few feet closer. She was too far away to make out the light green of his eyes, and she rather fancied the idea of seeing them widen in fear at her first volley. But, like his forked tongue and cloven hooves, she didn't need to see them to know they were there. Just as she didn't need additional proof that his handsome face, with its sharp cheekbones and broad jaw, hid a devious mind and that his charming smile hid an icy heart.

She watched as Samuel joined him and felt her hands curl into fists. Even at six feet, Owen ought to have looked smaller while standing in Samuel's towering shadow. Most men did.

But not Viscount Renderwell. Oh, no. The man had always possessed a larger-than-life presence. In the naïveté of her youth, she'd imagined that presence stemmed from virtues like courage and integrity and strength of purpose.

But now she knew it was simply pride and ambition that gave the man his grand stature. He reminded her of those colossal balloons she'd seen as a child—highly impressive when puffed up and looming over humanity like a guardian angel. Upon closer inspection, however, it became clear there was nothing of substance to be found inside.

It had been something of a disappointment to learn those giant balloons were empty.

It had been devastating to learn Owen Renderwell was just as hollow.

She'd built fantastic dreams around the man. Such impossible, ridiculous dreams. How could she not, when he'd offered up everything she ever wanted on a platter?

When she'd first met Owen, he'd held no illusions

about her family. He'd known exactly what her father was and enough of what her father had done that he ought to have tossed the man in prison and been done with it. Instead, he had extended a hand in friendship, even offered a chance at redemption.

Work for me and give your family a chance at a normal, decent life. Or, you may see them when they take leave of the poorhouse to visit you in Newgate.

Esther had once pointed out that the redemptive properties of blackmail were somewhat suspect. But Lottie hadn't cared. She'd been willing to accept any chance of redemption obtained via any means available. And if the only means happened to be the noble, charming, and handsome Lord Renderwell, Detective Inspector of Scotland Yard and decorated veteran of the Crimean War, well…

In the four years they'd worked together, Owen had never made her feel as if her family was under threat. He'd been infinitely respectful to her, offering every kindness and courtesy. He'd gone out of his way to make her laugh and make her think. He'd treated her like a person of worth. In time, she'd even begun to believe she might one day become that person.

But it had all been lies.

Owen Renderwell had seen a means to an end in her father and nothing more. God only knew what he'd seen in her. A means to keep her father in line, no doubt.

"Blighter."

The bedroom door opened and Esther padded across the carpet. Stopping next to the desk, she

brushed Lottie's hand away from a heavy inkwell.
"You can't do that, and well you know it."

"I wasn't going to kill him, just…" She wiggled her
fingers around the side of her head. "Graze him a bit.
Expose his horns."

"You haven't the aim." She nudged Lottie aside.
"And these are my things. Bloody your own inkwell."

Lottie wanted to smile at that but found she
couldn't, not while Owen was still in her line of sight.
"Ugh. The nerve. The *nerve* of them coming here. I
should have refused to see them. I should have told
Mrs. Lewis to toss them out on their ears." Or have
Mrs. Lewis send for a footman to see the job done,
which was a hair more realistic.

Esther gave her a quizzical look. "Why didn't you?"

"Because…" Because she'd thought, just for a
moment, that Owen might have come for something
other than a favor. That, perhaps, he had come to
make amends. She wasn't at all certain she wanted to
make amends, but, despite all better judgment, the
idea that he should try again after so many years had
intrigued her. "Because I'm an idiot."

"Rarely." Esther studied the scene outside the
window. "Although you'd certainly qualify if you
marred that perfectly lovely visage. Lord Renderwell
has aged quite handsomely."

"So has Mr. Nips," Lottie grumbled. "We don't let
him in the house."

Esther craned her neck for a look at the ancient,
white-muzzled pony standing serenely in his pasture.
"I doubt Lord Renderwell bites."

"You'd be surprised."

"Well, I doubt I'd mind the nibble—"

"*Don't.*"

Esther laughed and turned from the window. "Never fear, my dear smitten sister. As I recall, his dapper friend was always more to my taste. Lovely sense of style, that one, and very little sense otherwise."

Lottie's eyes narrowed. It would be like Esther to ease a distasteful situation with a touch of humor. Unfortunately, it would also be like her to hide a distasteful truth in a bit of teasing.

The girl was every inch their father's daughter. She was just as charming, just as cunning, and just as manipulative. A conniving rogue in a sweet pink gown, that's what she was. And it was foolish to make assumptions about rogues.

Lottie jabbed a finger at her sister. "You listen to me, Esther Walker. These men are not to be trifled with. They're nothing like your Harold Briggins or Timothy Wait or any of the other gullible boys in the village who are so eager to see the best in you. Try to make these men dance to your tune and call you a pretty piper, and they'll break that fife over your head for all the world to see. They will *ruin* you."

Esther raised both eyebrows. Of the three Walker children, she was the only one incapable of arching just one brow. "Your memory of them is quite different than my own."

"You were a child and they treated you like one. You'll not receive the same consideration now."

"I was well past nineteen when they left."

"But scarcely fifteen when they first…" She shook her head. This particular line of argument would have no impact on Esther. "It makes no difference. Esther, these men are not good marks."

You've got to pick your mark, poppet. Why risk toying with a tiger when a kitten will do just as well?

Esther had likely never heard that particular gem from their father, but she'd recognize the wisdom in it. Her habit of causing trouble without actually getting into any was a result of careful calculation, not luck.

"You would remember them better, I suppose," Esther conceded at length, and she shrugged. "I'll be good."

"Your word?"

"Yes, my word."

Lottie breathed a sigh of genuine relief. Her sister might be a rogue, but she was a smart rogue, and she was loyal to the family. She would keep her word.

Esther smiled pleasantly and leaned against the window frame. "Well, now that I've successfully distracted you from your murderous intentions, will you tell me the real reason Renderwell and his men have come and why you've allowed them to stay?"

She'd rather not, but there was no getting round it. "They want to search Father's journals for clues to an encrypted letter."

Esther made a scoffing noise. "You refused them, of course."

"I wanted to—"

"You agreed? You *are* an idiot."

"The letters were left behind by a murderer." Lottie's heart twisted at the thought and at the dim memory of the woman who'd taught her to waltz and how to hide a dagger in her décolletage. At eleven, Lottie's décolletage had been nearly indistinguishable from her waist. Still, it had been a sweet gesture. "Mrs. Popple was the victim."

Esther straightened, her blue eyes rounding. "Mrs. Popple? Father's friend?" She swallowed audibly when Lottie nodded. "Good Lord. I... Good Lord." She swallowed again. "I...I don't remember her well, to be honest. Do you?"

"Some." But not as well as the woman deserved. It had been years since Lottie had even spared a thought for her. "She was kind to us when we were young."

"I do remember that. I remember her laughter." Esther glanced out the window and back again. "And Renderwell hopes to find the same encryption in father's old notes, does he?"

"I doubt they expect to find an actual cipher, or a codebook for the letter, but even a piece of the puzzle would help." If they could discover an encryption of similar make, it was possible they could trace its origins to a particular group or groups in London, which might narrow their search.

"Do they realize how many journals father kept?" Esther asked.

"I don't know. He was supposed to have made all of them available to Owen's men when—"

"So they don't know."

"Likely not," she admitted. The journals had been turned over just days after her father's capture. He'd still been a mite...resentful of his new circumstances.

"It will take considerable time to go through them all."

"More time than they have, I imagine. Once they realize the extent of their task, I'm sure they'll insist on taking the journals back to London." And if they didn't insist, she'd find a way to ship the journals off herself and tell Owen to go fetch. She wasn't eager to remove the books from the house, but it was preferable to risking Peter's accidental exposure to the family's true history.

Esther shook her head. "Even a day or two of them here might cause problems. Peter is absolutely beside himself with the anticipation of talking to someone who knew Father."

Lottie blew out a small breath to settle her churning stomach. "I know."

For years, Peter had been fascinated with their father, or, more accurately, with the almost entirely fictional Mr. William Bales, devoted family man and respectable tradesman, who Lottie had created in an attempt to give the boy some semblance of a normal life. The only genuine similarities between their real father and the man Peter imagined to be their father was a first name and the ridiculous portrait in the parlor.

Someday, Peter would learn the truth—that William Bales was actually William Walker, infamous swindler. But Lottie had always envisioned that day to be of her choosing and that it would occur sometime in the vague and distant future.

She'd always thought they had plenty of time.

She now had approximately twelve hours.

Peter had agreed to go into the village for additional provisions—Lord knew the boy was more than happy to personally procure the freshest bread and best cuts of beef for their guests. And when he returned, she would explain that the gentlemen were resting from their long journey and would likely not emerge from their rooms until tomorrow.

What the devil was she to do tomorrow?

"What if they were to feign illness?" she suggested. "Something catching?"

Esther shook her head. "The more catching, the more likely Peter is to insist you and I remove ourselves from the house and leave him to play nursemaid. You'd accomplish nothing but provide him with a captive audience."

"Damn it." Lottie briefly squeezed her eyes shut. "This would be so much simpler if we had told him everything from the start."

"Everything?" Esther echoed in disbelief. "That we've changed our names because our father was a confidence man turned snitch and we don't want anyone to know? That's not a secret a child of six could have kept."

"We kept secrets at that age. We knew what father was before—"

"Allow me to rephrase. It is not a secret a six-year-old Peter could have kept. It is not a secret we can be certain he would keep now."

Lottie opened her mouth to argue, but Esther held up her hand. "I adore our brother. You know that I do. But he is good to his *very core*, Lottie. He'd give the shirt off his back to a prince picking his pocket."

"He's a pigeon," Lottie translated dully.

"God help us, he is the *fattest* of pigeons. A nearly perfect mark—well-heeled, trusting, and too proud and forgiving to make a fuss when he discovers the knife in his back."

"Peter is not stupid. Nor is he an angel."

"Not at all. Lord knows, there's no one less pleasant to be around than Peter in a temper. But his general nature is one of generosity. He loves without reservation. If you tell him the truth now, when he falls madly in love with some little twit at sixteen, he won't be able to stop himself from sharing every single secret in that enormous heart of his. And then it'll be blackmail and threats. Men and women pounding on our doors demanding the money father stole from them."

"Or it'll be father's old comrades out for revenge."

Esther nodded grimly.

"Right. You're right." She took another deep breath to steady herself and nodded. "We can do this." They had to do this. "I'll speak with Renderwell. Any stories they tell of Father will match our own."

"We couldn't possibly tell them everything in a few short hours or expect them to memorize it."

"No." She rested her first three fingers against the window frame and tapped them in an alternating drumming pattern. The light, rhythmic sound and movement always helped her to focus. "They needn't memorize everything, only the basic facts. They can claim ignorance on the rest. How well do men doing business together know each other, really? Particularly if that business is of short duration. Say…six months, do you think?"

Catching on, Esther nodded. "Long enough to take an interest in his children but not so long as to require a sustained interest."

"Right. There's no need for them to remember and repeat everything we've told Peter. If they can remember that Will Bales was not a heavy drinker or gambler, that he was adventurous, and that he had a great love of horses, then they can create a few diverting anecdotes for Peter—trips to the races, riding the first underground railway, lively debates over investments."

That wouldn't be hard. At least half of it was true. It was always best to keep a lie as close to the truth as possible. Her father had not been a heavy drinker or a gambler in the traditional sense. And he quite liked horses. Stealing them, specifically, but that was close enough.

"Stories only loosely connected to our narrative," Esther murmured thoughtfully.

"Yes, and the looser they are, the less chance there is for contradictions to occur."

"Anything new will make Peter happy. It could work." Esther jerked her chin toward the men outside. "Will they to do it?"

"Lie, do you mean? Of course. Why wouldn't they?" They certainly didn't appear to have any philosophical objections to deceit.

"But can they do it *well*?"

"Not so well as a Walker," she said frankly, not because she was proud of that, but because it was true. "But they manage." They'd managed to fool her for four years, after all. They could certainly fool Peter for two days. "This can work. We'll make it work."

Feeling calmer with a strategy in place, Lottie slipped an arm around her sister and stood with her at the window, silently watching the dwindling action on the front lawn.

The horses had been unpacked and led back to the stables, but the men remained on the terrace, all three of them now. Their heads were bent together in conference, and Lottie could only assume they were formulating lies and plans of their own.

Let them, she thought darkly. Renderwell could scheme to his small black heart's content. She was not her father, and she was no longer a stupid young woman to be taken in by a silver tongue and handsome face.

She'd not fall victim to his lies a second time.

The men could stay until they found what they were looking for, until they accepted that what they were looking for wasn't to be had at Willowbend, or until Peter began to grow suspicious. Whichever came first, provided none of it took longer than two days.

Two days, and Owen Renderwell would be out of her life. This time for good.

Lottie squeezed her sister lightly. "Esther?"

"Hmm?"

"I am *not* smitten."

Three

Ordinarily, Lottie loved the night.

During the day, Willowbend was filled with the commotion of everyday life. It seemed there was always someone stepping in or out of the room, footsteps thumping overhead, pots banging below in the kitchen, or voices filtering through the walls. The smell of baking bread and roasting meat filled the house and mixed with the heavy scent of lyc in the maids' buckets. Flittering birds and rustling trees outside created a constant dance of shadows across the floors and walls. It was endless. Lovely and heartwarming, but endless. No matter how hard one might try to find a quiet corner and moment for oneself, there was simply no escaping the light and sound and movement of day.

But nighttime offered a world without distractions. A still and silent world that extended only so far as the light of a single candle.

Lottie had always found peace in that small world and clarity in the solitude it afforded. She had spent countless hours at her desk in the dead of night, happily detached from everything but the book or work before her.

But as she walked softly down the upstairs hall at midnight, what Lottie wanted most was for this particular night to be over.

There would be no peace at Willowbend. Not until Owen and his men were gone.

Slipping a key from her pocket, she came to a stop in front of Owen's door and blew out a long, slow breath. Steadied, she unlocked the door and let herself in without knocking—in part because she didn't want to risk the noise carrying down the hall but mostly because she didn't like the idea of asking permission from Owen to enter a room in her own home. It was the principle of the matter, she told herself, and studiously ignored the fact that both the matter *and* the principle were just a little bit petty.

After quietly closing the door, she took quick stock of her surroundings. Most of the familiar room was shrouded in darkness, but a crack between the drapes let in a thin stream of moonlight that cut across the bed and lightly illuminated Owen's sleeping form.

It didn't surprise her to see that he'd retired still wearing his trousers and shirtsleeves. Her father had done the same, every night.

Always be ready to run, my girl. Always.

Lottie glanced at the foot of the bed and noticed Owen's toes sticking out from under the rich green counterpane. At least he didn't sleep with his boots on.

Careful to keep the glow of her candle from disturbing him, she crossed the room and stood beside the bed. Although she was in a hurry to see her task done, she spared a minute to take in the sight of the invincible Lord Renderwell lying vulnerable in his sleep before her. His shirtsleeves were rolled up, exposing tanned and muscled forearms, and the fine cotton had twisted a little when he'd turned onto his stomach, causing the fabric to pull tight across his broad shoulders. His face was turned from her, but she could make out the hard outline of his jaw and the way his lashes, the same deep walnut color as his hair, sat lightly against his skin.

Owen Renderwell didn't look the least bit vulnerable in sleep, she decided. Something of a disappointment, that, but it made sense. A wolf in repose didn't cease to appear threatening—it simply looked like something you shouldn't wake.

She frowned at that thought and kicked the bed. She wasn't afraid of this man.

"Get up."

He didn't jump, as she'd rather hoped. Instead, he pounced, drawing a blade from under his pillow and coming off the bed in a movement so quick and fluid, the candle flame barely flickered. Before she could even think to dodge out of the way, the knife was two inches from her face, gleaming sharp and silver in the moonlight.

She merely blinked at it. "*Charming.*"

Owen blinked in return, the glaze of sleep lifting from his eyes. He yanked his arm back, spinning the knife in his hand to face the blade away from her. "*God*, Lottie," he hissed. "You bloody well know better."

Admittedly, she did. She also knew he wouldn't hurt her, half-awake or not.

He glared at her a moment before turning away to set the knife on the bedside table. It bothered her a little to see the hand holding the blade tremble slightly, but it bothered her more that she should be bothered at all. What the devil did she care if she'd unnerved the man?

"If you damaged my linens, Renderwell, you'll pay for their replacement."

Another glare, this one more irritated than angry. "You used to be a bit more cautious."

On the contrary, she used to be a great deal more reckless, but she had no intention of sharing that with him. "And you. I could have done you in a half-dozen times just now."

"Oddly enough, I fancied myself safe here."

"Yes, that is odd. Particularly in light of that knife."

"Habit."

"Habit," she repeated dryly. "You must pay your mistresses a fortune."

He drew his hands down his face, the very picture of an aggrieved man. "What are you doing in here?"

"Retrieving your journals. Fetch a candle. If you want them, you'll have to help."

"Fine." Grumbling, he found a candle on the nightstand. "I'll get Samuel and—"

"No. There isn't room."

"Room?" He lit the candle off her own. "Where are they, exactly?"

Lottie strode to the far wall, took hold of a hanging tapestry, and pulled it back to reveal the striped wallpaper behind. "Here."

Joining her, Owen ran his hand across the wall until he found one of two small seams hidden along the edges of the stripes.

"A door," he guessed. "How very like the Walker household to have a secret room." He held his candle aloft and glanced about the bedroom. "This house doesn't appear old enough for a priest hole."

"And it was built by devout Protestants." Crouching down, she pulled away the loose floor molding and searched for a small latch hidden on the exposed bottom of the door. "There was a maid's room. Esther and I sealed it as soon as we arrived."

While Peter was still young enough to be distracted with toys and sweets.

"And hung the tapestry to cover your less than expert work. Clever."

"Necessary," she returned. Her father had taught her everything there was to know about removing complicated systems of locks from all manner of hidden doors, but he'd never taught her how to install such a system, nor the door. It had taken them weeks to finish the job. "Ah…here it is."

She flicked a latch, and a small panel in the door slid open in front of Owen, exposing an old lock.

"You were thorough," he commented, then frowned when she set down her candle and pulled a set of lock picks from her pocket. "Don't you have the key?"

"We couldn't take the chance of it falling into the wrong hands. We threw it away."

"Thus ensuring only a thief could get in."

"Thus ensuring Peter could not," she corrected, selecting the appropriate tool. She inserted it into the lock, pressed, and turned the way she had a thousand times in her youth, and she found herself perplexed when the door failed to open. There had been a time when picking a lock had come as easily to her as writing her own name; her hands could form the movements almost without thought. But it had been years since she'd last put the skill to use. Evidently, her fingers no longer remembered the correct steps.

"What about the servants?" Owen asked after a moment. "Didn't they notice a room go missing, or—"

"The room was sealed off before staff arrived…" She grimaced when her second attempt to open the door failed. "From outside the county."

"No connection to the local villagers," he murmured, stepping closer to better light the lock. "Less chance of gossip. For a time."

"Yes, and the tapestry is a priceless family heirloom. No one touches it but me, or Esther, if she was ever inclined to clean."

"People don't always do as they're told."

"Mrs. Lewis keeps everyone in line." She clenched her jaw when she failed to open the door again. This was ridiculous. Lock picking was the simplest of skills. She wished she could tell Owen to step back. It didn't help matters to have him looming over her like one of those damned balloons. But she needed the light from his candle.

"Have something on her, do you?" Owen asked.

She shot him a hard look. "She's a good woman. Let her alone."

"I've no trouble with your Mrs. Lewis. I do have some with how long this is taking, however." He held out his hand. "Give me the pick."

She wanted to refuse him—she was a Walker; she could bloody well pick her own lock—but there was petty, and then there was stupid. Allowing pride to further delay Owen's departure from Willowbend was most assuredly the latter.

She gave him the pick and watched with some annoyance when the lock clicked open on his first try.

"Thank you." She smiled sweetly when he returned the pick. "I suppose that makes you the better thief."

Before he could respond, she pushed open the door, stepped inside the room, and held her candle aloft to light the contents.

Owen followed but didn't get far inside. There simply wasn't space. "Oh, hell."

The room wasn't large, no bigger than was needed to house a lady's maid and her limited possessions, but nearly every inch of available space was filled with trunks, piled upon trunks, piled upon more trunks. All packed with her father's writings. Even the space between the top trunks and the ceiling was stuffed with loose journals. There was scarcely enough room for the two of them to hold their candles up without setting the journals, or each other, aflame.

Owen turned a tight circle. "Your father did not give us all his work."

"You don't know that." She suspected as much, but she had the right to disparage her father. He did not.

"I can see with my own eyes, Lottie. Our notes on your father's work wouldn't cover a quarter of this."

"Of course they don't. They... Oh, I'd forgotten." She lowered her candle. "You didn't help transcribe the journals, did you? Father and I worked with Mr. Bradley."

"And that changes things?"

"Yes. These are *all* of my father's journals. Every word he's ever written about anything at all." And her father had always had quite a lot to say about everything. "They're filled with childhood exploits, sketches." Bad ones. "Ciphers, random thoughts, poetry." Dreadful, dreadful poetry. "Schemes, plots, even a political manifesto."

"A manifesto." He looked at her, a little bit horrified. "You jest."

"Not at all. It's an exceptional piece of work." That was a lie. It was also dreadful. Dreadful and *lengthy*. "He wrote about everything."

Except her. At least, not directly. Her father had been unforgivably careless in so many ways, but he'd always been adamant in keeping names to himself. He spoke of her in his journals, but in his musings about their shared criminal activity, he referred to her simply as "the Tulip."

"The notes you have in London are just that," she continued. "Notes on what little information amongst all of this Mr. Bradley felt might prove useful."

Owen swore again. "It could take weeks for the two of us to go through all this."

"Yes. And before you ask—no, Samuel and Gabriel may not help. We can't have four people talking and clambering about in here at night. Someone would hear. And no, we can't go through them during the day. I'll not risk it."

"We don't have weeks, Lottie."

"I know. And I have decided you may take them to London, if you must—*if* you promise to return them as soon as you are through. I can tell Peter you're taking some of Father's old paperwork to London with the intention of having it searched for any forgotten business that might benefit the Bales family. And I can make sure that both he and most of the staff are out of the house when you haul out the trunks. That will keep anyone from looking too closely at the journals."

The story might pique Peter's curiosity a little, but it was highly unlikely a boy of fourteen would fuss over a lost opportunity to dig through piles of old papers. He was fascinated by their father's life, not his ledgers.

"And what reason would you give him for my having offered such a favor after so long?"

"The same reason I gave him for your sudden interest in the Bales children after ignoring us for eight years. You fancy yourself a kindly benefactor, but like most members of the nobility, you are inconsistent, self-centered, and something of a dolt."

He stared at her wordlessly.

"Fortunately," she continued, "the men in your employ are not. If I tell Peter there are none better qualified to see to the work, he'll be content to let the papers go."

"You're a small woman, Lottie."

"It's the little things," she explained with a happy sigh. "And it is Miss Bales."

"Well"—he ran his tongue over his teeth and eyed her with menace—"it would appear I haven't much of a choice, have I, Miss Bales?"

She shrugged, as if it all made very little difference to her.

Only it did, of course. Because, the reality was, Owen had no shortage of choices, and most of them could end badly for the Walker-Bales family.

If he wanted to drag the trunks out in the middle of the day and read the contents aloud to Peter, the staff, and the rest of Christendom, there was little she could do aside from putting up a grand fuss. That fuss would be very grand indeed and would include a substantial amount of bodily harm done to Owen's person. In the end, however, it likely wouldn't be enough to stop him.

"I'll see to obtaining a wagon tomorrow," he said at length. "We'll pare down what we can in the next day or two."

Lottie turned away and quietly expelled the breath she'd been holding. "Well then," she managed in a respectably even tone. "Let's get started."

She grabbed a few loose journals at random and, grateful that she'd traded the modesty of a corset and crinolette for the practicality of a tea gown, settled herself on the floor, her back against the open door and her legs tucked up to make room for Owen. A chair in the bedroom would have been far more comfortable, but the trunks provided a sound barrier and the tapestry effectively blocked the candlelight.

Owen must have understood this as well, because he didn't mention her awkward position. "You know, I had hoped your anger might have dissipated with time."

"I'm not angry with you, Renderwell. That would

require a level of interest and energy I have not been inclined to spend on you in years." She opened the first journal. "I simply do not like you."

"Disliking someone takes a fair amount of work."

"Everyone ought to have a pastime. Idle hands, as they say."

"Could you try for civil?"

"I wasn't the one swinging cutlery about," she reminded him and flipped the page.

She refused to look up from the journal, but she could imagine he was grinding his teeth, and she found the image, fanciful or not, immensely gratifying.

"I'll take that as a no," he said.

"Take it however you like," she told him. "Just do it in silence."

He went from grinding his teeth to staring daggers at the top of her head. Or so she gathered from the narrow view she had of his feet. They were very still, and they were pointed at her. What else could he possibly be doing?

At last, he moved. Owen snatched up a journal, took a seat across from her, and went to work.

Four

UNFORTUNATELY, THE SILENCE FOLLOWING OWEN'S capitulation proved to be far more discomforting to Lottie than an argument about her anger. Particularly as she'd been winning that argument.

She didn't feel as if she was winning now. Not unless winning was defined by an inexplicable and maddening inability to keep one's mind focused on the task at hand. She tried to train her eyes and thoughts on the journal before her, she really did, but it was distracting beyond measure to have the man who had once been the center of her universe sitting three feet away.

He'd been everything to her. Everything all the other men she'd met in her life had most assuredly *not been*—noble, strong, reliable, trustworthy, safe.

Good.

She watched him flip the pages of his journal, rapidly taking in the contents. She used to love watching him work. His mind operated with remarkable speed, taking in information, separating and retaining what he needed, and discarding the remainder with enviable efficiency.

He was a man who could disassemble and reassemble a puzzle in the time it took most men to simply comprehend what they were looking at, and she found his keen mind to be one of his most attractive attributes.

Had found, she corrected. She *had* found it attractive.

"None of this makes sense," he said suddenly, surprising her.

"Beg your pardon?"

"Much of this is written in some sort of shorthand... mess." He held up his journal, pages out. "What the devil is this?"

Lottie looked at the seemingly indecipherable array of lines and shapes, angles and letters, and hid a smile. Given the tenor of her thoughts a moment ago, she found his confusion more than a little funny. "It's a diagram, of sorts."

"Yes, I can see that. What does it mean?"

"It's..." She reached to point, drew her hand back when he turned the book so he could make out where, exactly, she was pointing, then tried pointing again. "See here, the..."

He turned the book again. "See what?"

"Oh, for heaven's sake," she muttered and set her journal aside. "Push over."

There wasn't much room for Owen to maneuver, but by pressing himself against the door frame, he managed to create sufficient space for Lottie to squeeze in between him and a stack of trunks.

She regretted the decision almost immediately. If it was disconcerting to have Owen loom over her, or sit across from her, then it was positively alarming to be pressed against his side with her knee touching his thigh and his familiar scent teasing her nose.

Wintergreen, she thought. He'd always preferred wintergreen in his soap.

Annoyed that she remembered, she pushed away all thoughts of soap and knees and thighs and tapped a series of small horizontal lines in the center of the journal. "This was a window in an alley near the corner of"—she pointed to the letters *F* and *B* inside a circle—"Fleet Street and Beard Lane. For a time, when I was very young, my father fancied himself a pickpocket. He'd do the thing neat and clean and hide the prize in the slats of the shutters here for...to be picked up later."

It was common practice among pickpockets to immediately hide or pass off a purse to an accomplice. More than one thief had been apprehended and searched a block or two from the scene of his crime only to be released when no stolen property was found on his person.

"I'm familiar with the scheme," Owen said, "but I cannot fathom how this jumble represents any portion of it. What does the rest mean?"

He'd turned his head when he spoke and his breath brushed against her temple, sending a pleasant and all too familiar shiver up her spine.

She cleared her throat. "It is everything within a six-block radius, more or less. See...letters inside circles are roads. If they're inside squares, they mark alleyways. Straight lines between the roads mean heavy foot traffic; dotted lines are streets with fewer people. This line with the squiggly marks means it's someone else's territory. There's no poaching. Nearby shops or buildings with back doors that could provide potential escape routes are indicated by diamonds. Filled squares mean there's no exit. A line through a diamond means the shopkeeper or home owner is likely armed."

"Why not just draw the thing out properly?"

"Takes longer, for one." Especially if you were a man of very limited artistic skill. "And it keeps any enterprising snooper from understanding what he's looking at."

"So, it's encrypted."

"If you like."

"The numbers in the top left corner? Dates and times, I presume?"

She nodded. "He kept a record of how often he used each particular plan."

Don't overfish a pond, love. Believe me. I know of what I speak.

"This down here." Owen tapped the bottom of a page. "Tulip. I remember that. A name, wasn't it? But not an actual person."

Her heart skipped a beat, then added an extra three in rapid succession to compensate. "Not a singular person. The name referred to any female accomplice he happened to have at the time."

"Do you remember them?"

"Not well." Perfectly well, in fact. "Father worked with a number of people, most of whom I was not allowed to meet."

"He was particular on that score," he agreed. "But is there a name that stands out to you? Someone he might have worked with more often than the others?"

Oh, yes. "None I recall."

Eager to be done with the conversation, she moved to leverage herself out of her cramped spot, but Owen grasped her arm, keeping her in place.

"A moment." He released her to flip back several pages. "What is this?"

It was another diagram, this one of a prosperous neighborhood her father had visited several times during his, thankfully brief, stint as a burglar. As soon as she finished explaining it, Owen flipped the pages again and asked after something else…and then something else. And on it went.

There were more diagrams, some sketches Owen mistook for diagrams as they were so badly done they actually appeared purposefully cryptic, and even the particulars of several popular dances, with notes on the most opportune moments to divest an unsuspecting dance partner of her ruby ring or sapphire brooch. Her father had never met a gemstone he didn't covet.

After a while, she gave up trying to leave and picked a journal to look through where she was. After several more interruptions, she abandoned the journal as well. And for the next two hours, they went through her father's entries together.

Despite the odd thought about soap, knees, muscled thighs, and Owen's funny little habit of twisting his lips to the left when he was puzzled, Lottie found that going through her father's writings was a rather pleasant endeavor. It engendered a sense of nostalgia she had not expected. Though she deeply resented the work her father had done, she didn't resent her memories of *him*. Not all of them, anyway. And it was lovely, really, to be reminded of some nice things about her father. Silly little things that had made him unique. Like the way he had turned a phrase or approached a job or a puzzle. The way his drawings of roses not yet in full bloom always turned out looking like sad little arrows with splintered shafts. And the way he'd laughed until he'd cried when Esther had stolen a journal and amended one of the sketches to include a close-up caricature of an astonished Prince Albert, mouth agape in a comical *Nooooo*, as he contemplated an immediate and inescapable death by rosebud-turned-misshapen-arrow to the right eye.

The pages before her were a far better representation of her father than the pompous portrait above the fireplace mantel could ever be. She wished now that she had taken the time to look through them years ago.

As the third hour ticked by, however, happy memories began to dim in the face of growing physical discomfort. The confined room was rapidly becoming overwarm with the tapestry trapping the heat of two candles and two bodies inside.

Lottie shifted her weight, seeking relief, but all she managed to do was press herself tighter against Owen's form. She felt a bead of sweat trickle down her temple, and she wiped it away with more fervor than was probably warranted.

She hated the heat. It didn't remind her of the happy times the way the journals did. It reminded her of the other times—the early years before her father had honed his craft and learned to save against the inevitable run of bad luck.

It made her think of summers spent in impossibly cramped rooms in cheap boardinghouses, where there was no privacy, no space, and no air. Where opening their sole window accomplished nothing but to carry in the sick odor of refuse rotting in the streets.

Winters had been miserable in those rooms, but Lottie had been able to escape the cold, if only for a few hours, by huddling with her sister under a mountain of blankets.

There had been no escaping the oppressive heat and stench of summer, and the memory of those endless miserable days made her vision blur and her stomach tighten and roll.

"Right. Up you go."

Owen's voice sounded unnaturally far away. She blinked away the blurriness and discovered he'd stood up without her noticing and was, once again, looming over her. "What? What are you doing?"

"You need fresh air." He bent down, caught her under the arms, and hauled her to her feet in one easy movement. "You're white as a sheet."

"I'm not." She likely was, but that was no reason to concede a weakness. "It's the light in here—"

"It's the heat," he returned. "You don't like it."

"I—" Surprised and a little dizzy, she didn't think to argue when he slipped an arm around her waist and turned her toward the door.

"Forgot you'd told me, did you?" he inquired, pushing the tapestry aside and ushering her forward.

The cool air that greeted them felt like heaven

against her skin and did a fair job of settling her nausea and clearing her head. She recalled telling Owen now. She also recalled that she'd never told him the reason behind the aversion. Thank God for small mercies.

Feeling stronger, she tried to extract herself from Owen's supportive grip, but he seemed not to notice the way she pushed at his hand. He led her to a chair and reached over her head to unlatch a window. The fresh air that blew inside felt better than heaven—it felt like sin. The sort one got away with scot-free.

When Owen stepped away, she gave into the temptation to close her eyes on a quiet sigh. Just for a second.

This was why she'd not made a habit of looking through her father's old journals. Yes, there was happiness in old memories. There was also fear, pain, shame, and more fear. It was better to leave well enough alone.

She opened her eyes and watched Owen return from the hidden room with their candles.

"Feeling better?" he asked. He blew out one candle and bent to set the other on the small table beside her chair…and also to take a close examination of her face, apparently. "You look better."

"I'm perfectly well." She had the most ridiculous urge to reach out and thump him on the nose. Not hard. Just a quick flick of the fingers. It would serve him right for looming. It would also serve to place her emotional age somewhere between four and four and a half. So she refrained. "We should return to work."

She really shouldn't. If she was contemplating the merits of thumping a grown man on the nose, then, clearly, she was not perfectly well.

"In a minute." Apparently satisfied with her improved color, Owen stepped away to take a seat in the chair across from her. "I'd like a rest as well." He undid a few buttons of his shirt. "Damnably uncomfortable in that room."

It was going to be damnably uncomfortable in *this* room if she had to sit there and watch him undress. "Why don't I—?"

"Would you like to see the other letters whilst we're sitting here?" he cut in.

"I suppose." She supposed she'd like just about any offer of distraction at the moment.

Stretching over the back of his chair, Owen reached for a small stack of papers sitting on the desk some distance away.

He snagged the papers with the tips of his fingers, brought them round, and handed them to her. "Think you might be able to make sense of them?"

"I don't know," she replied, squinting at the fine print.

"Here." Owen stood again, this time to light a nearby lamp.

She waved him away when he tried to hand it to her. "No. Put it out. Someone could see the light."

He set the lamp on the small table and took the candle for himself. "It is well past three in the morning and Peter's room is at the end of the hall, nearest the back stairs. On the very slim chance he wakes hungry or thirsty, he will go down those stairs to the kitchen. He will not come down here to investigate the space beneath my door."

"You don't know that."

"Do you really think he might?"

She really couldn't say. Peter was fourteen. He still secretly (he thought) slept with the small embroidered blanket she'd purchased during his infancy, and he ogled girls like a randy old man. He was a good boy. He truly was. But sometimes he raged over nothing or seemed to become indignant over everything, and he still insisted that the time the vicar tripped on the hem of his cassock and spilled the Eucharistic wine atop Mrs. Cooper's bent head was the funniest damned thing he would *ever see.*

The mind and motives of a fourteen-year-old boy were, in many ways, inscrutable.

"I don't know," she said.

Owen heaved a sigh. "Very well."

Taking that as capitulation, she expected Owen to put out the lamp. Instead, he went to the bed, pulled off the counterpane, and stuffed it up against the bottom of the door. "Will that do?"

She thought about it. "If we keep our voices down, yes."

Owen nodded and resumed his seat, and Lottie returned her attention to the letters.

She noted that the contents were of similar length and style. It was likely the same encryption on every page. Without doubt, they were constructed by a single author. "You took them to someone else first, I imagine?"

"Mr. Bradley," he confirmed.

"He's still alive?" A picture of a wizened face flashed in her mind. Mr. Bradley had been ancient when she'd known him. By now he had to be…practically eternal.

"Yes," Owen replied. "And still fond of you."

What rot, she thought. "Not so fond as to write a word in the last eight years."

He gave her a chiding expression. "He doesn't know where you are." Owen shrugged when she glanced at him. "There were very few people made aware of your relocation to Norfolk. I thought it best at the time."

"He could have given a letter to you."

"And you would have returned any letter from me unopened."

He had a point. And because he did, she dropped the subject and went back to studying the letters. In the parlor, the long list of letters and numbers had initially looked to be a simple substitution cipher, something like a Caesar shift. But at second glance, she'd realized the code was nothing of the sort.

Simple substitution ciphers were the most basic forms of encryption, the patterns they created obvious. In any given correspondence, certain letters like e and a would always be used with the greatest frequency. Disguising them as z and q or even the number four didn't change that. The repetition of the most common letters remained. The pattern was more or less unchanged.

Lottie didn't recognize the pattern in the code before her. She couldn't even find it, no matter how many times she flipped through the pages.

It was there. She knew it was there. She caught hints and glimpses of it, like intriguing flashes of light in her peripheral vision. But pinning it down was akin to studying a faint star in the night sky. She could see it twinkling out of the corner of her eye, but the second she turned her head to get a proper look, it disappeared.

She wondered if it was a particularly involved polyalphabetic cipher. Her father had been fond of using the Vigenère cipher, manipulating it a bit to give it his own personal touch. In that way, she supposed the encryption rather did look like something he might have created. The numeric values might represent stops, or punctuation. Perhaps they were included merely as a distraction, or as nulls or traps.

But that didn't fit. Without a keyword that sort of encryption might take months, even years, to decipher, if it could be done at all. A man who wrote four lengthy letters clearly felt he had something important to say. He didn't want to wait to be heard or take the chance he might never be heard.

Then again, if he'd designed the keyword to be easily guessed, he wouldn't have to wait. It could be the name of one of the artists or one of the victims. She should make a list of the possibilities. Obviously, she'd need a Vigenère table.

"Do you miss it?"

"Hmm?" She glanced up to find Owen watching her with a curious expression. "Miss what?"

"This. You used to help your father. Used to help us. And you enjoyed it, as I recall."

"I did." At the time, she'd thought she was doing something worthwhile for someone worthwhile. "No, I don't miss it."

"Liar," he accused softly. "You like the challenge."

He was right. She had missed the challenge, along

with the knowledge that she was doing something important, something noble.

Above and beyond that…she had missed Owen. It was a difficult admission to make, even to herself, but she *had* missed him. Or at least the Owen she'd once imagined him to be. The stalwart guardian. The trustworthy hero. The man she could laugh with, confide in, lean on. Her friend.

She had missed that Owen. Desperately.

"I might have missed it a little," she whispered and told herself there was no shame in missing an old lie. Believing it—*that* would be both shameful and dangerous. But missing it was mostly harmless.

"More than a little, I should think." Owen gestured to a clock on the mantel. "You've been at it for nearly an hour, and I'd wager you had no idea more than five minutes had passed."

She lifted a shoulder, secretly annoyed at herself for losing track of time, and a little perturbed that he might have been staring at her the whole time, and quite a *lot* perturbed that the thought made her heart race just a little faster. "I don't like leaving a puzzle undone; that's all. I'm stubborn."

"You are the single most obstinate human being I have ever known," he agreed readily. "You're also one of the cleverest." He leaned forward in his chair and reached out to tap the letters on her lap. "Can you decipher it?"

"I don't know," she answered honestly. "My father employed a variety of techniques and styles. Sometimes the codes he made or acquired were relatively simple, because they were designed to be used by relatively simple men as a means to communicate with other, ofttimes even simpler, men. Other times, an advanced understanding of the mathematics was required."

"You've a rare talent for the mathematics, as I recall."

"Not so very rare. My education was limited." But something told her that an extensive education was not what she was missing. It was the damned pattern. "But I might be able to decipher this with time."

"How much time, precisely?"

She gave him a sardonic look. "Two days, twelve hours, forty-three minutes, and six and three-quarters seconds."

Precisely? *Honestly.*

Owen's lips twitched, which made hers want to twitch, so she found something interesting to stare at on his collar. His open collar, unbuttoned almost to the center of his muscled chest. The familiar shiver returned.

This was a terrible idea.

Instinctively, she dropped her gaze, away from the sight of his golden skin…and straight to his lap.

Infinitely worse.

She tried his face again with the hope that his lips were done twitching.

They were. In fact, Owen no longer appeared the least bit amused. He was watching her with a quiet intensity she found far more unnerving than the sight of his open shirt.

She'd seen that look before. During their last year in London, she would catch him sometimes staring at her from across a room with the same determined look in his eyes.

She'd liked it then. She'd liked the way his piercing gaze made her skin tingle and her breath catch.

But tonight…tonight her skin tingled and her breath caught in her throat, just as before. But she didn't like it. She couldn't.

"I've no idea how much time," she said with more volume than was probably wise. It was worth it. Owen's gaze had drifted down to her neck, but it snapped back up at the sound of her voice. "I can't promise to decipher it at all."

He surprised her by shifting in his seat. She'd never known him to be a fidgeter.

"Will you try?" he asked, his voice a bit hoarse. "We can't look through the journals during the day, or when the room grows too warm, but you can work on this."

"While you do what, *precisely*?"

"Help?" He smiled when she snorted. "We made a good team, once upon a time."

"We did, yes. Until you tossed my father to the wolves."

"Lottie—"

She held up a hand, sorry she'd made the comment. Now wasn't the time to have that fight. *Never* was the time to have that fight. The man hadn't come to apologize. He wasn't sorry for what he'd done. And no amount of berating on her part would change that.

"I'll do what I can," she offered. She owed it to Mrs. Popple.

"Excellent."

"Under my original condition," she continued. "Peter is to know nothing of this. Nothing of what we are doing now nor what any member of this family has done in the past."

"Understood."

"Good." She set the papers aside, sat up straight, and gave him her full attention. "Then we need to discuss how we are to proceed tomorrow."

"And by discuss, do you mean to say you will tell me and I shall agree?"

"Yes."

"I see." He leaned back in his chair, stretched out his long legs, waved his hand in a prompting manner, and said, "Proceed." Putting Lottie to mind of a royal granting audience to one of his subjects.

It was tempting to issue a set-down, something to knock the imaginary jewels out of his imaginary crown, but she decided against it. At the moment, she needed Owen's cooperation more than she wanted his humiliation.

And so Lottie patiently explained her plan to the annoyingly regal Lord Renderwell and provided him with the information he needed to proceed without bringing down the lowly house of Walker-Bales.

The entire process took far less time than she anticipated, primarily because Owen didn't argue. He sat, listened, asked a few questions for clarification, then simply nodded and said, "It's a sound plan. I'll see Samuel and Gabriel follow it."

And that was that. He agreed to her scheme without an argument—without so much as a criticism.

She'd forgotten that about him. She'd forgotten how well he listened and how comfortable he was incorporating the ideas of others into his own plans.

"Do you intend to tell Peter the truth some day?" Owen asked in an offhand manner.

"Hmm?" How was it possible she remembered the smell of his soap and not how well he listened? Listened in a way no one else had before. Or since. "Oh. Yes. I'll tell him."

"Well, if you don't want him to learn of it yet, you should return to your room and have a few hours' sleep. It might look suspicious if we're both exhausted tomorrow."

Peter was familiar with her nocturnal habits. But under the circumstances, it was probably wise not to invite complication.

"Right. Well." She rose from her chair, brushed a hand down her wrinkled skirts, and, for no discernible reason at all, suddenly felt rather awkward. "Good night, Renderwell."

Without waiting for a response, hoping there wouldn't be one, she headed for the door. He was silent as she crossed the room and while she pushed away the counterpane. But the moment her fingers wrapped around the door handle...

"I don't think you dislike me at all," he called out softly, and she froze. "I think you are angry."

She kept her back to him. For reasons she couldn't name, she felt that if she turned round and looked at him, really looked at him, something inside her might break—or worse, melt. And she couldn't allow that to happen.

Anyone can be duped once, poppet. Anyone at all. There's no shame in it.

But there is nothing more pitiful on God's green earth than the dupe who comes back for seconds.

"Does it matter?" she asked softly. It shouldn't matter. Anger or dislike—either way, she wanted nothing to do with him.

"It does." A long pause followed. "Good night, Lottie."

Five

Owen worked out the stiffness of a sleepless night with an early morning walk about the grounds.

There were, in his estimation, few things capable of putting a man at his ease quite so well as a solitary walk in the country. There was something uniquely calming about the openness of the land, the rustle of the trees, and being the only person for…well, not that far, really. He was still in plain view of the house. But it was more distance from humanity than could generally be had in London, unless one cared to take one's walks through Hyde Park in the dead of night.

Even then, it wouldn't be the same. In London, vigilance was required the moment one stepped foot out the door. A man needed to be constantly alert, keenly aware of who and what was around him. There were pickpockets, footpads, ruffians, and cutthroats about—he rubbed absently at a healing bruise across his ribs—some of them waiting in dark alleys, eager to express their displeasure at having spent six weeks in gaol.

But out here, a man could relax.

He dropped his hand and considered the various weapons currently attached to his person.

A man could *probably* learn to relax.

He thought of Lottie last night, standing in front of his knife.

God *Almighty*, he needed to learn how to relax.

He rolled the painful tension out of his shoulders. He wouldn't have hurt her. He knew that and, clearly, she'd known that too. But it had been a terrible thing to find Lottie positioned at the wrong end of his blade.

Which was one reason his mistresses, when he had one, slept in their own beds. And why he would keep his knife out of arm's reach of his bed for the remainder of his stay at Willowbend.

Satisfied, if not completely soothed by that decision, Owen forced his mind back to his peaceful surroundings. Lottie had chosen a fine home for her family, he decided. The old stone house, with its lightly weathered green shutters and low-pitched roof, had a comfortable and settled air about it he found appealing. A small turret, no doubt a recent addition designed to hide a water tank, added a disarming whimsy.

And the grounds were superb. The front lawn was extensive, lightly dotted with trees, but otherwise open to the road. The back lawn, he soon discovered, was quite a bit smaller, hemmed in by the woods after only sixty yards or so, but that was more than adequate space for an extensive flower garden complete with meandering paths and what appeared from a distance to be a sizable fountain.

Owen stopped at the edge of the garden. It was

tempting to wander on, to take a few more minutes for himself, but there wasn't time.

He turned round and headed back to the house. By now, Lottie would be awake. He wanted a private word with her before the rest of the family arose and the charade began.

A minor alteration of plans had occurred. Very well, a significant alteration had occurred, and it would be best if she learned it from him and not one of his men. Owen supposed there was slim chance she'd take the news well. Then again, *slim* chance did afford the possibility of *some* chance. More, certainly, than he might have expected twelve hours ago.

Last night, Lottie had softened. Somewhat. The change had been so subtle, it could easily have gone unnoticed.

But he had noticed.

He'd noticed when she'd cast furtive glances his way over the top of her journal and when her lips had twitched with suppressed laughter. He recognized that sometime during the night her eyes had gone from sharp to wary, and her words from caustic to merely sarcastic. He sure as hell noticed when she'd looked at his lap.

Which led him to an unsettling observation about himself.

He wanted her. Or, more accurately, he still wanted her.

Eight years ago, Lottie had been forbidden fruit, a torturous little itch he couldn't scratch. To scratch would be to take advantage, and not the sort of advantage wherein a gentleman convinces his bride-to-be to anticipate their wedding night. It was really more of a *your family's future lives and dies at my pleasure, but don't let that sway your decision* kind of advantage.

There were words for men who made advances toward women in no position to rebuff them. All of them insufficiently foul.

Owen sidestepped a series of jutting tree roots and frowned. There were also words for men who bedded a countrywoman one day and left for London the next.

He traded frowning for scowling at his boots. Probably, there were also words for a man who tried to seduce a woman who had recently threatened to set him ablaze, throat first. But those were just embarrassing.

"Renderwell!"

Owen lifted his head to discover Lottie already halfway across the lawn. He waved at her.

She did not wave back.

Still, she made a lovely picture. He stopped where he was and let her come to him, for no other reason than to draw out the pleasure of watching her.

The morning sunlight was behind her, illuminating her lithe form with a soft glow, while a gentle breeze fluttered the skirts of her forest-green gown and caught a small lock of ebony hair, releasing it from its pins. That was sure to annoy her, Owen thought with a smile. Lottie was careful how she presented herself. She didn't like to appear undone.

"Care for a morning stroll, Miss Bales?" he inquired when she drew near.

"No," she said without heat, but also without hesitation. "Peter will be up soon. Have you spoken with Samuel and Gabriel?"

"After you left last night," he assured her. "They

understand what's to be done." She wasn't going to like what was to be done, but they would get to that in a minute. "Did you sleep?"

"Some." She brushed the errant lock of hair away from her face. "You?"

Well now, that was nice.

"I did," he replied and caught his hands behind his back. "Thank you for inquiring."

"Habit."

"Liar."

"Lottie!" Peter's young voice positively boomed across the lawn.

Owen tilted his head to look around Lottie and saw the boy walking toward them, Esther at his side. So much for a few private words. He couldn't tell her of the change in plan now. Well, he could, but he wouldn't have time to convince her it was for the best, so why bother with the argument?

"Healthy set of lungs on that one," he observed.

"He's fourteen." Lottie turned to wave at the newcomers. "He'll settle."

"He has a lifetime of settled before him. There's no hurry."

"Insightful of you," she said with a glance over her shoulder.

He stepped up beside her. "You needn't sound stunned. Some people consider me a man of exceptional insight."

Other people considered him a barbaric reprobate and a disgrace to titled gentlemen the world over.

She looked at him with great pity. "Might these people be your mother?"

His mother belonged in the category of "other people," but he appreciated the barb nonetheless.

"It requires a perceptive and intelligent woman to recognize brilliance." He gave her a consoling look of his own. "Trust me."

That pulled a laugh out of her. The sound was clear and sweet and made him feel as if he'd won a coveted prize. It was just as he remembered.

"You're delusional," Lottie informed him. "Both of you."

"And you're amused," he returned softly. "It is nice to hear you laugh, Lottie."

He waited for the laugh to die abruptly and braced himself to see her eyes go cold. But it never happened. Instead, the laugh faded slowly. The tone became less sure, more hesitant.

At last the laughter drifted away completely, and a weighted silence followed. He wanted to fill it, to find the words that would make her smile again.

But there wasn't time. A few seconds more, and Peter and Esther were upon them.

"Good morning, Lord Renderwell," Peter offered cheerfully and a little slowly, as if he was taking extra care with the words.

Good God, surely Lottie had not *actually* disparaged his intelligence in front of the boy.

Owen kept his tone light and easy, despite a rising irritation. "Mr. Bales. Miss Bales. Fine morning, is it not?"

"It is," Peter agreed. He smiled broadly. Much, much too broadly. "Have you plans?"

"I've some pressing correspondence." She *had*.

The little hellion had told her brother that Viscount Renderwell was a dolt. "But Sir Samuel and Sir Gabriel have expressed an interest in visiting your village."

Peter shook his head and continued to speak slowly. "There is little amusement to be had there, I'm afraid."

"There are ruins to the south, I've heard."

"There are," Peter confirmed, perking up and, thankfully, speeding up. "A twelfth-century motte and bailey with the remains of a keep converted to stone. I've spent a fair amount of time exploring them."

"Ah, a guide. Excellent. If you're amendable, of course."

Lottie's gaze snapped to his. "I'm afraid that's not—"

Peter spoke right over her. "Delighted to be of service, my lord. It is a bit of a ride, mind you. The better part of two hours by carriage."

Lottie shook her head. "Entirely too far. I am certain…" She sent Owen one of her extra-sharp smiles. "*Quite* certain the gentlemen have had their fill of travel—"

"Nonsense." Owen smiled right back. She was angry. Good. So was he. Dolt, indeed. "My men would like nothing better than a *leisurely*"—he drew the word out, just to be a little mean—"ride through the countryside."

"It's settled then," Peter announced.

Lottie's lips parted, she took a breath on which to object—strenuously, no doubt—just as the breeze picked up…and she found herself with a mouthful of hair.

She spit it out with a remarkable lack of grace for a woman best known for her unflappable poise. Owen did his utmost not to laugh. Lady luck might be a fickle mistress, but her little sister serendipity made for one hell of a friend.

Esther winced sympathetically, but she said, "A visit to the ruins does sound lovely," in a perfectly cheerful tone of voice.

"You mean to come?" Peter asked.

"Well"—she wrapped her arm through his—"someone must keep an eye on you, else your mischief will land our guests in hot water before midday."

On the surface, the comment appeared to be a playful bit of teasing. But the subtle nod Esther sent to Lottie held a promise, not a jest. Esther meant to keep an eye on everyone.

"Bit of a scamp, is he?" Owen asked while Peter blushed and stammered.

"Complete rapscallion," Esther assured him with a look that was neither playful nor reassuring. It was as hard as Lottie's eyes. Clearly, Esther didn't care for this turn of events any more than her sister.

"Hardly that." Peter laughed.

"Prove it," Esther challenged and placed a sisterly peck on his cheek. "Come inside and help me see to the arrangements, like a gentleman."

"I suppose we should pack a meal," Peter agreed. "Will you be joining us, Lottie?"

"I…" She pushed her hair back up with its pin. "Thank you, no. I've things to look after here."

Owen understood that to mean she had *him* to look after here. Under no circumstances would she allow him unsupervised access to her home.

Peter looked genuinely disappointed, once again raising him in Owen's estimation. It wasn't every fourteen-year-old boy who sought out the company of his sisters. "Certain? It won't be the same without you."

"We shall tell her all about it upon our return," Esther promised and gave his arm a gentle tug. "We should begin our preparations straightaway if we wish to leave by a reasonable hour. You will excuse us, my lord?"

He inclined his head. Peter bowed low. Esther curtsied prettily. And Lottie gave a merry wave.

A companionable lot were they.

Up to the very second Esther and Peter were removed from earshot.

"Four hours," Lottie ground out, spinning on him. "You couldn't keep to an agreement for *four* hours?"

"Four hours ago, I agreed to tell Peter a fictional variation of his family's past. That hasn't changed." He held up a hand. "Allow me to finish. With Peter out of the house, we can search your father's journals without fear of discovery."

"I have staff."

"Many of whom can be sent to attend those going to the ruins. Certainly the maids and footmen may go. I will find something else for the rest to do."

Her eyes turned murderous at the word *I*, but the overall effect was somewhat mitigated by the reappearance of the errant lock of hair. It slid back out of its pin slowly, the middle section first, creating a silken loop that grew larger and larger until finally the very end slipped free and came to rest on the gentle curve of her breast.

He decided he would not look at it. "*You* can find something else for the rest to do."

"Your men were to limit their time with Peter, not seek him out."

"Samuel and Gabriel know what they're doing. Deceit is not new to them. It is not new to you, either," he pointed out, eager to switch from defense to offense. "I cannot believe you would tell Peter I'm a dolt."

Her brows lifted. "Can you not?"

"It was reckless, Lottie. Don't you think he'll grow suspicious when he discovers the truth?"

A short pause followed. "I don't foresee the truth becoming a problem."

"Oh, for—"

"I didn't tell him you were a dolt." She rolled her eyes with supreme impatience. "Honestly, when did you become so gullible?"

Owen frowned and looked back at the house. "He was acting oddly. Didn't you notice?"

"Of course he was acting oddly. He's nervous." The wind caught her hair, lifted it to her face. She brushed it away. "You're the first viscount he's ever met, and you knew our father. He wants very much to make a good impression."

"Ah." He nodded as irritation drained away. "Yes, that makes sense. I—" He stopped before he could apologize for having assumed the worst. The whole thing had been her jest. He was not going to apologize for being the butt of it. "He has already made a good impression."

"Well, he doesn't know that," she bit off. "He doesn't know anything and I wanted to keep it that way. You *agreed* to my plan."

Owen studied her face. Her jaw was clenched tight, and her eyes kept darting to the house and back again. She wasn't angry, he realized. He studied her some more.

Yes, actually, she was. She was exceedingly angry. But she was also worried, maybe even a little fearful.

And now he felt like a heel. Using Peter to provoke her had been bad form.

"I did agree," he said carefully. "And I should have told you I saw need to alter it. I certainly should not have surprised you with it in front of Peter. That was badly done. I apologize."

She said nothing, just stared at him through guarded eyes. Not a trusting woman, his Charlotte.

"Your secrets are safe with me, Lottie. They always have been. They—" He broke off when she brushed at her hair again. "Here." Stepping close, he drew his finger across her cheek, catching the loose strand and gently tucking it behind her ear.

She stood very, very still during the process, like she couldn't quite decide if she wanted to lean into the touch or break his hand off at the wrist.

The breeze caught her scent and brought it to him. "You smell different," he said softly.

She took a quick step back. "I beg your pardon?"

Though he was reluctant to break the contact, he let his hand fall away. "I noticed it last night. You used to smell of flowers. Roses and lavender and such. Now you smell..." He bent closer and took in a breath. "Like lemons. Tart."

"If the scent offends you, I'll go inside—"

"Didn't say it offends me."

"—and bathe in it."

"It isn't offensive," he pressed on. "Quite the contrary. It suits you." He gave her a smile designed to charm. "It suits me too."

The design failed.

"Don't," she warned and turned to leave.

He caught her arm. "Wait—"

"*Don't.*" She yanked herself free. "You haven't the right to tease me, Renderwell, and you damn well haven't the right to flirt with me."

"I'm not attempting to flirt with you." He was, a little, but only in a bid to make her smile again. He held his hands up. "I am trying to form a truce, Lottie. If you would be reasonable—"

"Reasonable?" She spat the word out as if it burned her tongue. "If I—"

"Yes. Reasonable." Irritation was starting to return. "Being at odds with each other accomplishes nothing but to make our current situation unnecessarily uncomfortable. I want you to put aside your anger, your entirely unjustified anger, I might add, for two minutes and be reasonable. I want—"

"Oh, to *hell* with what you want."

The venom in her voice took him aback. So did the depth of rage in her eyes. There was more here than old, irrational anger, he realized. Even more than fear for her brother. There was something else mixed in. Something he couldn't put his finger on.

"The unbelievable gall of you." Lottie stepped up to him, hands fisted at her sides. "After everything that happened, you show up on my doorstep and expect friendly cooperation? Are you completely unhinged?

Why should I bother myself over your comfort, Renderwell? Why on earth should I dance one step to your tune? I tried that once. My father tried it. He danced a merry jig for your and your men for four years, and look what he got for his trouble."

"Now wait a min—"

"An unmarked, untended grave nobody knows where. That was his reward. Did you think I would forget? Is that your definition of reasonable—that I should pretend I don't remember or that my anger is unjustified, so you might be *comfortable*?"

What he'd done, Owen thought darkly. Sent her father out to single-handedly rescue the kidnapped Lady Strale from the nefarious Horatio Gage—that was his crime. He had sealed Will Walker's fate by ordering him into a building full of armed criminals.

Only Owen hadn't done it. He'd never given that order. And she bloody well knew it.

"Right." He considered his options, calculated the risks, and made a choice. "Right."

Determined now, he took hold of her arm and marched toward a nearby bench hidden from the house by the low-hanging branches of an ancient oak.

She pulled at her arm fruitlessly. "What do you think—?"

"We're having this out."

"I am not interested in—"

"I am." He spun her around, positioning her in front of the bench. "Sit down and listen."

"No."

"I have the advantage here, Charlotte. And we both know it." He moved an inch closer. "Sit *down*."

She stood just as she was. But only for a moment more, just long enough to make it perfectly clear how little she thought of him and his threats. Finally, she sat, slowly and without taking her eyes off him. Her black gaze promised unholy retribution.

She'd make good on that promise, no doubt. And well she should. A man who engaged in high-handed tactics with a woman deserved to lose a finger. A man who tried it with Lottie should expect to lose two.

But, by God, it would be worth it. Damn well worth it to have this argument out and done with at last.

He glanced down at his hands, then held them out for her to see. "Do you know how much blood I have on my hands, Lottie?"

She narrowed her eyes, suspecting a trap. "No."

"Neither do I," he admitted. "Enemy soldiers, mostly. It can be difficult in battle to know if it was your shot that felled a man or if the soldier standing next to you fired first. But it stands to reason I hit my mark at least some of the time, doesn't it?"

"Yes."

"Yes. And then there are the men I've killed since the war. Criminals like Daniel Potts, George Brunten, and a half-dozen others, maybe more. Again, difficult to tell when there are men beside you and the smoke of shot all around. But I can tell you the name of every man who died whilst under my command. Every man who was lost because I missed a shot or because, maybe, I hesitated too long to sound a retreat or not long enough before a charge. It is an ungodly amount of blood. The weight of it is staggering." He turned his hands over and studied the backs of his fingers. "I put it there, and I will live with it."

"I don't see—"

"But I will be *damned* before I let you add your father's blood to that weight."

She blinked, reared back. "What?"

"Your father chose his path. He chose to build his fortune through deceit and theft, and when he was caught, he chose to work with us rather than face punishment."

"I know that."

"And he chose to face Horatio Gage alone." She bloody well knew that too. "He was ordered to stay away. He knew better than to walk into a building brimming to the rafters with Gage's armed men. I was miles away. We were all miles away. There was nothing we could do to help him. He knew that." He leaned down, caught her gaze, and held it. "I am *not* responsible for the death of your father. Do you understand?"

"I… You…" she sputtered—something he had never seen her do before—then closed her mouth and for nearly a full ten seconds simply stared at him as if he was some sort of exotic and possibly dangerous beast.

And then, at long last—

"You really are a dolt," she said breathlessly, rather as if she was as surprised to discover this as he was to hear it.

He straightened again. "I beg your pardon?"

"How could you possibly think…?" She stared at him some more. "I *loved* my father. For all his vices, I loved him dearly."

"I know," he said, uncertain as to the current direction of the conversation.

"Do you?" A small, baffled laugh escaped her. "And yet you imagine I would choose for his murderer the *blistering* revenge of a cold shoulder?"

"Your options were limited. And I thought—"

"I was a Walker," she reminded him ominously. "I'd all manner of options at my disposal. I know who killed my father. I have always known. Horatio Gage. And had he not met his demise at the end of a rope, I'd have seen to it that it arrived at the end of a knife. Slowly."

Owen found himself at a loss. "Then why in God's name are you so angry with me?"

She shook her head slowly. "You really don't know, do you? It meant so little to you—"

"How am I to know what it meant to me if I don't know what *it* is? I'm not a gypsy woman, Lottie. I can't read your mind—"

"You disavowed him," she cut in, stabbing an accusatory finger at him. "You tossed him aside like garbage."

Garbage? What the devil was this? "I did nothing of the sort."

"Didn't you? Did you acknowledge what he did for you? Anything he did for you? Did you give him credit for rescuing Lady Strale from Gage? Did you *ever* speak one public word about my father?"

"You know I couldn't reveal your father's involvement," Owen returned, utterly confounded. "He was a thief." Public opinion on the matter of the police working with the very thieves they were meant to catch was unforgiving, to say the least. Moreover, it would have put the entire Walker family at risk. "He was a criminal—"

"Yes, and now that is all he will *ever* be," she snapped, rising from her seat. "He should not have gone into that building. It was stupid. It was stupid and reckless, and it was brave. For once in his selfish, sordid life, he did something good. He saved that woman. He died for her. But it was you and your men who received all the accolades and all the commendations. The heroic Lord Renderwell rescued Lady Strale, taking down the infamous Horatio Gage in the process. You went into that house a solid hour after my father dragged Lady Strale to freedom. But you became a hero and a viscount, your men were knighted, and my father went to the grave a pathetic, petty criminal and nothing more. He deserved better. He deserved—"

"The hell he did," Owen bit off, equal parts baffled and furious that *this* should be the source of contention between them. He'd understood an irrational anger born of grief. He'd hated it, but he'd understood. But this? It was ludicrous.

Eight years. *Eight years* she had punished him for breaking a promise he'd never made. He had never intended to reveal his association with Will Walker, and Will had never expected it of him. They'd both understood the rules and rewards of the game. They had all understood. "Your father *was* a criminal, Charlotte, and well you know it. When I first met him, all he deserved was a cell in Newgate."

Possibly a trip to the three-legged mare. The man's past had been more criminal than petty.

"Yes, when you first met him," Lottie argued. "He was a scoundrel, then. He wasn't a scoundrel when he died. It wasn't a scoundrel who saved Lady Strale."

Oh, yes. It had been. "Lady Strale would have been rescued that day regardless of your father's actions." There had been a plan in place. One that did not include Will charging in on his own.

"Lady Strale was rescued regardless of yours," she shot back.

"Mine did not result in the creation of three orphans. His did. And for what? A chance to pocket the diamonds she'd been wearing. Or claim Lord Stale's reward for himself."

She shook her head. "That's a lie. He wouldn't have—"

"Of course he would have. God, Lottie, you knew him better than anyone. You know he was capable."

"Yes, he was capable. But he *wouldn't* have done it," she insisted. "Not after four years of working with you. It changed him. He wasn't perfect, but he was a better man."

What a load of rubbish. "He was—"

"He was your *friend*!"

Owen opened his mouth, intent on calling her out on that absolute whale of a lie—*the devil he'd been a friend*—but he bit the words back before they could form.

She believed it. He could see it in her eyes. There was hurt there. That was what he'd caught a glimpse of earlier but hadn't been able to sort out from the anger and worry—pain.

It astounded him, even more than the true cause of her animosity. Will Walker, a better man. It seemed an impossible bit of fantasy for a woman like Lottie to have about a man like her father, but there it was. She truly believed her father had changed, that he'd become a hero, a friend. And she honestly believed that his redemption had been stolen away, the friendship betrayed.

Oh, hell.

For the first time, Owen was forced to entertain the disturbing notion that Lottie had, in fact, been a mite fuzzy on the aforementioned rules. Clearly, he'd been mistaken in thinking she knew her father best. Because the truth was, given the chance, Will Walker would have offered Owen's soul to the devil for halfpence. He had not become a better man.

And they had never been friends.

"Lottie…" He trailed off, at a loss for words.

When he'd begun the conversation, he'd done so with the expectation of putting to rest any misunderstandings about her father's death. He had not expected to encounter misconceptions about her father's life nor any bizarre notions that the man had made a miraculous transformation from sinner to saint on his last day.

The sudden change in perspective left him unsteady, as if the ground beneath him, relatively solid only minutes ago, had abruptly transformed into a high wire. And now he was afraid to move.

He desperately wanted to spare Lottie the pain of the truth, almost as badly as he wanted to strip away the lie that hurt them both. For the life of him, he could not find a means that led to both ends. He couldn't find his way off the wire.

And so he just stood there like a fool without a word to say for himself. Until, finally, his silence spoke for him.

"You're not the least bit sorry for what you did, are you?" Lottie accused quietly. She shook her head. "I knew you wouldn't be. I knew having this out would be a mistake. I knew..." She swallowed hard. "I'm going inside. I have work to do."

With a final shake of her head, she turned her back on him and walked away.

Six

It wasn't difficult to hide a foul mood from Peter.

People see what they expect to see, poppet.

Lottie considered this perfectly trite piece of wisdom as she smiled her way through the preparations for the trip to the ruins. Even at the age of nine, she had known her father's statement to be inaccurate.

People might see what they expected to see, but they looked for what they wanted to see. If a gentleman expected that a lady might be put out with him, then he would notice her averted gaze, her stiff posture, and her pinched mouth. But if he wanted forgiveness, then he searched for a softening of the eyes or a curve of the lips.

If one wished to dupe a person, one had to take into consideration that closer look. One had to remember both the expectation and the desire.

Fortunately for her, Peter's assumptions and wishes were in perfect accord. He expected her to be happy and he hoped she was happy. Therefore, when she smiled broadly and laughed freely as they packed a picnic lunch in the kitchen, he believed she was happy.

It was a joyless role to perform.

She disliked playing Peter for a fool. Keeping secrets from him was bad enough, but active manipulation carried with it a lack of respect that served only to deepen the guilt.

And it was all *his* fault, she thought grimly as Owen's dark form came into view through the windows.

She stuffed a ham sandwich none too gently into a basket and indulged in a spot of covert glowering even as she mentally retracted the accusation. It had been, and continued to be, her decision to lie to Peter and no one else's. There was plenty for which to blame Owen—no sense in diluting righteous anger with false recriminations.

Trouble was, she was more hurt than angry.

She watched Owen cross the back lawn in long strides, head bent in thought. She had expected him to defend himself differently. She had been prepared to listen to some long-winded, pompous justification for his actions. He was a gentleman, a nobleman, a man of honor and worth entitled to the adoration of the masses. He had only taken his due. She had thought his ambition and selfishness would be so evident that they would leave no room for anything but outrage and disgust.

But he hadn't defended himself at all. Instead of making a case for himself, he had made a case against her father. And by extension, against her.

Once a thief, always a thief.

Owen hadn't said those exact words, but the sentiment was clear, and it had cut to the quick. He had given no thought to the possibility of redemption for her father, no credit to the notion a person might change for the better. Will Walker had been a black-hearted scoundrel and, really, what else was there to say?

She shoved more sandwiches into the basket while Peter chattered on about the upcoming adventure.

Owen was wrong. People changed. People changed all the time.

She had changed.

Maybe she deserved a cell in Newgate. Maybe she deserved an unmarked grave next to her father's for the terrible things she had once done. But didn't she also deserve recognition for the good she had accomplished since those dark times? Didn't she deserve a chance at redemption? She had to believe the answer to both questions was yes.

Risking another glance at Owen, she saw him disappear around the corner of the house. No, he hadn't done what she'd expected, but he'd made it perfectly clear he wasn't going to offer what she had once hoped.

Across the table, Peter grabbed an apple and bit in. "Aye hood heck—"

"Swallow, then speak."

He chewed and swallowed dutifully. "I should check on the carriage and horses."

"I believe Sir Gabriel and Sir Samuel are seeing to them."

"They're guests. They shouldn't be." He took another, smaller bite and spoke around the food. "Did you know they're famous? Renderwell, particularly."

She froze with her hand in the basket. "I beg your pardon?"

"He's the Gentleman Thief Taker. Surely you've heard of him. Everyone has heard of him."

"How did you hear of him?" And when, and who had told? She was certain Peter hadn't the faintest idea who Owen was yesterday.

"I told you; he's famous. He rescued a kidnapped duchess." He lifted both brows and widened his eyes as if to say, *Can you imagine?* "A duchess. She went missing from her own ball whilst wearing the family jewels. Renderwell found those too, but they say she was so frightened by the experience, she *never* wore them again."

"You're not old enough to have heard of any of this. How did you come to know who Renderwell is?"

Peter wiped his mouth with the back of his sleeve as he studied her with a bland expression. "I'm not sure how many different ways one can impart the notion of famous. Renowned? Celebrated? Legendary?" He bobbed his head thoughtfully. "Legendary. I like that."

Legendary seemed a bit much. "How famous could he be if I didn't realize he was famous, and you didn't know who he was yesterday?"

"I knew who he was yesterday," he replied, a little defensively. "Well, I figured it out. Mr. Derby mostly called him the Gentleman Thief Taker. That's what the papers dubbed him. I had forgotten he was Renderwell."

"Mr. Derby told you?" The sliver of unease that had been working under her skin dissolved under the weight of a new, more prickly sensation. Surely Owen wasn't so famous that his actions eight years ago could still be of interest to a country schoolmaster who took pride in never having stepped a single foot in the god-less city of London.

"That must have been where I heard it first," Peter decided. "We were discussing... I don't remember." He waved his apple about. "The need for reform or some such. Mr. Derby is of the opinion that private investigators should be paid by the Crown, instead of taking on private commissions. He says some people suspect Renderwell left the Met so he could work as an agent for the Crown in secret, but those are only rumors. He says most of what was printed in the papers and broadsides were rumors."

"Broadsides?" She heard the stunned disbelief in her voice and prayed Peter would interpret it as eager fascination.

Had there been broadsides? She couldn't remember seeing any at the time. Then again, she was in the habit of ignoring the single sheets of paper sold on street corners, even crossing to the far side of the road to avoid the peddlers. Too often they heralded an upcoming execution. The condemned's name was written boldly across the page, directly under a macabre sketch of a lifeless form dangling from a rope. Though it was unlikely her father's crimes would have sent him to the gallows, it had nonetheless been much too easy to envision her father's face, her father's form hanging from the rope. Sometimes she even saw herself.

She knew that Lady Strale's rescue had received some attention. How could it not? There had been the bit in the *Times* detailing Renderwell's heroic actions, and she had seen the announcement of his elevation to viscount and departure from the police along with the soon to be knighted Sergeants Brass and Arkwright.

After that, she'd stopped reading the *Times*, stopped looking for any sign or news of Owen and his men. There had been so much to do. There had been a home to purchase, a family to move, staff to find, a father to grieve. For a time, she had stopped paying attention to the world outside her small family and their precarious future.

Peter bobbed his head. "He showed us some. Bit faded. There haven't been new ones made in years. A man can't go rescuing duchesses every day, I suppose. But Mr. Derby says there used to be new ones every day, for weeks, even months."

She wanted to swallow, but her mouth had gone dry. "Mr. Derby has a lot to say."

"About everything," Peter confirmed, with feeling. "But not so much as Michael Ernswot. He says his sister knows Renderwell's sister. One of the middle ones. Victoria, I think. Bragged on and on about it."

"His sisters?" Peter knew the name of Owen's sister? She knew the names of only two (neither of them Victoria), and those had been dragged out of him years ago. He rarely spoke of his family. "Are they famous as well?"

Peter shrugged and added utensils to the picnic basket one-handed. "There were sketches of them in some of the broadsides. Renderwell was a sensation. Ergo, the Renderwells were a sensation."

"I see." The prickly feeling grew into a disorienting blend of shock, trepidation, and another feeling she was reluctant to study too closely, but a small, distant part of her admitted might be hope.

Papers, broadsides, sketches. A sensation. Not just talk, as she had assumed, not merely the latest *on dit*, but a sensation. Owen hadn't mentioned a sensation. Why hadn't he mentioned it?

"Wait until he finds out we know him," Peter chimed.

"What?" She struggled to focus on the boy before her.

Peter rolled his eyes, laboriously chewing a piece of food he evidently assumed had muffled his words. "I said, wait until Michael finds out we know the man himself." He made a thoughtful face at the apple. "How do we know him? What sort of business did father have with the police?"

"Investments," she said quickly. "Father advised Renderwell on investments."

"Oh, right. Riiiight." He drew the word out, relishing how very amazing it all was. "Our father advised the Gentleman Thief Taker. That is bloody brilliant. Beg pardon."

"It was a long time ago, Peter," she said and busied her hands in the picnic basket to hide the way they shook.

"Doesn't matter." Peter tossed away the remainder of his apple, wiped his fingers down the front of his waistcoat, then grinned at her impishly as he headed out the kitchen door. "Still bloody brilliant."

"Language," she called out after him, but only because he would find it odd if she didn't. He could have left a mile-wide string of curses in his wake and right now she would not have cared.

Grateful for the momentary solitude, Lottie sank

onto a nearby stool and tried to wrestle her disordered thoughts into submission. Her carefully guarded world was shifting, pieces rearranging and falling into a pattern she didn't recognize.

Was Peter right? Had there really been a sensation?

She searched her memory of the weeks leading up to Lady Strale's rescue for signs of a public drama to come, for anything she might have missed. Nothing of significance came to mind.

Owen and her father had spent a good portion of their time out on the streets, sometimes together, often separately.

Her own involvement had been limited, as her skills did not run to pounding on doors and browbeating informants. As a result, she'd heard of Lady Strale's predicament in bits and pieces, and she could not recall reading of it anywhere.

It had been a subdued affair overall, likely at the family's request. A missing wife was much too sordid a tale for a peer of the realm to want bandied about. Why then had her rescue turned into something more?

Into something she had more sense than to wish on the Walker family?

She had wanted a bit of praise for her father, a forgiving word spoken here and there when he was remembered, but fame of the magnitude Peter described was something else altogether. It was dangerous.

Owen would have known that.

"I want a word with you."

Lottie's heart lurched at the sound of Owen's voice. He was standing in the open doorway, his hands caught behind his rigid back, and his face set in implacable lines. Somehow, he succeeded in looking both regal and mulish.

Slowly and carefully, she slid off the stool. "I think—"

"I know we had words. When the others are gone, we'll have more. We are not finished."

An hour ago, she had been certain they *were* finished and equally sure it was for the best. A minute ago, she had been afraid of it.

"No, we are not," she agreed and watched as her quick agreement caused surprise and suspicion to flash across his face.

"Right. In the parlor," he ordered in a tone that brooked no argument. "As soon as they leave."

She was stricken with the sudden urge to salute or drop into a dramatic curtsy or say something utterly ridiculous like, *Aye, Captain*, and she wondered if she'd always been prone to random acts of absurdity when nervous or if Owen's presence was a prerequisite for this new affliction.

She shoved the impulse aside. "As soon as we are alone."

～

In under an hour, the travelers set off with most of Willowbend's staff in tow. If Peter thought it odd that one picnic should require two footmen and both maids, he didn't mention it. Lottie assumed he was either too excited to think of it or had been too distracted by the discovery of a spot on his forehead. She caught him poking at it while squinting at his reflection in the brilliantly polished base of an antique candelabra.

The silliness of that act, and the simple normalcy of reassuring him that no, it was not the size of Wayton's chapel spire, had eased the worst of her nerves. But as the retreating carriage sent a plume of dust down the drive, those nerves came sliding back.

She stood in the parlor with Owen. She, next to the oversized writing desk. He, leaning against the back of the settee. Both of them dead silent.

Despite the tension in the air, she didn't feel foolish. Not yet. There was still the possibility that Peter was mistaken, that there had been only a handful of broadsides and one bored and infatuated headmaster.

She did, however, feel miserably conflicted.

It was a distressing predicament to stand at the crossroads of justified fury and complete remorse with no clear sense of which direction one ought to step.

In the end, she went with instinct. "Were you friends with my father?"

Owen was slow to answer. "I…"

"Don't think; just answer." People who had time to think had time to think of lies. "Were you ever friends with my father?"

He stiffened, though whether it was in response to her question or his coming answer, she couldn't say. "No. We worked together well enough, but we were not friends."

"Do you think my father became a better man?"

"No." A small sigh. "I'm sorry, no."

One thing at a time, she told herself and pushed disappointment aside. "If he had been, if he had changed, would you have given him credit for rescuing Lady Strale?"

"No. Lottie—"

"Why did you take credit for saving Lady Strale?"

"To keep you safe," he ground out, straightening from the settee. "Why else?"

"For the viscountcy," she replied and could not recall a time she had ever wished so much to be wrong.

Owen's expression darkened. "Let me be clear on this. I did not receive the viscountcy for rescuing Lady Strale. The Crown is aware of your father's act. I received it for years of exceptional service to the Crown culminating in the capture of Horatio Gage and a dozen of his men. I'd not have accepted it otherwise."

"But you accepted the credit given to you by all of London."

"Yes, and I would do it again." He stepped forward, impatience all but coming off him in waves. "For God's sake, Lottie. Did you not stop and think what would happen to you if your father's actions that day had become known?"

"Of course I did. It is what I wanted, for people to know the truth. Only..." She grimaced and found something fascinating to stare at in the grain of a side table. "Only I did not think it would be of great interest to most." Just sufficient interest to ensure her father's legacy consisted of more than a long list of black-hearted deeds. "Lady Strale's kidnapping received very little attention. I assume people spoke of it, but—"

"No one spoke of it. Her disappearance from her own ball whilst wearing the Strale diamonds was a closely guarded secret. The ransom note we received demanded silence in exchange for her continued well-being."

"Gage. Of course." Gage would not have wanted all of London searching for him. "I assumed that her family wished to keep it quiet and that Lady Strale would not care to become a spectacle after—"

"Lady Strale has always been a spectacle, even when she's sober. A more self-absorbed, melodramatic human being I've yet to meet, unless it is her stepson, the current Lord Strale. They run head-to-head. After her rescue, she related the tale of her abduction to anyone willing to listen and embellished it with the skill of a seasoned actress. She reveled in the attention, dining off the story for months. We could only count ourselves fortunate she was unconscious at the time of her rescue and unable to recognize your father."

"You told her it had been you."

"It was the Crown's decision. I'd have chosen someone else, but it was insisted that as a baron..." He waved his hand in the air as his voice trailed off. "Neither here nor there. Had your father received the credit for Lady Strale's rescue, he would have become a tremendous sensation, likely more so because of his death. That is what mattered."

"He was already well-known—"

"But *you* weren't," Owen insisted with growing heat. "The name Will Walker might have been spoken in hushed whispers in thieves' dens and ballrooms all across London, but scarcely a handful of those whispering could have picked the man out of a crowd. The details of his life were shrouded in mystery. Details like the names and location of his children. He made sure of that. I made sure that didn't change."

"I wanted it to change," she murmured, more

to herself than to him. The conversation tied her in knots. It felt as if she was somehow both winning and losing, and though she knew which she preferred, it made her miserable all the same. "I wanted it to change for the better."

"It wasn't possible. It still would have been necessary for you to leave London with a new name for your own safety."

"I know that." One good act, however heroic, would not have appeased every man her father had duped nor every former associate he had betrayed in his work with Owen. "But I thought his legacy might be different. I thought—"

"That legacy would have put you in harm's way."

She nodded and risked a glance at him. "Peter said your sisters became the subject of talk as well."

Though she was no longer arguing with him, Owen appeared not to notice. The less resistance she offered, the more emphatic he became. "My sisters. My parents. My long-dead grandparents. My tutor when I'd been eight. They picked my life apart, Lottie. For months after Lady Strale's rescue, every detail of my existence was fodder for the presses. Nothing was too small to omit. Where I went, what I ate, what sort of boots I wore, the brandy I preferred. That would have been you. With your father dead, his orphaned children would have been the focus of every gossipmonger in England."

"No one knew us," she pointed out. "No one ever knew our given names."

They'd not had live-in staff, and even Mrs. Popple had only known her as Walker Daughter the First. It had been that small act of care on her father's part that had allowed them to keep their given names upon moving to Norfolk.

"Mystery would have only fanned the flames," Owen argued. "There would have been descriptions of you and Esther and Peter, even sketches, drawn from the memory of one of your father's former accomplices or a servant or neighbor. Anyone who might have caught even a glimpse of the Walker children. Your likeness would have been printed in broadsides and papers all over England. No matter where you went, there would always be the risk of someone recognizing you. And it would have been only a matter of time before word of your location reached London. I couldn't protect you from that. I could hide you from your enemies in London—I could not shield you from an entire nation."

She nodded again. There was nothing else she could do. In her visions of what might have been, her father's act of courage had been a minor footnote in a larger tale. Worthy of mention, not dissection.

"Your father understood all this," Owen pressed, his voice lowered and insistent. "He understood and agreed to the risks and rewards of working with me. He never expected accolades. He never wanted them. Not for his sake. And certainly not for yours."

Needing something to do with her hands besides twist them, she picked up a glass paperweight from the table and ran her palm over the smooth surface. "It is…difficult to know what to believe."

Owen closed some of the distance between them. "Believe this. I am the one who told you how your father died. I came to your house, sat you down, and told you exactly what had happened. If my intentions had ever been to deceive you, I'd have done so that day. A lie would have served me far better than the truth."

"I know." She remembered thinking of that years ago. It had given her pause, before it disappeared under the weight of anger and grief. "I need to think."

"Think here," he snapped when she stepped past him toward the door. He caught her arm and turned her round again. "I am tired of watching you walk away, Lottie."

"I'm not walking away." Not like he meant. "I need a moment to think. Please."

"Think here." His voice softened, and his grip gentled. "Lottie. Your revenge. Your cold shoulder… It was blistering to me."

She looked down. "I am sorry. I—"

"Think here," he repeated, quietly this time. His hand slid down her arm in an unmistakable caress.

If he had continued to demand, to press, she might have found the will to leave, but his words were more plea than they were an order.

"Yes. All right. A moment."

"A moment," he agreed. He stepped back, studied her warily for a second, then nodded once and turned away to gaze out the window.

Lottie let out a breath of relief. She needed that small distance between them. As much as she wanted to oblige him, she could not stay in the room if he insisted on watching her. No one could think while they were being watched by a man like Owen Renderwell.

One could, however, think quite clearly while they

watched someone else. Her gaze traveled up his long back, the wide breadth of his shoulders, the slight curl of hair at the nape of his neck. Everything about him was as familiar to her as it was foreign. How could she know someone so well and still be so wrong?

She pulled her eyes away and frowned at the ribbons of color twisted through the paperweight in her hands. She wasn't *entirely* in the wrong. Owen was mistaken on a fair number of points. Her father *had* changed and deserved some sort of recognition for that. And there had been options other than danger and immediate discovery in the aftermath of his death. The Walker family might have emigrated, for example.

She didn't want to emigrate, but that was beside the point.

She stifled a sigh. The point was that she had been wrong about what mattered most right now. She had been wrong about Owen's intentions. They hadn't been greedy and selfish. They had been good.

As far as she was concerned, the road to hell was not paved with good intentions. It was paved with bad deeds. Most of them her father's. A few of them her own.

Good intentions provided a light in the dark. It lit the spot for a new road, one that led up and out. All a body had to do was pave it.

It was what she wanted most in the world—to build a new path forward for herself and her family, to be given a second chance and the benefit of the doubt.

How could she deny Owen what amounted to the same thing?

❧

Owen was accustomed to reading people. He could spot a shift in mood or a reversal of heart from the most subtle change in expression, the slightest adjustment in posture. It was an essential skill in his line of work. It was also one that required a clear head and a fair amount of concentration.

He was concentrating, to be sure, but his mind was anything but clear. It rarely was when it came to Lottie.

As she stared at the paperweight, turning it over in her hands, he studied her profile—the soft line of her jaw, the downcast eyes, the long sweep of lashes.

He hadn't the foggiest notion what she was thinking.

If she'd been another woman, a different sort of woman, he could be sure how this scene would end. The truth was there, standing before her large as life. She only had to see and accept it.

But it had been Owen's experience that the more often one encountered lies, the less adept one became at recognizing the truth. A falsehood here and there could be disregarded as an aberration. A few more lies and a person began to wonder what could be believed and what could not. When there was more deceit than honesty, it became easier, safer, to assume everything was a lie.

It is difficult to know what to believe.

It was difficult for everyone, Owen thought, but immeasurably more so for a woman raised in a world where deceit overran honesty by leaps and bounds. Lottie's excessively cautious nature was understandable, and heartbreaking.

And made him want to shake her until her teeth rattled.

It was for this reason that he had insisted she stay in the room. He would give her the time and space to think things through, but not too much time nor too much space. He wouldn't give her the opportunity to talk herself out of the truth.

After another minute, Lottie set her paperweight aside and faced him. "It is not easy to alter one's perspective of eight years over the course of a few minutes."

"I know."

"And I want…I want to say I am sorry."

He didn't want another damned apology. Her feelings, or some of them, were clear now. Her expression was troubled, her voice uncertain. He hated seeing both, but she continued before he could argue. "I am not a stupid woman. I should have known your reasons for…for many things, I suppose, were valid."

"And I should have made my reasons clear from the start." It simply hadn't occurred to him that she was unaware of how things stood. An unforgivable error on his part. He should never have assumed that Will Walker would be forthright with his daughter or that Lottie, so often isolated in the Walker home, should have guessed the truth herself.

"But I want you to understand…" She lifted her chin. "You are wrong about my father. He changed."

He swallowed an oath. "Lottie. You don't—"

"And you were wrong to disavow him completely. I understand why you did not, or could not, give him credit for rescuing Lady Strale. But you could have acknowledged some of the work he did for you. You should have."

He was tempted to agree for no other reason than

it would prove expedient. If he gave her the words she wanted, they could put the whole unpleasant business behind them and move on. But it would be just another lie, he thought, just one more layer of deceit.

Though it cost him, he shook his head and stood his ground. "We will not agree on this."

"I know." She straightened her shoulders and took a breath. "I do not require absolute harmony of opinion complete—" She stopped mid-sentence and sighed, her shoulders drooping. "How ridiculously pompous," she muttered, and he almost smiled. "What I mean to say is…" She caught and held his gaze. "Sometimes friends do not agree."

Though her words were a statement, he heard the question in her voice. More, he heard the offer.

He reached for it with both hands. "Sometimes they do not."

A curious stillness fell over the room. There was no awkwardness or tension between them, but a sense of settling, as if they'd come up from a long underwater dive and needed the moment to catch their breath and find their bearings.

When he felt certain they'd accomplished a little of both, he stepped close and brushed the backs of his fingers across the smooth skin of her cheek, letting the touch linger.

"We should look through the journals," he said at length. He could have stayed just as he was, lost in the thrill of seeing Lottie's eyes free of anger and mistrust for the first time in eight years. But there was a job to do. Also, there was a limit to how long a man could stay lost in a woman's eyes while he caught his breath. At some point, he was just staring and panting.

He let his hand fall away.

"The journals," Lottie echoed. "Yes. I...," She gestured vaguely at the parlor door. "I sent Mrs. Lewis and Cook to the village for various supplies. Mary, the scullery maid, will be busy in the kitchen for most of the day. We can work without interruption."

"More supplies?"

Humor danced across her pretty features. "They are astounded at the extent and variety of your demands."

"I am a trial," he agreed solemnly.

She laughed lightly, and the sound of it was as thrilling to him as the sight of her clear eyes. *I've missed this*, he thought—the easy banter and teasing that had once come so naturally.

When they were sure of themselves again, when the friendship was on solid ground once more, then he would decide what else he wanted. He would decide what came next.

Seven

LOTTIE REFUSED TO LISTEN TO THE LITTLE VOICE IN her head that insisted she was making a colossal mistake. It whispered in her ear, persistent and nasty. She believed too easily, capitulated too quickly, trusted too readily. She was the worst sort of dupe.

The voice belonged to her father. The doubts were echoes of lessons she had learned at his knee. Years ago, she would have given credence to those echoes, but not now. She loved her father, and she was grateful for some of what he had taken the time to teach her. But she did not want to be her father nor govern her life according to his suspicious view of the world, believing the worst of everyone, seeking out their weaknesses and cataloging them away for future exploitation.

It had been the right thing to admit her own error and to give Owen the benefit of the doubt. She knew it was right because it *felt* right. In fact, it felt marvelous. There was something uniquely liberating in letting go of old anger. And it was exciting, almost intoxicating, to take a chance on someone, to discover she still possessed the capacity to trust, even if it was a partial and rather cautious trust complicated by doubts, qualifications, and the existence of an ugly, nagging voice.

It still felt marvelous.

Smiling to herself, she waited for Owen to find another journal page requiring explanation. At his insistence, they had abandoned the small secret room for the comfort of the armchairs in the bedroom. Owen had placed the two side by side, forming a sort of miniature settee with a divider. It was an arrangement Lottie found quite comfortable, despite Owen's propensity for throwing his elbow over both armrests.

He had a tendency to sprawl like a big cat. She pursed her lips a little at the assessment. *No, not a cat.* Gabriel struck her as more the cat—smooth and a little sneaky. Samuel would be a bear, naturally—large, forbidding, surprisingly quick.

And Owen… Owen was very much the wolf she'd imagined the night before. Clever, dangerous, powerful, a little unpredictable perhaps—she lifted a brow as his arm slid farther onto her side of the chairs—and decidedly pushy.

"They ought to make these larger."

Owen glanced up from his book. "Beg your pardon?"

"Armrests. They ought to make them larger to accommodate individuals with oversized elbows."

"Oversized elbows."

"Yes." She used two fingers to very deliberately push his *oversized elbow* off her chair.

"Ah. It isn't the size of the elbow, sweet; it's the length of the arm."

She blinked once at the careless endearment and the

little dart of pleasure it brought her. "Then perhaps you have overlong arms."

"They are in proportion to the rest of me, I assure you." His green eyes twinkled with a humor she didn't understand a moment before he tapped the page. "Tell me about this."

She leaned over for a closer look. "It's an old encryption. Father was hired by a man he called… oh, let me think…Stump. That was it. From Devon. Stump hired him to decipher a letter he took off a land smuggler. He wanted it for blackmail. Father told him he couldn't make heads or tails of it and then blackmailed the smuggler himself." A freighter, as she recalled. It had been a profitable, if short-lived, venture. A smart blackmailer didn't linger or push for more than his mark could afford to pay.

"No honor amongst thieves," Owen muttered and once again edged his arm a little closer to hers.

"No mercy for the weak would be more accurate." She shrugged when he lifted a brow. "Stump was an inept thief with no connections and even less intelligence. A pigeon in swindler's clothing, if you will. That made him fair game. If he had been a man capable of defending his own, Father would have done the job fair."

"There is no honor in that, either."

"No, but no less than is found in the rest of the world. Demanding exorbitant rent from a tenant farmer for a leaky cottage and a patch of infertile ground or paying a maid slave wages might be legal, but they're hardly honorable." She relaxed back in her seat. "The strong have always taken advantage of the weak."

"You pay your maids quite well."

"How did you know that?"

"I know you," he said simply. He studied her quietly a moment. "I should probably mention whilst you're still smiling that I also know your Mrs. Lewis rather well. I remember her trial."

She considered that admission as the little voice did its best to undermine her resolve to trust. "Owen, Mrs. Lewis has friends in the village. She has built a life for herself here."

"If I had any interest in destroying that life, I'd have seen to it years ago. I looked into all your staff when you settled here."

"Oh." She wondered what it said about her that she found that bit of intrusion sweet instead of suspect. "I see."

She also saw that his arm was continuing to encroach on her space. Amused, she nudged it away.

He put it right back. "I am curious as to why you chose to bring Mrs. Lewis from London. Were you aware of her history when you hired her?"

"Yes, of course."

"Do you think she stole Mrs. Smith's brooch?"

Lottie chose her words carefully. "I think that after decades of loyal service to the Smith family, Mrs. Lewis deserved better than to be dismissed for theft after her grandniece was seduced by their son and Mrs. Lewis insisted he take responsibility for his child. The accusation left her destitute and unemployable by most standards. It was unjust."

His lips twitched with humor. "You haven't answered my question." He leaned closer, letting his arm come to rest against hers. "Do you think she stole the brooch?"

Lottie was certain of it. Despite being alone and unemployed, Mrs. Lewis's grandniece had managed to remain out of the poorhouse during Mrs. Lewis's incarceration and trial. As few had believed the Smith family accusations, Lottie found Mrs. Lewis's guilt to be a delicious bit of irony. "I do, yes."

"Her guilt doesn't concern you?"

No more than it did him, apparently. "As I said before, she is a good woman. She did what was necessary for her niece."

"There are better ways to accomplish the necessary than through thievery."

"And there are worse ways." Uncomfortable with how that sounded, Lottie sought to explain herself. "I don't condone stealing." Anymore. "But I'll not condemn Mrs. Lewis for it. A man ought to provide for his children."

"Agreed. But the question of whether two wrongs make a right..." Owen shrugged. "It has always been an interesting moral dilemma."

Given the dire circumstances, Lottie doubted Mrs. Lewis had put a great deal of thought into the question of morality before she'd pocketed the jewelry. "My father used to say morality was a currency. The very poor sell it off quickly because it is the only thing of value they possess, and the very rich spend it frivolously because they've other commodities with which to replace its value."

"And the middle class?"

"They're stuck with it. They don't want it, necessarily, but neither can they justify its expenditure."

"Do you believe that?"

"No." She drummed her fingers against the arm-rest and tried to ignore how warm Owen's arm felt pressed against her own. "I think people just enjoy feeling superior."

"No, you don't."

She gave him a pointed look. "It is certainly the case with some."

"With me?"

"You don't believe yourself superior to those men you catch and put away?" Or those he would have put away, given the opportunity. People like her.

"I know I am a better man than most of them, if that is your question. I don't hurt the innocent for profit. But understanding that my actions make me a better man by comparison is not the same as enjoying a sense of superiority." He tipped his head to the side thoughtfully. "Although, in fairness, I do sometimes enjoy a great sense of superiority at the inevitably successful conclusion of a challenging hunt. I find it gratifying."

She lifted a brow and smirked. "Inevitably?"

"The opportunities to prove one's superiority to one's fellow man are bountiful. I enjoy any number of them."

She laughed at that. "You make it difficult to have an earnest discussion."

"You make it difficult to have an easy one. You should laugh more often. With me," he qualified and leaned over to lightly cup her face in his hand. "You should laugh with me."

She wished she could laugh right then. She

wished she could swat away his hand with a careless laugh and witty rejoinder. Yesterday, she might have managed it, though the laugh would have been cutting, the wit scathing. Today, however, things were different.

Without anger and mistrust as her shields, without the assumption he meant to manipulate or mock her with the inviting smile and gentle caress, she was unsure how to react.

Strange, she thought, that she should be more certain of him now and less certain of herself.

She reached up, intending to draw his hand away.

Instead, she simply covered it with her own. For one brief moment, she held it against her cheek. She didn't want to push him away. She didn't want to relinquish his touch.

But nerves got the better of her. "Perhaps I shall," she said in an unsteady voice, and, releasing him, she returned her attention to the book on her lap. Avoidance might not be the most noble course of action, but it was often the safest.

೫ಾ

Owen drew his fingers away but couldn't force his gaze to follow suit.

Lottie was blushing a little, a fact that charmed and fascinated him. The scent of her teased his nose. Tart, he thought, wondering how she managed it. It wasn't merely lemon juice in the laundry. He didn't smell it anywhere else in the house, and there was an earthy quality to it, lending an unexpected warmth.

"Is it perfume?"

She glanced up from her book but didn't quite meet his gaze. "Sorry?"

"The tart. Is it perfume?"

"Oh. No. Soap. It was a gift from Esther." Her lips curved in affection. "She has a fondness for surprising people with presents and a talent for picking just the thing."

"Where did she find it?"

"Kithan, two villages over. It's quite dear, I'm afraid. I shan't have it much longer."

"I'll buy you more." A barrel of it.

She gave him a quizzical look. "Why would you?"

Because it was sweet and sharp. It was Lottie. But he didn't say that. Instead, he leaned in closer, breathed her in. "What's in it?"

"I don't know." Her gaze traveled to his mouth, snapped away, then traveled back again, almost reluctantly. "I never asked."

He considered that, and her. "Don't," he decided. "Don't ask. I like the mystery of it."

That, too, was Lottie. Mysterious, enigmatic, secret. He'd never been able to resist the lure of a secret.

She smiled at his comment and he leaned closer still, even as he called himself a fool. This was not why he had sought to make things right between them. He had counted it as a possibility, even entertained the notion of that possibility blossoming into solid probability, but it was not the reason.

He'd only wanted...

He couldn't remember. For the life of him, he could not remember what his intent had been yesterday, or earlier today, or even five minutes ago.

He could think only of what he wanted now.

She was beautiful. She was smiling at him. That wonderful secretive smile that wrapped around and drew him in as thoroughly as her intoxicating scent.

And he wanted her. Right now.

"I should wait," he heard himself murmur as he slipped his hand around her neck and brought her, unresisting and flushed with surprise, closer. "We should wait. I was going to wait."

He didn't wait. His mouth settled over hers almost before the last word was out.

He tried to tell himself that it was just a test, just a little experiment to see if reality held up to imagination. God knew, he had spent an exceptional amount of time imagining how Lottie would taste, how she would feel in his arms. It was only natural a man would take the opportunity to satisfy a curiosity that had hounded him for years.

But he wasn't fooling himself. It wasn't simple inquisitiveness that drove him. It was *desire*—but in its infancy yet, a low burn rather than a raging inferno. He could keep it there. For both their sakes, he could keep that fire banked.

Not every kiss was the prelude to something more; not every moment of passion need burn out of control. A kiss could be simple and carefree. It could be fun. He would like that for her, for both of them.

Mindful of the flame, of his intentions, he kept the kiss light and easy, brushing his lips over hers with care. He found the sweetness he'd imagined on her lips and in the soft mingling of their breath. And he discovered the hint of tart beneath, tempting him to take a deeper taste. But he held back. Even as she sighed, a whisper of air against his mouth, and brought her hand to his face, he held back.

It was only a test, he reminded himself. It was only a sampling. Later he could think of more. Later, when he knew what to expect, how to prepare himself for that first intoxicating taste of her, that first feel of her lips moving under his with a mesmerizing blend of hesitancy and confidence. It wouldn't shock him then when she responded to his touch—not with a bid to take charge as he'd anticipated, but with a soft yielding that threatened his own control.

He would be prepared for the way she shivered when he pressed kisses along her jawline and the way she melted when he lingered at the corner of her mouth. He would know that the feel of her small hands coming to rest against his chest caused the flame of desire to burn brighter and that when she moaned, soft and sweet in the back of her throat, his good intentions would start to evaporate in the heat of that fire.

He realized he was gripping the back of her gown too hard and forced himself to edge the kiss back into safer territory. He nipped at her bottom lip gently and swallowed her soft gasp of surprise.

Fun. The kiss could be fun and light and playful, he thought…until she nipped back. Which he ought to have expected, really. Lottie might yield to temptation, but she wasn't one to back down from a challenge.

He felt his own shiver, his own need to yield. Suddenly, the kiss no longer felt playful. It felt poised on the brink of something far more significant and far more dangerous.

He needed to end it, needed to pull away. And he would. In a moment. Just a moment more, he told himself, just an inch closer. Just one minute to know the sensation of holding Lottie Walker fully in his arms the way he'd always imagined.

Pressing forward, he tried to wrap his arms completely around her, but he was stopped short by a solid barrier at his waist. He had the fleeting thought that armrests should not be made larger, but rather removable, or possibly eliminated altogether. He couldn't get close enough. It didn't matter that he was drowning in the taste and texture of her; it wasn't enough.

A plan of action formed in his mind—one that began with hauling her out of her chair and culminated with the both of them on his bed. The image was so real, so tempting, and so monumentally foolish that it succeeded in shocking him back to sanity.

This was not the way, he told himself as he pulled back. This was not the time.

His resolve wavered again when he looked down into Lottie's face. Her lips were swollen, her eyes were closed, her skin was flushed, and her hair was mussed. His formidable pirate queen, always so composed, was now beautifully, perfectly undone. It took everything he had not to reach for her again.

He would do well to remember his loss of control. He would remember and he would prepare.

Also, he would never, ever again purchase a chair with a thrice-damned armrest.

He cleared his throat in an effort to break the spell

of the moment. It mostly failed. "I'll apologize for that, if need be."

Her lids fluttered open and she regarded him with hooded eyes. "Are you sorry?"

The taste of her lingered on his tongue. "No."

"Neither am I."

He dug his fingers into the chair to keep from reaching for her again. He was staring and panting now, and he didn't care.

Lottie's gaze dropped to his mouth. She leaned forward. Her lids slid closed—and then flashed open again when a long, low rumble shook the house. "Is that *thunder*?" She shoved away from him without ceremony and darted to the window. "Damn it. Damn it. It is."

Owen stayed where he was and struggled to find the composure he hadn't expected to lose. His gaze flicked to Lottie. Out of reach. And that was for the best. He needed time to think things through, to decide what he wanted.

The physical was easy. There was no question of his desire. But what else? What came after?

What had come before? he wondered. For eight years, he'd kept an eye on the Walker family, but he'd not followed Lottie's every move. He knew nothing of her daily activities, the small events in her life— her day-to-day routines, her habits and hobbies, her friendships and acquaintances, her lovers. Had there been lovers?

She was thirty years of age and in possession of a fluid sense of morality. It was difficult to imagine she'd not indulged herself at some point.

It was even harder to decide if he cared for the idea or not. It stung to think of her in the arms of another man, to imagine some nameless, faceless libertine taking down that silky black hair, pin by pin, and stripping away her clothes, putting his hands on her.

Jealousy, selfish, dark, and acidic, burned under his skin. With a roll of the shoulders, he acknowledged the emotion and did his best to set it aside. He didn't mind the sense of possession and competitiveness the feeling engendered, but the sharp edge of desperation cut painfully into his pride.

Besides, it might be to his benefit if she'd had affairs. Virginity complicated things. Tremendously. A man didn't go about seducing virgins. A *good* man didn't.

His gaze flicked back to Lottie's profile and latched on to that deliciously secretive mouth.

Good was such a relative term. Open to all sorts of interpretation.

He would give some thought to that, and then all the rest, later. Much later, when her taste wasn't still on his tongue, clouding his judgment.

For now… He took a steadying breath, scrubbed his hands over his face, then rose to join her at the window.

The sun was still shining overhead, but a hulking wall of clouds billowed and swirled on the horizon. Beside him, Lottie was quiet, her back rigid.

"Are you afraid of storms?" he asked. He couldn't recall her ever mentioning it.

"No, but Peter and Esther will be caught in it."

"Not necessarily. They'll see it coming."

As they stood there, the wind picked up, sending loose leaves tumbling across the lawn. Blowing toward the storm, he noted, and he hoped Lottie didn't recognize it as an ominous sign.

"Perhaps they already have," Lottie said. "Perhaps they will cut the day short and make it back before the storm arrives."

It was moving too quickly, Owen thought, but he kept that observation to himself. He wasn't concerned. There was plenty of time for the group to seek shelter. And, if not, there was still no cause for alarm. People were caught in storms all the time—rarely did they emerge the worse for wear.

But Lottie was worried, so he ran a soothing hand up her back and pressed his fingers gently against the tight knot of muscle at the base of her neck. "Perhaps."

❧

The storm arrived in under a quarter hour, dashing Lottie's hopes that the travelers might beat the weather home.

"They'll not make it back tonight," she murmured, watching from the windows as the trees outside swayed under the onslaught of rushing wind and pounding rain.

Next to her, Owen craned his neck a little to study the swirling black sky. "It's moving quickly. Should be cleared before dark."

"There's too much rain. The road to the village routinely floods. A horse and rider could get through, but it takes a half day of sun or more for it to dry out to a degree that a carriage might be managed. If there's more rain to come…"

"They'll be fine, Lottie."

"Better, were they here." She tried to shake off the worry. "You can still secure a wagon, once the storm has passed. You'll not be able to bring it back, but…"

"Tomorrow is soon enough. We should take advantage of Peter's extended absence."

She flinched at a bright flash of lightning and the answering boom of thunder. "We should."

"Come away from the windows." He nudged her back gently. "Why don't you work on the letters for a bit?"

The suggestion surprised her into turning from the storm. "You need my help with the journals."

He took hold of the drapes and pulled them shut. "I'll ask for it when needed."

She couldn't work like that. "I'll not be able to concentrate properly with distractions."

"Distraction is exactly what you need at present. But I'll keep mine to a minimum," he promised, urging her toward the desk. "I'll keep track of what I am unable to decipher, and we can come back to it later."

He insisted she work in his room, and Lottie put little effort into arguing otherwise. It made more sense to work in her own room, at her own desk, but she didn't feel like being sensible. She didn't feel like being alone.

And so they sat in companionable, if not entirely comfortable, silence as the storm raged over Willowbend. Like a child's fit of temper, it bellowed and blustered and passed in the course of a half hour, leaving behind a weak leak of rain and hiccups of wind.

Owen began his distractions after that. He was subtle about it, offering a comment or question here and there designed, she knew, to take her mind off Esther and Peter.

It was several hours more, however, until Lottie was able to fully relax. When the clock on the mantel chimed six, she breathed a quiet sigh of relief. By now, sufficient time had passed for the storm to move over the travelers, and if mishap or injury had occurred, someone would have brought the news to Willowbend by horse.

She set her pen atop the paper she had used to take down notes. It was mostly blank. "I've accomplished very little, I'm afraid."

"You can make up for it here." Owen tapped his finger against a small stack of journals in the seat next to him. "I've marked a number of pages requiring your attention."

She rose, bent a little to stretch a sore back, then crossed to Owen on stiff legs. She picked up one of the journals, opened it, and paused with her hand hovering over the pages.

"You've folded them. You've folded down the corners."

She wasn't upset. She wasn't even mildly irritated. Her father hadn't been particularly careful with his journals when he'd used them. As a result, most were already worn, stained, and even torn in some places. But it surprised her that Owen had been careless as well, and she wasn't quite sure why.

He looked slightly affronted. "I didn't damage them."

"You've creased them. Do you do this with your own books?" Her mouth fell open when he kept his silence. "You *do*," she accused, and the surprise grew. "It is a terrible habit."

And therein lay the surprise, she realized. Owen wasn't a man of bad habits. Faults, certainly. Everyone had faults. He had many. But folding the pages of a book was a trivial bit of foolishness, and to discover it in a man who was neither trivial nor foolish was both unexpected and rather charming.

Though she didn't approve of the habit itself, she quite liked the idea of Owen possessing the funny little quirk. More, she liked the idea that there might be others—unexpected foibles that made him...more human, she supposed. And less wolf.

Owen closed the journal in his hands. "I'd offer an apology, but it would appear one is not required. Why are you smiling?"

Sometimes, she thought, honesty could set a person off balance more efficiently than a lie. "I find myself intrigued by the idiosyncrasy."

He said nothing as she bent to scoop up the journals stacked on the seat. Curious about his sudden stillness, she lifted her head and discovered his face near her own.

His own smile was slow, sure, and decidedly wolfish. "Intrigued, is it?"

Her heart tripped, her blood warmed, and her mind raced. If she leaned in, just a hair more, she could put her mouth over his. They could continue what they'd started before the storm. It would be so easy. And because it would be, she pulled back.

In less than twelve hours, they had dragged out an eight-year-old argument, apologized, and kissed. That was sufficient reconciliation for one day. Anything more crossed the line straight into recklessness.

"I'll just take these to my room, shall I? Note anything of significance."

"Hmm."

There was no telling what he meant by that, and she thought it best not to inquire. She sidled over to the desk to gather the letters and her notes, piling them haphazardly atop the journals, and she was off.

Eight

LOTTIE WORKED LATE INTO THE NIGHT. SHE PORED over the journal pages Owen had marked first, jotting down information he might find useful or interesting. Then she turned to the letters again to search for the pattern hidden in the encryption.

It was a slow, methodical process, further complicated and delayed by random thoughts of Owen that continuously popped into her head.

She had not given in to the embarrassing urge to peek down the hall at his door, but she knew he was still awake. He would be up for hours more, reading the journals, turning down the corners of pages.

It was easy to envision him just as she'd left him, sprawled out in the chair.

Or maybe not quite as she'd left him. Surely he had made himself more comfortable by now. She imagined he had taken off his coat and necktie and probably his waistcoat. He'd likely rolled up his sleeves and unbuttoned his shirt to expose a bit of muscled chest and the tawny patch of skin she had made such a poor effort not to look at the night before.

Perhaps, in her absence, he had made himself even more comfortable.

Settling back in her chair, she pictured him with his shirt further unbuttoned. Then further. Then she had him take the thing off altogether. Because if a woman was going to indulge in a scandalous fantasy, it ought to be worth the embarrassment she was sure to feel later when she had to face the object of that fantasy. So she fantasized, in leisurely fashion, what he might look like without his clothes—long arms, broad chest, golden skin, rippling muscle—and felt an answering spread of warmth through her veins.

Desire. She knew what it was and where it could lead.

She wasn't a worldly woman, exactly, but there had been worldly women in her life and a father who had paid one of those women to educate his eldest daughter on one of the very few topics he was unwilling to discuss himself.

Said woman had done so with an enthusiasm and thoroughness that had left a girl of ten absolutely stupefied. And terrified. For years.

But she was grateful for the knowledge now. She was aware of what went on between a man and a woman behind closed doors, aware that Owen was interested in developing a physical relationship with her, and she could admit without reservation that she was interested in return.

There was little to stop her from pursuing that interest. She had no moral or philosophical objections to bedding a man outside of wedlock. She'd not been raised with them, and, more to the point, she was unwilling to relinquish all hope of ever experiencing what the worldly woman had promised could be an act of affection and unparalleled pleasure when performed with the right man.

Marriage was not an option for someone like her. It pained her sometimes to know that she could never have a husband and children of her own, but she tried not to dwell on the matter. She preferred to remember that *affection* and *pleasure* remained within her grasp.

There were, however, several practical considerations that could not be ignored. In a small, isolated village like Wayton, gossip was always a risk. Which is why she'd not fully pursued the handsome butcher in the village who had taken her eye and offered his attentions several years ago.

There was also the matter of trust. She had kissed the handsome butcher. Under an ancient oak in the heat of late summer, Mr. Whitlock had taken her in his arms and put his lips over hers. It had been a perfectly lovely experience. Until his increasingly eager mouth had traveled to her ear and whispered, "*Oh, Miss Bales.*"

At which point the pleasant little fire he had sparked under her skin had been snuffed out.

She was not Miss Bales. And she could not reconcile giving herself, even if it was a small part of herself, to a man who had no idea who she was and who could not be trusted with the truth.

Restless now, she pushed away from her desk and worked out the stiffness in her limbs with a slow pace between the bed and the fireplace.

The townspeople of Wayton were all like the butcher. They did not know her, and they never would. She was not the well-bred daughter of a respected tradesman. She'd not had a governess named Mrs. Thew, nor had she spent her summers on a small country estate in the south of Scotland. She'd not been taught to waltz by a French dancing master nor learned embroidery at her mother's knee.

These were all lies in a great, long list of lies that, when combined, created the fictional character of Miss Charlotte Bales.

Any relationships she built were based on that fiction. She wanted a friend, possibly a lover, of her own. Someone who knew she was Lottie Walker, eldest daughter of William Walker, the notorious criminal. She had spent her summers learning how to lie and cheat and steal in London or Bath and had been taught how to dance by the madam of a whorehouse. It had been her father who had taught her to read and write and how to mimic the accent of her betters, because they made more lucrative marks.

Owen didn't know all of these things. But he knew some of them. Enough that he could be a friend. He could be more.

She would have to think it through carefully, weigh all the possibilities, all the dangers. The more time she spent with him, the greater the risk he would discover the truth about the Tulip. But if there was even a chance they could...

When the floor trembled softly beneath her stocking feet, all thoughts of Owen, Wayton, handsome butchers, and passionate love affairs disappeared in a heartbeat. Her hand froze in mid-reach for a bedpost, and her mind went blank, utterly blank, except for the baffling realization that the vibration had come from a door being quietly opened and closed downstairs.

Someone was in her house.

It took only a second more for the shock to clear and fear and determination to fill the void. Her mind raced through her options and through a quick count of where everyone was in the house. In an instant, she considered and dismissed the idea that someone might have returned early from the ruins. There was no possible reason to risk the poor roads at night just to carefully sneak inside. Her eyes darted to her door, and she valiantly suppressed a yelp when she found Owen standing there in his shirtsleeves, a gun gripped in his hand.

Her palms grew sweaty at the sight of the weapon. Her mouth was dry as dust, and she saw red. Blood red, specifically. Heavy streams of it flowing from her father's nose and mouth. A thin film of it slicked over broken teeth exposed in a grimace.

Where's the money? Tell me where the money's gone!

Not in front of my girl, Fensley. Have a heart.

Mr. Fensley had been in possession of a heart. He'd taken her into another room, given her three pounds, and told her to get her father out of Bath within the fortnight. Then he'd left the house, shooting her father in the leg on his way out.

She hated guns.

She shook her head at Owen, for all the good it did her. He ignored her order completely. Instead, he looked at her, expression cool and unyielding, and mouthed the word, *Stay*.

Which was both insulting (she wasn't a hound to

be ordered about) and unnecessary. Of course she was going to stay. Where was the sense in going downstairs? Mrs. Lewis and the rest of the staff where all safely ensconced in their beds a floor above. Certainly, if the intruder meant to come upstairs, she would pick up a weapon and protect those who depended upon her. But if all their intruder wanted was a few items to pawn, then let him have them.

They were just things. She was attached to some of those things, and the idea of a stranger pawing through them made her skin crawl. But not so much as to wish him dead for the offense and certainly not so much as to risk Owen's life.

They were just *things*.

She pointed at the weapon in his hand and shook her head more emphatically.

No.

He blinked once, then shook his head in return, slowly, as if to say, *What the devil is wrong with you?*

Unable to answer any other way, she fell back on shaking her head. Again.

His face went from implacable to annoyed and he crossed the room, moving with preternatural stealth. She heard no footsteps nor a single creek of floorboard.

"I am not going down there without a gun," he whispered harshly.

Did he think that was what she was after? No wonder he was looking at her as if she might be daft. Of course she didn't expect him to confront an intruder unarmed. She didn't want him to confront the intruder at all. "Stay here."

Now he was looking as if he simply didn't have

time for whatever the devil was wrong with her. "I am not staying here."

"Then neither am I."

That was a lie, one she prayed he would believe. Owen operated under a strict code of conduct. She couldn't claim to know everything about him, but she knew him well enough to be certain there were some things he simply would not do. Allowing a woman to confront a burglar seemed like it might be one of those things.

"I will stay," she promised, "if you stay."

His response was to reach under his coat, pull out a set of manacles he must have grabbed for the intruder, and dangle them before her on the end of a finger.

"You wouldn't dare," she hissed.

Only he might dare. If that code was very strict, he just might.

He brought the manacles up one inch. "Stay. Here."

She considered them, then Owen, then the gun. Someone was going to end up shot. That someone could be Owen. She could see it, see him as she had seen her father, writhing on the parlor floor, screaming while the life seemed to pour out of him in a thick red stream.

Desperate, she chose a path she knew she would come to regret only slightly less than the alternatives.

She lifted a foot and stomped her heel against the floor as hard as she could. "I *say*, Renderwell!" she all but bellowed. "Do you hear a ruckus downstairs?!"

Owen slapped one end of the manacles over her wrist, latched the other end to the bedpost, and was out the door in the blink of an eye.

She could have told him not to bother. The intruder would bolt from the house and be into the woods before Owen could make it downstairs, but mentioning it seemed perilously close to a taunt. So she kept her mouth shut, took a seat on the bed, and waited for the inevitable retribution to come.

The wait was short, though short was a relative space of time when one was manacled to a bedpost. No more than ten minutes passed before Owen was back again, standing in her doorway with gun in hand.

"What the devil is *wrong with you*?"

She almost laughed. There was a bubbling nervousness at the back of her throat that begged to be set free. It was oddly comforting to know she could read his thoughts so well. And it was an immense relief to see him standing uninjured before her.

She held back the mirth on a choking little hiccup of breath.

Owen took two steps forward, clearly alarmed. "Are... You're not...?" He took one step back. "Are you going to cry?"

"What? No." Though his reaction to the possibility of tears had her swallowing another bout of laughter. "Are you going to...?" She held up her manacled arm.

He considered her carefully as he crossed the room. "No."

The urge to laugh was thoroughly squashed. "No?"

"Why did you help him?"

"*No?*" She rattled her restraints. "Unlock these at once."

"Why did you help him, Lottie?"

"I didn't help him," she snapped. "I helped you."

"Helped me?" He swore, vividly. "I wanted him caught, not gone. I needed to question him, find out why he was in your house."

"Find out why?" What sort of question was that for a man called the Gentleman Thief Taker? "Good Lord, however did you capture anyone? Ever?"

"Lottie." Her name came out on a growl.

"He was in my house to steal, obviously."

"Possibly."

"Oh, most assuredly." She couldn't believe she had to explain this to him. Wasn't the man supposed to be legendary? "It is no secret Willowbend has a viscount in residence. Either he was here to see if we left the good silver out after dinner, or he heard the residents of Willowbend were waiting out the storm at an inn, and he was here to steal from what he imagined to be a mostly unoccupied house. Whichever the reason, there was no need to kill him."

"I wasn't going to kill him."

"Then why bring a gun?"

He looked perfectly baffled by the question. "To defend myself."

"Which is *exactly* what he would have done upon seeing your gun. He would have lifted his own weapon to defend himself, and before you knew it, the two of you would have defended yourselves to death."

"That would not have happened. Damn it, Lottie. I'm careful—"

"But he may not have been," she ground out. Oh, how she hated this sort of arrogance, the absolute conviction that he was, and always would be, in complete control of every situation.

No one had control all the time. Or even most of the time. Life was filled with an infinite number of unknowables—distractions, traps, surprises, lies, betrayals. Control was something a body reached for, grabbed, lost, and reached for again. The only thing constant about it was the regularity with which it slipped through the fingers and how quickly the assumption of its possession could put a man in his grave.

"You could have been *killed*, Owen."

"I am good at what I *do*, Charlotte."

Now she had pricked his pride. God help her. She gestured at the gun in his hand. "Put that away, if you please."

"I don't see—"

"I don't like guns," she snapped. "If you wish to continue this argument, you will put it away."

"You don't like…" It was a toss-up as to which emotion played longer over his face—shock, horror, or fury. "Are you telling me there are no guns in this house? That you have spent the last eight years in an isolated country home without the means to protect yourself?"

"Of course I have guns. I have two pistols and a rifle right there." She pointed to the trunk at the foot of the bed. "And had the intruder thought to come upstairs, I would have retrieved them without hesitation."

"You know how to use them?"

"No," she drawled and dropped her arm. "At the time of purchase, I just thought them terribly pretty."

He glared at her.

She ground her teeth. "Yes. I know how to use them." The lessons had been terrifying, exhausting, and self-imposed. Contrary to what Owen appeared to believe, she was quite aware of where she lived and for whom she was responsible. "I know how to protect my own home."

"Do you? Because it seems to me you allowed a man to come into your home—"

"I did not *allow* it."

"You helped him escape."

"I chased him off. Without anyone becoming injured."

"Without anyone being apprehended for a crime." He stepped closer. "Is that what this is about? Proving there is honor and loyalty amongst thieves?"

"I am not a thief." It was almost true. She wasn't a thief now, and even when she had been a thief, she'd never gone skulking about someone's house. She'd merely picked the lock and kept an eye out so her father could go skulking about. It was the thinnest and flimsiest of distinctions, but she clung to it with both hands.

Anger fired hot in Owen's eyes, then died just as quickly. His features softened and he sighed. "But your father was," he murmured. He was quiet a moment, and when he spoke again, his tone was filled with understanding. "I'd not have killed the intruder, Lottie."

"I'm sure it would not have been your intention."

His lips twitched. "I don't kill people accidently."

Self-defense was not accidental, but she didn't see the purpose in starting the argument anew, not when they were so close to a truce.

"I'm sure you don't." Repetitive, perhaps, but it was the best she could do.

"Did someone shoot him? Your father?"

She hesitated, uncertain how to answer. She didn't want to lie to him, not about this. Why this should be the case, she couldn't say. Perhaps because it was such a big part of her life and that would make her denial of it a big lie. And, really, there were only so many big lies one could tell a person and still retain the hope of a true friendship. *I'm not a thief* likely topped out that threshold.

But neither did she wish to discuss the matter. At all. It was an ugly memory. Painful, frightening, and for reasons he'd not understand, unbearably humiliating.

She would wager every penny she owned that Owen had never been forced to watch his father crawl and beg in a pool of his own blood.

But telling Owen she didn't wish to discuss the matter was tantamount to saying yes, indeed, someone had shot her father. And once she admitted the truth, however indirectly, Owen would *insist* on discussing the matter.

She shook her head and rattled the manacles. "Doesn't matter. Let me out of these."

To her relief, he neither pressed the matter nor denied her request. After digging out the keys, he released her hand and tossed the manacles on the bed.

A crease formed in his brow. "Did I hurt you?"

"Hurt me?" She looked down to where she was rubbing her wrist. "Oh. No." It was like taking off a tight or heavy bracelet—one rubbed afterward without thinking about it. "No, I'm—"

He took hold of her hand gently and turned it over to study the wrist. His thumb caressed the palm of her hand. "Has this happened before?"

"Manacles? Yes, but—"

"No, not manac—" His head snapped up. "Wait. Yes? *Yes*? Who the hell put you in manacles?"

"My father. He felt it was important I know how to get out of them. And I can, generally, if I have a hairpin or the time to work my hand through, or if I have access to a hard surface or object and enough room to maneuver. With a little luck, a well-aimed swing can break one of those open, you know."

"I do know. I also know that two of those processes have the potential to break bone."

"Unlikely." Though her efforts had resulted in some colorful scraping and bruising. "They were lessons, not life-or-death scenarios."

"And how many times did your father have you practice this particular lesson?"

"Until I got it right."

❦

Until I got it right.

Owen banked the sudden rage that threatened to boil up and out on a string of invectives aimed at Will Walker. What sort of man, what sort of father put his own child in manacles? Worse, watched as she struggled to free herself? The iron was sharp and unforgiving; it would have cut and bruised the skin. The thought of it, the image of Lottie bound and hurting, turned his stomach and squeezed his heart.

Carefully, so as not to expose the tenor of his

thoughts, he asked, "Did he do this whilst I knew you in London?"

"No. I told you. He changed."

He had nothing to say to that—at least nothing she would care to hear.

As if sensing the direction of his thoughts, Lottie pulled her hand away, and her voice took on a defensive tone. "He was only looking out for my well-being. He wanted to know I'd be safe."

"*He* should have kept you safe."

"He did. He—" She pressed her lips together and made an exasperated sound in the back of her throat. "I don't wish to fight with you again tonight."

Owen clenched and unclenched his fists. He didn't want to fight with her at all. He wanted to go back a decade or more and beat Will Walker to the ground. Because he couldn't, he shoved the anger aside and changed the topic.

"This changes things, you understand."

She shook her head. "What has changed what?"

"A man broke into your home tonight."

"Yes. I am aware."

"And I am staying."

"*Staying?*"

"Yes. Just until I can be certain the man downstairs was only here to nick the silver."

"Well of course he was here to steal."

That had been his initial assumption as well. Just a common burglar, easily managed. But the muddy footprints he'd found downstairs told a different story. "He walked right through your parlor without taking a thing."

"Perhaps there wasn't time."

"There was time." The tracks across the rug were those of a man walking, not running. "You've a small pair of silver candlesticks on your fireplace mantel. They're sitting in plain view. Why didn't he take those?"

She hesitated, looking uncertain. "I don't know. Maybe he wasn't after valuables. Maybe he was just hungry and in search of the kitchen."

"Then he would have broken in through the kitchen, not a side door." The kitchen would have been easy to find from the outside. Its drapes had been wide open. "Do you have an item of exceptional value in the house? Something the local villagers know about?"

"You think he was after something in particular?" She shook her head. "The only things out of the ordinary to be found at Willowbend are my father's journals."

There were also the letters, he thought.

And there were the Walker children.

He took Lottie's chin in his hand and held it steady. "Listen to me—every precaution will be taken to ensure your father's past remains a secret. Peter will not hear it from me or my men. I swear it. I'm sorry if that's not sufficient to ease your fears, but until I can be sure this man was nothing more than an inept burglar, I am staying."

"You're really rather worried, aren't you?" Her mouth turned down at the corners in a thoughtful manner. "Very well. You'll stay."

"Very well?" he echoed, suspicious of the agreement.

"I think you're wrong, but if there is even a remote possibility my family is in danger, I'll not argue against your protection. Why would I?"

Loath to break the contact, he let his fingers linger a few seconds before releasing her. "Because argue, darling, is what you *do*."

She opened her mouth, then snapped it shut. He watched with satisfaction as she struggled with the impossible task of disputing that point without actually producing an argument.

"Surrender, Lottie."

"I disagree with your assessment," she announced. "And were I in a mood to do so, I would explain to you the nature of your error."

"That is still an argument."

She ignored him. "I do feel compelled, however, to explain a possible complication of your decision to stay."

"Oh, elucidate, by all means."

She leaned a hip against the bedpost. "You could be here a very long time, Owen."

"Eager to be rid of me?" It troubled him how much he didn't want her to say yes, even in jest.

"No. Not anymore. But you are needed in London. Mrs. Popple deserves justice. Her family does as well. I think…" Her brow knit. "She might have mentioned a sister once."

"In Leeds," he confirmed. "At the moment, your father's journals are the best chance I have at finding Mrs. Popple's murderer. I can always send Gabriel or Samuel to London if the need arises." They'd need to check in on other investigations and other clients at any rate. "You knew Mrs. Popple, didn't you? She wasn't just a friend of your father's."

"I knew her for a time when I was quite young."

Her voice and tone softened in memory. "She was very kind."

"That is the way people speak of her. Her employees and patrons both."

"But I rather doubt her sweet nature would make Inspector Jeffries take note of her. I remember him. He wasn't the sort to trouble himself over murder amongst the criminal class." She shook her head. "No, he didn't ask for your assistance, though I suspect he was eager to hand you the work. Who hired you? Mrs. Popple's sister?"

"She is the wife of a respectable shopkeeper. She wanted nothing to do with her sister in life, or death. Inspector Jeffries did seek me out, Lottie. So did Lord Sevarton when one of his oil paintings disappeared."

"Oh, yes, the missing art. That would garner the inspector's sympathies." She ran a finger down a long groove in the bedpost. "I'd not thought so much about that part of it."

"It is not the part that matters." It was an easy statement to make, and he thought nothing of offering it, until Lottie looked at him with eyes that shone bright with understanding and gratitude.

"You're right. It isn't."

She smiled at him then. A rare, soft smile that held no trace of disdain or regret or mistrust. She smiled at him as if they shared something essential. As if *he* was essential.

It had been so long since she'd looked at him like that. In truth, he couldn't be certain she'd ever looked at him like that. But he was damned sure he wanted her to keep looking at him *just* like that. It stunned and unnerved him, the power and intensity of that one wish. There were probably things a man would not do, lengths he would not go or depths to which he would not sink, to assure a woman kept looking at him just like that, but damn if he could think of a single example at present.

He took two full steps back. "You should get some sleep."

"And you."

"Yes." No. He would not sleep tonight. But he needed to end the conversation, needed to leave before he did something imprudent. Like take her in his arms, and not with the breathless but relatively manageable desire he'd known in his room, but with the strange desperation that was clawing through him now.

"Go to sleep," he repeated with an embarrassing catch in his voice. Then, to top off that indignity, he all but bolted from the room, slamming the door on his way out.

He struggled with a mix of need and anger as he stood in the hall and took several steadying breaths. Ill at ease with the need, he concentrated on the anger. Anger could be controlled, even diminished in part, if he could only settle on one target and let loose. But he couldn't decide where to aim.

There was Will Walker: worthy of retribution but unreachable in death. There was the man who'd broken into Lottie's home: a deserving target but not yet in his line of sight. And there was himself: a target both justified and available.

From the start, he'd handled the business with

Lottie poorly. Or, at the very least, with less finesse than a man his age and experience ought to be able to muster.

He had finesse, damn it. He was a careful man, a man well prepared for every circumstance. He'd learned early the value of forethought, discipline, and careful planning, and had experienced the ugly consequences of forgoing all three. Until the day his father died, the Renderwell home had been in a constant state of chaos. The sword of utter ruin had dangled over the house for years. There'd been no control, no safety, no thought given to the future. There had been only the endless, mindless pursuit of immediate gratification.

With a stifled oath, he headed for his door. He knew better than to charge ahead without thought for the consequences. He knew how to take charge of a situation, how to bring order out of chaos.

Why, then, did he find himself off-kilter and struggling for balance in Lottie's presence? Why did he feel as if there was another sword hovering about his head, ready to lop off an ear?

Because he'd *not* prepared. That was bloody why. He hadn't planned what to do about Lottie. He'd simply arrived at Willowbend and charged ahead, allowing himself to be governed by… He had no idea. Emotions, he supposed.

He stopped outside his door.

No, he did *not* suppose. Small children and hysterics were governed by emotions. A grown man might, however, be governed on occasion by… He tipped his head back, considered various options, and finally landed on…instinct. A grown man might be guided by instinct.

Satisfied with the internal edit, he let himself into his bedroom, then began a slow pace across the carpet. Utilizing instinct was not a failing in and of itself. He used it often and he used it well when the occasion called for it. But it was a poor alternative to reason and strategy when there was time and call for both.

There had been time, and there had certainly been call, but he'd chosen to concentrate instead on his primary purpose in coming to Willowbend. Namely, to seek out Will Walker's journals.

Reconciliation with Lottie had been secondary in his consideration. While Owen preferred to think he'd put murder first because, well, it was murder, he could admit now that it had also been easier, even safer, to concentrate on an objective he could be sure of achieving.

He'd been quite sure of his success in obtaining the journals and had planned accordingly.

He had not been sure of Lottie, had not been comfortable pondering the countless ways an attempt to make amends with her might ultimately lead to his humiliation, and had therefore failed to plan for either defeat or victory.

Which had left him with the aforementioned reliance on instinct.

Perhaps he'd kiss her again, perhaps not. Perhaps he'd bed her, perhaps not. Oh, he'd just see how things ambled along, work the whole business out as they went, would he?

Lottie was right. He was a dolt.

Worse, he'd been a coward. Or perhaps it had been more a matter of neglect.

Owen ceased pacing and sought out the blade he'd put away, a second pistol, and his resolve. Failure, cowardice, or neglect—no matter the error, it would be remedied. Tonight, he could plan. He would keep watch over the house, and he would formulate a sensible strategy for dealing with Lottie. Come morning, he would be prepared.

Nine

THE STORM LEFT WILLOWBEND'S GARDEN BRUISED AND battered. Foliage was torn and flattened, the shredded remains of blooms littered the pathways, an old trellis had been snapped clean through, and now only the tenacious grip of a climbing rose kept the two halves in place.

Lottie surveyed the damage as she strolled down the familiar path. The trellis could be repaired and the plants would rebound and thrive. Within days, there would be new blooms on…whatever that squat little bush with the blue-tinted leaves happened to be. She had no real knowledge of gardening. In fact, she wasn't sure the blue plant flowered at all. But there would be blooms on something somewhere. And Owen would be there to see them.

She looked at the drive and wondered when he might be back. She'd slept later than she intended, rising well past nine. By the time she'd dressed and made it downstairs, Owen had already taken breakfast, informed Mrs. Lewis of the previous night's events—wisely editing out any mention of manacles, it seemed—and taken himself off to the village. That had been nearly three hours ago.

She wondered if his delay meant he'd obtained information on last night's intruder or if he'd found Peter and Esther.

Hoping for the second more than the first, she resumed her stroll and nearly tripped over her own feet at the sound of Owen's voice calling her. Whirling about, she found him striding up the path behind her.

A lovely thrill of anticipation sent her pulse racing. He was such a pleasure to look at—the long legs that ate up the ground between them in easy strides, the windblown locks reflecting the barest hint of copper in the sunlight. There was the relaxed grace, the hard jaw, the verdant eyes... Eyes, she noted as he drew near, that were shadowed by the faint bruise of fatigue.

"You're tired." This was not, she admitted, the most eloquent greeting a woman might offer a handsome man on a fine summer day. The words had just tripped out.

"I was up a time or two to check on the house." He stopped before her and offered a brief smile. "Did you sleep well?"

"Better than I should have, clearly. Why didn't you wake me? I might have helped."

Something about her statement made his lips twitch. "I walked about the house. What sort of assistance do you imagine I required?"

It didn't matter what he required. It was her house. If someone needed to stumble about it in the dark, that someone ought to be her.

She opened her mouth…and shut it again as she recalled Owen's words from the night before.

Argue is what you do.

Not today, she decided. Not in the first thirty seconds of his return, anyway. Not when he looked so tired. "Never mind." She gestured toward the drive. "I didn't see you return."

"Cut through the woods," he explained. "Faster."

"Oh." As Peter was the only member of the family who could seat a horse properly, she'd never given a thought to alternate routes.

His features briefly tightened in annoyance. "I instructed Mrs. Lewis to keep everyone inside whilst I was away. Why are you outside?"

"Because I want to be," she said and winced. "I didn't mean for that to sound so disagreeable. I wanted to take a walk before I started on the letters again, that's all. I've stayed in the garden, well within sight of the house. And Mrs. Lewis, you'll note." She pointed to a ground-floor window where, a moment ago, the elderly woman had been watching her like a hawk. She was gone now. "Well, she *was* watching me."

Owen relaxed a little, and his lips hooked up in a small smile. "Yes, I noticed her earlier. Your idea?"

"Yes." No. The woman was just bold as brass. "So, you see, I was quite cautious, and perfectly safe. Now, tell me what you learned in the village. Are Peter and Esther there?"

"No, but the innkeeper graciously provided an introduction to someone he believed could be of help in locating them." He paused dramatically. "The physician's wife."

"Oh. Oh, no." She bit the inside of her cheek to keep from laughing as the image of a ruddy-cheeked woman with a penchant for flounces and fussy lace collars popped into her head. "Mrs. McKinsey."

"The very same. You've made her acquaintance, I assume?"

Everyone made Mrs. McKinsey's acquaintance. There was no escaping an introduction to the mostly harmless, but exhaustingly effusive woman. One could escape further interaction, but to do so required an uncommon amount of work, a fair amount of guile, and, sometimes, a little bit of hiding.

"I have," she replied.

"Then you will not be surprised to learn that Mrs. McKinsey was delighted to inform me, over the course of three-quarters of an hour, that her neighbor, the widow Smith, heard from her maid, Bridget Hamm, that her brother, a farmer, had cause to pass through the village of Fisckrem last night after visiting a sister with whom the aforementioned Bridget Hamm *Does Not Speak*. And during a brief respite at the local tavern, but not brief enough in Mrs. McKinsey's estimation—the farmer has a weakness for drink, you know—"

"I did not."

"Yes, well, during his shamefully extended respite at the tavern, he happened to learn from the innkeeper's wife—Mrs. McKinsey's second cousin once removed, in case you were interested—"

"I was. Awfully."

"I was not. Nevertheless, Mrs. McKinsey informed me that her second cousin once removed mentioned to her maid's brother, the farmer, that Mr. Peter Bales and Miss Esther Bales of Willowbend and two gentlemen said to be traveling with Viscount Renderwell were lodged at an inn eight miles down the road. Where, it was mentioned, one cannot find a respectable leg of lamb."

"I see." Amused and relieved, she tipped her head at him. "Who said it?"

"I beg your pardon?"

"Who was it that told the farmer that Peter and Esther were down the road?"

A weighted pause followed. "I do not know."

"Then it would appear you wasted three-quarters of an hour." She had to bite her cheek again when his expression turned baleful. "It is a sad day when the Gentleman Thief Taker is unable to ascertain any sort of useful information from the likes of Mrs. McKinsey."

"Shall I escort you to town so you might inquire yourself?"

She hopped back when he stepped forward. "Thank you, no."

"It's no trouble—"

She danced away from his grasping hand, delighted to see his fatigue lightened by humor. "Generous of you, I'm sure, but it's quite impossible. The carriage is gone, and I don't ride."

Not well. She wouldn't admit it to Owen under threat of death, but Lottie had not come by her poise naturally. As a child, she'd been ungainly and uncoordinated. The dignified elegance she was capable of displaying now was the reward for years of hard work and practice, most often in the form of walking about the house with various objects atop her head. Sadly, the reward did not extend to a show of coordination during equestrian pursuits. Her ability to glide into a room like a ballerina and her propensity for gliding off a saddle like a sack of potatoes were fairly well matched.

Owen fell back a step and lifted a brow. "Do you not? I could teach you, if you like."

"Perhaps sometime." Or never. She'd just as soon he not witness her take a fall on her backside. "You didn't go into the village to ask after Peter and Esther. Did you learn anything about our intruder?"

Annoyance flashed over his face. "Your family did not come second in my consideration."

"I didn't mean that."

"I know." He made a dismissive gesture. "I know. I learned nothing, and it has left me irritated."

"Perhaps he came from another village." She didn't mention that she was a little relieved by the news. Not out of concern for the man's well-being but because she was quite concerned about the length of Owen's stay. It was selfish of her, but she hoped to have him for at least a week. Maybe even a fortnight. She could keep Peter distracted for a fortnight. It no longer seemed quite so terrifying or impossible a task now that she could trust Owen's intentions.

One fortnight, she thought, as they began a leisurely stroll along the garden path.

Let me have him for one fortnight.

"Where did you hear of my moniker?" Owen asked after a time. "The Gentleman Thief Taker?"

"Oh. Peter. You've an admirer in his Mr. Derby."

"Ah."

He seemed to take this as a matter of course. Did he face fawning admiration everywhere he went? How did one ever become accustomed to such a thing? "Are you still a sensation?"

He laughed softly. "Old hat now, thank God. As a viscount, I warrant an occasional mention in the society pages, nothing more." He slanted her a cautious look. "That would change, if your father's work came to light now. It would change for all of us."

"I know."

He nodded and seemed content to let the matter drop. "Your garden needs repair," he commented as they walked past a large, knee-high reflection pond overfilled with rainwater.

"Esther will see to it, and Peter, if she can bribe or threaten him into it."

"You haven't a gardener."

"An unnecessary expense," she explained. "The gardens were well established when we arrived, and Esther takes pleasure in caring for them now."

"Would you hire the help, could you afford it?"

"No." She kicked absently at a pebble in the path. "Not unless Esther wished it."

"I am relieved to hear it." He cleared his throat. "I know you do well enough, but…I want you to know, I did argue that you should be able to keep the thirty thousand pounds."

"It doesn't mat—" She stopped in her tracks. "Thirty thousand pounds?"

That could not be right. Surely she had misunderstood. What thirty thousand pounds?

"The reward," Owen said, as if that explained everything. "For the return of Lady Strale." A line formed across his brow. "You didn't know there was a reward?"

"Of course I did." In a vague sort of way. She remembered the mention of a reward. But not thirty thousand pounds. It was a staggering amount of money.

"Lord Strale offered, in secret, thirty thousand pounds for the safe return of his wife and the Strale diamonds. A bargain, considering the exorbitant ransom Gage was demanding. I argued that as the surviving family of the man who rescued the duchess, you were entitled to the whole amount, but I was overruled by Strale and the Queen. Two-thirds was split amongst the men who brought in Gage and his men. You should have received the remainder."

"I did." The ten thousand pounds had come as a tremendous relief, as had the news that an annual allowance was to follow. "I assumed it was the result of my father's contract with you. A sum upon his death. That sort of thing."

"No. There…" He hesitated, cleared his throat again, and took a suspicious amount of time choosing his next words. "There was only the allowance."

"That is not what you were going to say."

Indecision played clearly over his features. It didn't worry her at first. If Owen meant to lie to her, he wouldn't be so obvious about it. But as silence dragged out, it occurred to her that it might not be reluctance that kept him quiet but a bid for time while he looked for a way to soften or skirt around the truth. And what was that but another kind of lie?

"I would have the truth, Owen," she said quietly.

That did the trick. He gave a short, resigned sigh. "There was no contract. Your father agreed to work for us in exchange for his freedom."

"I see. And the allowance I receive?"

"From the Crown's coffers."

"I have always assumed as much, but…" That assumption had been based on the belief that Owen was a selfish, untrustworthy liar and therefore highly unlikely to share his own wealth, even to honor a contract. The only logical source for her income had been the Crown. Until now. "Did you have some say in that?"

He bent his head a little so they were looking eye to eye. "That allowance is yours and always will be. I want you to know that. You are not dependent on me nor beholden to me in any way. Your family's finances are not under my control."

Not under his control, perhaps, but probably within the scope of his influence. Then again, he was a viscount. Most everything fell within his scope of influence.

"But the allowance was your idea?" she pressed.

He straightened and found something to stare at over her shoulder. "There was a consensus. It was only fair."

"Liar. You'd not have hesitated over a consensus." She didn't understand why he should hesitate at all or why he should look embarrassed. "I would thank you—"

"Unnecessary. It is the Crown's money, as I said. Besides, you earned it."

"Earned it?"

"Your assistance was vital on a number of occasions."

Vital was probably excessive, but why argue with flattery? "Thank you. I would—"

"If you are going to apologize again for our estrangement, I don't want to hear it."

His brusque and implacable tone seemed excessive, as well. "Why not?"

"I wish for things to be comfortable between us. I don't want our friendship weighed down with apologies any more than I wanted it weighed down with anger."

It hadn't been weighed down so much as it had been thoroughly crushed, but she didn't mention it. "I wasn't going to apologize, as it happens."

"Weren't you?"

Yes, she was, but it was only a little lie to pretend otherwise. "I was going to say I wish someone had informed me of the details from the start."

"Do you want me to apologize?"

"No." That was the truth. She offered him a smile. "I should like for us to be comfortable as well."

There were a half-dozen reasons she ought to feel distinctly uncomfortable just then—the continued absence of Esther and Peter, the fact that someone had broken into her home, Owen's sudden reappearance in her life—but Lottie didn't feel those matters pressing on her as they continued their leisurely stroll. Well, Owen's company was certainly felt at present, but it was a welcome weight.

It felt right, just right, to be walking in companionable

silence. As if a midday stroll on a sunny day was a diversion they'd indulged in a hundred times before and would indulge in a hundred times again.

No doubt it was unrealistic to hope for a hundred strolls with Owen, but a dozen might be feasible if she had her fortnight. Maybe more, if he returned to Willowbend in the future.

"Will you write me again?"

"What was that?"

Lottie wished she could steal the words back. They sounded like a plea to her ears when she'd meant them to be casual and careless. She shrugged, hoping that would add an element of disinterest, and knowing it didn't. "I was wondering if you meant to write after you leave, or..." Or if their alienation had merely been a frayed string to him, one he now considered trimmed and knotted off. "Or not."

"You could write me."

"I couldn't possibly," she replied with an affected primness. "It would be unforgivably forward."

"True."

"Besides, I have no idea where you live. I assume you no longer keep rooms above a bookseller?"

"Ah, no. I've a house in Mayfair now. Park Lane."

Fearful she might trip over it, Lottie bit her tongue. Park Lane? She hadn't expected Park Lane. That was the realm of wealthy aristocrats. Owen's blood was blue enough, but it was still strange to think of him there, attending balls and dinners and soirees and...and whatever august and lavish festivities Park Lane inhabitants devised for themselves. Strange and disheartening. Did he dance with the pretty little debutantes, she wondered. Did he flatter their mamas and kiss the hands of their maiden aunts? Did he spend evenings sipping brandy with gentlemen who looked down their aristocratic noses at the lesser creatures of the world? People like the Walkers?

He must, she supposed. It was what respectable men did.

Suddenly, it seemed as if the great chasm they'd managed to bridge opened before her once more.

"How very fashionable of you," she said with affected good cheer.

"I had little choice in the matter. It was Caroline's decision."

The disgruntlement in his voice did wonders for her mood. "Your sister?"

"The eldest," he said. "She wanted seasons for the younger girls and a proper address from which to launch her campaign for decent husbands."

The chasm began to narrow again. "You don't wish to live there?"

Please say no. Please, please…

"It's no great hardship." He absently trailed his fingers along the tips of a tall, thready plant that had managed to escape significant damage. "But I preferred the seclusion of my old rooms and the disinterest of my old neighbors. I find Mayfair inhabitants to be…"

"Pompous?" she offered. "Officious? Haughty? Ostentatious? Genuinely horrible people?"

He laughed at the last. "Obtrusive. I find them obtrusive."

That was good enough. "I think I should dislike it as well. Peter wants to take a house in London."

"Does he? Bit young, yet, to be contemplating the sowing of wild oats."

"He doesn't want it for himself."

"Seasons for his sisters?" He nodded with approval. "There's a fine boy."

"Happy are they who have not walked in the council of the wicked," she murmured, more to herself than Owen. The quote often popped into her head when she thought of Peter.

He gave a quizzical look. "Shakespeare?"

"The Bible, more or less. The Bales are a respectable churchgoing family." A change that had first required several weeks of proper study and planning. Lottie figured she had probably seen a Bible at some point in her life before Willowbend, but that was as far as her religious education had progressed.

"Speaking of Peter," Owen said. "I find myself curious. Why is it you didn't ask how I knew the details of his schooling? You were surprised to hear I knew of Mrs. Lewis but not of Peter."

"I was surprised to hear you knew of Peter as well," she admitted. "But I reasoned it through quickly. We are Walkers and you are a man of the law. It is hardly surprising you kept apprised of our activities."

A cloud settled over his features. "Your father is not the reason for every—"

"Do you hear that?" Lottie spun about at the sound of hoofbeats and rumbling wheels turning onto the drive. "Oh, they're home!" Excited, she pulled Owen back the way they'd come. "I thought it would take longer for the road to dry out."

"The storm was more a wash than a soak. And

Samuel is a fair hand at the reins." They veered around a muddy patch of ground, then continued down the path at a brisk pace.

"I'll need a private word with him," Owen said after a few moments. "And Gabriel."

"About the intruder?" Frowning, she stopped and looked at him and discovered she was still gripping his arm. Embarrassed, she pulled her hand away. But not too quickly. The only thing worse than being embarrassed was being obvious about it. "It isn't a secret."

"Nevertheless."

She waited for him to add something meaningful to that statement. And waited. And waited.

"Oh, for pity's sake," she finally huffed. "I'll keep Esther and Peter in the house. You may use the stable for your little assignation."

He laughed, bent down to give her a sweet but all too chaste kiss on the cheek, then took off for the stables.

Lottie changed course again and headed for the house. She made it no more than a few steps down the path before a sharp blast rent the air. A half-dozen yards away, a small decorative maple shook violently, its delicate trunk splintered.

Gunshot.

She threw her hands up over her head out of instinct, but when those same instincts demanded she drop to the ground, she shoved them aside.

Owen. She had to help Owen.

Crouching low, she spun around, pushing off the ball of her foot. She'd not made it halfway through the turn before Owen's voice boomed out like a cannon.

"*Down!*"

She dropped to the dirt. There was no hesitation, only relief as she covered her head with her hands and made herself as small a target as possible. If Owen knew it was safest on the ground, then he would be on the ground too. He wasn't an idiot.

Except that he was, apparently. She heard his pounding footsteps before she saw him, tearing up the path.

"Idiot!" Terror bloomed as another shot rang out, clipping a holly bush a mere six feet behind Owen. "Get down! Get—!"

He got down. Mostly on top of her, his weight shoving the air out of her lungs.

He pushed an arm under her shoulders, threw another around her waist, and then they were rolling. Once, twice, three times… Her back slammed against something big and hard. Dizzy, it took a moment to orient herself. The reflection pond. Her back was pressed against the stone edge of the pond, and Owen was pressed against her front.

He was moving, reaching for something under his coat.

"Are you hurt?" she demanded. She struggled against him, trying to maneuver so she might see properly. "Are you hurt?"

"He missed. Keep your head down, darling."

It was his tone rather than the words that stilled her. It was shockingly calm, almost conversational. Shifting slightly, she angled her head for a look at his face.

Had she the air, she would have gasped. She'd never seen Owen like this. She'd never seen that brutally cold, utterly detached look in his eyes. How could someone sound so calm, seem so controlled, and still look so fierce?

His hands were steady, his movements methodical and precise as he retrieved a double barreled pistol and cocked it.

She felt Owen's hand and the weight of the gun settle on her hip. Fear and the horror of old memories washed over her, threatening to overwhelm her. She shoved the encroaching panic aside. If she was going to die in her garden then, by God, she was going to die with some dignity, not whimpering like a trapped animal.

"Owen?"

"Shh."

"Do you have another?" She swallowed the bile rising in her throat and wished she could will away the trembling of her limbs. "Give me a gun. Let me help."

"It's all right. Just lie still."

He wasn't listening to her, she realized. Pulling away from her slightly, he studied the damaged maple behind him, then the holly bush. He moved back, cocked his head slightly, and aimed over the edge of the reflection pond without looking.

He was judging the angle and distance from the shots to the shooter, she realized.

That couldn't possibly work. "You won't hit him. You can't—"

"Don't need to hit him. Just need him to move a little."

"What if he already moved—?"

Before she could finish, Owen adjusted his aim and pulled the trigger.

She felt the recoil pass through him and reverberate through her. Her ears rang from the blast, a high-pitched whining that made her jaw clench. Her nostrils filled with the heavy scent of spent gunpowder, and her tremors grew as the memory of her father came flooding back once more. Squeezing her eyes shut, she struggled to keep calm. She had to do something, anything.

"I need a gun," she whispered. "Give me a gun."

She felt him shake his head a moment before a second shot fired from the direction of the house. The vision of her father was instantly replaced with the image of Owen with a bullet in his back.

"Behind you. Move." She shoved against him, tried to leverage herself over him with the vague—and she would admit later, fairly ridiculous—idea she could protect him from the other side. "You have to move. He's behind you."

"It's Gabriel. It's done." His free arm slid under her, and he rose, pulling her to her feet.

"No! What are you doing? Get down. For God's sake—"

"Lottie, it's over." With his arm still wrapped around her waist, he pulled her close, holding her tight. "It's all right. He's gone. It's done."

"You can't know that. How can you know that?"

"Because." His lips brushed her hair. "Gabriel took his shot."

And therefore hit his mark? The audacity of that statement wasn't sufficient to push aside her fear, but it did add a fine layer of incredulity. "You can't *possibly* believe—"

"He's not shooting now, is he? No one is. It's over. I swear it." Another kiss, brushing gently next to her ear. "Do you think I would risk it? Risk you?"

Maybe not, she conceded, but she noticed he placed himself between her and the woods, and he kept his gun at the ready.

Gabriel's voice boomed from the front of the garden. "Renderwell! Miss Bales!"

"Here!" Owen pulled back, and his gaze traveled over her as the sound of rushing footsteps drew near. "All right, are you?"

"I... Yes." She took a full, proper breath as the fear began to subside. "Yes. You?"

He nodded once and gave an absent "hmm," as his men rushed up to meet them.

"Hit him?" he asked Gabriel.

"He missed," Samuel offered with a smirk.

"I didn't miss. He was too far away."

"Or a little too far to the right," Samuel countered.

"I didn't miss." Gabriel gave Lottie a smile that managed to be both charming and menacing. "I don't miss."

She had nothing to say to that.

Samuel glanced at Lottie, then shared a look with Owen. "Damned poachers."

Lottie shook her head. Who in their right mind poached in a garden? "I think it—"

"Lottie!" Esther's frantic yell blended with Peter's as the pair flew from the carriage.

Gabriel swore softly. "Had the devil's own time keeping them in the carriage."

"Peter is quite protective."

"Not Peter," Samuel corrected on a grumble. "Your sister. The woman is a menace."

❧

As the Walker siblings raced toward the garden, Owen took hold of Lottie by the arm. Wordlessly, Samuel moved to flank her and Gabriel took up the rear. Together they headed toward Esther and Peter at a near run.

"Keep them in the house," Owen ordered Lottie. "Lock the doors and close the drapes. Keep everyone inside."

It was a costly and likely unnecessary delay, taking her back to the house, but it couldn't be helped. He couldn't send her across the lawn alone.

Lottie pulled on his arm. "I've a stable boy and grooms and—"

"I'll see to them. All of them. Go." He ignored the barrage of questions and exclamations from Peter and Esther, pushed the group toward the house, then shoved them up the terrace steps. "Get inside. Now. And stay there."

The second the front door closed, he spun about and faced his men.

"Wasn't a poacher," Gabriel stated with conviction.

"No. We had an intruder in the house last night." He looked to Samuel. "What did you see?"

"The back of him. He was already in retreat by the time we spotted him. Dark coat, black hair cropped above the ears, no hat, stout build, five feet, seven to nine inches. Liver chestnut mount, maybe fifteen hands. Matching tail. White socks…" He frowned a little at the ground. "No. Fetlocks. White fetlocks in the rear."

Owen nodded. No one remembered details like Samuel. "You've three hours." He jerked his chin toward the trees. "Track him."

Samuel grunted once in assent and took off for the woods.

Owen took Gabriel's rifle. "See what you can charm out of the villagers."

"Charm or coerce?"

He preferred charm, but it had been of little benefit that morning. "I'll leave it to you."

"Excellent." Gabriel's smile was grim as he headed for the stables.

"Three hours!" Owen called out to his back.

He didn't wait for a response before heading into the house. Though he would have preferred to follow Samuel into the woods for the hunt, the safety of Willowbend and its occupants took precedence.

Ten

IT REQUIRED THE BETTER PART OF THOSE THREE HOURS
for Owen to make certain the orders he'd given Lottie
were followed, then turn the horses out to pasture,
haul in sufficient firewood, bring in the staff, and
otherwise see Willowbend secured.

By the time he dragged himself into the front parlor
to speak with Lottie, he felt as if he'd fought a war,
swam the English Channel, traversed the Alps, and
aged several decades.

Physically, the work had been easy. The coordination of men and tasks was a simple business. Ideally, it
should have taken no more than an hour, one and a
half at the most.

But there had been talking. Dear God, the *talking*.

Every order—every damned one of them—had to
be discussed by the staff and explained and commented
upon and, on two occasions, enforced by threat of
violence and/or dismissal.

Was his lordship absolutely certain *everyone* need
move into the house? Was it really necessary to close
all the drapes? Would his lordship consider putting

the mares in the far pasture, instead? Wouldn't it be wise to send for the constable? Had Miss Bales agreed to this? Or that? Or that other thing? One could not imagine she had agreed to that other thing. That other thing would need to be discussed.

On and on it went. It was maddening.

And on top of all the questions and arguments had been the theories.

Everyone had an opinion on who the shooter might be, what he wanted, where he could be found now, and what was to be done with him upon his capture. And everyone had to make their opinion *known*.

"It was not a poacher."

Owen stopped three feet inside the front parlor and looked at Lottie standing in front of the glow of a lamp. He opened his mouth. Shut it again. *Lottie's* opinion was welcome. "No, it was not."

"And the intruder last night was not after a few baubles to pawn."

"It might be a coincidence," he allowed and crossed the room to lower himself into a wing chair, manfully swallowing a grateful moan. "But it is unlikely."

"Is he after you or the Walkers?"

"I don't know." He grimaced and swore. He bloody well did know, and the knowledge sat like lead in his gut. "Me. Or Samuel or Gabriel. Damn it."

"How can you be certain?"

"Have you had trouble before this?"

She shook her head and took the chair next to his.

"Then it is unlikely to be you. He's after me or maybe the letters I brought—"

Esther voice's, unusually apprehensive, interrupted from the doorway. "I think perhaps not."

"I thought you were with Peter," Lottie said, half rising. "Where is he?"

Owen gestured for her to keep her seat. "Mrs. Lewis put him to work clearing out a room for the grooms. What do you know, Esther?"

"Very little, I'm afraid." Pale blue eyes darted to Lottie. "But I saw someone at the inn last night."

Someone who clearly frightened her. Owen rose and ushered Esther to the settee. "Sit down. Tell us everything."

"We were taking dinner. It was early; there was some light yet. I saw him crossing the yard." Her fingers bunched in the rose taffeta of her skirts. "He saw me too. He recognized me. I'm sure of it."

"Who?" Lottie asked.

"An acquaintance of father's."

Every drop of color drained from Lottie's cheeks. "Are you certain? Are you absolutely certain?"

"Yes. I met him. I was very young at the time, eight perhaps, or nine, but I do remember meeting him."

"His name?" Owen inquired. Too restless now to sit, he took up position next to Lottie's chair.

"I don't know. Father rarely used names. Never ours. But he called him"—Esther scrunched her face up in annoyed concentration—"oh, something unflattering. The man didn't like it. I don't remember."

"Maybe I would," Lottie said.

"No. I don't recall you being there. Father and I were alone, walking somewhere, and we ran into the man on the street."

❧

"When? What street? Where were you going?"

Lottie didn't mean to fling all three questions at once—they simply rolled off her tongue in quick succession. It was so odd that Esther and their father should have been on an outing alone. Their father rarely took Esther anywhere. If he had need of a daughter, he took Lottie. Every time. It had been a constant source of hurt and humiliation for Esther, to consistently come second to the favored older sister. Initially, Lottie had been too young to know how to bridge the emotional gap between Esther and their father. Later, she'd know better than to try. Esther had been too needy, and Will Walker too selfish before his work with Owen. He might have loved his younger daughter, but that love wouldn't have stopped him from using her in his work.

Esther threw up her hands in frustration. "I don't know. It was years ago. I was a child."

"Old enough to remember meeting him," Owen replied.

"He frightened me. That's why I remember him. I didn't like his eyes." She wiggled her hand in front of her face. "They were black and beady—" She broke off suddenly and snapped her fingers. "Ferret. That's what father called him. The Ferret. Because of the beady eyes and pointed face."

"Do you recall anything else?" Owen asked. "Build? Voice?"

Esther's expression turned apologetic. "Average build. Dark hair? That's all I remember. He wore an overcoat last night. And it happened so quickly.

I only noticed his face, really. Lottie told me of the intruder last night. Was it him, do you think? And in the garden, as well?"

"It could be," he muttered bitterly. "Bastard might have followed or tracked us from London. We might as well have come by railway."

Lottie nodded. It would have been easier to determine their destination had the men come by train, but even on horseback, the men would have gone through several villages, stopped to change or rest the horses, passed other travelers on the road. It wasn't terribly difficult to follow someone if you knew the road they'd started on and knew how to ask the right questions of the right people. "How could he have known you were headed here?"

"I don't know. No one knew where we were going."

"Your men knew," Esther pointed out.

Owen sent her a stern look. "My men have known where to find you for eight years."

"I did not intend to disparage their loyalty or honor, Renderwell. I was merely questioning their discretion."

Lottie knew that, in Owen's eyes, they were one and the same. She shook her head at Esther, but her sister ignored the warning.

Esther continued, "If they were in their cups, or—"

"They don't talk."

"People make mistakes."

"My men do not talk."

Lottie could see Owen's temper rising in the face of Esther's persistence. He was still, his stance relaxed, but his clipped tone was taking on a sharp edge.

"I would have a word with my sister," Lottie said quickly.

The last thing she needed now was an all-out row between Owen and Esther, and that's exactly where they were headed.

When Owen hesitated, she laid a hand on his arm. "Owen, please."

The muscles beneath her fingers bunched once, then released a second before he drew away. "Very well."

Esther watched his departure before turning to face Lottie with raised brows. "Owen now, is it?"

"It is. I'll explain later." She had no qualms about telling Esther of her reconciliation with Owen, but now wasn't the time. Owen wouldn't stay away for long. "He is right, Esther. If Owen was followed here, it wasn't due to the carelessness of his men."

"You don't know that."

"I believe it. Moreover, we cannot be sure it was the Ferret who shot at us today or came in the house last night. We have no way of knowing who is out there, how he got here, or why he has come, and casting blame about does nothing to improve the situation."

Esther slumped a little, but she wasn't ready to give in entirely. "We'll not have answers unless we ask the questions."

"Yes, but it must be the right questions. For all we know, the Ferret stumbled upon you at the inn by accident. He might have been simply passing through Fisckrem, and there you were. Renderwell's presence here may have nothing to do with this."

"You cannot believe this is coincidence."

"I find coincidence more plausible than a betrayal by Owen's men." Lottie rose from her chair and slid onto the settee next to her sister. "They have kept the Walker family secrets for twelve years. Eight since we've come to Willowbend. They have earned the benefit of the doubt."

Esther blinked at her, brows raised. "This is a fine change of tune to have over the course of two days."

"It is, I admit, but two days ago I believed Owen had betrayed father, and cheated him out of a hard-earned legacy. I was wrong." She thought of his insistence that her father had remained a black-hearted scoundrel. "Half wrong," she amended and brushed off her sister's questioning expression with a wave of her hand. "Later, I promise. The point is, I never feared he would compromise our safety. Never."

Esther's lips twisted. "It might be compromised now, regardless."

"It might." She wanted to close her eyes on a heavy sigh as the life they had built in Wayton, the future she had imagined in her lovely little piece of Norfolk, faded away.

If one man from their past had found them, then others might follow.

Willowbend was no longer safe.

The knowledge of it broke her heart, but for Esther's sake, she smiled and reached for her sister's hand. "There is no sense in borrowing trouble."

"Trouble finds us anyway."

"If it does, we shall make the most of it. It might be exciting, moving to a new village. Think of it as an adventure, and think of all the new subjects you would have for your artwork, all the new architecture." Esther had always loved sketching interesting houses and buildings and had often complained of the lack of variety to be found in Wayton.

"Perhaps." Esther pulled her hand away and rose. "I have to go. I need to think." She gave Lottie a smile that was closer to desperate than hopeful. "If I think on it, I might remember something useful."

"You already have," Lottie assured her, but Esther appeared not to hear. She walked away without reply.

Lottie gave into the sigh as she watched her sister leave. She'd barely finished exhaling when Owen appeared in the empty doorway.

"Were you waiting in the hall?" she asked, uncertain if she should be amused or annoyed.

"Eavesdropping, do you mean?" He crossed the room to her but didn't take a seat. "No."

"You needn't worry about Esther."

"Has she revised her opinion of my men?"

"Doubtful," Lottie admitted. "But she is not the vengeful sort. Your men are safe."

His lips twitched in amusement. "I shall allay their fears directly." He leaned lightly against the side of a chair and tilted his head at her. "Are you all right?"

Lottie's first inclination was to square her shoulders and respond with sarcasm complemented by a strong undercurrent of bravado.

Naturally, she was all right. She could smile and dismiss his concern with a careless wave of the hand. She was a Walker, wasn't she? She wasn't afraid of anything.

Just the idea of putting up such a pretense exhausted her. Later, she would be strong for Peter and Esther. She would rally and reassure. She would pretend a courage and confidence she did not feel, just as she had always done. But for a few minutes, before all the lying began, she wanted to indulge in the luxury of honesty.

She slumped against the back of the settee. "We have to leave Willowbend."

"No, you don't. I'll catch him, Lottie. I promise."

"Perhaps, but it changes nothing. Whether or not the Ferret is the shooter, his presence so near can't go ignored. He saw Esther. He knows we're nearby. He may have told others by now. He might—"

"He may have seen her," Owen cut in. "It doesn't necessarily follow that he should remember her."

"She said he recognized her."

"She was a child when they met. Too young to even properly recall his appearance at the inn. It would be difficult for a man to recognize a child he met years ago in an adult he caught a fleeting look at through a window. If this Ferret recognized anything, it was intense interest from a lovely woman. Any man subjected to the stare of a Walker sister is going to take a moment to stare back."

Despite her worries, her cheeks warmed at the easy compliment. "She was certain."

"She was scared."

"Yes. Yes, she was." And being scared, Esther would have jumped to conclusions. And being a Walker, that jump would have landed dead center of The Worst Conceivable Outcome.

A sliver of hope worked its way into her gloomy predictions for the future. She struggled to find the balance between allowing that small measure of light and not allowing it to blind her to reality. It was too soon, yet, to draw any conclusions.

It was not, however, too soon to take precautions. "I want to send Esther and the staff away with Peter. They can visit Scotland, or—"

"No."

Just *no*. Not an offer of explanation, not an invitation to discuss. Just *no*. Arrogant, irritating man. "If it was not the Ferret who shot at us today, then we've two threats to consider. I want them safe. I want—"

"As do I," he assured her. "I don't know what the man who shot at you today wants nor how far he is willing to go to obtain it. It's too easy to track someone traveling by train, and I'll not send any of you off in a carriage that can be run down. I'll not allow him to use any one of you as leverage."

"The shooter may be long gone by now."

"In which case, there's no call to run, is there? Are you willing to chance it?"

She drummed her fingers against the settee cushion as she considered his argument. "No. I'll not risk it. They'll stay. But your men are not to continue seeking out Peter's company."

"Very well. Now"—he rubbed the back of his neck—"we've another dilemma. Some of the staff have asked whether we should send for the constable, but they've not yet insisted upon it."

"They won't." This, at least, would not be a problem. "No one wants to send for Mr. Barclay. He's a drunk. We can tell them you've wired your former colleagues in London. That will satisfy Peter and the staff."

"Excellent. You'll inform them. And remind them they are to stay inside. All of you are to stay inside.

Away from the windows. Drapes remain drawn. Do you understand?"

"Yes." She took in the overcoat he'd yet to remove and the pair of gloves in his hand. "Do you?"

"What do you mean?"

"Do you understand the need to stay inside as well?" He sighed.

"I'll take that to mean no," she said blandly.

"I have to catch him."

"And if he catches you first?"

His smile was pure arrogance. "I am not easily caught."

"Hubris makes a better target than it does a shield."

"I use it for neither."

"Then why bother with so much of it?" she grumbled.

"Because it irritates you." He grinned at her scowl. "Will you give me a kiss before I go?"

The attempt at distraction was no less effective for its blatancy. "I…" She cast about for a deflection of her own. "You mean to go back outside right now?"

"Samuel and Gabriel will return soon. We'll take shifts, searching the woods, watching the house." He straightened from the chair. "Come here, Lottie."

She might have, but the movement briefly brushed aside his overcoat, revealing that he had not one, but two pistols hidden beneath.

"You have another gun."

He glanced down. "I do, yes. I've several."

Several? On his person? Good Lord. "Did you have it in the garden?"

"Yes."

"But I asked for one. You refused."

"You don't like guns," he replied in a reasonable tone.

"I like feeling useless even less."

"Anyone would." He was quiet a moment before asking, "Will you tell me the reason for your aversion?"

She found a loose thread on the cushion. "What does it matter?"

"If you'll not trust me with the reason, how am I to trust you with the weapon?"

"It has nothing to do with trust." She plucked at the string. "I am capable of handling a gun. I practice."

"With targets. It is not the same."

"I know that."

He was silent for a long time, and though she could feel his gaze, she couldn't lift her head to meet it. "You were shaking."

"I was afraid. That doesn't mean—"

"It means you were unlikely to hit your target and apt to hit something of value."

Bristling at the implication, she abandoned the string and glared at him. "I don't kill people accidently, either. Were you not nervous the first time you raised a weapon at something other than an inanimate object?"

"I was, but it was different."

"How?"

"It was war. I had no choice. You had a choice."

"I—"

"You had me."

The words were glib, even a little smug, but Lottie heard the hard edge buried beneath.

"And I am grateful for it," she said carefully. Did he believe otherwise? "I didn't mean to imply that I am not grateful, but—"

"You didn't." He brushed her comment away with a short sweep of his hand. "Tell me your secret and we shall discuss your future participation in armed conflict."

Discuss, she noted, was not the same as a promise. "It isn't a secret. I don't like to speak of it, that's all. I don't like to think of it. May we speak of something else?"

He shook his head at her, and when he spoke, his voice sounded a little strange, as if he was sad, or possibly just annoyed. It was difficult to tell. "You've too many secrets, Lottie. And too little trust."

"I don't." Oh, but she was a liar. Her time as the Tulip might be just one secret, but there was no doubt in her mind it would be one secret too many for Owen. She needed to move the conversation into safer territory. "We'll not agree on this," she said and wondered just how long the list of things on which they would not agree had now become. "Haven't we enough to worry over at present?"

"We have," he replied after a moment, then surprised her by jerking his thumb over his shoulder. "Where the devil did you acquire that desk?"

"What? Why?"

"We've enough to worry over, as you said. I'd like this particular concern of mine put to rest. Why would a woman of taste and sense allow that insult in her home?"

She leaned a bit for a look around him at the carved monstrosity in the corner. His was a fair question, she had to admit. "It is hideous, isn't it?"

"A gross understatement."

"At last, we are in agreement," she replied, mostly because it felt nice to be able to say. "It was willed to

Esther three years ago by Mrs. Stanway, the vicar's late grandmother. Esther saved her little poodle from being trampled in the road."

He made a face at the desk. "Does Mrs. Stanway have family about who would make a fuss if you sold it off?"

"No. Esther insists we keep it."

"She likes it?" He looked positively astonished by the very notion.

"God, no. Who would? Aside from Mrs. Stanway, apparently. But Esther liked the poodle and Mrs. Stanway. Possibly in that order." She leaned again for another look. "I don't mind it, really. It is a nice reminder."

"Of a woman and her dog?"

"No, of a good deed. A selfless act." She shrugged, but it was stiff, and she knew she came off less like a woman who didn't care and more like a woman who was trying very hard to look as if she didn't care. "Rarer than diamonds in the Walker house."

He tapped his gloves lightly against his leg. "I've seen generosity in Peter and devotion in Esther."

"Yes, but—"

"Only days ago, you despised me. And yet you allowed me into your home and agreed to work with me because you wanted justice for a woman who was, briefly, kind to you when you were young. If you do not see the good in the Walker house, then it is a result of your own willful blindness."

She wasn't convinced by his staunch defense of her family—of her in particular—but she was touched. "I shall endeavor to open my eyes."

"See that you do."

He came to her then and bent his head to press a kiss to her forehead. As he straightened, his eyes flicked to the door and back. The movement was quick, but she saw it.

He wanted to leave, she realized. He was edgy and restless, refusing to sit, fiddling with his gloves. Was that what she'd heard in his voice earlier? Irritation? The desire to be away from her? Surprise and hurt lasted only as long as it took for common sense to intrude. Of course he wanted to leave. He was making conversation in the parlor while his men were out working. The inactivity had to be eating at him.

Yet he made no move to go.

When he stepped back, she studied him, much as she had in the garden, but this time she looked beyond the appealing surface and beyond the obvious layer of arrogance. There was, she thought with some amusement, probably more arrogance under that initial layer, but there was such patience in him, as well, and a vast selflessness she wished, with all her heart, she had remembered eight years ago.

Owen frowned a little under her watchful gaze. "What is it?"

You're a good man, Owen Renderwell.

She bit back the words. She wanted to offer them, but it wasn't the sort of thing one could just blurt out. Even if it was, it wasn't the sort of thing one could blurt out without the expectation of a conversation to follow, and she'd kept him in the parlor long enough.

"Nothing. You should go." She waved her hand at him when his frown deepened. "Go. I need to make certain Mrs. Lewis and the rest of the staff understand what's to be done."

"Are you all right?"

"I am. I promise. Go."

He was already moving. "I'll return soon," he promised over his shoulder. A second more, and he disappeared out the door.

Two seconds later, he, and the frown, reappeared. "You'll stay inside. Away from the windows."

"I will."

One brusque nod and he was gone again.

No doubt he had wanted to leave almost from the start, but he had stayed. He had taken the time to settle her fears about leaving Willowbend, ask about her aversion to guns, and speak with her about her family. He had taken the time to make sure she was all right.

Because the words still wanted out, she whispered, "You're a good man, Owen Renderwell" into the still room.

Maybe too good, the little voice said.

Too good for the likes of you.

Eleven

FOR TWO DAYS, FAMILY AND STAFF REMAINED INDOORS, and a tense and heavy gloom fell over a house that was essentially under siege.

Owen and his men took turns searching the surrounding woods and countryside, going out one or two at a time, and returning every few hours to switch off, eat, and rest. They had little to show for their efforts but the occasional discovery of new tracks, dousing what hope Lottie had that the shooter had left for good.

The man was still out there, drawing close to the house at times but never leaving the cover of the woods. There was no sign or word of him in the village, and his tracks always led through the backwoods and out to a busy crossroad, where they were lost among the signs of other travelers. He was camping in the woods on the other side of the road, that much could be assumed, but there was no telling how far he traveled down the road—or in which direction—before disappearing into the trees once more.

Eventually he would need to emerge for supplies,

or he would be apprehended on approach to the house, or the tracks leading off the road would be discovered. Eventually, Owen would catch him.

In the meantime, there was nothing for Lottie to do but worry and wait.

She passed the long hours by keeping busy, spending every free moment she had studying the letters and small stacks of journals she secreted into her room at night. Some of those journals had pages with corners turned down and little notes from Owen tucked inside, asking her for clarification or for an explanation of some diagram or encryption. She wasn't sure where he found the time or energy to sift through her father's work. She could only assume he spent some of the hours in his room reading instead of sleeping. He had to be utterly exhausted. And still he was working to find Mrs. Popple's murderer.

The remainder of her time was divided between finding work and amusement for the staff and fulfilling her regular household obligations.

Esther helped with the chores as needed but spent her free time isolated in her bedroom, refusing all offers of company.

Lottie wished Peter would take it upon himself to follow suit. Alas, he chose instead to air his dissatisfaction with the current state of affairs publicly. He skulked from room to room, mumbled and snarled his way through conversations, dragged his feet about the house with an uncommon amount of noise, and took advantage of every opportunity to glower at Owen and his men, who had, it would seem, plummeted in his esteem.

The sustained display of temper was quite unlike him and highly annoying, but Lottie could scarcely blame him for it. He wanted explanation and action, and she could offer neither.

"We don't know who it is, Peter," she explained on the second afternoon. "It might be a poacher, just as Owen, his men, and his colleague in London suspect."

"Bollocks. We are not holed up in this house because of a poacher."

"It is only a precaution," she said again. Was this the third time they'd had this discussion or the fourth? It felt like the hundredth. "And mind your language."

"Then let us be cautious," Peter said stiffly. "I want you out. I want you and Esther and the staff far away from here."

Lottie abandoned the set of ledgers she'd spent the last two hours struggling to reconcile with the possibility of an upcoming move and turned to run a loving hand down her brother's arm. "I know, dear, but on the very, *very* small chance we are not dealing with a poacher, the wisest course of action is to stay protected inside the house at all times."

"He is alone in the woods. Sir Samuel says it appears as if he approaches the house for only a brief time, then leaves again and camps elsewhere at night. We can use the cover of darkness to slip away."

If it was the man's intention to follow them, then there was every reason to believe he had someone watching the roads. Possibly several individuals. One or more could reach him and return on horseback much faster than they could get away in a caravan of carriages traveling down a dark road. She couldn't explain this to Peter, however, without implying that they were almost certainly not dealing with a poacher. "I am sorry, Peter, but I am tired of discussing this. It is safer to stay in the house. We are not leaving. And that is that."

Peter puffed his chest up in a manner she could only assume was meant to be impressive. It put her in mind of a little boy playing soldier. "That, I believe, is for me to decide."

That sentiment was a hair more pompous than sweet, but she made allowances for age and circumstances. "It is not."

"Who else, then? Renderwell? It is his fault, like as not—"

"It is not. And it is my decision."

"I am the man of the house."

This was a new tactic and not the least bit sweet. She rose from her chair to pin him with a single, cold stare. "You are a young man in *my* house, Peter. Understood?"

His lips thinned into a single angry line and his hands fisted at his sides until his knuckles turned white. Lottie braced herself for the verbal firestorm to come. But Peter said nothing. He simply spun on his heel and strode from the room.

After that unfortunate incident, Peter's surliness grew into a veritable thundercloud of anger that rumbled and roiled over his head, pouring resentment and temper down on anyone so unfortunate as to cross his path.

To Lottie's considerable dismay, and Peter's great delight, Owen rectified the situation by taking matters into his own hands on the morning of the third day.

"Peter will aid me in a search of the woods today." Owen announced this unwelcomed bit of news as Lottie walked into the front parlor to discover Peter loading a rifle.

"What? No. Absolutely not. Absolutely *not*." She stabbed a finger at Peter. "Put that away. You've no idea how to use it."

"Yes, I do," Peter countered, sparing her a glance. "Mr. Whitlock taught me."

"Mr. Whitlock?" The handsome butcher? "When? Why?"

"Two years ago, to start. When I've had the opportunity since. And because I asked it of him. He agreed the *only* man in a house ought to know how to protect it."

"That rotten—"

"You like Mr. Whitlock," Peter interrupted, and he sent her his first smile in days. "He quite likes you."

"This is not a source of humor, Peter."

He shrugged and went back to his gun. "If you wish to sulk about it, I cannot stop you."

For one infuriating moment, she was stunned speechless.

Owen cleared his throat. "Peter, I am not certain it is wise—"

"*Me*?" Lottie found her voice and, with it, a fair amount of volume. "You insufferable child. You have tried my patience, and the patience of every person in this house, for days. We've had nothing but sullen, peevish behavior out of you. I swear you were better company as a squalling infant. He had colic." This last was snapped at Owen, to whom she felt compelled to offer some sort of explanation.

"I see."

She jabbed her finger at Peter again and took a step toward him. "I couldn't put you over my knee for that, but by God—"

"Do you know," Peter chirped and took a quick step back toward the door. "I believe I've forgotten my…er…my hat." He set his rifle aside without taking his eyes off her. "I need my hat. Back in a thrice."

"Don't you dare walk out of this… *Oh*, that little brat." With the object of her fury gone, she whirled on Owen. Had she thought him a good, selfless man only a few days ago? She was an idiot. "What have you done?"

Owen merely shrugged and checked his own weapons. "He needs something to do. He needs to feel useful."

"Oh, well, if a desire to feel useful is the only prerequisite for indulging stupidity, allow me to fetch my pistol."

"Rifle would be preferable. Greater range."

Temper was briefly overtaken by surprise. "You would take me?"

He didn't look up from his task. "Did you think I would make the offer to your young brother and deny you?"

"Yes." And his answer, she noted, had come in the form of his own question. "You said you don't trust me with a gun."

"No, I implied that I do not trust your

ability to properly handle a weapon during a time of danger. Which, in this case, is not a concern." He leaned his rifle against the wall and finally gave her his full attention. "I would suggest, however, that you choose another time to accompany me. Peter is likely to take exception to having the butt of his rifle tangle in the leading strings."

"I am not interested in Peter's exceptions." And she still was not convinced Owen would be willing to take her along to search the woods, but it was the lesser of two concerns at the moment. "I am interested in his safety."

"He'll be fine. He is a clever, capable young man."

"He is a child," Lottie countered.

"I am nearly fifteen," Peter countered, reentering the room. He stopped near the door, hat in hand, and gave Lottie a speculative look. "You're not really going to try to put me over your knee, are you?"

She'd never put him over her knee in his life, but Lottie thought it best to keep a boy of fourteen on his toes. "That remains to be seen."

"I am not a child, Lottie."

"You are. He is." When Peter shook his head and turned his attention to donning his coat and gloves, she stepped close to Owen and whispered so only he could hear. "He should be. Don't take that from him. Not yet."

A mix of understanding and sympathy passed over Owen's face. He shot a quick glance at Peter, then leaned closer and gently ran his hand down her arm. "Lottie. I'd not take that from him for any price. He will trudge about the woods with me for a time, nothing more."

"You can't be sure."

"I can, or I'd not have made the offer to Peter." His fingers brushed lightly over the back of her hand. "I'll keep him safe. I promise. Samuel has already searched the area northwest of the house. There are no tracks there nor signs anyone has been through there at any time. There is no one there, but Peter will feel the better for having looked."

"I don't…"

"Let him help you. He will never forgive himself for not helping you."

Her resolve wavered. Owen was right. Peter wanted so badly to do well by his family. He needed so much to take care of those he loved. She wanted the same thing herself, but she was not a boy of four-teen, standing on the cusp of manhood. She hadn't so much to prove nor a confidence so easily damaged.

She gave a shaky nod and reluctantly stepped away from Owen's reassuring touch.

"You have one hour," she announced loud enough for Peter to hear.

"Five," Peter countered.

"We will return in three." Owen threw Peter a sharp look before the boy could protest. "It is the same for Samuel and Gabriel. There is nothing to be gained in staying out longer than necessary. And take off the hat. Nothing to be gained by making yourself a larger target, either."

Peter nodded, tossed his hat aside, and hitched his rifle to his shoulder with a practiced ease that made Lottie's heart twist. Hadn't he just been struggling to learn his letters? Hadn't it been only yesterday that he'd needed her to kiss a scraped elbow or knee? How could he be standing before her now, with a man's cocky grin on his face and a weapon in his hands?

"Don't be afraid, Sis." He gave her a cheerful grin. "I'm not."

"You are. You *are*," she repeated coolly when he would have argued, "because I did not raise a stupid, selfish boy."

His cheeks flamed red with insult, then quickly dulled to a faint blush of shame. "I'll be around to flatten spiders for you a while longer," he offered sheepishly. "Please don't worry."

"I always worry," she replied, but she smiled. There didn't seem to be any other choice but to force a smile and keep it in place as she followed them through the house, then saw them out a side door.

Owen paused on the other side of the threshold. "Who is Mr. Whitlock?"

"The butcher." She thought of the wiry strength in Mr. Whitlock's arms and his sharp set of knives and let the smile go. "Bring Peter back with so much as a scratch, and I'll arrange an introduction."

"Wouldn't mind an introduction."

"You would mind his cleaver," she promised and shut the door.

❧

Three hours later, Peter returned as promised, without a single visible scratch and without the miserable temper of the previous days. His fine mood was further buoyed when Owen suggested later that afternoon that Peter join him during his night watch.

Lottie didn't argue. Walking about the house with Owen was hardly dangerous work. Still, it rankled that Owen had, once again, not sought out her approval, or even her opinion, before involving Peter.

"You cannot presume to take over the running of this house and this family after mere days in residence." He shouldn't expect it at all. It was her house, her family. It was her parlor they were in. That was her settee he was sitting on. It was her carpet he'd muddied with his boots. "I appreciate what you have done and what you continue to do for us, but neither gives you the right to take charge of this house."

Owen's lips turned down at the corners. "You're quite right."

"Furthermore, if you… I beg your pardon?"

"I said you are correct. I should have discussed the notion with you first." He shrugged. "I am accustomed to leadership."

When further explanation was not immediately forthcoming, she tamped down annoyance and tried to help him along. "You are accustomed to issuing orders, therefore you issue orders?"

"Without consultation or interference, yes. I meant no discourtesy. It's habit. One I'll make a concerted effort to alter whilst at Willowbend."

"Well. Good." She thought about it as she took her own seat and decided that, no, it was not good. Quick capitulation was always suspect. "In the future, you'll not involve Peter, or any other member of this house, without my permission?"

He rubbed the backs of his fingers under his chin. "Well, now, I'll certainly discuss it with you first."

"I knew it."

"Tell me of your Mr. Whitlock."

The abrupt change of subject left her reeling. "What? Why? No, never mind. It doesn't matter. We are not discussing Mr. Whitlock."

"We could be. I'd rather be."

"But we're not."

"I think we are," he returned, a teasing glint in his eyes. "We have now made four consecutive statements—five including this one—of which your Mr. Whitlock is the topic. That constitutes a discussion."

They weren't discussing Mr. Whitlock; they were discussing whether or not to discuss Mr. Whitlock or possibly whether or not Mr. Whitlock was currently being discussed. Whatever the case, it was entirely different than a discussion *of* Mr. Whitlock. Lottie hesitated to point this out, however.

There was little chance they would come to an immediate agreement on who was currently in charge. It would take time to make Owen understand the difference between discourtesy and disrespect. So she would give him a few hours, or maybe the night, and then they would revisit the matter.

In the meantime…she rather liked the idea of discussing Mr. Whitlock.

A part of her—a small, juvenile part—was intrigued by the idea that Owen might be jealous. She'd never made a man jealous before. She knew how. She'd been given lessons in all manner of manipulation. But the opportunity to put this particular lesson to use had never presented itself.

A larger part of her warned against playing games with Owen. He was not a dupe. She was not a schemer. And she didn't *want* there to be games between them.

The second part was older, wiser, and safer. But it wasn't nearly as interesting.

"He is not my Mr. Whitlock," she said carefully, undecided as yet which part of herself she would heed. "He is Wayton's butcher."

"The butcher who quite likes you."

"He did, once."

He stretched out an arm on the back of the settee. "And now you are mortal enemies?"

"Now we are friends."

"But you were more than friends, once."

She brushed a fictional piece of lint from her sleeve. "He was a suitor for a time."

"How much time? How long ago?"

She had to think about it, which gave her some pause. Until her kiss with Owen the other night, Mr. Whitlock's courtship had been the closest thing she'd known to a great love affair. But if she couldn't easily recall when this momentous event had taken place then, clearly, neither "great," nor "love," nor "affair" actually applied. *Inconsequentially affectionate episode*, that's what she'd had. It was depressing.

"Three years ago," she replied, fairly certain it was the same summer Esther had saved the poodle.

And, again, wasn't that a sad statement of her affairs—or lack thereof—that she should remember those months as *the summer in which my sister rescued a dog and acquired a desk*, when it ought to have been *the summer in which Mr. Whitlock kissed me*. To combat the sudden desire to sag in her seat, she inched closer to the edge of the chair and straightened her shoulders. "Not for long. Two months, perhaps three."

"You encouraged his attentions, then. The courtship would not have lasted a day unless you were agreeable." He tipped his head at her, his eyes inscrutable. "Handsome, is he?"

"Naturally," she drawled. "Why else would a lady bother?"

"Why indeed? Who ended it?"

"Does it matter?"

"It does." He regarded her quietly for a moment. "It was you."

"Do you think?" She didn't mind telling him it was, but she minded a little that he should be so quick to draw his own conclusions.

"You're embarrassed, but you're not hurt," he explained. "Was he angry?"

"I'm not embarrassed." She was a trifle embarrassed, but there were appearances to maintain, even with Owen. "And no, he wasn't angry. It was all quite civil. I told him I could not return his affections, and that was the end of it."

"Was it?" He asked softly. "Do you think he let you go so easily?"

"I don't know as it was *easily* done." That wasn't at all flattering.

"Wailed and gnashed his teeth, did he?"

"There was a brief spot of gnashing. No wailing. And now we are friends. Friendly acquaintances, really. There are no sweet words of devotion nor hopeless gazes of longing."

"Not on your end, I'm sure." He stretched his long legs out before him. "But it is naïve to assume a man doesn't look, even when he shouldn't. Especially when he shouldn't."

"There is no assumption. He lets me alone."

"Doesn't mean he isn't looking." His voice took on a silky quality. "I can't imagine a man not looking."

Something warm and liquid started in her chest and spread. "You didn't."

"Beg your pardon?"

She bit the inside of her cheek and prayed she wasn't blushing. *In for a penny*, she thought.

"In London. You never looked." That wasn't entirely accurate. He'd looked that last year. She often wondered if he'd looked before without her notice. And since it appeared she hadn't the gall to provoke his jealousy, she could at least have her curiosity assuaged.

"Is that what you think?" Owen asked.

"Did you?"

"Not initially, no," he replied, and she felt herself deflate. "You were an infant when we met."

"An infant? I was eighteen." And worldly with it, in comparison to the sheltered misses he knew.

"And had I been eighteen as well, I might have commissioned a poet to herald your beauty. But I was five-and-twenty, if memory serves. Too old for a girl just out of the nursery."

Most gentlemen were not of a similar mind, but that wasn't the portion of his statement that snagged her attention.

"Commissioned a poet?" She laughed at the very notion. "Good Lord, you *are* a viscount."

"Wouldn't you like a poem written for you? And don't say no," he warned with a smile and a pointed finger, "or I'll know you're lying. Anyone would be flattered."

"You'll know I'm lying when I inform you I've been lying," she told him with a smirk. "Would you be flattered?"

"I'd prefer a ballad, truth be told. Everyone likes a ballad. And I would prefer it told of my cunning wit and unparalleled courage, but if it must regal its listeners with tales of my dashing good looks, then it must."

She cast her eyes to the ceiling. "You should write your own ballad. I daresay no one could praise Viscount Renderwell quite like Viscount Renderwell."

"Ah, but I haven't the talent for verse. That's why I'd have commissioned the poet for you."

"A woman would prefer a poem written from the heart, not the purse."

"Any woman worth poetry is worth good poetry. And no woman deserves to have her name immortalized in bad verse."

She could only shake her head. "You are the single most unromantic human being I have ever met."

"I've romance," he assured her. "But I do not press myself upon young women under my care."

"I am not a young woman under your care now."

"You're partially right. Come here."

"I beg your pardon? Are you saying I am not under your care, or are you calling me an old woman?"

"Neither." He laughed. "Come here."

She scooted back in her seat. "Why?"

"You're a clever woman—I imagine you can work that out for yourself."

Of course she could work it out. That's why she'd scooted. "You want to kiss me."

"No." His lips curved in a beguiling smile. "I want you to kiss me."

Unbidden, a vision of doing just that popped into her head. Standing up, walking to him, bending down, and placing her lips against his while he sat still and unmoving under her attentions, the king on his throne, or possibly the wolf in repose. Either way...

"Absolutely not."

"How do I know I'm not another Mr. Whitlock—another temporary amusement whose attentions you simply endured?"

"That's not... I did like Mr. Whitlock."

"Enough to cross a room and kiss him?"

"I don't have to answer that." There was no good way to answer that.

"I kissed you last," he reminded her. "It's your turn."

She made a face at him, unhappy with his choice of words. "Are we keeping score?"

"Think of it as a transfer of control. Isn't that what you want? To have control?"

"I never said I had to *do* everything."

"Just tell others what to do?"

She opened her mouth and then closed it. There was no denying that issuing orders came with being in control.

"Ah." Owen rose from his seat. "In that case..."

Stepping close, he took her hand and slowly pulled

her to her feet until they were standing mere inches apart. Her skirts rustled against his legs, and she caught the subtle blend of wintergreen soap and woods. He bent his head, and his breath was warm and soft against the skin of her cheek. "In that case…" He brushed his lips across her jaw. "Tell me what to do, Lottie."

Without thought, she turned her head in an effort to catch his mouth, but he moved away, staying just out of reach. His lips found the corner of her mouth for one tantalizing second, then pulled away again.

"Tell me," he whispered, and she could feel his smile against her skin.

For one brief second, she wondered if she should take offense, but when she pulled back and looked at him, all thought of insult drained away. There was humor in his eyes, a bright, devilish light that danced and teased, but there wasn't a hint of arrogance nor a trace of smugness.

This wasn't an attempt to embarrass her, she realized, nor a bid for dominance.

It was an invitation to play.

A new kind of pleasure warmed her blood and had her fighting back a smile of her own.

"Tell you?" She pretended to consider that for a moment, then wrinkled her nose at him. "No, I don't fancy kissing a man who has to be told how it's done."

And with that, she slipped her hand from his and headed for the door with an exaggerated flounce.

She made it two steps before he caught her waist and spun her around again.

He was laughing when his mouth found hers, and she was laughing right back. It was a peculiar sensation to kiss a man while laughing. Peculiar, a fair bit awkward, and quite possibly the most wonderful experience she'd ever known.

There was no trace of nerves as there had been in his room. There was no ugly little voice whispering in her ear, no shadow of a mistrust so recently set aside. There was only the laughter, the fun, and the sheer pleasure of being held.

This, she thought, twining her arms around his neck, *this will* always *be the summer with Owen.*

She let herself fall headlong into the moment, teasing him with light kisses, nibbling playfully at the corner of his mouth. She even heard herself giggle, a silly little sound she was certain she had never made before in her life.

But when she grew bold and flicked her tongue into the warmth of his mouth, the mood shifted.

Owen tensed, his arms banding tight around her waist. Intrigued, she tried again and was rewarded with a low, masculine growl. She had only a second to wonder at it, at the knowledge she had the power to pull the primitive sound from his throat, and then he was kissing her again. Kissing her differently.

His mouth slanted over hers, hungry and demanding, again and again. It robbed her of thought, left her boneless and breathless. The world around her spun away in a disorienting rush. There was no more laughter, no more giggling, no more parlor. There was only Owen, the intoxicating kiss, and a biting urgency unlike any she'd ever known.

She kissed him back with equal fervor, meeting his every demand with one of her own, and her response seemed to enflame him further. He walked her backward toward the wall in quick, stumbling steps, then pinned her there, pressing the hard length of his body into hers. His hands roamed over her possessively, molding her waist, caressing her hips, her thighs, brushing along the sides of her breasts.

He trailed hot kisses down her neck, following the beat of her pulse to the tender spot above her collarbone, then lower still, to the heated flesh just above her neckline. He lingered there, tasting with wicked little flicks of his tongue, teasing with the gentle scrape of teeth. Slowly, he drew his thumb along the seam of her gown, letting the backs of his knuckles drag softly across the hard peak of her nipple.

Her breath hitched and caught at the dazzling sensation, then released in a ragged moan when he pressed his knee into the folds of her skirts, finding the relentless ache between her legs.

Frustrated by the layers of taffeta and linen that separated her skin from his touch, she writhed against him in a desperate bid to be closer.

She dug her hands into the hard muscle of his shoulder, pulled at the fabric of his coat, speared her fingers into his hair.

In some distant, disregarded corner of her mind, she was stunned by her own wild behavior. Shocked at the sound of gasps and moans and wordless murmurs and…footsteps.

She heard footsteps.

Both of them froze, went absolutely stock-still, as the heavy fall of boots outside the parlor doors intruded into their world. To Lottie, they sounded like cannon fire, and still she strained to make them out over the mad rush of blood in her ears and the silent prayer in her mind.

Don't stop. Don't come in here. Please, don't stop.

They didn't stop. They passed by harmlessly, slowly disappearing down the hall.

She told herself to move. She *knew* she had to move. And yet she stayed just as she was, wrapped in Owen's arms, unable to do anything but drag in one unsteady breath after another. After what seemed an eternity, Owen shifted and spoke softly against her ear. "We're in your parlor."

Her own voice came out a tremulous whisper. "Yes."

"Anyone could walk in."

"Yes."

He loosened his hold a little and leaned away, putting a few inches of space between them.

The sudden loss of warmth sent a chill racing over her skin.

Owen ran his hands down her back, chasing it away. "It's all right."

"Yes." Good Lord, could she think of nothing else to say?

Embarrassed, and more than a little lightheaded, she began a hurried and shaky attempt to straighten her dress, smooth her hair, and collect her scattered thoughts.

Owen stepped back to give her room. "We should be more careful."

Oh, *yes*.

She was considering an illicit affair. *Illicit.* How could she have lost control so completely, lost all sense of where she was and who else was in the house? "I cannot believe we were so reckless."

Reaching up, he twined a loose lock of hair around his finger, then surprised her by carefully pinning it back up himself. "It's all right. Peter is occupied elsewhere."

"Peter isn't the only other person at Willowbend." She took a small step away from him and jabbed another pin back into place. "This can't happen again. Not like this."

"No reason it should," he returned easily. "Next time, just kiss me when I tell you to."

She paused with her hands still on her head. "*What?*"

He laughed softly, but it came out a bit breathless, a bit rough, and she realized he was still every bit as affected as she. He was just better at hiding it.

"You could try flouncing away a little quicker." He stepped up and pressed a soft kiss to her mouth. "But we both know I'd catch you."

❦

Owen returned from the woods with mud caked on his boots and the anger of thwarted vengeance eating at his patience. At Mrs. Lewis's insistence, he scraped off the former by the kitchen door before heading upstairs. The latter he set aside to be called upon when needed. He knew how to wait. When the time was right, he would get his man.

And his woman, he thought.

The plan he'd formulated two nights ago was serving him well where Lottie was concerned. And why shouldn't it? It was a well-reasoned, well-constructed plan.

Well, no, it wasn't really. It was more of an outline of a plan than an actual plan. But it did have an objective (obtain Lottie) and strategy (charm and seduce and, above all, protect) and even a contingency plan in the event the initial plan should fail (be better at charming and seducing). Obviously, the contingency could use a spot of work, but it was a start. It was sufficient to afford him a sense of control and balance.

He just needed to flesh things out a bit more. He still needed to figure out what came next.

Did he want Lottie for a dalliance? As a mistress? As his wife? A swell of pleasure and possession washed over him at the thought. So did the fear that it might not be possible.

There were countless obstacles standing in his path. Some of them were merely logistical—marriage to a woman with an assumed name, relocating her family, the paperwork, the finances. It would take an incredible amount of work. But it could be done. He was a titled gentleman of wealth and influence—he could make it happen.

He had far less control over the remaining barriers.

He was a man of the law. She was a Walker.

She didn't trust him. She wasn't always honest with him. She kept secrets from him.

She might not have him.

The possibility of rejection made him distinctly nervous. Lottie was clearly agreeable to a romance, maybe an affair. But she might not be willing to accept something as permanent and binding as marriage.

He wasn't sure he could be satisfied with anything less. He'd spent so many years trying to forget her, trying to pretend he didn't still dream of her, didn't compare other women to her, didn't mind the way her image was always sitting in the back of his mind.

Would he go back to that when the affair ended? Would it be worse than before? He wasn't sure he could do it. He caught sight of her through the open door of the study at the end of the hall and, God help him, felt the world tip.

And he knew in that moment that he would take whatever she offered. As long as he could have her.

She was so lovely, utterly captivating. And rather serious at present. Her head was bent over her work, her hand scribbling industriously over a stack of papers. Though he was too far away to see, he knew there would be a furrow of concentration across her brow. He wanted to smooth it away and watch her smile. He wanted to see all of her smiles—the mysterious, the wicked, the carefree, the inviting. Most of all, he'd like to see that soft smile again, the one that had made him feel essential, made him feel powerful and humbled all at once.

No other man could make her smile like that, and she smiled like that for no other man. He was sure of it.

Gabriel's voice sounded behind him. "There's a pretty picture."

The sudden intrusion didn't startle Owen; he was accustomed to the ways of his men, but it was a damned inconvenient business having stealthy friends. They were always popping up unexpectedly. "Indeed, it is."

"I was wrong, you know," Gabriel commented after a moment's study of Lottie. "She has changed."

Owen glanced at him, surprised at the comment. "Do you think?"

"She's happier now than when we knew her in London."

"Certainly, living with her father put—"

"She's far more generous with her smiles."

That wasn't at all what he wanted to hear. "Not that generous."

"Haven't you noticed? Well"—Gabriel sniffed and shot his cuffs—"maybe the extra smiles are only for me."

Owen had the singularly irrational urge to plant his fist in the man's face. "You'll keep your distance from Charlotte."

"Is that an order?"

Only because basic civility and a long-standing friendship wouldn't allow for a threat. Yet. "It is."

Gabriel laughed lightly and shook his head. "Thought that might still be the way of things. Don't bother dusting off the dueling pistols, Renderwell. I've no designs on your Charlotte. A Walker woman would be entirely too much work. Although..." He went back to looking at Lottie, which made Owen go back to wishing he could punch him. "I imagine there aren't many who would agree with me on that point." He paused for a moment. "And there are a fair number of unattached men in the area, you know." He paused again, longer this time. "The vicar's son in particular seems a promising fellow—handsome, well set-up, and near to Charlotte's age... Do you suppose they might...?"

"Go to hell, Arkwright," Owen suggested, amused despite himself. He knew for a fact that the vicar had no son but rather four unwed daughters of what many would say was too much education, two orphaned nieces with hair a most unfortunate shade of red, and a spinster aunt who did her reputation no good by making eyes at the widower Mr. Burns. *Thank you, Mrs. McKinsey.*

Gabriel laughed again. "In good time, no doubt. But I'm for Kithan first. Jeffries will be expecting a wire."

Owen dragged his gaze from Lottie. "You know what to tell him."

"We're passing through Kithan from the south."

That was still too close to Wayton and Willowbend for comfort, but it couldn't be helped. They couldn't be cut off from London completely. Jeffries would grow suspicious. "Give him two hours to respond, then I want you back, with or without an answer. Keep sharp on the roads."

"Always." He gave Owen a hearty pat on the back. "I'll leave you to your pining, then."

"I am bloody well not—" Devil take it, the bastard was already halfway down the hall.

But he wasn't pining, damn it. Pining wasn't in the outline.

Twelve

THE NEXT DAY, LOTTIE STOOD IN THE FRONT PARLOR
and basked in the warm glow of the late afternoon sun.

It was lovely to be able to look outside again. She
had insisted on finally opening the drapes, and a few
of the upper floor windows.

The closed and darkened house had started to take
on the feel of a prison, and her staff was beginning to
show the signs of confinement, growing anxious and
short with each other. She sympathized with them,
feeling rather edgy and short-tempered herself.

Her lack of progress in deciphering the murderer's
cipher only added to her anxiety. She'd spent the
entire night poring over the letters and the journals
she'd smuggled into her room. She'd searched tire-
lessly for something, *anything*, that would help the
investigation. The closest she'd come was discovering
an old polyalphabetic cipher of her father's that looked
strikingly similar, with a mix of letters and numbers.
But it wasn't the same. The decryption method and
keyword he'd used didn't work on the letters.

Frustrated and exhausted, she'd fallen asleep at her

desk and awoken with a terrible crick in her neck and a sour temper. She didn't even have Owen to cheer her. He spent most of the morning in and out of the woods, and he'd been in bed for the last few hours.

No progress, no freedom, no Owen, and a staff that was beginning to sound more and more like Peter. It made her skin itch.

Which is why she opened the windows. They needed sunlight and air. There was little danger in seeking both in the parlor. Only a fool would attempt to sneak across the predominately open expanse of the front lawn.

Nonetheless, she kept back a few feet and kept a wary eye on the spots a foolish man might hide. The giant oak at the edge of the drive seemed a likely choice.

She caught a flicker of movement and light out of the corner of her eye and absently turned to look for the source. A bird, she thought, or a squirrel running across the stable roof at the side of the house.

She saw flame, a thin, sneaking lick of it, dart out from the far end of the open stable doors.

Disbelief came first. She stepped forward to press against the glass and craned her neck for a clearer view of the side lawn. Surely she'd imagined it. It was a trick of the light, an illusion created by the setting sun.

But the flames came again—thick, grasping fingers that curled over and gripped the eaves.

For a few seconds, she simply stared as twin sensations of horror and relief washed over her. There was nothing of true value inside. All the staff had been moved to the house, the horses were pastured, and

Isis, the stable cat, had elected to have her kittens in
the carriage house. Everyone and everything was safe.

She opened her mouth to shout for Owen, but the
breath whooshed out of her at the sight of Esther's
slight form racing across the side lawn, straight for
the stable.

Lottie's hand flew to the glass as if it could reach
through and grab her sister back.

"No!"

Shoving away from the window, she bolted out
of the room and down the hall, then threw open the
side door.

Her mind found the pattern she needed without
looking. *Run past the trio of young birch trees, keep low
behind the line of bushes and the stone bench, veer to the left
to reach the half wall, and then make a straight dash to the
stable doors.*

She darted from the door, feet pounding against
stone and dirt as she followed her course. She was
faster than Esther. Taller, longer of leg. She could
still catch…

Esther's blond locks flashed into view, then disappeared into the stable.

Lottie was only moments behind, running into a
haze of smoke but no flame. The fire was still confined
to the back half of the stable, its greedy claws crawling
slowly up the wooden walls and into the rafters.

"Esther!"

"Mr. Nips!"

A few more strides and Lottie was on her, grabbing
hold with both hands. "He's in the pasture! Right
outside! Damn it—!"

"He's here!" Esther strained against her and pointed farther into the stable. "Here! I saw him!"

Lottie saw it then too, the blur of movement in the fourth stall. Just a flash of chestnut ears and mane as the frantic pony reared and kicked at the door.

Disbelief warred with terror. He shouldn't be there. He'd been pastured. And the fourth stall hadn't been used in weeks; the bottom half of the exterior door was warped, making it impossible to open.

Lottie shoved Esther toward the stable doors. "Get out!"

Esther stumbled, shook her head, and spun around for the stall. She charged ahead, throwing her arm out behind her. "Go! Go! Leave!"

They reached Mr. Nips at the same time. Esther threw open the latch and pulled the door. It didn't budge.

Lottie ran frantic hands and eyes over the wood and discovered a small chunk of wood wedged in between the top of the half door and the post.

"Wedged! It's wedged shut! Pull!"

They grabbed and yanked and strained as the fire grew around them. Lottie could feel the heat build and smoke thicken as the flames drew closer.

It was no good. She knew it was no good. If Mr. Nips's panicked kicks couldn't budge the wedge, the struggles of two women didn't stand a chance.

"We have to pry it loose!" Esther shouted. She grabbed a hoof pick from a nearby hook.

Lottie snatched it out of her hands, shoved it against the exposed lip of the wedge, and bore down.

The fire was a roar in her ears now. But she could

still breathe, and the path to the stable doors was still clear. They had time.

The pick slipped free twice and sent her tumbling back. But on the third try, the wedge splintered and popped free.

Lottie jumped back as Esther threw open the stall door and Mr. Nips took off like a shot, charging for the open doors just as the fire caught hold of a thick layer of straw spread across the floor. It flashed over the stable aisle as if caught on a wind. Lottie had a brief glimpse of the pony's rear end on the other side of the doors as he gave a last indignant backward kick at the stable, and then there was nothing but flame.

It surrounded them, closed in like a fist. Lottie turned a panicked circle. The fire had caught hold of the bedding in the stalls, jumping from one enclosure to the next with terrifying speed. Those exterior doors were lost to them now.

Her eyes darted to the tack room. If they soaked a horse blanket in the aisle trough, they could throw it over their heads and...

The tack room was already in flames.

There was no way out.

She had waited too long.

Smoke and fumes filled her lungs. Heat curled around her, burning her cheeks and eyes. She turned another circle, searching for something, anything that might help, but there was nothing but the large water trough butted up against the aisle wall. Grabbing hold of Esther, she dragged her over and shoved her down and into the water. It was a clumsy and desperate move. Esther's head smacked against the wall. The wooden sides of the trough jammed into Lottie's legs, knocking her to her knees.

She pulled up Esther's sodden skirts and held them to her sister's face, then slammed an arm over the trough when Esther tried to rise. Using her free arm, she dunked the hem of her own skirts and breathed through the wet layers.

Lottie would never be able to sort out how she managed to keep Esther in the trough. She could hear her sister scream, struggle, and fight against the restraining arm, but the noise and movement was a dim echo in the roar and heat of the fire.

It would give Esther time. Maybe Owen would find a way in. Maybe a section of the fire would burn itself out in time for them to escape. Straw went up bright and fast, but it didn't burn for long. There was a chance. Esther had a better chance in the trough.

Squeezing her eyes shut against the stinging pain of hot smoke, she curled into herself as the inferno grew and Esther's struggles slowly weakened into wrenching coughs.

A searing pain stabbed at her calf and her eyes flew open on a scream. A thin ribbon of flame had followed a trail of loose straw across the floor and taken hold of her dry petticoat. She kicked out wildly and slapped her wet skirt over the small flame while her lungs seized up from the excruciating intake of boiling air.

She was burning alive. She was going to *burn alive*.

She heard her own screams, and wondered in a daze of pain and terror where she found the air. Her frantic efforts succeeded in snuffing the fire, but there was more straw. Everywhere she looked there was more straw. It was all around her. It would succumb to the flame at any second, and so would she.

Knowing it was futile, she kicked out at the straw nearest to her and the trough.

She didn't see the dark figure moving through the flames until it was almost upon her. Then something heavy and wet was thrown over her head, and she was being lifted from the ground. "I have you. I have you."

Owen. His voice was rough in her ear and terrifyingly muted by the raging fire, but his hold was strong and the damp material of his coat was cool against her cheek.

Relief, hope, and fear flowed through her in equal measure. She couldn't leave Esther behind. She tried to call for her sister, but the words came out on an excruciating cough. Blindly, she reached toward the trough.

Owen tucked her closer. "Samuel has her."

She wanted to see for herself, but there wasn't time. Owen shifted the blanket, wrapping it around them both, and then they were moving. For one awful second, a scorching heat exploded around her, and then, in a flash, it was gone. The blanket was thrown off and fresh air, blessedly cool and clean, washed over her face and into her lungs.

They were out of the stables.

She tried to shift in Owen's hold and struggled to open her eyes and find her sister, but her body wouldn't cooperate. Her lids were too heavy. Her arms felt clumsy and half-numb, oddly detached from the rest of her. They loosened from around his neck even as her fingers dug involuntarily into the back of his coat as a wave of heaving, shuddering coughs hit her. Her thoughts, racing and scattered like shot only a moment ago, slowed to a sluggish crawl.

She heard Owen barking orders, but the sound was distant and tinny in her ears, scarcely audible over the sound of her own struggle for air.

"Gabriel!"

"No shots! No movement!"

"Everyone inside! Where's the boy?"

"Footman's still holding him!"

"Staff?"

"Mrs. Lewis is taking count!"

"Physician?" Samuel called out.

"Now!" Owen snapped.

"No." Gabriel again. Closer this time. "We met him in Wayton. He is eighty, if he is a day. He can't—"

"I don't bloody care how old he is. Put him on the floor of the carriage if you have to. Just get him here."

"Think, man. It is too great a risk. Wait and see—"

The rest of the argument was lost to her. A door opened and slammed shut and she was surrounded by noise and movement. There was Peter's frantic voice. Mrs. Lewis's brisk tones. Esther's wracking coughs. Her own painful struggle for air. Owen shouting more orders. The pounding of running feet.

Safe. All of them safe, she thought, and she let the waiting darkness and the painless oblivion it promised swallow her up.

✑

Lottie's eyes didn't open as Owen settled her on her bed, but he was certain some part of her faded in and out of consciousness. She couldn't possibly remain under while her body heaved and shuddered, trying to expel the smoke from her lungs.

With every wrenching cough, he expected to see blood, some sign that he'd been too late, that there was too much damage.

Mrs. Lewis nudged him aside with competent hands and a brisk voice. "It is time for you to leave, my lord. She needs out of her corset. It will help her breathe. Mary, your assistance, please."

Owen backed away but stayed in the room, his eyes trained on Lottie. "Hurry."

A young maid brushed past him and assisted Mrs. Lewis in turning Lottie onto her side.

He watched in mounting frustration as they struggled with the buttons of her bodice for what seemed an eternity while Lottie coughed, hiccuped, and gasped.

"Hurry."

"The material is damp, my lord. We are doing our best—"

"Move," he bit off, and he pulled a knife from his boot with hands that shook.

The maid's eyes grew round. "What do you think—?"

He pushed her aside and, forcing his hands steady, took hold of Lottie's gown. He sliced the back of it to the waist, then he took hold of the corset beneath and slit it clean through. "There. Get it off her."

Mary hesitated. "I believe you should—"

"*Now!*" For Christ's sake, she was *hurting*. Couldn't they bloody see she was hurting?

In contrast to his furious tones, Mrs. Lewis's voice was calm and soothing. "You need to wait outside, my lord."

"No." Hell, no.

"It would be best."

"I'll not leave her." He needed to be there, where he could see with his own eyes that Lottie was still breathing.

"There is nothing more for you to do here." Taking his arm, she pulled him away from the bed with a gentle but persistent pressure. "You are frightening Mary."

"I don't care."

"I do. I need her calm and collected if she is to be of use. Do you understand?"

No, he didn't. Lottie was hurt; she was suffering. How could he leave her? How could they ask it of him?

"I can help." There had to be some way he could help her, something he could do to ease her pain. He couldn't stand it.

"The best thing you can do for her now is leave."

He watched, never so helpless or frustrated in his life, as Mary's nervous eyes darted to his and she fumbled with the wash basin in her hands.

"Milord," Mrs. Lewis whispered. "*Please.*"

She was right. He knew she was right.

He bit back a long and particularly foul string of expletives.

"I'll be in the hall."

Thirteen

HE COULD STILL HEAR HER COUGHING.

Leaning against the wall next to Lottie's door, Owen bowed his head and curled his hands into fists. He struggled to find the calm so necessary for control. He'd had it earlier. When he'd first spotted the flames from his upstairs window, he'd been calm.

His heart had performed one long, sick roll when the maid came tearing down the hall sobbing that Miss Bales and Miss Esther were nowhere to be found, then it had settled into place—or, rather, it had become cemented in place, cold and bloodless, as unyielding determination took over. His hands had been steady when he grabbed two blankets off the bed and tossed one to Samuel in the hall. His voice had been strong when he ordered a footman to keep Peter inside and strong still when he'd spotted Gabriel running out from the woods and had shouted at him to watch the tree line.

He'd crossed the lawn at a dead run, but he'd been in control. Until he'd heard the screams. Lottie's screams. And a terror unlike any he'd known had grabbed him by the throat.

He'd fought it back. He'd chained it down so he could do what needed to be done, shoving his blanket in a trough outside the stable, throwing it around him before charging into the flames. There had been a wall of them. He hadn't stopped to think how thick the wall might be, how deep the flames might go. How useless his efforts might be.

The relief he'd felt when he'd found her, kicking out weakly at the straw, had nearly brought him to his knees.

She was alive and conscious. He wasn't too late.

He'd scooped her up, carried her out, and made the mistake of letting his control slip.

Sometime during the trip from the stable to the house, the fear had seeped back in, and with it came a viscous rage. He couldn't separate the two now, the sick panic of seeing Lottie in danger and pain and the fury for the man responsible for both. The need to hit something, to swing and pound until he saw blood, tore at him. He wanted aching fists and swollen knuckles. He wanted the satisfaction of hearing bone crunch beneath his blows.

But more than that, more than anything, he wanted back in Lottie's room.

With neither option available to him, Owen blew out a shaky breath, let his head drop back against the wall, and resigned himself to his third, final, and most difficult choice of action.

He waited.

❧

The physician came and went, leaving behind a small measure of real relief. The ladies would recover. He recommended bed rest, cooled tea with plenty of honey for the throat, and laudanum for pain once the coughing eased. A close eye would need to be kept on Miss Bales's leg. The injury was not severe, but the possibility of infection could not be ruled out. Any sign of the wound turning septic, and he should be fetched immediately. Preferably by someone other than Sir Samuel Brass—the man drove like a lunatic.

It had been a risk, taking to the open road atop a carriage, but even Gabriel had been forced to admit there was little choice but to send for help once he'd taken a look at Lottie's leg.

From his chair next to her bedside where he'd taken up vigil for the night, Owen studied the wound. The burn was no larger than his palm and showed only minimal blistering. But he knew it had to be acutely painful.

His chest tightened, and a new wave of anger washed over him. There seemed to be nothing he could do about the former, but the latter he acknowledged and set aside before it could settle and take hold. It had taken him hours to regain his calm. Hours of waiting, pacing, snapping at the staff and physician, and otherwise making a general nuisance of himself.

It wasn't a nuisance Lottie needed.

For what he was sure was the hundredth time, he leaned over to brush a damp lock from Lottie's forehead. "What were you thinking?" he whispered. "Why didn't you call for me?"

She stirred, moaned, and then woke with a suddenness that startled him.

"I won't die like that." Her voice was scratchy and

panicked. Her gaze darted wildly about the room, latching on to nothing. "I don't want to die like that."

"No. Here now." He stroked her hair gently. "You're safe."

"I won't."

"No, you won't. I promise you won't. Look. Look at me, Lottie." He took her face in his hands. "I'm here. You're safe."

Glassy, reddened eyes focused on his, then fluttered shut.

⤳

Lottie drifted in and out of a fretful sleep.

She was aware of movement around her, of soft voices, dim light, and the ever-present pain. She tried to pull herself completely free of sleep. If she could wake up, then she might be able to do something about the pain. She could tell someone about it, at the very least. But she just couldn't manage it, any more than she could ignore the pain and slip fully back into sleep.

It was like suffering from a terrible thirst brought on by a raging fever. She was thirsty because she was sick, she was too sick to do anything about the thirst, and she was too thirsty to let the sickness drag her into the painless dark. She was trapped and frustrated, struggling between awake and asleep while pain radiated from her leg and throat…and, damn it, now she *was* thirsty.

"Thirsty."

That wasn't what she meant to say. She wanted to tell someone about the pain in her leg, but the act of speaking alone propelled her that last laborious step into the conscious world.

With a groan, she pried lids away from eyes that felt like hot, dry coals.

Owen's face loomed over hers in the dim light. "There you are."

"Esther?" Was that really her voice? It was so weak and ragged.

A hand stroked over her hair. "She's safe. She's sleeping."

"My leg hurts." Oh, but that was an understatement. Her leg burned, throbbed, and, when she shifted in a bid to find comfort, screamed. "*Hurts.*"

"I know. I'm sorry. Here, drink a little." He slipped an arm under her neck and propped her up for a few sips of lukewarm tea. She tasted the sweet hint of honey, felt it coat and cool her raw throat. "A little more," he urged. "The physician won't allow laudanum until your lungs are clear. In the morning, I promise."

Physician? "Is it very bad?"

"No, sweetheart." He laid her down again, then bent over her and gently brushed a soft kiss on her brow and another on her temple. "No." His lips moved to the sensitive skin of her eyelids. First one. "You're all right." Then the other. "Everything will be all right. Rest now."

She sighed as his mouth moved leisurely over her face, trailing soft kisses across her skin. It was better than laudanum, sweeter and more soothing than honey. The darkness settled around her again, ready to pull her under. She didn't fight it.

"Will you be here?" she whispered.

"I will." He kissed her cheek. "I promise." His lips hovered over hers and his breath whispered warm against her mouth. "Trust me, Lottie."

She wanted to tell him that she did. In that moment, she would have trusted him with anything. But she fell asleep before the words could form.

❧

The next time Lottie woke, she felt relatively lucid. She still hurt, everywhere, but the pain no longer carried the sharp urgency it had earlier, and the thick dregs of exhaustion and fear no longer dragged at her body and mind.

Turning her head, she found Owen standing at the windows, his back to her, awash in the warm glow of sunshine peeking out from half-open drapes.

"Owen?" She pushed herself up onto her elbows. "What time is it?"

Turning, he studied her. "Are you awake?"

Was she awake? What an odd question. She was speaking to him, wasn't she? "Of course. Why would you ask?" Good Lord, had she spent a portion of the night speaking to him without being awake? Surely not. "I was awake before."

He came to her bedside table and occupied himself with the various bottles, jars, spoons, and other accoutrements associated with a sickbed. "Which time?"

Apparently, she really had spent a portion of the night talking in her sleep. How mortifying. Because her arms were beginning to shake, she shifted back to lean against the headboard. "When you gave me something to drink."

He poured a cup of tea and reached for one of the bottles. "Again, which time?"

When you kissed me, she thought, but she said nothing, afraid his reply would be the same. "Did I say anything untoward at any time?"

He glanced at her, offering a small, reassuring smile. "No."

That was something, anyway. She frowned when he reached for a bottle she didn't recognize and uncorked the top. "What is that?"

"Laudanum."

"I don't want it." She'd had it once, when she'd twisted her ankle and it had swelled up to twice its natural size. The drug had done an admirable job of relieving the pain but had left her fighting nightmares and nausea.

Without a word, Owen poured a small dose of the drug into her cup and handed it to her.

"I said I don't want it."

"Didn't ask what you wanted."

"Owen, please—"

"You're in pain," he snapped.

She was. Her leg throbbed like the devil. But she didn't see why he should be so angry about it. "It makes me ill. I would take it otherwise. But it makes me ill. I don't want it. I just want…"

Relenting, he lowered his arm. "What?"

Her lips curved in an embarrassed smile. "A bath. I want a bath."

The stench of smoke clung to her hair and skin—a

thick, offensive perfume that billowed around her every time she moved. Even the linens smelled of it now.

"A bath, then," Owen agreed. "To start."

It required a level of coordination and dexterity that bordered on acrobatic to take a bath while keeping the entire bottom half of one leg dry, but Lottie managed it with the aid of two maids, a small wooden footstool, and what she could only assume were the limbering properties of utter desperation.

It was heaven to be rid of the smell and soot.

She was changed and comfortably settled back in a cleanly made bed when Owen returned with a small tray holding a bowl of stew and two thick slices of bread.

She waved the sight of it away. "Thank you, but I couldn't possibly."

"You need to eat."

She couldn't imagine why. She'd been roasted, not starved. "Hot stew sounds most unpleasant."

"It's cold."

"Oh." She wrinkled her nose. "That's worse."

"Mrs. Lewis thought you might prefer it chilled for your throat. She sent Samuel down to the ice-house." He set the tray next to her on the bed. "He risked life and limb for this repast, Lottie. Will you snub his gallantry?"

"It is cold, day-old stew," she said blandly and felt that was answer enough.

"Sop up the broth with the bread and we'll consider your duty discharged."

"Just the broth?" She waited for his nod before reaching for the tray. "Oh, very well."

She still didn't want it, but it had been thoughtful of Mrs. Lewis and rather sweet of Samuel. She wouldn't go so far as gallant. Something a bit more palatable ought to come out of gallantry. The stew was not improved by age or altered temperature.

Still, it was pleasant to sit and eat while Owen kept her company. He explained Esther's condition, which was rapidly improving, and made idle conversation that distracted her from the continued throb of her burn. Despite the pain, and cold stew, she felt a lovely warmth spread through her limbs. It felt wonderful, almost blissfully normal, to sit and speak of the weather and staff and family. Or it would, were she not reclining in her nightgown in her bedroom.

She gestured at her leg with a piece of bread. "I suppose I'll not be able to join you for that tromp about the woods for a time."

"Yes. Pity that."

She tilted her head at him, then quickly righted it again when it wobbled. Must have strained her neck sometime in the stable, she mused. "Would you truly have taken me?"

"Did you want to go?"

"Not an answer," she mumbled and smacked her lips experimentally. They felt oddly thick. Or maybe it was her tongue. She seemed not to have its full cooperation. And the warmth had grown into a foggy sensation all of a sudden. Scowling, she looked at her bowl. "I think the stew's gone off."

Oh, wouldn't that top things off splendidly? She'd survived a fire only to be done in by bad broth.

How dreadful, she thought. And giggled. Which

wasn't right at all. Death by stew wasn't the least bit funny.

"'S definitely gone off."

"It couldn't have." He reached out, dipped the tip of his pinkie finger in the broth, and had a taste. "Ah. Mrs. Lewis added a little something extra, I think."

"Something that made it go off."

"It isn't off, darling. Let me have the bowl."

She barely felt him slip the bowl from her fingers. "I feel most pecoo…" She smacked her lips again. "Pe-cu-li-ar." She enunciated each syllable slowly and carefully, and she still wasn't sure she'd gotten it right. "Tricky word, that."

Her head lolled and snapped back up.

The broth, she thought drunkenly. There was laudanum in the broth. Outrage bloomed and vanished just as quickly. She couldn't hold on to it. She couldn't hold on to a single thought.

She pulled herself together long enough to glare at him. Or hims, rather, as he was currently multiplying exponentially before her eyes. First two, then four, then eight…

It was fascinating, really.

"So *many* of you."

She was delighted to see he found this as amusing as she. Wasn't it lovely, to share a spot of laughter with someone for whom you cared?

"Close your eyes, Lottie."

She would rather watch the Owens. They were moving now, slipping arms around her back, settling her down on the pillows. And didn't that feel delicious? Absolutely delicious.

"You're better 'n stew."

She wasn't sure he heard her. There were too many of him, making her dizzy.

She closed her eyes and slipped back into the waiting darkness.

Fourteen

"YOU PUT LAUDANUM IN THE STEW."

Lottie delivered this accusation—one she'd been waiting to hurl for the last half hour—the moment Owen walked in the door carrying a tray with a small teapot and cup.

If he thought she would take so much as a whiff of what was in that pot, he was mistaken.

"Good morning, Lottie."

"Is it morning?" she snapped. How was she to know? She'd woken disoriented, alone, and in the foulest of tempers, which was, she now recalled, another unpleasant side effect she'd experienced after taking laudanum for her ankle. The clock on the mantel said it was a quarter past six, but she couldn't tell if the light peeking in through the drapes was morning or evening light.

"Early yet," Owen returned. "But yes. Most of the house is up. How do you feel?"

"As if someone put laudanum in my stew," she bit off. And like she'd spent a full day sleeping off the effects.

"That someone was Mrs. Lewis. I had nothing to do with it."

"Oh." Feeling thwarted, she folded her arms across her chest and hunched her shoulders. "Then I apologize for the accusation."

"Yes," he replied dryly, "you sound remorseful. She was trying to help, you know. She was worried about you. Now she's worried she'll lose her position."

"Mrs. Lewis isn't going to lose her position." She was, however, going to get a tremendous earful.

"Do you feel ill?" he asked, setting the tray down. "The food should have helped, but Mrs. Lewis brewed up a pot of something soothing if you need it."

"Something soothing," she repeated, suspicious. "Like laudanum?"

"No, I tried it myself first. It has chamomile and…" He waved his hand about at the pot. "I don't know what. Soothing sorts of ingredients. Who knows where housekeepers acquire their recipes. Do you want some or not?"

"It won't be necessary." She felt sluggish, but not ill, and she hadn't had any nightmares that she recalled.

"Are you feeling better? You look and sound as if you're feeling better."

"I am." Crabbiness notwithstanding, she felt markedly improved.

Moving closer, he studied her face. "Certain?"

"Yes."

"Your throat? Your leg?"

They pained her, particularly the latter, but not enough to risk another dose of laudanum. "Both better."

He bent over her and subjected her to a long,

narrow-eyed examination that made her distinctly uneasy. Apparently satisfied with his own assessment, he leaned down even farther, planted his hands on either side of her pillow, and ground out, "Then you can tell me… What in the name of *God* were you thinking?"

She pressed farther into the pillows. Later, that would sting the pride, but she couldn't help it. He was furious. The muscles of his arms were bunched, and green eyes snapped in a face otherwise hard and unyielding as stone.

Carefully, slowly, she chose her words. "Owen…"

Too careful, too slow. He barreled on without her explanation.

"You ran into a burning building, Lottie. Into fire. What sort of madness—?"

"I'd not have done it but for Esther." She shook her head, determined that he should hear her out, that he should believe her. "I swear it. I'd not have left the house at all. But I saw Esther. She went after Mr. Nips. Someone put him inside. They put him in the fourth stall. It won't open from the outside."

"You would have died for a pony."

"No," she insisted, and though she knew it was the right thing to say, would have been the smart thing to do, she felt the pain of shame at the admission. "I'd not have gone in, even for him. I went in for Esther."

"You should have called for me."

"I did." Hadn't she? The moments before she rushed to the stable seemed a blur to her now. "I thought I did. It all happened so fast. There was so little time."

"You didn't," he snapped and pushed away from the bed. "There was time. A body can run and yell simultaneously."

"I thought I did. I know I meant to call for you. I remember that I…" She remembered opening her mouth to shout for him. Then she'd seen Esther fly across the lawn. "Oh."

"*Oh?*" he repeated incredulously.

"I did mean to call for you." She licked lips gone dry. "Then I forgot."

"You forgot."

"Well, people *do*," she returned impatiently. She had intended to call for him. The thought ought to count for something. "I was a trifle distracted."

"Distracted."

"Repetition of what I say is not a conversation. It is an echo."

"You don't want to hear my own thoughts just now."

"Then you may listen to mine. Esther is my sister. I have cared for her since her infancy because, Lord knows, our mother was not fit for the task." The woman had been perpetually absent, preferring the company of her lovers to her own children. "Forgive me if I did not instinctively abandon a lifelong responsibility to a man who has been here less than a week."

Something flashed across his face. Anger, maybe. But something else as well. "You've known me longer than a week."

"I have," she said, happy to find at least one point on which they could agree. "Which is why I intended to call for you. Certainly, I should have called for help from someone. But when I saw Esther, I simply acted.

I did what came naturally. That may not have been the wisest course of action, but it was the best I could do. I will not apologize for it."

He opened his mouth, then snapped it shut and dragged a hand down his face. "You owe me no apology, Lottie."

She was happy to have that point on which to agree as well. "No, but I do owe you a great debt of gratitude."

"You're not in my damned debt."

She gritted her teeth with impatience as he swore, shook his head at her, then took up pacing at the foot of her bed. "Do I wish to know your thoughts now?" She ventured after a time. He didn't look a great deal less angry than he had a few moments ago, but he'd gone from stomping to merely striding, which she took as a promising sign.

"I am thinking of how best to go about not killing Esther."

"Owen, don't. It was my decision to go after her. She tried to make me leave."

"Not hard enough," he ground out.

"She was trying to save Mr. Nips."

"A damned pony," he snarled with an angry gesture. "Over her own life, over the life of her sister."

"He's not any pony. He is so much more to her than that. He was a gift from our father. He..." How to explain it? She busied her hands with the counterpane while she searched for the right words. "Father had a tendency to forget Esther. I was his firstborn. Peter, when he came, was his only son. He loved Esther, of course. He loved all of us. But..."

"But what?"

She bit her lip and glanced at the open door. "Will you close that?"

He grumbled, stalked to the door, slammed it shut, and stalked back. "But what, Lottie?"

"Esther is likely not his natural daughter."

He considered that with a furrowed brow. "Did William know?"

"I believe so. He was so often distant with her. I think, perhaps, he wasn't sure what to make of her. So he set her aside, in a way. Ignored her, or… Esther loves to sketch, and she's wonderfully talented. She made dozens of drawings for Father over the years. But he only ever bothered to frame one of them. Just *one*. And he would forget her birthday sometimes." She sighed and, annoyed with her nervous fidgeting, pushed the counterpane away. "He forgot most of her birthdays, to be honest. But he remembered her fifteenth. He brought her Mr. Nips. Esther has a great affinity for animals, and for Father to remember that, and her birthday…" She shrugged and wondered if Owen could understand what a gift like that, on a day like that, would have meant to a girl accustomed to being shunted off to the side by a father she adored.

"I assume Esther doesn't know. How do you?" he asked when she shook her head.

"The journals. He wrote about our mother whilst she stayed with us and made a note of each time she left. It isn't a clear picture, but the pieces are there, if one cares to put them together. Our mother returned from one of her travels, as she called them, approximately seven months before Esther was born." It was fortunate that Esther had never been one for puzzles. "I know Mr. Nips is just an old pony to you, but—"

He held up a hand. "I would have gone after him for you. For Esther. You should have called for me."

And back to this, Lottie thought. "Good God, you are so immovable in your positions. Completely intractable."

"I beg your pardon?"

She cocked her head, studying him. "I don't know how I failed to notice before now. You've called me stubborn, but it is you who wins arguments through sheer obstinacy."

"This isn't about winning."

Every argument was about winning, or else it would be a conversation. But that was a separate argument. "You might concede a point or two or change your tactics a little, but your position never really alters. You simply refuse to budge until you have your way. Obstinate."

Every difference of opinion they'd had thus far had played out in the same manner. She might disagree, debate, or explain, but, in the end, he walked away the victor. Even when the disagreement had led him to issue an apology of some kind, he still had his way in the end.

"You chased off the intruder," he reminded her. "That was not what I wanted."

"But I stayed upstairs whilst you ran off with a gun. You insisted on the trip to the ruins, and the trip was taken. You insisted on Peter's involvement, and Peter became involved. The gun, the stew, the—"

"Is there a point to this?"

Mostly the point had been to change the point, but

it was worth pursuing nonetheless. "Only that you can't always have your way."

His expression shifted suddenly, his handsome features hardening with anger. "If I had my way, you would stay locked in this room and chained to that bed until I found the man responsible for hurting you and peeled the skin and muscle from his bones in quarter-inch strips."

"Oh. Well. That is…really quite gruesome." And rather creative, she had to admit. "But I've no objection to the sentiment."

Something like a laugh escaped him, softening his countenance once more. "You'll not object to any of it."

"I'll not be put under lock and key."

"No, but you'll rest for a day or two."

"If it suits me, yes. I imagine it will," she added when he looked a bit exasperated. "That's not a capitulation, mind you. Merely a reasonable assumption given the circumstances."

"Noted," he said dryly.

Lottie drummed her fingers against the sheets. "I suppose there's no chance at all that what happened in the stable was an accident."

She took some satisfaction in setting him off balance with the unexpected change of subject. It wasn't quite so bold as demanding he cross the room and kiss her, but it was gratifying all the same.

"None," Owen supplied.

"I thought not. He took a risk, coming out of the woods to lead Mr. Nips into the stable, wedging the door shut, starting the fire. That took time."

"He's growing desperate."

"He's cruel. Why would anyone do such a thing? How could someone seek to hurt a helpless old pony?"

Owen shook his head and abandoned his pacing to take a seat at the end of the bed. "To attract our attention."

"That couldn't be his only reason. He already had our attention."

"To make a point, then, or deliver a message." Frowning thoughtfully, he tucked the edge of the blanket under her foot. "Would the Ferret have known what Mr. Nips means to Esther?"

"I cannot imagine how. Esther was a child when she met him. She'd not have acquired Mr. Nips yet. He was simply convenient, I think. Pastured right up against the stable, wasn't he? On the side away from the house?" She waited for his nod. "That's likely why he was chosen. He's a crabby old fellow but docile on a lead." She cocked her head and smiled. "Rather like you."

He barked out a laugh and rose from the bed to peek out the drapes. He was impatient again, Lottie realized. He wanted to work, to be in the woods with his men, but there was one more matter they needed to discuss first.

"Owen? If you catch this man—"

He flicked a glance over his shoulder. "When I catch him."

"Very well. When you catch him, it will be necessary to turn him over to the police for his crimes." And once he did, the existence of the Walker-Bales family in England would no longer be a secret.

"I can arrange for his quiet removal out of the country."

"Without a trial?"

He turned to face her, his brows drawn together. "He nearly killed you, and your sister, and you would worry over his fate?"

"No," she replied, wincing a little at the admission. She'd always loathed the idea of vigilante justice. Funny how quickly the loss of objectivity could turn one into a hypocrite. "Perhaps I should be, but my concern is for you, not him. The law says he must have a trial. You're a man of the law, Owen, not a criminal."

She wouldn't have him change that, not for her, not for any price.

"Ah. You needn't worry on that score. When you disappeared eight years ago, it was with her majesty's blessing, and when I send the bastard off in chains, it will be with all the proper permissions."

Lottie didn't see how it could be that easy, but a soft knock on the door barred additional questions. Esther padded inside, looking pale and small in her flowing white dressing gown. "May I speak with you, Lottie?"

"Of course." Recalling his earlier threats, Lottie tensed as her gaze flew to Owen.

He took a step toward Esther, brow furrowed. "What are you doing out of bed? You should be resting."

Relieved, Lottie relaxed again. Concern before anger, she thought. Was it any wonder she'd once been half in love with the man? Was it any wonder she was more than three-quarters of the way there now?

She shot straight up in the bed.

Was she? Was she, really? That didn't seem the sort of thing that should sneak up on a woman. She'd been infatuated with him once, and she was attracted to him now. She respected him, liked and admired him, but—

Esther took a step closer to the bed. "Is something wrong, Lottie?"

"What? No."

"What is it?" Owen demanded. He was at her side in two steps. "It's the pain, isn't it? I knew it. You need to take the laudanum."

"No, it isn't." Reaching out, she slapped his hand away from the laudanum bottle. "Don't touch that. I was only stretching a bit."

"It didn't look as if you were stretching."

"Well I can't help what it looked like, can I? Put that away. Better yet, take it away. I would like a private word with my sister."

"You need rest." He threw a look over his shoulder at Esther. "Both of you."

"What I need is a word." She gave him a saccharine smile. "Owen, please. Don't be obstinate."

She watched amusement and frustration play across his features.

"Ten minutes," he decreed. "You have ten minutes."

She'd have as long as she bloody well liked. "Why thank you, Your Highness. Most generous of you."

He eyed her through lowered lids, then eyed the laudanum bottle, then her again, then finally strode to the door and let himself out.

Esther took a seat on the bed, pulling up her stocking feet and scooting close to face Lottie. "How are you feeling?"

"Singed." And confused and a little frightened. "You?"

"Much the same." Esther's gaze traveled to Lottie's

injured leg. "It would have been worse for me, if not for you. You should not have followed me into the stables."

"We should not have been in the stables at all."

Esther briefly closed her eyes and let out a shaky sigh. "I know. I wasn't thinking. I saw Mr. Nips from my window, just a flash of his head as he reared in the stall, and then I was running. I didn't stop to think. I just ran. I couldn't let him die like that."

"I understand, Esther."

"But I should have. I should have let him go. I put him first." Esther's voice trembled, and Lottie knew she wasn't speaking only of Mr. Nips. "I put him first, and that was wrong of me. I don't know why I did it. I don't even know why."

"Because you love him." Had loved their father, Lottie thought, and had never been certain that love was reciprocated.

"I love you more," Esther whispered, a moment before a faint smile danced on her lips. "I love *me* more, come to that."

"Oh, I know," Lottie replied, with feeling. Humor lit her sister's pale features, but all too soon, it was gone.

"I should have remembered that, instead of…other things." Esther took her hand. "I am sorry, Lottie. I'm very sorry."

"I know that too."

"I have so many amends to make."

"Not so very many," Lottie replied in a bolstering tone. "You've already made things right with me. There's only Owen and Sir Samuel."

Esther curled her lip. "I don't want to apologize to Samuel. He's a brute."

"Samuel?" She'd always thought him the most congenial of the three, if only by virtue of being the least likely to open his mouth.

"I tried to speak with him once already." She snagged an extra pillow from the head of the bed and hugged it to her chest. "He called me a selfish imbecile and walked out of the room."

"Samuel?" Now she was just echoing herself.

"He might be right about the selfishness," Esther conceded in a quiet voice. "But I am not an imbecile. It was one stupid act. It doesn't make me a stupid person entirely."

"It certainly does not," Lottie assured her. "But you need to find a way to make peace with him, all the same. He pulled you from a fire, Esther."

"I know." There was a wealth of bitterness in those two words. "I'd rather it had been Gabriel. He's such a nice fellow."

Lottie recalled the smile Gabriel had offered while informing her that he *did not miss*. Nice did not apply. "Sir Gabriel is many things, apparently."

"So is Sir Samuel. All of them unappealing."

"Well, you needn't deal with any of them right now." Lottie gave her sister's hand a bolstering squeeze. "No one expects you to settle matters immediately. Go back to bed. Rest for a while. Things will look better later."

"People always say that." Esther sighed again and lightly tossed the pillow back with the others. "And they're always wrong."

Fifteen

LOTTIE REMAINED CONFINED TO BED FOR THREE DAYS. On the first day, she was unable to keep her eyes open for more than an hour or two at a time, rendering her a pleasant and compliant patient. On the second day, she grew restless despite the distraction provided by working on the encrypted letters.

By the middle of the third day, not even the threat of another dose of laudanum could convince her to remain tucked up in bed.

"I will personally force it down your throat," Owen threatened at her bedside.

She didn't believe his threat for a moment, but she met his threatening glare with one of her own. "You are welcome to try."

"Let her alone." This from the newly arrived Esther, fully dressed and looking like her old self.

"Why does *she* get to be out of bed?" Lottie demanded.

"I didn't injure a leg," Esther replied without rancor. "Let her up, Renderwell. She can rest dressed and on the settee in the library just as well as sitting about in here."

"She can nap in here," Owen replied.

Lottie's fingers curled into the sheets beneath her. "I don't want another damned—"

"She can nap on the settee," Esther countered.

She was not going to nap on the settee, but if the possibility swayed Owen, she'd let him believe it.

"Besides," Esther continued, "the healing process can be slowed by temper and quickened by fine spirits."

Lottie had no idea if that was true, and neither did Owen by the looks of it, but she nodded vigorously all the same. "It's true."

"It's rubbish," Owen returned.

"It certainly won't be aided by a physical altercation. I *will* get out of this bed."

Even if it was only for the ten seconds she could manage before he dumped her back into it again.

"You'll stay seated in the library?" His tone held both skepticism and demand. "You'll stay where I put you?"

She took some offense to the phrase *stay where I put you* (she wasn't a bloody doorstop), but she was willing to pick her battles. "I shall recline on the settee and work on the encrypted letters." She wished she could bring some of the journals as well, but they couldn't be as quickly or easily hidden under other paperwork should Peter come into the room. "It's a fair compromise. Also, it will allow me the opportunity to speak with Samuel and Gabriel. I've questions."

"Questions you can't ask me?"

"I shall ask you as well, if you sit with me in the parlor. Otherwise I will speak to everyone in here." She waved her hands down her prone form, indicating the nightgown, the loose hair, and her injured leg sticking out from the blanket, exposed from the knee down. "Like *this*."

Twenty minutes later, she was up and dressed. Though a few testing steps indicated she could walk without significant discomfort, Lottie made no protest when Owen lifted her in his arms and carried her down the stairs. There was no sense in risking further aggravation of her injury nor in denying herself the pleasure of feeling weightless in Owen's arms.

Owen settled her on the settee and brought her the letters and a small lap desk on which to work until Gabriel and Samuel returned from their excursions outside.

It was the first time all four of them had been able to meet for more than a passing exchange of information, and it came with a cost. She heard Samuel in the hall before he entered the parlor, grumbling about getting back to the hunt.

"This will only take a few minutes," she promised as Gabriel appropriated the open chair next to Owen, leaving Samuel to haul over a wooden chair from a nearby table.

"Where's the lad?" Samuel asked.

"Keeping watch over the west woods from the attic. Esther is with him." And would keep him there, Lottie thought.

"You've questions?" Gabriel prompted.

"I do." She shifted to sit a little higher against the arm of the settee. She didn't care to look a complete invalid, even in front of men she more or less trusted. Invalids were vulnerable. "I've been unable to make

heads or tails of these letters. I'm missing something."
Or everything, if one wished to be precise. "I'd like
you to tell me more about the crimes."

She knew names, dates, and times, but that was very
nearly all. If the key to deciphering the letters wasn't
to be found in the letters themselves, then it had to be
someplace else. Someplace she'd not yet looked.

Owen's face turned wary. "Such as?"

"What was the value of the stolen items? Was the
intruder tidy in his thefts, or did he leave a mess?
Were the occupants home at the time? Where did
he leave the letters, exactly? What was the weather
like? What—"

"The weather?" Gabriel smiled, amused by the
notion. "Why should that matter?"

"I don't know that any of it matters. Humor me,
if you will."

Both men looked to Owen.

"The value ranged between six hundred and four
thousand pounds," he supplied. "The occupants
were away during two thefts, in bed for the last.
The letters were left in the open near the missing
art. One on a small table, one on the floor, and one
on the bare nail left in the wall. Mostly, he did the
jobs neat, but he did break a window at Mr. Landie's
town house."

"Is that how he got in?"

"Presumably."

"How did he get in the other homes?"

"Picked the locks on terrace doors leading into a
study and drawing room, respectively. I don't recall
the weather. Samuel?"

Samuel tipped his head back and closed his eyes for a moment. "Rained two nights out of the three."

Good Lord, he actually remembered the weather? She'd not been serious about that. "I see. And Mrs. Popple?"

Owen shook his head. "Nothing was stolen at Mrs. Popple's."

"Yes, I know. How was she murdered?"

"We don't need to discuss it."

"We do." She huffed impatiently when all three men remained tight-lipped. "I can't help if I haven't even the basic facts with which to work. Owen, please."

He hesitated a beat longer before answering. "She was strangled."

Though Lottie's heart squeezed painfully, she kept her expression void of emotion. No sense in giving Owen an excuse to end the conversation before it had really begun. "And?"

"And what?"

"How did he get inside? Did she still keep rooms at the brothel? Was he tidy? Where was the note? Et cetera."

He considered her questions and seemed to relax at the realization that she wasn't asking him to paint a picture of the death scene. "Mrs. Popple had a private house. The staff were off for the night save a pair of grooms in the mews and a maid sleeping in the kitchen two floors below on the opposite end of the house. It looked to us as if he gained entry through an unlocked window in a sitting room. He was not tidy. There was a struggle. The letter was left next to her on the floor in her bedroom."

"No rain."

"Thank you, Samuel."

"What does all this tell you?" Gabriel asked. "That he is inconsistent?"

She hitched up a shoulder. "Yes, or that he is intelligent and imaginative and wishes to appear inconsistent."

Gabriel folded his arms across his chest and smiled. "In other words, it tells you nothing."

"It provides no immediate answers," she admitted. "But it may be of use later. Either something will lead us to a keyword, or I am wrong about the nature of this encryption and it's... I don't know. Gibberish, or entirely mathematical, or—"

Gabriel looked to Owen. "You're skilled in the mathematics."

"Not so much as Lottie. And I've no talent for this sort of thing. Encryptions and such." He tapped his finger against the armchair in a thoughtful manner. "I wonder why that is."

"Poverty of imagination," Lottie offered, and she answered his annoyed expression with a teasing smile. "Unlike our murderer, you seek consistency. You demand control. How can you see what is different when you are forever endeavoring to make everything the same?"

"You think he's not in control?" Samuel asked.

"He is in some ways," she replied. "But not all. He burglarized men of power, murdered a women, and left behind the means by which to catch him. Those are not the actions of a man in complete control of himself."

Gabriel's brows lowered. "You make it sound as if he had no choice."

"Perhaps he didn't, in a way."

"Bollocks," Samuel grunted. "He knows what—"

"I wasn't attempting to exonerate him. He is accountable for his crimes." Pursing her lips, she searched for a way to explain. "But you must know men of his ilk. We all do. Men who can't control their desire for something. Men whose passion for drink or power or money"—or the next scheme or confidence game—"is so overpowering they become a slave to their own need."

"Yes," Samuel agreed.

"Those men will do anything to obtain the object of their desire." She gestured at the papers on her lap desk. "Even if it comes at their own expense."

Gabriel shook his head. "The expense has been the life of a woman and several works of art."

"Yes, but thievery and murder are clearly not the sum total of his desires, are they? He left these behind to be found. He wants them to be deciphered."

Samuel leaned forward in his chair, intrigued. "How do you know?"

"Why else would he leave them?"

"Merely the ugly taunt of a monster," Gabriel offered.

She shook her head. "Taunts aren't particularly effective, or gratifying, when the intended recipient is unable to understand what is being said."

"Perhaps he gains satisfaction from gloating over our ignorance," Gabriel suggested.

"If he wanted you to be completely ignorant of him, he would have walked away from his crimes and gloated in silence." She looked down at her lap desk. "He wants us to decipher these letters, so that we might either comprehend his insults or, as is my guess, follow whatever clues they hold."

"Your guess?" Samuel repeated.

"Until I know what these say, an educated guess is the best I can offer," she said and shrugged. "Perhaps he is unhinged. In which case, there is simply no telling what he means by leaving these."

Unwilling to dismiss the letters as the indecipherable ramblings of a madman just yet, she continued her quest for useful information for another quarter hour. She asked after the location of the artwork within each house, the location of the houses themselves, the age of the art and its owners. She confirmed dates and times, took notes on family, staff, friends, and anyone and everything else that came to mind. Until, finally, the men grew visibly restless and she was forced to let them go.

Owen stood but didn't immediately follow his men from the room. "Will you rest now?"

She tipped her head back and groaned. "I *am* resting."

"No, you're working."

"I won't sleep. I'm not tired, and if I force myself to sleep now, I'll be awake all night."

"You like being up at night." He held his hands out, palms up, when she glowered at him. "Very well. You don't have to sleep. I'll fetch a book for you."

"This needs to be done," she argued, motioning at the letters. "I've tried everything I can think of, Owen. Every possible keyword involving the artwork, Mrs. Popple—"

"And now you'll have a few more keywords to try, won't you?"

"Yes, but…" She let out a frustrated breath. "Every day that passes is another day he—"

"I know. We'll stop him." He stepped near and slid the desk from her lap before she could argue. "A compromise. Rest for a few hours and work tonight. You do your best work when the house is quiet. You told me that."

It was a reasonable suggestion, just not one she cared to hear. "If I say no, will you give me back the desk?"

"No."

She crossed her arms over her chest. "I could take it from you."

"I could fetch Mrs. Lewis and the laudanum."

"No," she replied pertly. "You really couldn't."

He set down the desk and pinched the bridge of his nose. "You tossed it out?"

"Don't be ridiculous. Of course I've not tossed it out." What if someone else had need of it? "I hid it." Just in case Mrs. Lewis started worrying again.

"You hid it."

He was echoing again—a sign, she was coming to realize, of mounting anger.

No, not anger, she amended, taking a closer look at him. He wasn't angry, or even annoyed. He wasn't tensed as if to pounce or pacing about the room. He simply watched her with shadowed eyes and a line of concern across his brow.

Worried, that's what he was, and from his own perspective, being reasonably cautious. She found his behavior smothering, presumptuous, and fairly irritating, but she could see his good intentions clear as day.

Which left her struggling to juggle her own wishes and the urge to accommodate his requests, if only to see him at ease and smiling again.

"I don't need a nap. And I don't want a book." She held up a finger before he could argue. "But I wouldn't mind a spot of Esther's company this afternoon."

The smile he gave her was small, but it reached all the way to his eyes. The sight of it was more than worth a few hours of compromise.

～～

Minutes later, Esther entered the room with a smirk. "You rang?"

"Yes." Amused, Lottie snuggled back into the cushions of the settee. "I must say, being an invalid has its advantages. I quite like summoning people."

"Feels regal, does it? Sadly, you'll tire of it soon. It takes twice as long to summon someone as to seek them out for oneself."

"It does," Lottie admitted. "Play a game with me, will you? One of the disadvantages of indolence is boredom."

"And overbearing gentlemen who believe indolence and boredom possess medicinal properties?" Esther guessed.

"Quite."

"Backgammon, then?"

"Naturally." It was always backgammon. Esther refused to play chess with Lottie, as she never won, and Lottie disliked playing cards with Esther, as Esther stubbornly adhered to the Walker family tradition of cheating.

"You look well," Lottie commented as Esther pulled a small table to the settee. "Have you made peace with Samuel?"

"I'm not certain." She took the backgammon board from a shelf and placed it on the table. "I tried. I did. I apologized again this morning, but I suspect he was only half listening."

"Was he otherwise occupied?"

"Not especially, as he was cornered in the larder at the time."

Lottie paused mid-reach for the board. "Sorry? Cornered?"

"Trapped, really. I went looking for him and found him in there hunting something up for Mrs. Lewis, so I took advantage of the situation. I stood in the doorway. He had to listen to me or pick me up and set me out of the way."

Amused, and a little bit proud, Lottie grinned at her. "Then he did listen."

"I don't know." Esther took her seat with a pronounced *harrumph*. "When I was done, he grunted. Just grunted."

Yes, that sounded like Samuel. "He is a man of few words."

"*Then* he picked me up and set me out of the way."

"Oh." Lottie winced, then sat back against the cushions, considering. "I think if he stayed to hear the whole of your apology before moving you, then you've made peace."

"And *I* think I don't care. I'm done with him," Esther declared. "My apology was sincere, as was my gratitude. He ought to have accepted or refused them. Not grunted. That could mean anything, couldn't it?"

"I suppose, yes."

"Well, I'll not go begging for an explanation." Esther brushed her hands down her perfectly smooth skirts. "I'll not force another apology on him."

"I think that's fair. If he chooses not to acknowledge or accept your apology, that is his business, but you've done what you can. You did what was right. Now you're finished."

"Yes." Esther reached for the dice and absently rolled them in her palm. "Finished."

It wasn't finished, Lottie thought. It couldn't be for Esther.

Lottie had always wished for a more respectable standing in the world, but she rarely troubled herself over the opinion of any particular individual. It did not, for example, bother her terribly that the vicar's wife thought her a fool for not bringing Mr. Whitlock up to scratch, nor that she'd angered Mr. Quimby by purchasing a horse from his neighbor, Mr. Crowlings.

She could live comfortably knowing a few people in the world did not care for her.

Esther could not. It would eat at her, wondering if Samuel was angry with her, thought poorly of her, had lost all respect for her. She sought approval, or at least acceptance, with the same unerring tenacity that Lottie used to solve a puzzle. Only Lottie found disappointment and frustration in failure, not heartache.

Wishing she could ease her sister's worries, Lottie strove for a light but encouraging tone. "Finish with him for now. Give him a few days. Then we'll see."

Esther tossed the dice onto the board. "Let us speak of something else. Have you and Renderwell come to an understanding?"

"I... An *understanding*? Do you mean an *engagement*?" Lottie's pulse raced at the very idea, though whether it was because of simple shock or shock with a dose of impossible hope tossed alongside, she couldn't say. And didn't care to guess. "No, of course not."

"Why not?"

Why not? There were a thousand answers to that question. Most of them could be neatly summarized with, "I'm a Walker, Esther."

"That's no secret to Renderwell. He knows what Father did."

"He doesn't know what I've done."

"Is it necessary that he should?"

Uncomfortable on several levels, Lottie fussed with the pillows at her back. "I'd not come to an understanding with a gentleman under false pretenses."

Esther snorted. "You're not a very *good* Walker."

She wasn't good, period. That was the problem.

"Well," Esther continued, "if he must know, then tell him."

"I couldn't possibly."

"Whyever not? You're fond of him. He's fond of you. You would like to tell him the truth and I suspect he'd like to hear it. Why keep quiet, then?"

"Because..." Again, there were so many reasons, but one stood out from the rest. "Because he's like Peter."

"He's no pigeon, Lottie. You told me so, and I can see it well enough for myself."

"No, not a pigeon. He's good." Completely, utterly, infuriatingly *good*.

"Oh. Oh, right." Esther paused thoughtfully. "He is, isn't he? To the very core."

"I can't tell him what I've done. He wants me to trust him, but…"

"You want him to trust you back," Esther finished for her.

"Yes. And that would never happen if he knew the truth. No one trusts a criminal. And even if he did…" She shook her head. "It would never work."

A viscount wasn't going to fall madly in love with a criminal and defy all convention and common sense by sweeping her away to Gretna Green for a few weeks so she could be married under her real name without anyone being the wiser and then return with her to his estate so his unsuspecting family and staff could properly welcome the new viscountess.

What preposterous drivel.

"I don't know." Esther shrugged. "I trust you. And Renderwell hasn't always been a viscount. His view of the world, his expectations, are different, I should think, than those of your average peer. I think you should tell him. What's the worst that could happen?"

"He could take me for a black-hearted villainess and haul me off to gaol."

"There is that."

Lottie hunched her shoulders. There were times she wished Esther wasn't quite so fond of lying to everyone else and was a bit more willing to lie to her.

"Do you think he'll hurt you?" Esther asked softly.

"No. I don't know. Not intentionally. Maybe."

She shook her head. "I don't really believe he'd haul me off to gaol. I don't know what he would do."

"Oh, he wouldn't haul you off," Esther said with total confidence. "He must already suspect some of what you did with Father, and you're still here."

She shot a quick, nervous glance at the door and kept her voice low. "Suspicion isn't knowing, and helping Father with a cipher here and there is not the same as being a regular accomplice." She had over a decade's worth of crimes chronicled in the hidden room upstairs. "Owen is a man of the law, and I was a proper criminal for a long time. What if it's just too much for him to forgive? What if he doesn't believe I've changed?"

Once a thief, always a thief. Just like her father.

He wouldn't arrest her. He would keep her out of prison. She *had* to believe she meant that much to him at least. But he could turn from her. He could walk away and never look back.

"I could lose him forever, Esther."

Life without Owen, without his smiles, his teasing, his touch. The very idea made her feel ill. She could never marry him, never have the dream of a husband and a family. But she could still have him in her life. Maybe, if she didn't try for more, if she kept her mouth shut, she could even keep him.

Esther set down a game piece and studied her with curious eyes. "You care for him a great deal, don't you? I hadn't realized how much."

"You thought we'd come to an understanding," Lottie pointed out.

"I assumed a mutual affection and attraction. That's

sufficient reason to marry for most people. But it's more than that, isn't it?" She paused, her eyes narrowing with intense interest. "Are you in love with him?"

"That would make me the worst sort of Walker, wouldn't it?" It would make her vulnerable. A laughably easy mark.

Worry flashed over Esther's features. She set the last game piece in place and handed Lottie the dice. "Only if you end up hurt."

❧

Later that night, Lottie pored over the encrypted letters and her notes by the light of her single candle.

She forced herself to focus on the task at hand with cold detachment, just as her father had taught her. There was no Mrs. Popple, no gentlemen whose homes had been invaded, no works of art that had disappeared. There was only a series of events, a list of actions and reactions occurring in a world of innumerable variables. The key was narrowing down those variables to the ones most likely to affect one man's world.

It's like walking a man down ten miles of gravel path. Some of the pebbles, he'll notice. A pretty stone here, a stone out of place there. Most he'll pass over without a second thought. It's reaching the end of the path that most interests him. But here's the secret, poppet. There is always one stone in the mix sharp enough to push through the sole and slice the foot. Sharp enough to make a man stumble, make him fall. And in that moment, that split second when he loses his feet, all other variables disappear. There are no other pebbles to him, no path, and nothing waiting for him at the end of it. There is only the fall, the fear of hitting the ground, and the overpowering instinct to right himself again.

"And me. I exist."

Aye, and you, my clever girl. You can catch him now, if you like. You can be certain he'll reach for you. Or you can let him fall. You can give him a nudge, if it suits your purposes, or offer him just enough assistance to keep him upright but off balance. You can do whatever you like.

But you've got to know where the sharpest pebble is, love, and you've got to know when to lead him to it. Find the pebble and, for a time, you can control his world.

Lottie trailed a finger down the letter in front of her.

Find the sharpest pebble.

What, in the murderer's vast world of smooth stones, made him react?

She tried several keywords inspired by the information Owen and his men had supplied earlier and wasn't particularly surprised when they failed. There was little to connect the crimes besides the missing artwork and the letters left behind. Certainly, there was nothing that stood out as a possible key to the puzzle. Nothing that stood out like a sharp stone.

She concentrated on the numbers next. Earlier, she'd found their corresponding letters in the alphabet and applied the resulting nonsensical string of letters, but it had resulted in nothing. Hoping those same letters might be an anagram, she'd combined them into every possible word or set of words she could imagine, but to no avail.

Now she added them up, halved them, added them in pairs, threes, fours. But in no order or arrangement could they be matched to letters that constructed a usable keyword.

"Damn it."

She glowered at the stacks of paper before her. She was alternately going in circles and standing in place while banging her head against a brick wall. Both approaches led her nowhere. She needed a new start, a fresh perspective.

"From the beginning, then. Slowly and carefully."

She grabbed more paper and, though she'd done it a half-dozen times already, listed the numbers in rows, between nine and sixteen on each letter, making four neat lines of numbers on the page. The result meant nothing to her, and her mind and fingers itched to move on, to try something else, but that was what she'd done every time before. She had rushed ahead.

This time, she made herself stop and look. She stared at the numbers and stared at them, and then, going on a hunch, rearranged their order and stared some more. And finally, she saw it—that twinkling hint she'd seen on the first night. The pattern was in the numbers. It was the only possibility that made sense. They were the only variable that stood out from the rest. Somehow, someway, the numbers had to add up to the keyword.

Unless Gabriel was right and the murderer didn't want the letters deciphered, or it was gibberish, or there was no keyword and the encryption was beyond her...

Lottie's hand hovered over the page.

No keyword. Not a keyword.

She tossed down her pen and rifled through her notes, pulling out all the attempts she'd made to manipulate the numbers into something useful—something that could be converted into the letters of a keyword.

But what if the numbers didn't correspond to the letters of the alphabet? What if they were a clue of their own? They could be an address, a date, time, longitude and latitude, a ransom amount for the art-work. They could be nearly anything.

Finding her last page of attempts, she set it atop her now completely disordered desk and studied the simple mathematical work with a new eye. All she had done was add the numbers in pairs, or threes, where necessary. The first two numbers, then the second two, and so on. But she hadn't taken the time to consider those immediate results. She'd jumped right ahead to trying to turn them into a keyword.

Now she took the time to look at the sets of num-bers themselves. The first set meant nothing to her, but the second set read 52772. That was something. She sifted through more paper and found her notes on the third crime. A painting had been stolen from Lord Thadwist on the night of May twenty-eighth.

"Dates," she whispered into the dark. "They're dates."

Well, one date—the night before the crime. The numbers from the other letters didn't add up to any-thing helpful. But surely the near match of one date was not a coincidence.

Lottie stifled the urge to rush to Owen with the news. If she could match one date, if it really was not a coincidence, then she could find them all.

She spent the next hour manipulating the numbers. It was easier, faster, and tidier to start over from the beginning than to sort through the notes she'd loosely organized on the basis of possible keywords.

"There was no keyword," she mumbled to herself. "Wrong sort of pattern, entirely."

Slowly, surely, she found success. When the numbers on the first page were added in threes, then divided in half, they became the day before the second crime occurred. Unlike the second letter, the year was not included, but it was still a clear match. After eliminating every third number and subtracting the second of each remaining pair from the first, the numbers on the third letter became the day before Mrs. Popple's murder.

Even as the pattern emerged and the excitement of success sent her heart racing, a chill began to spread through her veins. A new pattern was coming to the forefront. One she'd never considered.

The numbers weren't hints at the keyword. They were time limits. And they had stopped when Owen came to Willowbend.

Sixteen

Much as she had the first night, Lottie let herself into Owen's bedroom without knocking. And just as she had before, she took a moment to study the supine figure on the bed. He was in his clothes, as he likely was every night. She rather doubted he even owned a nightshirt. But unlike that first night, she had the sense to stop midway across the room, out of arm's reach.

Filled with eagerness and anxiety, it was all she could do not to close the distance between them and rouse him with a shake and a shout. "Owen. Owen, wake up."

Owen bolted upright before she'd gotten his name out the second time. "Lottie? What's wrong?"

Though it made her feel rather silly, she couldn't stop from dancing from foot to foot in her excitement. "Owen, it's me."

"I can see it's you. What—"

"No, it's *me*. Well, it's us, really. The Walkers." She came close and held up the papers she'd brought along. "We're the sharpest pebble."

"The sharpest…? The what…?" He leaned forward, eyes narrowed. "Why the devil are you walking on that leg?"

Ignoring the third question altogether, she forced herself to start from the beginning. "I deciphered part of the letters. The numbers. They're dates. The dates before each crime."

Owen pushed aside the covers and swung his legs over the edge of the bed. "Let me see."

She lit a lamp while he squinted at her notes. "Every letter is the same," she explained. "The numbers on each note indicate the date before the next crime occurs."

"You figured it out."

"Only the numbers. It wasn't especially difficult in the end. Perhaps that's why I didn't see it at first. I expected something more complicated, more involved. This was just a bit of adding, subtracting, and so on. It was more a guessing game than anything else. Does that seem odd to you?"

He glanced up from the papers. "Should it?"

"I thought he'd be cleverer, I suppose."

"Haven't you been guessing at the keyword?"

"Only because I couldn't find another way. I assumed he left a way for us and we just needed to find it. But this was rather like the codes passed between men with whom my father often worked."

"Simple men," he said and handed her the papers.

"The simplest, in this case."

"There are the rest of the letters, yet."

"True." She didn't understand why anyone would want to use two codes, each a different level of complexity, in a single letter. It didn't make any sense. But she could start on that part of the puzzle tomorrow. For now, the results from the numbers concerned her most. "There's a pattern in the dates."

"A pattern of pointy rocks, by chance?"

"No, it leads to the pointed rock. You found the first letter at the site of the first burglary. It held a time limit, I'm sure of it. Here. See?" She held up her notes and pointed at the top page. "The day after it passed, there was another theft, another letter, and another date." She indicated the next set of numbers. "The day after it passed, there was yet another theft and so on. Mrs. Popple was murdered the day after the third time limit. I've deciphered them all and they're all the same. Until the fourth letter. The one you found with Mrs. Popple." She shuffled the papers in her hands and held up a single page. "That time limit passed the day after you arrived at Willowbend."

"That can't be right. Gabriel contacted London just a few days ago. There hasn't been another theft or murder."

"Because you beat the time limit. Our villain has what he wants. The Walkers."

His eyes flicked to the papers, then back to her. "No."

"Yes. You brought the letters to me before the last time limit."

"Coincidence."

"Not if one is aware of the nature of your work with my father. And me." She shook the pages a little. "Look at these burglaries. The victims were men of station and means. Men who—"

"He wanted items of value," Owen broke in.

"Where else would he find them but at the homes of the *ton*?"

"If it was coin he'd been after, he would have targeted modestly well-to-do tradesmen and nicked items that could be easily and safely pawned. No one but the victims would have batted a lash. But he stole art, which is notoriously difficult to fence, from men of power, and he left behind letters encrypted in a style similar to something my father might have done. The crimes brought him attention. The attention and the letters brought you. You brought him to Willowbend. And then the letters stopped and the attacks here began."

He swore softly and shook his head. "Mrs. Popple was not a member of the *ton*, nor did she possess any art of value."

"No, but she knew the Walker family. Two people my father knew drawn into this—?"

"Lottie," he cut in, again. Then he trailed off and seemed to struggle to produce any additional argument, until he finally arrived at, "You're tired."

"What?" Offended, she drew herself up. "Don't patronize me."

"I'm not. I'm stating the obvious. You're exhausted. No one thinks clearly when exhausted."

"I am thinking clearly." He was the one who appeared to have lost the ability to reason properly. "Listen to me. It is a good principle to explain a phenomena by the simplest hypothesis possible."

"I… *God*." He briefly pressed the heels of his hands to his eyes. When he dropped his arms, his expression was one of resignation and thinly stretched patience. "Ptolemy. More or less."

"Yes. Or William Punch, if you like. Thomas Aquinas, Sir William Ockham. There are others, but they all professed the same principle. A convoluted explanation is unnecessary when a simple explanation is at hand."

"I'm finding this conversation and your theory exceedingly convoluted."

"Our villain stopped when the letters came here." How was that not simple?

"It does not necessarily follow that he stopped *because* I came here. You've found a correlation, that's all. It could be nothing more than a coincidence."

"You would insist on explaining this away as a mere coincidence?"

"Damn right I will," he all but snarled.

"Why?" she demanded. "Why are you so adamant in your denial? I might be wrong, yes, but it's a sound hypothesis and the best—no, the *only*—one we have. Is it so difficult for you to admit I might be right?"

"Yes."

The quick dismissal took her aback. "I'd not have thought you… Why did you ask for my help at all, if you hoped I would get it all wrong in the end?"

"That's not it." He dragged a hand through his hair, leaving the dark locks in tousled disarray. "I don't want you to be wrong in a general sense."

"Only about this?" she asked incredulously.

"Yes. For pity's sake, Lottie."

"I don't understand—"

On an oath, he snatched the pages out of her hand and shook them at her. "These are the letters of a murderer. And you tell me they're meant for you?

Addressed to you? Yes, I bloody well want you to be wrong."

"Oh." Insult slipped away. When viewed in that light, she rather hoped she'd come to the wrong conclusion as well. "I don't know that they are addressed to me, exactly. It's really more that they were addressed to you and pointing toward the Walkers."

Not surprisingly, he had absolutely nothing to say to that.

"*And*," she continued in a bid to allay his fears, "looking at the circumstances objectively, I'm not in any more danger than I was ten minutes ago."

"Cold comfort, Lottie."

It was, rather. Unfortunately, it was the best she could manage at present. "They're from the man in the woods, aren't they? The Ferret."

"There can only be so many coincidences. He followed my trail from London." He glared at the papers in his hand. "I wish to God I'd never brought these letters here."

"They're my notes, actually. It's good you brought the letters," she added quickly when his expression darkened and his fingers curled into the pages. Gingerly, she reached out and retrieved her notes before he could damage them further. "Isn't it better that we know? If his desire to find the Walkers was so great that it led him to murder a woman, then he would have found us eventually. One way or another, he would have found us. I'm glad you brought the letters here. I'm glad you're here." She scowled at her own words. "That sounds selfish. I didn't mean—"

"It didn't. It doesn't." Stepping close, he stroked a finger down her cheek. "I'm glad I'm here too."

Without thought, she reached up and closed her hand over his. Here was warm comfort. In his strength, his touch. It was tempting to lean into that comfort, to lean into him, but now wasn't the time. There was still work to be done. "Father must have stolen from him. Crossed him somehow."

"And he seeks retribution the only way he can," Owen replied, letting his hand fall away. "Through the children. But why target you now? Will has been gone for eight years."

And honest for four before, Lottie thought, though it was possible her father had betrayed the Ferret in working for Owen. "It is a long time to wait before seeking revenge."

She had no doubt that there were men and women who would strike out at the Walker family for the sins of their father, but she suspected many wouldn't bother unless the Walker family happened to be standing in front of them, or at least easily found. The Ferret had gone to terrible lengths to discover the family's whereabouts. Why, if his need for revenge was so great, had he waited years to begin his search?

"He may have been imprisoned," Owen said thoughtfully.

"Or he has been looking all along," she ventured. "And frustration at repeated failure has pushed him to take extreme measures. Or perhaps he is mad, above and beyond being a murderer, that is."

She saw by Owen's expression that the latter

possibility had occurred to him. "If that madness is recent—" he began.

"It would also explain why he is only now seeking his revenge," she finished for him. "I've no experience with madness. Can a man create such a scheme as this without full use of his faculties?"

"It's possible."

"Possible," she repeated. There were so many possibilities. Maybe the dates really were a coincidence. Maybe the Ferret wasn't out to settle a score with her father, but with her. She couldn't recall having met a man matching Esther's description of the Ferret, but that didn't mean their paths had never crossed. He could be one of many her father had cheated while she worked behind the scenes.

What if he knew it? What if all of it—the thefts, the shooting, the fire, the murder, the danger Owen had put himself in—was because of her past as the Tulip?

"Lottie, what is it?"

She glanced up from the papers to find Owen looking at her with concern. "Sorry? No. Nothing. I was just thinking." She cast about for a suitable diversion. "It's all connected. My father, the murder, the man in the woods. We can't hope to keep the police out of this now. You can't simply exile him without anyone being the wiser. Your colleague in London will want answers."

"He'll have them. I promise."

"But not the truth," she guessed. "You'll lie."

He stepped closer and bent his head to catch and hold her gaze. "I will keep you safe."

"The safest thing to do would be for the Walker family to leave Willowbend once this is all over." *And you've gone*, she added silently, and she discovered the former no longer troubled her nearly so much as the latter. Strange how greatly things could change in a few short days.

"It would be best," he agreed, straightening. "At least until we can be certain the Ferret is acting alone." He smiled warmly, then, and reached out to toy with the ruffled lapel of her dressing gown. "I'll take the lot of you to Derbyshire, to Greenly House."

She found herself smiling in return, reassured by his confident tone, enthralled by the sensation of his fingers dancing along the very edge of her gown. "Greenly House?"

"The Renderwell country estate, though few know it. It's a secluded country manor I purchased as a haven for my family during the height of my fame. It isn't a grand residence, mind you, but I think you'll like it, and my sisters. I make no promises where my mother is concerned."

"You…you would introduce us to your family?" Introduce her to his *mother*? Hope, fear, and confusion filled her so quickly she couldn't hope to keep them hidden. "Owen, you can't. We're not respectable." As the Bales family, they were, certainly. But they were not the Bales family to Owen. They were the Walkers.

He gave her a look of rebuke. "On the contrary. I have a great deal of respect for you, Charlotte."

It was not the same thing, not by miles and miles and miles, but just then, she didn't care. Hope and warmth edged out fear and confusion. "I respect you too."

That wasn't what she wanted to say. It felt like a careless exchange of compliments.

Lovely hat, that.

And yours.

No, not what she wanted to say at all.

"I respect you more than any man I've ever known," she offered and silently wished she had the nerve to add the rest.

I love the way you smile, and laugh, and fold down the pages of your books. I admire your unyielding sense of right and wrong, your bravery and tenacity, even your arrogance and stubbornness. I want to walk in the garden with you again. I want to kiss you in the sunlight and again under the starlight.

I want the courage to tell you the truth.

I want the courage to tell you I love you.

But she didn't have it, not tonight.

"It's late," she said softly and, gathering what courage she had, stepped close to place a single kiss on his cheek.

His arm curved around her waist, but she backed away, slipping out of his reach. "Good night, Owen."

❧

Though it was not his turn to keep watch, Owen relieved Gabriel of his guard duties for the remainder of the night. He couldn't hope to sleep, and if he was going to pace about like a trapped animal, he might as well pace where it would do some good.

He would have preferred the thrill of the hunt in the woods, but he knew better than to signal Samuel back to the house early. Tracking at night required a clearer head and sharper focus than he could manage at present.

He checked doors and windows instead and scanned the front and back lawns from the attic windows. Then he began his patrol of the house, keeping his ears and eyes trained for anything out of the ordinary, while his mind went over his conversation with Lottie again and again.

After all this time, after all that had been done, all that had been sacrificed to keep the Walker family safe, in the end, he'd brought a monster to Lottie's door.

He thought through his trip from London to Willowbend, scrutinized and second-guessed every choice to stop and rest, water the horses, stretch the legs, check a shoe. He brought to mind every face, horse and rider, and carriage they passed on the road or met at an inn. Had the enemy made himself known only to be overlooked? Had the signs they were being followed been there all along only to be missed?

Where the devil had he gone wrong?

For the life of him, he couldn't find his mistake. He couldn't nail down the point where he should have taken a second look, or a third, or turned right instead of left, or pressed on instead of stopping. It was infuriating.

And pointless to boot, he told himself.

One way or another, he would have found us. I'm glad you brought the letters here. I'm glad you're here.

Lottie's words made sense. He knew they made sense. The Ferret's determination would have met with success at some point. At least, this way, Lottie didn't have to face the threat alone. This way, Owen thought darkly, he would have the opportunity to deal with that threat personally.

But even the promise of vengeance did little to ease his guilt.

"Cold comfort," he muttered into the darkness. "Damned cold comfort."

Seventeen

Though the next day dawned warm and clear, a thick cover of clouds rolled in by afternoon, carrying in an unseasonably cold rain. The miserable weather didn't keep the men indoors during daylight, but when night fell, they had no choice but to call off the search in the woods.

"Black as pitch," Gabriel informed Lottie as he and the rest of the men joined the family in the library. "Can't see my own feet."

"He leaves at night, doesn't he?" Lottie asked. She glanced at the closed drapes and tried not to imagine someone lurking on the other side of the windows. "Makes camp farther out?"

"Appears that way."

She exchanged a skeptical look with Esther. Appearances meant little.

Peter set aside the book he was reading. "He won't come to the house with all of us here. It would be suicide."

"It would," she agreed and didn't mention that a madman might not care overmuch.

She rose to ring for refreshments, then froze in a half-standing position as a muffled pop of gunshot reached her ears. There was an unmistakable crack of glass and a pained grunt from Samuel as he stumbled back into the bookshelves and slid to the ground.

Everyone else in the room dropped to the floor like a set of abruptly abandoned marionettes.

"Stay down!"

"Samuel!"

"Alive! He's alive!"

"Lottie! Esther!"

"Stay down, Peter!" Lottie yelled, torn between terror for Samuel and blinding relief that Owen and her family were alive and unharmed.

"The hall!" Owen's booming voice drowned out the chaos. "Everyone in the hall!"

As a group, they crawled, bellied, and, in Samuel's case, were dragged across the floor and into the hall.

Owen kicked the library door shut with his foot before scrambling to his feet. "Peter, I need you to get to the staff. Put them in the hall. Don't go in the rooms, any room—just call them out to the hall and make certain they stay there. Can you do that?"

"I can." Peter's voice wavered, but he nodded and gained his feet. "Won't you need us here? Shouldn't we arm ourselves?"

Owen aided Gabriel in propping Samuel against the wall. "No. It was a single, distant shot. He's not trying to get in."

And even if he was, Lottie thought, Peter and the staff would be safer upstairs. "Do as he says."

"Right." Peter nodded once and took off down the hall.

Standing on legs that wanted to buckle, Lottie reached out and grasped Esther's hand without looking. Her eyes were fixed on Samuel. He was awake, but his skin was ashen, his face drawn tight with pain.

Owen and Gabriel maneuvered him out of his coat. They were brisk but careful. Still, Samuel's already pale face turned a sickly gray when they pulled the material down his right arm. Blood had soaked through his shirt at the shoulder and continued to slowly spread down his side and across his chest. It would keep coming, Lottie thought. It would keep coming and coming until there was a pool of it on the floor. They had to stop the blood.

Owen tore off his own coat, his waistcoat, and finally his shirt. Gabriel followed suit and promptly bunched one shirt against Samuel's shoulder and pressed the other against his back.

Bandages, Lottie thought. They needed bandages. "Esther and I can fetch bandages."

Owen didn't look at her. "No."

"We can find them in the dark."

"No." Owen pulled a knife from his boot. "Your petticoats. Sleeves. Skirts. Whatever is easiest. That will do for now."

"Yes, of course." Her hands shook, but Lottie accepted the knife and immediately got to work.

While Lottie and Esther sliced away strips of material, Gabriel gingerly cut and pulled the shirt away from Samuel's shoulder and back to inspect the wound. "Clear through. Missed the collarbone.

Missed bone altogether, by the looks of it. Christ, you're lucky. Number four, my friend."

Samuel bared his teeth as his friends poked and prodded the wound. "Hurts…every…bloody…time."

"Bullet wounds are subject to the law of diminishing returns, same as everything else," Gabriel told him. "Just need a few more to feel the effects."

Samuel's only response was an obscene gesture with his good hand.

Esther paused in her awkward efforts to remove one of the detachable sleeves from her chemisette without taking off her gown. "Four?"

"Fourth bullet he's taken," Owen supplied. "One in the leg. One in the side. One in the arm. Now one in the shoulder."

"Ah, variety," Gabriel chimed. "The spice of life."

Samuel gave a choked laugh, paled, and grimaced. "No laughing. Will kill you."

"You can try later. Don't want that fifth bullet so quick after the fourth, do you?"

"Soon." Samuel closed his eyes on a ragged sigh. "Kill you soon."

Esther took a hesitant step forward as Samuel slumped farther down the wall. "Samuel? Is he… He's not…?"

"No," Gabriel assured her. "Fainted, that's all. Always does. He'll come to in a few minutes."

Owen edged Gabriel aside and took hold of the shirt against Samuel's wound. "I have it. I want every room in this house lighted. No fires. Lamps near the windows."

"Understood."

Lottie didn't understand, but she said nothing as Gabriel jumped to his feet and disappeared down the hall. Instead, she focused on the task at hand, methodically stripping lengths of fabric from her and Esther's overskirts and petticoats to replace the linens as they became soaked with Samuel's blood.

"That should be sufficient," Owen said after a time, measuring up the small stack of extra bandages. "The bleeding has nearly stopped."

Lottie let out a small breath of relief. The slow of blood was a good sign.

The news that she would not be required to strip bare in the hall was also welcome. She'd already gone through several inches of skirts and undergarments.

Samuel groaned and his eyes fluttered opened.

"There you are." Owen patted his friend's face, then changed out another bandage. "Enjoy your lie down?"

"Kill you too."

"You'll have to stand first. Can you manage it?"

"Aye."

Supporting Samuel's uninjured side, Owen hauled the wounded man, grunting and swearing, to his feet.

"Stop it." Esther's voice cut through Samuel's cursing. "You're hurting him. He needs a physician. And something for the pain."

Samuel curled his lip. "Don't want either."

"You'll have both. Where are you taking him?"

"The sitting room." Owen jerked his chin at a nearby door just as Gabriel came down the hall at a brisk trot, carrying a small stack of linens. "We need light in there."

"Right." Gabriel handed Esther the linens and Owen a clean shirt as he brushed past the group. "Right. Give me a minute."

They waited in the doorway until Gabriel had lighted every candle and lamp in the room and placed them all as close to the windows as possible without threatening to set the closed drapes ablaze.

"Stay away from the lamps," Owen ordered as he settled Samuel on a settee and Gabriel set off to light other rooms.

Lottie studied the odd arrangement. Of course, she thought. The light made sense now. They couldn't remain in the hall indefinitely, and they couldn't stumble about rooms in the dark. But lighting only the rooms they used told the shooter where they were, as did walking in front of the lamps and candles, creating shadows.

"He can't tell where we are," she murmured. From the outside, the whole house would be glowing and still. "That's very clever."

"Well, this isn't," Esther protested, motioning at Samuel. "We can't leave him here. Fetch the footmen, Renderwell. We'll carry him upstairs."

"The devil you will," Samuel growled. He turned angry eyes on Owen. "Make her stop."

"Make him listen," Esther countered. "He needs a proper bed."

"I need a bloody whiskey. And some peace in which to drink it."

"You've no idea what you need." Esther snatched up a linen and folded it into a new bandage. "Clearly."

Owen wisely backed away as he donned and

buttoned his shirt. Far away, until he was standing next to Lottie by the door.

"Will he be all right?" Lottie asked.

She felt his hand, warm and strong, come to rest on her back. "He will. Gabriel was right—nothing vital was injured. It's a flesh wound. We'll keep it clean and keep him rested." He moved his hand in a soothing circle as they watched Esther fuss over her snarling patient. "Your sister appears to have the job in hand. She makes a formidable nurse."

"She makes a formidable everything."

Owen winced when Esther thwarted Samuel's attempt to sit up by delivering a quick thump of the fingers to his nose. "Indeed."

"Huh. Maybe it's familial."

"Beg your pardon?"

"The urge to thump irritating men on the nose." She glanced over and saw his baffled expression. "Never mind. Is he always so recalcitrant when injured?"

"No. He's usually worse. But she's a woman. He isn't allowed to thump her back." He considered this a second. "Wish I had thought to hire a woman to nurse him the last time."

"Did he thump you on the nose?"

"He broke it."

Lottie looked at him with horror. "Good Lord."

"In Samuel's defense," Owen added quickly, "I was holding him down at the time, whilst a surgeon extracted a bullet from his leg."

"Oh," she said, weakly. She'd not watched the surgeon pull the bullet from her father's leg all those years ago, but she'd heard the screams, and she'd seen the state of her father's bedroom after. She'd seen the bloodied tools and bandages, the ruined bed linens, and the bowls of rose-red water. It would have been much the same for Samuel, she thought, and she felt a little nauseated. "I see."

Owen's hand moved against her back again. "Esther is safe, I assure you. Why don't we leave her to her work for a moment?"

She nodded in agreement but took a small step away from his supporting hand. She wasn't a child, or a silly woman indulging in a fit of the vapors. She could walk out the door on her own two feet.

Once in the hall, however, she did indulge in a long, steadying exhale as she leaned back against the wall. "Is he out there, do you think, watching the house?"

What did it say about her, she wondered, that she found it easier to think about a murderer in her woods than a decades-old memory?

"I very much doubt it." Owen settled next to her so that their shoulders brushed. She found that small connection every bit as comforting as his hand against her back.

"I thought he camped elsewhere at night."

"He does. Perhaps he lingered too long and became hemmed in by the dark."

"Or he could be growing brazen in his impatience."

Owen nodded and grew thoughtful. "We'll stick to rooms at the front of the house and keep watch over the lawn and tree line. Gabriel will have taken care of that by now. Your Peter has a sharp eye. So does your footman George."

"But how can they see anything?"

"They would see a flash from a muzzle," he explained. "And he knows it. It's why he didn't risk a second shot and why he won't risk another tonight. We're safe."

She closed her eyes, exhausted now that the immediate danger had passed. "Safe for now."

"Now is what matters." He shifted beside her. "Bearing up?"

"Yes." She opened her eyes and found him leaning close, studying her face. "You?"

"I am. But I wasn't the one…" Frowning, he tucked a loose lock of hair behind her ear. "I'd say it was a toss-up who looked paler when we first crawled into the hall, you or Samuel."

"I don't doubt it." For a moment, it had been a toss-up whether or not she'd follow Samuel into a faint. She managed a half smile. "You'll not give me that gun now, will you?"

"Depends. My offer still stands."

"Your offer," she echoed. Tell him the story of why guns frightened her, and he would consider giving her a weapon. "It's ridiculous. How would my telling a story prove I am a capable shot?"

"It wouldn't. I'm not asking for proof of your marksmanship. I am offering an exchange of trust."

"You're offering a bribe," she corrected and stepped away from the wall. "And not a very good one. I have my own guns. I don't require yours nor your permission to use my own."

"This isn't about the guns."

"No, it is about trust, but trust doesn't work like that. It isn't currency, Owen. You can earn it, yes, or offer it, but you can't barter with it, or bribe someone with it, or owe it. You shouldn't." She shook her head. "It isn't a game. I'll not play games with you. There's no trust in that, at all."

One dark brow winged up. "We play games all the time."

"Not when it matters," she retorted and immediately knew that wasn't true. "Or perhaps we do. But it isn't what I want. Not anymore. Not with you."

The corners of his mouth curved up. He took a step toward her. "It isn't what I want either."

"Then no more bribes," she said softly. "No more games."

"It was not my intention to play a game with this. It isn't—" He stopped mid-sentence, snapped his mouth shut, and grimaced. "But that's exactly what I've done, isn't it?" He dragged a hand down his face. "Damn it."

Wishing to end the matter altogether, Lottie shook her head again and offered them both a way out. "This is of little consequence, really. We should get back to Samuel."

The words sounded like a lie to her, and she didn't know why. She didn't mean them to be, and she didn't understand why they should be. And yet the moment felt important somehow. Another crossroads, she thought. Only this time she wasn't sure how she had arrived or where either path led.

"Wait." Owen held up a hand to stay her. "Please. Listen." He took a step closer and then another. "Trust can be more than earned, or offered. It can be manufactured. A person can manipulate another into trust. I am accustomed to manipulating people. I'm good at it. Better than I want to be."

"That is not real trust."

"No, it is not. And it isn't what I want with you. It isn't what I meant to do. I'm sorry, Lottie. I am."

In some respects, Lottie thought, their worlds were not so different. Both were filled with lies and deceit, manipulation and mistrust. It was no easier for Owen to set aside the lessons of his world than it was for her to do the same.

"Intentions count for quite a lot," she replied. "So do apologies."

"You're not angry?"

"No. We do what we know, I suppose. And make amends when we get it wrong."

He reached for her hand and took it in both of his. "What I know is that I want your trust. I will be here when you are ready to offer it. I will… Wait, no." He made a face. "That's not right, either, is it?"

"I thought it rather nice." Not a bribe or a game or manipulation. Just an offer. Quite nice, indeed.

"But it isn't right. It isn't…" He pulled her hand up to press a kiss against her palm. "I will be here, Lottie."

She waited for him to finish the thought, to add an "until," or "when," or "if."

He said nothing, and she realized then that he'd not made an offer, but a promise. One without qualifiers or caveats or ulterior motives. Just a single, simple promise to be there.

Oh, yes, the offer had been nice, but this was so much better.

She looked at their connected hands. Again, a

simple thing that felt like so much more. "I don't know what to say."

"You don't have to say anything." He smiled at her. "That's rather the point."

"You were right before," she said suddenly, surprising herself. "Someone shot my father."

He shook his head and rubbed his thumb against her palm. "You don't have to tell me."

"I know." That's what made the difference, she realized. That's why she could. "I want to. It isn't an exchange. I want to tell you."

"All right." He squeezed her hand once. "All right. Who was it?"

"A man named Mr. Fensley. Not his real name, I'm sure."

"How old were you?"

"Nine. It was two weeks after my ninth birthday." It was the autumn her father was shot and always would be.

"And this Mr. Fensley," Owen prompted. "Was he a friend of your father's? Or a victim?"

"Neither. He was what my father would have considered a poor mark."

"And yet your father tried to steal from him?"

"No." She pulled her hand away gently, and for one brief moment considered ending the conversation. She wanted to tell him everything, the whole terrible story of that night, but the closer she came to the memory, the more her courage waned.

Foolish, she thought. It was only a memory, only a story.

"It was his sister my father was after," she explained.

"Father lured Mr. Fensley's young sister into an investment scheme. Something involving ships and sugar. I don't recall the specifics, but he'd taken the money, claimed the ship was lost, and that was that."

"That sort of scheme requires a considerable amount of planning and work. What went wrong?"

"Nothing my father could have predicted. Mr. Fensley returned from abroad months before he was expected home. He looked into his sister's financial affairs and immediately knew my father to be a cheat."

"Immediately?"

"Like recognizes like," she told him with a half smile. "Miss Fensley's money came courtesy of her brother, and it was as ill-gotten as our own."

"Another swindler. What happened?"

"He came to the house late one evening and kicked in the kitchen door." She tried not to think of the terrible noise, the awful confusion. Owen didn't need every little detail, and remembering them only served to make her feel anxious and a little ill. "Esther was in bed. She slept through the whole thing. Or maybe she hid. She was very young. Fensley demanded the return of the money. He was…insistent."

"Insistent," he repeated grimly. "Did he hurt you?"

"No, he barely looked at me. All he wanted was the money. But Father didn't have it. Most of it had been spent on the lease of the house. The rest he'd invested in another scheme. There was no way Father could return the funds. Not right then."

"Fensley didn't believe him," Owen guessed.

"Not at first, I think. Or maybe he did, and he was after a bit of revenge. The result was the same, either way. But he gave up, after a time. He gave me three pounds, shot my father in the leg, then left."

There, she thought, *that wasn't so bad*. She'd told Owen the story, and she was no worse for wear. There was a mild ache in her belly and an uncomfortable prickly sensation behind her eyes, but the discomfort was manageable and likely had less to do with the conversation than it did with having been shot at less than a half hour ago.

Owen cocked his head at her. "He gave you three pounds?"

"He did. Strange, isn't it? He wanted us out of Bath." She shrugged, her confidence returned now that the hardest telling was over. "I suppose that's why he did it. Father couldn't have walked out of town. He needed a physician first and transport after."

"You might have pawned items from the house."

"There was little to pawn," she explained. "It was hardly a grand manor. A few clean rooms and a roof that didn't leak, that was all. But, yes, there were things we could have sold. Perhaps he felt bad for beating and shooting a man in front of a child. Even violent people can be capable of the odd act of sympathy or charity. Or maybe it was just expedient to pay for our removal. I suppose I'll never know."

Owen took in Lottie's detached expression and cool tone. There was so much more here, he thought. So much she wasn't sharing. "You speak of it as if it happened to someone else."

"It did. It happened to my father."

He didn't bother acknowledging that bit of flippancy. "You'll tell me the story, but you won't share the memory."

"They are one and the same."

"They're not. You know they're not." He took her by the hand again and pulled her farther away from the sitting room door. "I don't want to manipulate the rest of the story out of you... Well, yes, I do. But I'm trying not to."

"The rest?" Shaking her head, she pulled her hand from his. "There's nothing left to tell. I used the three pounds for a physician and transport out of Bath."

"No, not what happened after. The rest of what happened during."

Her mouth thinned into a frustrated line. "I don't understand what you want. What else would you have me say?"

The hint of temper was good, so much better than the muted and distant tone of before. He only wished he knew how best to answer it. He couldn't push, but neither could he risk letting her walk away now, alone with the memory of that night fresh in her mind. "I can't tell you what to say. I won't."

She laughed a little, but the sound was small and tired. "You're trying very hard not to be manipulative, and I'm trying very hard not to be manipulated. We're so careful. We'll never get anywhere this way."

"Nothing wrong with being cautious."

Her expression turned thoughtful and a little sad. "Except that it so easily slips into fear."

"You don't have to be afraid. Not with me."

She said nothing, but he could see the struggle

between her desire to finish what she'd started and her need for caution. She glanced back at the sitting room door and worried her bottom lip with her teeth.

Tell me, he thought. *Tell me the story. Don't walk away now.*

Finally, she shrugged, just a slight hitch of the shoulders. "You have seen what a bullet can do."

"I have. Too many times."

She shrugged again, as if she couldn't quite let go of the need to pretend indifference. "He was my father."

"And you were nine years old."

She was quiet again, fidgeting with the waist of her ruined gown. He wanted to reach for her, tilt her chin up so she'd meet his eyes, but he couldn't be certain she would perceive the gesture as the encouragement and comfort he intended rather than a push.

She wouldn't hesitate to push back. The fear she spoke of, the instinct to see manipulation at every turn, it would make her jump at the excuse to walk away.

Uncertain of his next move, afraid of frightening her away, he kept quiet and still and watched helplessly as she struggled on her own.

She traded fidgeting with her gown for playing with her own fingers. Twice she opened her mouth as if to speak, only to close it again with a trembling breath. At last, on the third try, she managed a shaky but clear whisper.

"He wouldn't stop screaming. He wouldn't stop, and I didn't know what to do for him."

"I'm sorry." Such a useless sentiment, he thought. And the only thing he could offer.

"He hadn't taught me what to do for a bullet

wound. So I stood there. I let him bleed. He had to care for the wound himself."

"You were a child."

"I was, yes." She let her hands fall to her sides, where they opened and closed into fists. "I feel no guilt for what happened. Only…"

"A determination not to see it happen again?"

"A fear that it *might*." Her voice was stronger now, tinted with anger. "I don't like weapons. I don't like the sight of blood. I don't like being afraid, and I don't like feeling useless and helpless. Is that what you were waiting to hear?"

"No." And if he had the chance, he'd find this Fensley and make him pay for all of it.

"I'm sorry." She rubbed her hands over her face. "I know it wasn't. There was no call for that. I'm sorry."

"It's all right."

❧

It wasn't all right.

Lottie battled to gain control over her emotions and the cowardly urge to bolt for the sitting room door and the safety of her sister's company beyond. Maybe then the sick fear crawling through her would temper back into the mild and manageable anxiety of earlier.

What had she been thinking, telling him everything? How could she have convinced herself that it was just a memory, just a story, when it was so much more than that?

She'd not kept it to herself for the sake of secrecy nor because it was simply unpleasant to think on. She'd kept it out of self-preservation. She'd kept the memory because, like so many others, it was dangerous.

It was a sharp pebble in ten miles of gravel path positively littered with sharp pebbles. There were boarding rooms that sweltered and stank and iron shackles that cut and bruised. There was the constant fear for Peter and Esther, nightmares of gaol and the gallows, the memory of her father bleeding on the floor, and her past as the Tulip. *Always* her past as the Tulip.

So many places to trip, so many vulnerabilities to guard. Sometimes it was easier to stand still. Always it was safer.

Instead she had led Owen straight to that sharp pebble and then taken off her shoe and stepped down as hard as she could. Now she felt off balance and exposed. She would fall in a minute. She could feel the tears pressing against the backs of her eyes. Worse was the need to reach for him, and in reaching for him, offer everything. Every secret, every truth. Who she had been. The things she had done.

How she felt.

I love you. I think I have always loved you.

She could see herself saying the words, offering everything. She could see herself falling toward his outstretched arms and landing directly atop the sharp pebble when he took a step back.

It wouldn't do.

"You should go. Be with Samuel." She heard the catch in her voice and it frightened her all the more. "There's so much to do."

"In a minute. Come here." He slipped his arms

around her and pulled her close. "Here. We can take a minute."

There was no demand in his voice, no seduction in the embrace, no judgment or manipulation in the offer, and no push for more. He was simply…here, she realized. Owen was *here*. And because he was, and because there was no place she wanted to be more in that moment than *here*, with Owen, she put her arms around him and held tight.

"A minute," she whispered into the crisp fabric of his clean shirt.

"A minute," Owen agreed.

Closing her eyes, she took that minute and held on to it, and him, until the tears dried without falling.

Eighteen

SAMUEL LOWERED HIMSELF CAREFULLY INTO AN ARM-chair in his bedroom. "God, I want to kill that man."

"Gabriel?" Owen inquired.

"Naturally. And always." Samuel rubbed his injured shoulder gingerly. "But I was referring to our friend in the woods."

"Ah." Owen settled on the edge of the bed. The clean, well-made bed, he noted. That would be Esther's doing. "Where is your nurse?"

"The devil knows, poor bastard."

Owen studied his friend carefully. Samuel was fairing remarkably well for a man who had taken a bullet two and half days ago. Owen suspected Esther's particular style of nursing had something to do with the rapid recuperation, though whether Samuel was getting well due to Esther's care or out of a desire to escape that care was unclear. "Gabriel tells me you mean to resume guard duties tonight."

"Sentry duty," Samuel corrected. "I'll take a chair to the attic, watch the woods."

"You'll take Peter for company."

"I'll not nod off," Samuel groused. "Not when we're so close. You found his camp again this morning."

"He's growing careless," Owen said by way of answer. "Making mistakes."

"Maybe." Samuel scratched the underside of his chin. "Maybe."

"He camped the last two nights on our side of the woods." And had left each morning, reversing his earlier pattern.

"The last two nights have been moonless," Samuel pointed out. "The weather looks to be clearing. He'll stay away."

"He'll risk another night."

Samuel's brows lifted. "You're very confident."

He had every reason to be. "There was a chill in the air last night. He built a fire."

"Did he?" Samuel sat up straight in his chair. "That was stupid."

Owen nodded in happy agreement. The light from the fire hadn't reached the house, but it might have. The Ferret couldn't have been certain it was safe. "Ten pounds says I have him tonight."

"I'll not wager against my own interests."

"Then I'll content myself with your fawning admiration." He smiled pleasantly. "Well, more of your fawning admiration."

Samuel snorted out a laugh. "Allow me five minutes alone with him after, and you'll have it."

"You'll have to wait your turn." Owen stood and gave his friend a bolstering pat on his good shoulder. "You should rest if you mean to be of use tonight."

Samuel's face turned surly. "Bloody hate sleeping in the middle of the day."

So did Owen. Nevertheless, he did his best and spent a full half hour lying in his bed, staring at the ceiling, and trying very hard not to think about Lottie. Had she been avoiding him? They'd not shared more than a handful of words in the last two days and always in the company of others. Had he tried for too much, too quickly? Then again, maybe this was one of those situations where it would be best to push harder or risk her walking away. Or maybe she wasn't avoiding him at all, and he was simply imagining things. They were all busy, and Peter had grown surly over the lack of progress again, requiring a good deal of her attention. Or maybe…

When he felt his eyes begin to cross, he gave up, got dressed, and settled in one of the armchairs with a drink and a book.

He'd only just opened the cover when a knock sounded on his door and Esther stepped inside at his answer.

"I'd like a word with you, Renderwell."

"Of course." He smiled absently, expecting a report of Samuel's condition followed by a quick exit. It surprised him when she closed the door behind her, took the seat across from his own, and regarded him with frigid blue eyes. Concerned, he set his book aside. "Is something wrong?"

She stared at him a moment more, then reached down, lifted the hem of her skirt, and revealed a small, unadorned dagger strapped above her ankle. "I saw you with Lottie in the hall two nights ago."

When they had embraced, he guessed. He couldn't see any other call for the knife. "I see."

"I am not certain you do." She pulled the dagger free and straightened in her chair. "This family became respectable three weeks after my fifteenth birthday. Just like"—she lightly jabbed the tip of the knife into the armrest—"*that*, and we were all good children of the God-fearing Mr. Bales, successful tradesman. At fourteen we were criminals and at fifteen we were not. Do you know how much changed for me then?"

"How much?"

"Not a damn thing." She lifted the blade and studied it. "My sister likes to think she is privy to all the secrets this family holds. She was my father's pet, you know. He saw in her the same talents, the same natural gifts he had in himself. She was clever in ways I'll never be—with numbers, with patterns, with strategies. She can read some people as if they were a page of simple verse she wrote herself. I get on well enough in those areas, mind you. I could lead the men of Wayton on a merry chase straight off the cliffs of Dover. But…" She shrugged lightly, fiddling with the end of the knife. "The sweet boys of the village are not so great a challenge, are they? Merely the best I can reliably manage. Lottie, on the other hand, could convince a man to put his own head on a block."

He reached for his drink and took a small sip. "Your father liked that about her."

"Oh, he did. He very much did. And I envied that, truth be told. But I had my own talents, my own uses, and Father was never one to let a gift go to waste."

"Am I looking at one of those talents now?"

"The dagger? Oh, no, it isn't weaponry, per se, that made me so valuable to Father." She gave him a bright smile that might have been charming, had it been a little less terrifying. "It was my willingness to use it."

"Ah."

"Not every scheme my father designed relied on a keen insight into human nature. Not every success was a result of nuanced manipulation. Sometimes, a little push was needed. A bit of fear to put one off balance. Nothing makes a man vulnerable like a healthy dose of unexpected terror, wouldn't you say?"

He lifted his glass in a small salute. "I wouldn't know."

"Liar. Everyone stumbles when they're afraid."

As you are now, he thought. "Do you mean to tell me you were your father's henchman, as it were?"

"Nothing so vulgar," she replied with enough affected amusement for Owen to know it had been exactly that vulgar.

A child playing with knives for her father's benefit? Christ, how could that be anything but vulgar?

"What were you, then?"

"Useful," she replied simply. "It is an easy thing for a handsome man to gain entrance into a crowded ballroom with a pretty young girl on his arm. And it is a difficult thing to ascertain whether it is a breathless boy of twelve holding a blade to your throat or a well-trained fifteen-year-old girl who'd slipped into trousers and a hat."

He could picture it easily, not because Esther struck him as a woman of violent nature, but because she'd been a young girl desperate for the love and approval of Great Britain's most manipulative bastard of a father.

The image of Esther playing the thug at her father's request made him ill, and the shame he saw in her eyes, shame too thick to be hidden behind a wall of pride and bravado, twisted something in his chest.

Careful to keep his tone neutral, he said, "Your father continued his work after he began working with me, then."

"He liked to dabble."

With his young daughter at his side, apparently. "I see. I imagine you are divulging this particular secret for a reason?"

"I want you to understand that the Bales family might be respectable, but I remember being a Walker. I remember what I once was. Hurt my sister…" With a speed and dexterity that surprised even him, she hurled the knife at his chair. It landed with a thunk in the wooden leg, vibrating mere inches from his knee. "And I will gut you like a trout."

"And pick my bones from your teeth with the same blade, no doubt." He set down his drink. "You are good, Esther." He glanced down at the knife and considered. "You are very, very good."

"Good enough. That is all you need remember."

"Possibly. You could use a spot of training, however."

"I don't need training from the likes of you."

"I knew you were bluffing ten seconds into this conversation. Also"—he reached down and pried the knife free with a quick yank—"it was shortsighted to have thrown your only blade." He offered her the knife, handle first. "Tell me, Esther. Do you think I kept up with your family for all these years for the purpose of one day hurting your sister?"

"I don't know why you kept up with us."

"Because I wanted to know you were safe and well."

She hesitated, then rose to retrieve her blade before returning to her seat. "Or you were afraid we would divulge secrets Father might have told us. Or you thought you might have need of us in the future. Or—"

"Good God, this family. You would question the motives of a saint."

"Anyone with an ounce of common sense would be suspicious of a man claiming to be a saint. Canonization requires that a man be dead first." In the ensuing silence, she made a rather obvious effort not to squirm in her seat and then, at long last, slumped and made her first openly honest statement since she'd walked in the door. "We can't help it."

"I know." And it broke his heart. "The last thing I want is for your sister to be hurt. For any of you to be hurt. Understood?"

"Yes." She tilted her head to the side. "I will rain all manner of hell upon your head if I discover you're lying. Do you understand?"

"Yes. Now, aren't you the least bit curious to know where you went wrong?"

"No. I know where I went wrong." She smiled a little. "Poor mark."

"Well, we all stumble when we're afraid. But there's more to it than that. Keep your seat a moment longer, and I'll explain. But first"—he sat back and subjected her to a cold stare of his own—"I want to know what you've done with the rest of your father's journals."

Her smile vanished. "I'm sure I don't know what you're talking about."

"I'm sure you do. Will kept a record of everything. If he was still dabbling in crime after he began work with me, then there are journals somewhere detailing those activities." He'd wondered before now if those journals might have existed at some point. He'd just assumed Will had hidden or destroyed them long ago. For the first time, Esther had presented a different possibility. "I think they're in this house, and I think you know where they are."

"That is quite an assumption."

"If you were the only person who knew Will was working again, then you're the only person to whom he could have entrusted the journals."

"Maybe he hid them away himself in one of the old chests or trunks sitting in the attic." Esther made a prompting motion toward the door. "Go search them, if you like."

He didn't bother with a reply. They both knew everything in the house had been searched years ago, and every hint of Will Walker's past had been removed for Peter's sake.

Esther dropped her hand and shrugged. "I daresay if there *had* been any journals and I'd found them, I would have burned them."

"You wouldn't have burned them."

"Why not?"

"For the same reason you nearly killed yourself saving an old pony." The same reason Lottie hadn't burned the others.

"Mr. Nips is a living creature."

"And a reminder of your father, of a day he finally loved you well enough to remember your birthday," he said and fought back remorse when she blanched. "Those journals are a memento of a time he trusted you above all others. Even Lottie."

It was difficult to watch her struggle to hide her emotions. Esther was a gifted actress, but there were some kinds of pain that were impossible to mask.

After a moment, she rose from her chair. "I have said what I came to say." Her voice sounded small and oddly subdued. "This conversation is over."

Nineteen

Twenty minutes later, Owen found Lottie in the study, hunched over the pile of papers on her desk.

"We need to talk," he said softly.

She barely spared him a glance. "Just one moment. I'm almost done."

He walked to the desk and stared at the top of her head. "Lottie, look at me." He didn't want to do this. He bloody well didn't want to be, yet again, the man who leveled ugly accusations at someone Lottie loved.

Frowning, she pulled her attention from the desk, then set her pen down carefully. "My apologies, I didn't realize you were upset. What's happened?"

"Did you know your sister helped your father?" He knew she didn't. But, somehow, asking the question felt like a gentler introduction to the topic than simply spitting out *your sister was a criminal and your faith in your father is rubbish*.

"I beg your pardon?" She shifted in her seat to face him fully. "Helped him with what? His work, do you mean?" She shook her head. "No, you're mistaken."

"I just finished speaking with her. She told me herself."

"I see. And what did she tell you, precisely?"

He offered an abbreviated version of his conversation with Esther, leaving off the question of the missing journals for now. Lottie winced when he mentioned the knife but offered no other reaction until he was done, at which point she laughed lightly.

"Henchman? Honestly. Never say you believed her?"

He did. Every word. But what concerned him more at the moment was that Lottie clearly did not. At a guess, she'd never even suspected Will had involved Esther in his work.

"Lottie, the truth is—"

"I'm *telling* you the truth," Lottie cut in. "Esther never worked with my father. Why would I lie about that?"

Looking to put off the inevitable for a few moments, he grabbed a nearby chair and positioned it in front of Lottie's so that their knees brushed when he sat. "I don't know why you bother lying at all. I can always tell."

"What rot."

"You get the faintest wrinkle, just here." He brushed the tip of his index finger just over her brow.

She lightly slapped his hand away. "I do not."

"You do, and I know why. You don't like lying."

"Irrelevant. I'm good at it. There is no wrinkle."

"Not this time." Or ever. Reading her would never be so easy. He told himself that the purpose of the offhand, and entirely fabricated, comment had been to make her smile for a moment, but *that* was a lie. He was stalling, distracting, looking for a way out or around the impending argument. He didn't want to be the accuser again. But there was nothing else for it. "I'm sorry you didn't know about Esther."

"There is nothing to know. Esther was never a part of our father's work. I told you, he took less notice of her than he ought to have. He certainly never invited her to join him in his crimes."

"That may have been true for a time. When was it he bought her the pony? Her fifteenth birthday, did you say?"

A reward for her help, no doubt.

"Exactly so," she said, pointing a finger at him. "He'd just started working for you. He'd stopped his criminal activities."

"Your father worked for himself. That never changed."

She sighed, a sound that was both annoyed and tired. "I don't wish to have this argument with you now. Possibly ever. We'll never agree about my father. Why bother?"

"This isn't about your father. This is about Esther. You cannot help your sister by sticking your head in the sand."

Temper flared in her eyes. "Do not presume to tell me how to handle my sister. I know her, Owen. You do not. She has played you for a fool."

"Do you think I imagined a knife being hurled at my chair?"

"No. I think you believed a preposterous story she concocted to accompany what is, admittedly, an unusual talent."

"A talent your father made certain was cultivated. For what purpose?"

"His own amusement," she replied with impatience.

"He thought it great fun to have a daughter with a penchant for hurling knives. Owen, I appreciate that you would come to me with your concern. But Esther…" She sighed heavily. "Esther is misguided in her motivations at times and a gifted storyteller. That doesn't mean my father used her as a henchman, as you so ridiculously put it. He may not have been the best of fathers, or even a particularly good one, but he was not a monster. He cared for the safety of his children. Even you said so."

"I assumed there was some degree of care, yes, but—"

"It was the correct assumption."

"I am no longer certain," he replied and swallowed an oath when she flinched. "I'm sorry. I am. But your father was unpredictable. More than I realized. His notion of what was safe and what was not may have been even more"—patently insane—"flexible than I assumed."

"He was unpredictable," she agreed in a tone that emphasized she was trying very, very hard to find some common ground between them. "And certainly he had rather unconventional, even poorly conceived, ideas on what sort of activities were appropriate for children. But neither of those facts has any bearing on the current discussion. My father did not involve Esther in his work before he met you, and he no longer continued his own work after he met you. Regardless of whether or not my father might have thought it safe for her to do so, Esther *did not* act as my father's henchman."

"Yes, she did."

She made a sound that was half groan, half growl,

and all aggravation. "This is *absurd*. You are asking me to believe—"

"I am asking you to consider the possibility that you were mistaken about this one aspect of your father's life. I am asking you to approach this in a calm and objective manner for Esther's sake."

"You expect calm from me? You would turn my father into an ogre and my sister into a thug. And I am to be calm and objective?"

"For God's sake, I've no intention of hauling your sister off in shackles, but—"

"I should hope not," she cut in, "as she's not committed any crime."

"Esther admitted to helping your father."

"Esther lies."

"So did your father."

"Yes," she agreed with mounting heat. "Regularly. Brilliantly. Without remorse, often without care for the consequences, and sometimes for no other reason except that the lie was there and he liked the way it tripped off his tongue. You are not in a position to enlighten me on the nature of my father's character. I know who he was. And I know who he became."

"You would believe your father became an honest man but Esther is still a liar?" he asked, incredulous.

"Esther didn't lie to me. She lied to you. That's entirely different."

"Only to a Walker," he ground out. "Lottie, listen to me. If your father continued his activities with Esther—"

"He *didn't*."

"Hypothetically," he pressed on, ignoring another growl of frustration from her. "If he did, he would have written about them. You said yourself he wrote about everything. There would be a journal or journals detailing his activities."

"Yes, which only goes to prove those activities never occurred. I've seen all my father's writings at some point or another, including the notes he kept during the years he worked for you. There is no hint of him running a scheme or confidence game during that time, and certainly no indication Esther was ever involved."

"Not in the journals you've seen, no."

"You think there are others? You think Esther has journals hidden away? Is that what she told you?"

"She denied it."

"Because it *isn't true*," she all but shouted at him.

"Suddenly she's telling the truth?" he snapped.

"Suddenly she's a liar?" she shot back. Her hands curled into fists. "We'll not agree on this. We will *never* agree. I am done speaking of it, and you are done with my sister." She shoved her chair back from his and rose. "Stay away from her."

Stay away? That cut it. He meant to keep his own calm, his own objectivity, but by God, the woman was infuriating. "The hell I will." He rose from his chair. "Your father was a blackguard, through and through, Lottie. He used your sister and—" He swore when she spun away and headed for the door. He caught her in two steps, snagged her arm, and whirled her about to face him. "There is a *murderer* in your woods. If there is any chance, any chance at all, Esther's journals can help us, I—"

"There are no other journals!" She yanked her arm. "Let go of me!"

He did, only to grab her again when the door flew open and Peter appeared, crimson-faced and trembling, with an old-fashioned dueling pistol at his side.

"Take your hands off my sister!" The hand holding the pistol shook as he lifted it to aim at Owen. "Now!"

"Peter. My God." Lottie shifted to stand in front of Owen. "My God, what are you doing?"

Eyes trained on the weapon, Owen shoved Lottie behind him. "Stay back."

She popped right back in front of him. "Stop it. He doesn't want to shoot *me*."

To avoid an extended shoving match, Owen caught Lottie around the waist with one arm, dragged her to his side, and angled his body to make himself the larger target. "He doesn't want to shoot anyone." But the boy was armed, angry, confused, and neck-deep in a dangerous bluff he couldn't hope to pull off. All the necessary elements for tragedy were present.

"This," Owen said grimly, "is how one kills people accidently."

As if to prove the point, Peter waved the gun at him. "I said take your hands off her."

"If I take my hands off, she'll move to stand in front of me again. Is that what you want?"

Though it didn't seem possible, Peter's face turned a deeper scarlet. "Lottie, step away from him!"

"Absolutely not. Set that gun down this instant, or so help me God—"

"What's all this?" Esther's baffled voice arrived a moment before she appeared in the doorway beside Peter. In the space of two seconds, she took in the scene, snagged Peter's wrist, twisted, and caught the gun before it dropped an inch from his hand.

"Ow! Bloody *hell*, Esther!"

"Idiot boy." She inspected the gun while Peter cradled his arm. "It isn't even loaded."

"Of course it isn't loaded. I wasn't going to shoot him." Peter gestured at Owen with his good hand. "I just wanted to scare him."

"Into shooting *you*?"

"He's not armed."

"The devil he's not." Esther arched a brow at Owen.

Owen pulled back his coat to reveal the gun holstered at his side. He'd never had any intention of drawing it, but he was willing to let Peter believe otherwise. It might frighten some sense into the boy.

Lottie spun on him. Horror flashed in her eyes, then disappeared just as quickly when he gave a quick, nearly imperceptible shake of his head. She offered a subtle nod of understanding in return, then yanked his coat closed again. "He is just a boy, Owen."

"A boy pointing a gun at your head."

"*Your* head, you bastard," Peter snarled.

"You could have missed, lad."

"It wasn't loaded," he ground out and winced. "God, Esther, you broke my wrist."

"No, I didn't. But I should have." Moving past him into the room, she tossed the gun onto the nearby wing chair. "Renderwell didn't know that was empty, you fool. Another minute, and he would have shot you dead."

"Well, not *dead*," Owen objected, willing to take the ruse only so far.

Lottie made a show of glaring at him. Then she glared in earnest at her brother. "What on earth were you thinking?"

"What was I...?" Peter's expression went from pained to outraged in the space of a heartbeat. "What was I *thinking*? Someone broke into our house, then shot at you, then burned down our stables nearly killing both of you, then shot at all of us, and that man"—he used his good arm to stab a finger at Owen—"knows why. That man knows everything. Everything about us, about our father. Everything you've not seen fit to tell me. *That's* what I was bloody thinking."

Owen bit back an oath. The boy had heard their argument. "Peter, listen to me. Your sister is not to blame—"

"Sod off, Renderwell."

"*Stop it*," Lottie snapped at Peter. She turned to Owen. "I would like a word with my family, please."

"Lottie, I..." With an oath, he reached out and snagged her hand. He didn't know what to say to her. Surely, there was something he could do to make the coming scene easier for her. There had to be something he could say to set things right between them. *Again*. It seemed as if he was always searching for the right words to smooth over some new argument, constantly struggling to bridge some new gap between them.

He wanted to believe that they would always find a way to build that bridge, that no matter how many times they argued, or walked away, they would always succeed in finding each other again. But there were times, like now, when he feared the worlds of a lawman and a Walker might be too far apart.

Because the words he needed eluded him, he settled for rubbing his thumb once over her knuckles before releasing her hand. "I'll be here, Lottie. I am here."

Twenty

A TERRIBLE SILENCE FELL OVER THE ROOM AFTER Owen's departure.

Peter stood hunched by the fireplace, while Esther propped a hip on the arm of the wing chair. Both of them looked to her expectantly.

They were waiting for her to speak, Lottie realized. Even now, when it was clear she'd made a mess of things, they expected her to lead.

She cleared her throat and straightened her shoulders. "Do you understand how foolish and dangerous it was to draw a weapon on another human being, Peter?"

He curled his lip in disdain but wouldn't look her in the eye. "If it is your intention to deliver a lecture, I'll leave."

"You'll stay where you are. Whatever you overheard tonight, however angry you might be, it was no excuse for what you did. You will apologize to Renderwell."

"The hell I will," Peter snarled. "I'm leaving."

"Don't you have questions?" Esther asked quietly as he moved past her. "You must want answers."

He stopped, turned, and glowered at her and then at Lottie. "Will I get them or just more lies? God, Lottie. Everything you've told me, everything about my life, all of our lives, has been a lie."

And everything, she realized with a rising panic, must have been what Peter had heard tonight. He'd not stumbled on a bit of the argument. He'd been eavesdropping.

"No," she said with a calm she didn't feel. "It is true that pieces of our history have been altered, but only pieces—"

"The important pieces," Peter cut in. "Who was William Bales? Was he really our father?"

"Yes, he was. I swear it." She swallowed around a lump in her throat. "His name, however, was William Walker."

"Walker," he breathed, as if testing the name. "Is that who we are? The Walker family?"

"We were, yes."

"And he was a criminal, our father?"

"For a time, yes. But he changed—"

"Into what?" Injury apparently forgotten, he gestured angrily at the door. "To hear Renderwell tell it, he was as much a blackguard at the end as he had been at the start."

"He is wrong. Our father started a new life, became a new man."

"You think he redeemed himself."

"He was on the path to redemption, yes."

"And that's why we are here," he scoffed, "in the wilds of Norfolk living under assumed names? Is that why there's a madman in our woods? Because of our father's great journey toward atonement?"

Esther made an impatient noise. "Norfolk is hardly a great wilderness."

Lottie shot her a quelling glance. "He was not given the credit he should have received. He saved a woman's life. He——" She cut herself off before she told Peter of their father's connection to Lady Strale. He didn't need another reason to hate Owen just now. She would explain it to him later, when he had calmed down a little. "He died saving a woman."

"I'm delighted for him. And her. How many lives did he destroy?"

"I don't know." She dug her fingers into the material of her skirts. "I don't know. Too many."

"And you?" Peter asked, his tone lowering. "Were you a part of it? Did you help him?"

Esther rose from her seat. "Peter. Don't."

Ignoring her, Peter kept his focus on Lottie. "That's what you were arguing about, wasn't it? Whether Father used you. Whether you helped him."

So he hadn't heard everything. Maybe their voices had been muffled through the wood of the door, or maybe he'd come late to the argument. Whatever the case, it gave her the opportunity to save some portion of the story he knew. It gave her the chance to keep some measure of his trust.

All she had to do was lie.

Yes, they'd been arguing about her. No, she had not helped their father. It would be so easy, so simple.

But she couldn't do it. She couldn't bear to tell him one more lie.

She opened her mouth to admit to everything, but Peter answered for her.

"You did, didn't you?" His young face contorted with disgust. "My own sister, a filthy criminal."

"Well," Esther drawled before Lottie could respond, "I was a criminal, anyway. I wouldn't say filthy."

"Esther, please don't," Lottie pleaded. "You'll only make this more difficult."

"It was never going to be easy," Esther returned. "Besides, it was me you were arguing about with Renderwell, was it not?"

"Yes, but—"

"There you have it," she told Peter. "It was me. I helped Father." She stepped forward from the chair, her demeanor suddenly hard. "But if you think for one moment, child, that you may now speak to me as if I'm shite you've wiped off your boots, you will think again."

"Stop it, Esther," Lottie snapped. This was not what they needed. "I will handle this."

"Then handle it." She waved a hand dismissively at Peter. "I'll not stand for the boy's insults."

"You'll not stand for it?" Peter echoed incredulously. "You fabricated an entire life. All of our lives."

"We did the best we could," Lottie said quietly. "What we thought was best."

"That is a pretty way of saying you failed."

The words cut quick and true. "Be that as it may—"

"You've not failed him," Esther bit off impatiently. "And neither have I." She pointed at Peter. "You've been sheltered, and cared for, and treated like a princeling since the day you were born. And not by our sainted mother or father, but by us. We've given you every privilege, every opportunity."

"You've given me lies," Peter shot back. "Everything I knew of our father and you, and…" His eyes grew round in renewed horror. "Our mother. God, our mother. She would have known as well. She wasn't the doting wife of a tradesman at all, was she? Who was she?"

"She was an unfaithful bitch," Esther informed him. "Just like her daughter."

"*Esther.*" Lottie rubbed her forehead where an ache was beginning to form. "You are *not* helping."

"I won't coddle the boy whilst he's kicking at us. And I won't give him the truth in fits and starts. You would drag this out for eternity." She focused on Peter, her voice cold and matter-of-fact. "Mrs. Walker had the morals of a stable cat and the parental instincts of an adder. She knew exactly what our father was, and it bothered her not one jot. His crimes provided her with the funds to disappear for years at a time."

"Disappear? For years?" The horror grew in Peter's eyes. "Years? Was he even my father at all?"

Esther reached up to pointedly twirl a lock of her pale blond hair. "Oh, he's *yours.*"

Oh, God. Oh, no. "Esther…"

"Oh, don't trouble yourself." Esther waved away Lottie's concern. "I've known for years. We can discuss it later. Will Walker was your father," she told Peter. "Mother was home a full ten months before your birth and died from a fever six weeks after, as we said."

"Generous of you," Peter muttered. "To allow me that bit of truth."

"That bit of truth wouldn't hurt you," Esther replied.

"We didn't *want* to hurt you." Lottie took a cautious step forward, desperate to close the distance between them in some tangible way. "We wanted to protect you."

Peter stepped back. "Me? Or yourselves? I had nothing to hide. I was never a criminal."

"We weren't hiding from our crimes," Esther returned. "We were hiding from Father's enemies."

"Men like the one in the woods? Is that why he's here, because of our father?"

"It's possible," Lottie admitted. It was also possible the man had come because of her, but she couldn't tell him that, she just couldn't.

"And Renderwell?" His gaze shot to the door and back. "What is he? Another enemy? Or another fraud?"

"He is neither. He was a police inspector eight years ago when Father worked for him. He is a private investigator now. And he is a friend."

"How am I to believe that?" Peter demanded, throwing up his hands. "How am I to believe anything you say?"

"We love you." She could hear the desperation in her voice, made no effort to disguise it. "I know you believe that." He had to believe it. "We only wanted to keep you safe. You were six. What were we to do?"

"I haven't been six for a long time."

"No, but you've been happy. We were scared, Peter. I was scared we would take that from you."

"You *have*." He backed away from her, shaking his head. "I don't… I can't look at you. Either of you. I have to go."

Head down like a bull, he made a straight line for the door.

"Not everyone lies," Lottie called out at his back.

He stopped, but he didn't turn around. "What?"

"There are people in this world you can respect and trust. That hasn't changed."

That was her greatest fear, she realized, that the truth would warp and break the trust that was so fundamental to his nature. That it would strip away all that was good and generous in him. That he would become the angry young man she'd seen holding a gun in the doorway. That he would become a Walker.

Peter digested her words silently, shook his head once more, then left.

"Damn it." Lottie scrubbed her hands over her face, wishing she could scrub away the entire, horrible day. "Damn it all. I thought you were going to help, Esther."

"I did. You would have coddled him."

"And what is wrong with that?" The boy's world had been turned upside down. The life and family he had known had been all but ripped from him over the course of a quarter hour. "Where was the harm in trying to make this easier for him?"

"Aside from the fact that he was pointing a gun at you only minutes ago?" Esther shook her head, her shoulders sagging. "There was no harm in it and nothing at all wrong with wanting to coddle him. But it is not what he needed. Nor is it what he wanted. He's angry, Lottie. He needed to kick at someone, and he wants to feel his behavior is justified."

Suddenly, her sister's purpose in antagonizing Peter became clear. "And you made yourself a target." She sighed heavily. "You should not have done that, Esther."

"He'll feel the better for it." She shrugged and offered a small smile devoid of real humor. "Or he'll feel guilty. Either will work to our benefit."

"It wasn't fair to either of you."

"Fair has nothing to do with it. It was the best thing for him. Let him fume at me today and burn away some of his anger. Then you can tell him the rest tomorrow when he has calmed down."

Good Lord, the pair of them, Lottie thought. The incompetent leader and the sacrificial lamb. What a terrific disaster they had created. "I don't know that this was the wisest course of action. It is but lies atop more lies."

"Lies," Esther repeated quietly. "Yes, there are always more lies, aren't there?" She turned cautious, guarded eyes on Lottie. "I want to show you something."

❧

In Esther's bedroom, Lottie watched with a sinking heart as her sister reached into her hope chest, shifted linens, and pulled out a single worn journal. "Here."

Lottie took the book slowly. It seemed such an innocuous little thing, no different than the stacks of books just like it sitting down the hall. But it was different. It changed everything.

"Oh, God."

"I lied to Renderwell," Esther said. "I told him there were no more journals. I thought to lie to you as well. Or continue to lie, really."

Lottie tore her eyes from the book to look at her sister. "But that's not what you've done."

"I've been studying it since Renderwell arrived.

I found nothing that would aid us," Esther added quickly. "Nothing that would help us capture a crazed man in the woods. If I had, I'd have given it to you straightaway. I hope you believe that. But I found nothing. Initially."

"Initially?"

"There is a small sketch of us inside. You and me, and Peter in your lap. I thought nothing of it, at first. I passed over it a dozen times. But last night I stopped to really look at it, just to remember, I suppose, how small Peter was, and what a terrible artist Father was. Then something about your dress caught my eye. Here, I marked the page…"

Esther took back the journal, opened it to the sketch in question, and returned it to Lottie. There they were, the three of them perched on what appeared to be a lopsided bench.

"Do you see?" Esther continued. "The ribbon along the hem of your skirts? I thought it decorated with flowers, but it isn't."

"They're letters." Tiny, perfectly formed letters hidden among some delicate, if poorly rendered, scrollwork. "A code."

"Yes, but not the same as the letters Renderwell brought. I checked."

"We can't be certain." But there were no numbers, and the text was broken into several short groups instead of written out in one long string. Esther was probably right. It would likely turn out to be nothing, merely a silly bit of nonsense their father had devised for his own amusement.

She closed the book and wished with all her heart

she could toss it across the room. "It's true, then. You worked with him."

Esther took a small step toward the window, away from Lottie. "Yes."

"When?"

"After Renderwell came and your focus turned to him."

And I never noticed, Lottie thought. Distracted by the handsome prince, charmed by the promise of a new life, she'd never even suspected. "You said nothing. All these years, you said nothing. Why, Esther? Did you think I would judge?"

"No, of course not." Esther winced, as if realizing her answer had come too quick. "Perhaps a little. It is different, what I did."

It was violent. Their father had used her for violence. In that moment, for the first time in her life, Lottie well and truly hated William Walker. "You should have told me."

"Like you should have told me of my real parentage?"

"Yes. I'm sorry."

Esther surprised her by huffing impatiently. "It was a rhetorical question, Lottie. No, you should not have told me."

"What?"

"I learned the truth long ago. Well before we came to Norfolk. I knew you had to know, clever as you are. And I knew, as I have always known, that you would never tell me. Not because you wanted to lie to me, but because it would have been the best thing for me. And it was. I wish I'd never…" Esther shook her head. "It doesn't matter. The point is not every secret is selfish. Sometimes we keep them to protect the people we love."

Lottie glanced down at the journal. "You lied to protect me?"

"I kept a secret. It's different. And I'd keep it still, if I could. I should have burned that journal. There's nothing inside that implicates me in a crime, but still…I should have burned it." Stepping forward again, Esther tapped the cover of the journal. "This is my past, my mistakes. I've no business laying them at your feet. You'll just pick them up now and shoulder them with the rest of your burdens."

"Esther, did you hurt anyone?"

Esther's mouth twitched with sad humor. "No. Not seriously. I delivered a mild warning prick to one or two of Gage's more unpredictable men, that's all. I didn't cause them real harm."

"Gage's men?" It couldn't be. Gage was a common enough name. "You can't mean Horatio Gage."

Esther nodded. "I do. Father was working with him. He wanted to keep in the game, but he hadn't the time to invest in it fully, not whilst Renderwell was breathing down his neck. Gage's resources allowed Father to keep invested, as he put it."

"He hated Gage." In her father's eyes, Gage had been little more than a glorified footpad.

"He did. And he feared him. That's why he kept me about. He liked the idea of having a guardian, as it were, and thought my gender added a lovely element of surprise."

"I'm sorry. I'm so sorry, Esther." What good was

that, she wondered. What good did it do Esther now, for her sister to be sorry?

"If it's empathy you keep offering, I'll accept it, gladly. But if you are issuing some sort of apology, I don't want it. None of this was your doing. Besides, you might want to wait until you've heard everything before you decide how sorry you are and why."

"There's more?" Good God, how could there possibly be more?

"Regrettably, yes." Esther blew out a short breath. "The man I saw at the inn. The Ferret. I did not meet him as a child. I met him when I worked with Father."

In her teen years, Lottie realized. Old enough for the Ferret to recognize her. "Was he one of Gage's men?"

"Possibly. Gage had men who worked for him and men with whom he worked. From what I could ascertain, the Ferret fell into the latter category. Gage preferred that his men have a sharp mind and a bit of education, if possible. The Ferret had neither. But I can't be certain of his relationship to Gage. We only dealt with him once." Esther grimaced. "It did not go well."

"What happened?"

There was a long, long pause before Esther spoke. "We were to relieve a duchess of her jewels. A diamond tiara, necklace, bracelet, brooch, and earrings. She wore them once a year at the family's annual ball. All at once. They were worth a fortune."

"Lady Strale." It couldn't be. It couldn't possibly be. "You're talking about the Strale diamonds."

"Yes."

"Oh, God, Esther." Weak-kneed, Lottie reached for a nearby bedpost. "Did you kidnap Lady Strale?"

"No. That is…" Esther hunched her shoulders and winced. "*We* didn't. A kidnapping was not the plan."

"What *was* the plan?"

"It was quite detailed, really, but the abbreviated version is, Father and I were to attend the ball as guests, lure Lady Strale out of the ballroom, divest her of her jewels, then hand them off to the Ferret in exchange for our share of their worth. He was to be waiting right outside."

"Your share before they were sold?"

"Father didn't want to keep the jewels," Esther explained with a nod. "He said it increased the risk. He was willing to take a smaller percentage if he was paid up front."

"Wait outside? That's all Gage's man had to do? Wait and take the jewels? Why would Father need him for that?" If all he'd needed was a fence, he could have gone to half a dozen others with whom he'd worked in the past. Men he'd liked and trusted a great deal more than Gage.

"I don't know. There was more to Gage's involvement than just unloading the jewels. I don't recall everything. He obtained our invitations, I think."

"How?" It was easy to sneak into some balls. One or two extra guests in a crowd of hundreds hardly signified. But the annual ball in which the Strale diamonds were showcased was likely another matter. Invitations would need to be shown at the door, and entrance to the home would be closely guarded.

"I don't know how. What does it matter?" Esther briefly pressed the heels of her hands against her eyes. "Nothing went as it was meant. At first, it went better than planned. Lady Strale was drunk. Staggeringly drunk. I didn't have to tear her train and insist on escorting her away from the guests to have it fixed. I merely suggested a turn about the room and she followed me out of the ballroom like a clumsy lamb. I cannot imagine what her family was thinking to allow her to come to such a state. She was so malleable that when I brought her to the empty parlor where Father was waiting and asked her to remove the diamonds for a good cleaning, she agreed. Pulled off every piece and put them right in my hands."

Esther shook her head. "Then Father opened a door to the terrace and passed the jewels off to the Ferret. That should have been the end of it."

"But it wasn't."

"The Ferret took the jewels, pushed right passed Father, snatched up Lady Strale, tossed her over his shoulder, and ran out." Esther opened her hands in a helpless gesture. "There was nothing we could do."

Overwhelmed, Lottie rested her forehead against the bedpost and closed her eyes. "Do you understand what this means?" Opening her eyes, she caught her sister's gaze and knew Esther understood perfectly. "Father didn't go into Gage's building for Lady Strale." It hadn't been to rescue her. It hadn't even been for the reward. "He wanted the diamonds."

"But he didn't come out with the diamonds, did he?"

"So he failed." Another Walker tradition, she thought bitterly. "And rather than leave empty-handed, he settled for the lesser prize of Lady Strale and the reward money."

"Lottie?" Esther wrapped an arm around the other

bedpost and leaned against the wood. "Do you think he loved us at all?"

"I don't know." Her eyes fell to the book in her hand. "I want to believe it. Despite everything, I want to believe he loved us. I don't know what that makes me."

"I think," Esther said softly, "that it makes you more like Peter than you realize."

Twenty-one

WHEN LOTTIE LEFT ESTHER, IT WAS WITH THE INTEN-
tion of seeking out the haven of her bedroom. She'd
always felt safest in her own space, among her own
things, sitting quietly at her desk with a pen in hand
and papers stacked and strewn around her.

She walked right past her room without so much
as a glance.

It wasn't isolation she wanted now. It was Owen.
It was the comfort of his voice, the sight of his smile,
the faint hint of wintergreen on his skin. It was the
promise that he would always be there. She wanted to
hear him say it again.

Her feet dragged to a stop just outside his door.

Did she want to hear it again? Should she?

He'd meant it. It was as solid and true a promise as
she'd ever received. Even after their terrible argument,
he'd offered it. But he'd done so without knowing
the truth about the Tulip. It was a promise built on a
false foundation. How could she be sure that promise
would hold when the ground beneath it fell away?

If she was careful, if she wove a clever web of lies

and half-truths, she would never have to be sure. They could go on as they were now, with Owen assuming the best of her and she hiding the worst. Nothing had to change for them. She would never have to risk losing the man she loved.

And she would never know if that one thing, the most important thing, was really true.

Sick at heart, she stared down at the journal in her hands and thought of everything it represented and whispered two words into the stillness of the hall.

"*It's true.*"

Then she lifted a shaking hand and knocked.

❧

Owen's first thought upon opening the door was that he'd never seen Lottie so tired. She was pale, her beautiful features drawn, her dark eyes shadowed. Without a word, he took her arm and ushered her inside, closing the door behind them.

"There are things I need to tell you," she said softly, standing still and alone in the center of the room. "But I want a minute. I need a minute."

He saw it then, the small book she clutched at her side. "Lottie—"

"May I have a drink?"

"Yes. Of course."

She said nothing as he poured two fingers of brandy. When he handed her the glass, she merely stared at it as if uncertain how it had come to be in her hand. "No, I don't want this."

"All right."

He reached to take the drink back, but she shook

her head and stepped away. "It is not all right. How can one person make such a bloody mess of *everything*?"

It took him a second to realize they were no longer talking about the drink. "Lottie, your father—"

"I am not speaking of my father. Why did I not see it, Owen? I'm the cleverest, aren't I? How could I not see it?"

"I... See what?"

"Esther," she whispered and squeezed her eyes shut, almost as if that simple act could hide her from the truth. "You were right about Esther. He taught her how to *hurt* people. I thought the knives were just for... I don't know. Defense or just amusement. I loved that he taught her. He ignored her so often, and...I should have made him stop. I should have protected her. I failed her. And I've failed Peter. And I failed you."

She pressed the binding of the journal against her forehead. "I took the promise of a man who lied to me my entire life over the word of the only man who was ever honest with me." She lowered her arm with a groan. "I blamed you for eight years because I couldn't see the truth perched on the end of my own damned nose."

"Lottie—"

"And now it's all fallen apart. I thought I'd made such a fine job of it, but it's all fallen apart." Her voice cracked, and the hand holding the drink began to shake. "How could I have been so blind to his true character? *How* could I not see what my father really was?"

"You saw what he could be. There's no shame in that."

"But not what he *was*. He was a villain." Her lips trembled and the anger in her voice drained away, leaving only awful resignation. "A villain," she whispered. "And he was never anything else."

Owen stood with his fists clenched at his sides and wondered why he had been so eager for Lottie to arrive at this truth. Was this really what he had wanted, to watch while she relinquished the last shred of hope for a father she'd adored?

He had no idea, not the faintest notion, of how that felt. He'd never had illusions about his own father. There'd never been hope there. Moreover, his father had been a selfish ass, not a dyed-in-the-wool villain. And Owen had never adored him. This was a loss he'd never experienced. He didn't know what to say to Lottie, how to comfort her.

"All of this is because of me," she said quietly.

He damned well knew what to say to that. "No. This is William's doing—"

"Do you know why he turned to Esther for help?" She turned away from him to set her glass down with great care. "Because I told him no."

"Better it should have been you instead of Esther?"

"You misunderstand... No, I misspoke. I didn't tell him no." She looked at him for one brief moment, then averted her eyes. "I told him *no more*."

"Ah." He took a small step closer. "He used you as well."

She released a long, ragged breath. "I was the Tulip."

"One of the women mentioned in the journals," he said with a small nod. "I had wondered if he'd put your lessons to use a time or two. It seemed probable."

"*No.* I wasn't one of the women." She turned to face him fully now and gripped the journal against her chest like a shield. "*I* was the Tulip. There was never another. It was just me. From the very start."

If she'd marched up and slapped him across the face, it would not have left him more stunned. All those journals, all those entries. Good God, all those years. How old would she have been at the start—five, six? Younger? It left him sick, and it left him speechless. He could not come up with one proper response to her admission.

It was just as well Lottie didn't seem to require one.

"I didn't want to do it anymore," she continued, looking away again. "I didn't want to be a villain. I told him it had to stop, and he agreed. And then you came and I thought, this is perfect. Isn't everything so perfect? Only it wasn't, and I didn't see it. I didn't help her."

And I didn't help you, he thought.

"I wish I had known," he murmured. "I should have known."

The last drop of color drained from her cheeks and she took a small, wary step back from him. "I won't hold you to any promises."

"Beg your pardon?"

"You're not obligated to keep them." Her eyes, dark and nervous now, darted to the door. "You were unaware of the truth when you made them."

"What are you…?" He trailed off as understanding sank in. His promise to be there. And her instinct to trust nothing, believe no one, and assume the worst.

A sharp needle of anger twisted beneath his own regret.

"I see. I'm to fetch the shackles now, am I?" He marched up to her, snatched the journal out of her hands, and tossed it aside. "For God's sake, Lottie. I am not taking you to gaol. I am not breaking my promise. Understood?"

She swallowed audibly. "But you said—"

"I said I wish I had known. Because if I had known, I would never have given William the opportunity to stay with his family whilst he worked with me. I would have taken you somewhere safe. All of you." As he should have done. "How could you think I meant to take you off in chains?"

"I didn't. I didn't. I just…" She gave a minute shake of her head and began to visibly tremble. "You're the Thief Taker. I'm a thief. Was a thief. I *lied* to you."

"Why not keep lying? If you thought I'd betray you, why did you tell me the truth?"

"I *didn't* think…" She shook her head again, stumbling over her words. "I told you because I didn't want to lie to you anymore, and… You promised to be here and I…" She covered her eyes with her hand. "I believed you."

And with that, she burst into tears.

As a man with six demonstrative sisters and one histrionic mother, Owen had been witness to every variety of tears. The loud, the loving, the embarrassed, the wounded, the furious, the manipulative—he knew them all. He knew how to handle them all.

He hadn't the faintest notion of how to handle Lottie's tears. He had never seen her cry. He rather doubted anyone had seen Lottie Walker cry in the last quarter century. It was heartbreaking, and a little bit terrifying.

"Don't. Lottie." Feeling helpless, he pulled her into his arms. "Here now. We'll make this right."

"Let me alone." Her words were muffled against his chest, but he heard the embarrassment, and he knew it was pride that made her pull away. "Let me alone a minute."

"Not this time." Not ever again. "I'm here, Lottie. I promise. I will always be here."

He drew her close again and held tight while her shoulders shook and her fingers curled into the fabric of his shirt. He held on until, slowly, slowly, the jagged catch and release of her breath began to even out.

"It's all lies." Lottie pulled back, but not away, and knuckled away tears that continued to fall. "My father lied to me, lied to Esther. Esther lied to me. I lied to you. I lied to Peter. Peter was right. Everything is a lie."

"It isn't. Darling. It's…" He wanted to give her something solid and true, something absolute to hold on to when everything else in the world shifted and disappeared.

He took her hand, placed her palm flat against his heart. "Look at me, Lottie." He waited until her gaze fixed on his, waited until he knew she saw him and only him. Not her father, not her siblings, not the lies that swamped them all. Just him. "I love you." Her hand twitched in his, but he held tight. "*I love you. That is the truth.*"

"No. You…" Her voice was little more than a whisper. "You can't mean that."

"I love you," he said again.

"I was a thief, Owen."

"You were." His hand tightened on hers. "You stole my heart."

She jerked and reared back a little, her eyes widening almost comically. A moment of stunned silence followed, and then…a giggle emerged. Then another. Then she burst into laughter. It came out ragged and drenched with tears, but it was loud and long and made him feel like a king.

"Good God, that was *atrocious*," she managed at last. She wiped her cheeks with the back of her free hand. "Oh, that was appallingly bad."

"Yes, I know." He grinned at her, wholly unashamed. "This is why I do not write poetry."

She looked down at their joined hands. "Do you mean it? You love me?"

"I do."

"I thought… I was afraid you'd not be able to forgive me. I was afraid you'd walk away from me."

"Never."

"I want…" She trailed off, pulled her hand away, and bit her bottom lip.

What did she want? To give him the words back? To be able to give him the words back? To ask him to take the words back?

"I want…"

"Tell me."

Her dark eyes met his. "I want you to show me."

"Show you?" Hadn't he shown her a hundred ways already? "What do you—?"

"Show me," she repeated and stretching up, laid her lips against his.

"Oh." *Oh*. He went perfectly still, suddenly

uncertain of himself, of the moment, of what he should do. "Lottie, I'm not certain—"

"I am," she whispered, and her hands began to move over his chest, down to the buttons of his coat.

Her mouth found his again, and he tasted the salt of her tears. "Maybe we should—"

"Stop talking."

"—think this through."

She undid the last button, pulled back to look at him. "Are you going to tell me I don't know my own mind?"

"No." He was worried. Maybe a little flummoxed. He wasn't an idiot. "Absolutely not."

"Good." She fumbled with his coat, pulling one side off his shoulder and halfway down his arm, where it bunched up on itself and flatly refused to move. She scowled at it. "I may not know what I'm doing, precisely." She gave the sleeve a solid tug, to no avail. "But I know what I'm *trying* to do."

She yanked at the sleeve again but only succeeded in bunching the material further. "This is ridiculous." She stepped back with a huff. "If it's not too much of an inconvenience, might you find it in your heart to *lend a hand*?"

In another time, another situation, he might have laughed. She was right. It was ridiculous. Also, he'd never seen her so adorably annoyed.

But what he saw beyond the flustered frustration gave him pause. There was determination there, to be sure, not the blind desperation he feared, but rather a clear, sharp resolve. Without a doubt, Lottie knew what she was doing. She knew her own mind. And that was all he needed to make up his own.

He had his coat off and her bodice half-undone in under ten seconds.

This wasn't how he'd imagined making love to Lottie for the first time—any of the ways he'd imagined. There were no candles and flowers, no soft blanket on a field of green grass, no serenade of birdsong. But none of that mattered now. The decorations of daydreams, however pretty, could not compare to the beauty of reality. Of Lottie, warm and willing in his arms. *At last.*

He wanted to touch her everywhere at once. He'd waited so long, been denied for so many years.

But he needed to slow down. His hands were too rough, his mouth too demanding in its pursuit of possession. The need for more, the desire to have everything, and have it now, threatened to overpower him. That wasn't what he wanted. He wanted to share and explore and love at leisure, not conquer in haste.

Struggling for control, he slowed his hands, gentled the kiss, and allowed them both the luxury of drawing out every moment. He savored the taste of her, reveled in the sight of her, relished the feel of her beneath his palms and the sensation of her curious, eager hands running over his chest.

She shivered when he nuzzled at her neck, trembled when he slid her bodice from her shoulders and followed the exposed skin from her collarbone to the soft swell of her breast above the confines of her corset.

They undressed each other in slow stages. There were so many layers to be stripped away, so many secrets to discover, and so much pleasure to be had in the reveal.

He touched her everywhere, just as he wanted, but he did it with the disciplined care of a man mindful of the treasure he held, of how close he'd come to losing her. His hands skimmed lightly over the gentle rise of hips as he helped her out of her skirts. His palms curved around the indentation of her waist as he slipped off her petticoats and crinolette.

Lottie undid his necktie and pressed a kiss to his throat as her fingers worked the buttons of his waistcoat.

Gradually, piece by piece, the layers slipped away until there was nothing standing between them but Lottie's light blush.

&

Touch me.

Lottie's skin was hot and tight, unbearably sensitive. The cool air against her exposed flesh sent shivers racing up her spine. Only she didn't feel cold. She felt wicked, delighted, cherished. And, yes, just a mite embarrassed. But all thoughts of modesty disappeared when Owen reached for her. His calloused hands pulled her close, lifting her effortlessly into his arms.

He settled her on the soft linens of the bed and then there was only sensation after sensation. His large body covering her own. The brush of lips and hands, the mingling of breath. His touch was everywhere, drifting across her heated skin, making her squirm and shift in a restless bid to prolong each moment of pleasure. Her hands trailed down the long plane of his back and found the firm muscle of his buttocks, eliciting a choppy groan from Owen. She reveled in that sound and in her own helpless sighs. She felt thrilled and impatient, emboldened and powerless. She felt loved.

She shivered and arched as his mouth traveled up her neck and caught the sensitive lobe of her ear between his teeth. A pull of need dragged a gasp from her lips when he bent his head and lazily circled a nipple with his tongue.

"Owen. I want…"

"I know." His whisper was tortuously hot against her flesh. "Wait for it. It's better when you wait for it."

It couldn't be better. Nothing could be better.

Oh, but there could be *more*.

He drew her nipple gently into his mouth, and she arched against him with a stunned cry. Slipping a hand between them, his clever fingers sought the ache between her legs, and then she was lost to everything but the dizzying pleasure. It grew and swelled, layering and building on itself endlessly until she thought she could bear it no longer.

"Owen, *please*…" She wasn't sure what she was asking for—she only knew that better was no longer enough, more wasn't what she needed. Everything. She needed everything.

Shifting over her, he carefully settled himself between her legs, and she instinctively brought her knees up to cradle his heavy form.

Hurry. Hurry. Hurry.

She needed him. All of him. Her Owen.

He wrapped his arms around her protectively and pushed forward with one long thrust.

There was pain, but it faded as quickly as it came, leaving behind only a curious ache that became lost to the relentless pull of arousal and the ecstasy of knowing that finally, *finally* he was hers.

Wanting more, she bowed up, encouraging him to move. But he simply held her, and held her still as his mouth took hers in a long, unhurried kiss. His hands began to caress her again, petting and soothing, teasing and exciting with exquisite care and boundless patience, as if he had all the time in the world.

She could feel him shaking with the effort to be still, felt the tremble in his arms and down the hard slope of his back. He was trying so hard to be gentle.

So careful, her Owen. Always so wonderfully, infuriatingly careful with her.

"Don't wait." She wrapped her arms tight around his shoulders in an effort to bring him even closer. "Don't wait."

He muttered something against her ear, an endearment, or a curse, she couldn't tell. It didn't matter, because he was finally moving, working himself inside her in careful, shallow thrusts that enflamed and frustrated.

"Please," she whispered. *More. Faster. Everything.*

With a groan of his own, he began a new pace, steady and strong, and every part of her sighed in relief, even as her muscles tightened and bunched with an anticipation she didn't fully understand. Something was coming. Something tremendous. Something necessary. Without hesitation, without a moment's trepidation, she gave herself over to the wanton, dangerous ecstasy of rushing headlong to meet it. Because she could. Because Owen was with her, pulling her along, holding her safe and tight in his arms.

She gave herself over to him. And finally, all at once, she had everything.

She cried out, shocked and dazzled by the pleasure, but even as wave after wave of it swamped her, she held tight to Owen, pulling him along, keeping him with her.

"My Owen."

At last, he buried his face in the crook of her neck, tensed, and shuddered in her arms.

Twenty-two

OWEN STARED DOWN AT THE DARK HEAD RESTING ON his chest. It was difficult to believe that, after all these years, it was Lottie in his bed. It was Lottie draped over him like a sheet.

Smiling, he ran a hand lightly down her hair and fought off the urge to close his eyes. He wanted to give into the exhaustion pulling at his body and slide into sleep with Lottie in his arms.

He already felt as if he was half caught in a dream, one he'd kept locked away for twelve years. There was more to that fantasy, a future that went beyond secret kisses and stolen moments of passion. He wanted endless hours with Lottie, countless nights of falling asleep next to her, and waking with her in his arms.

He'd have them. One day, he promised himself, and pressed a soft kiss on the crown of her head. One day soon. He'd find a way.

But for now, there was a house to secure before nightfall and an angry young man sulking somewhere downstairs.

Taking care not to wake Lottie, he maneuvered out of bed, donned his clothes, and gathered his weapons.

He paused at the door and cast a glance over his shoulder.

She hadn't given him the words back, not even in the throes of passion. That worried him—even as he told himself to have a little patience, it worried him.

He did his best to set it aside, however, and went in search of Peter. Owen found him in the study, sprawled in a worn leather chair and glowering at a beam of early evening sunlight that sneaked around the edges of the drapes to cut a sharp line across the faded carpet.

The boy spared him a furious glance but said nothing until Owen had poured two glasses of brandy and taken the seat next to him. "What do you want, Renderwell? Come to shoot me?"

"No. I've come to offer an olive branch." He handed Peter one of the glasses. "As it were."

"I don't drink spirits." A corner of his mouth hooked up. "I'm not allowed."

"Because you're only fourteen."

"Nearly fifteen."

And the drink was so diluted as to nearly be water. He held it out again. "Exactly so."

Peter made a face but accepted the glass. "Is it true, what Lottie said—that our father worked for you?"

"It is. Lottie did as well."

"But not Esther." He snorted derisively. "Too busy helping our father, I suppose."

"I wasn't aware of it at the time. Neither was Lottie."

Peter traded scowling at the fireplace for scowling

at his drink. "She doesn't even have the decency to be ashamed."

"Ah, now that is where you are wrong."

"I'm not. She stood there and admitted to it, bold and proud as you please."

"I'm sure she did. A rare breed, our Esther." He pictured Esther playing with her dagger. "Shame is a tricky thing, Peter. There are some, like Lottie, who will let the fourteen-year-old boy she raised with selfless devotion kick at her like a dog because she feels she deserves it."

"That's not—"

"And there are those, like Esther, who prefer to do the kicking themselves."

"She ought to have the decency to at least appear ashamed."

"Your father ought to have had the decency to keep a child out of his affairs," Owen returned. "You want someone to blame, blame him. You've a right to your anger. No one will argue otherwise. You've a right to feel cheated and put on. But you have no business judging whether or not your sisters appear adequately sorry for the failings of your parents."

Peter's expression was both skeptical and mulish. "No one forced them to help our father. They made their own choices."

"I imagine that twelve hours ago, you would have been willing to call a man out for impugning the honor of William Bales. You would have risked your life for no other reason than that he was your father. Think what you would have been willing to do had you actually known him."

"I'd not have become a common criminal," Peter muttered into his glass. "I can tell you that."

"Maybe not," Owen agreed, not because he believed it, but because it was best if the boy did. "We'll never know for certain, will we? Your sisters made certain of that. They made certain it was a choice you would never have to make."

"You think I should thank them?" His voice was thick with indignation and disbelief. "For lying to me? For making a fool out of me? I've gone on and on about our father—at school, in the village, to you and your men. I bragged about him, about our mother. And it was all lies. They made me a fool and a liar."

And for that, Owen thought, the boy had his sincere sympathy. "No man likes to feel a fool. But every man does, at some points in his life. You'll find the pain of it fades with time."

"This won't," Peter grumbled.

Owen took a sip of his drink to hide a smile. Everything was so certain in youth. So permanent. "Regardless of what your feelings may be in a few years' time, you must admit now that your sisters made the correct decision eight years ago. They lied because you were a child. It was their duty to protect you, even from yourself."

"I'm not a child now."

"No, you are a young man in possession of a dangerous secret. There are other men like the one in the woods. Men who would not hesitate to harm your sisters because of who your father was." He saw that hit the mark, saw the flinch of worry and fear. "You are Lottie and Esther's brother. However angry you are, whatever your feelings for them might be at present, you are bound by duty to keep them safe."

"I know that."

"Will you?"

Peter stared at his drink a long time before answering. "Yes."

∽

For nearly a quarter hour after waking, Lottie stayed just as she was, stretched out in Owen's bed, tangled in the linens. Her body felt weighted and sore and absolutely wonderful. Oh, she felt glorious. She shouldn't. It was the wrong time, absolutely the wrong time to feel as if she had swallowed an army of wicked little butterflies, but she would be damned if she felt even a second of guilt over stealing this moment of joy. Owen loved her. Owen had loved her, and she him.

When the time was right, she would give him the words. She had almost offered them when he had, but she didn't want to offer them as an exchange. She meant to give them as he had, as an unconditional gift.

Soon, she thought. She'd offer them soon.

She let herself seep in the thrill and wonder of the moment for a minute longer, then she slipped out of bed, retrieved the discarded journal, and sneaked back to her own room to work.

∽

It didn't take Lottie long to correctly guess the keyword to the code adorning the hem of her dress in the sketch.

"The cipher was on my skirt," she explained as

everyone but Peter gathered at a small table in the library. "Not a terribly difficult clue to follow. The keyword was 'Tulip.'"

Next to her, Esther rolled her eyes. "Of course it was. God forbid it be 'Kitten.'"

"Kitten?" Owen inquired.

"I was Tulip," Lottie explained. She met his gaze and looked away quickly when her cheeks warmed at even that small connection. "She was Kitten."

"I see. What does it say?"

Lottie handed a single piece of paper to Owen and waited while the group inspected the short, simple message it contained.

You blocks, you stones, you worse than senseless things.

And then, in postscript:

Love, Your Papa.

Samuel scowled at the page and shook his head. "What does that mean?"

"Probably nothing of use," Esther replied. "Like the rest of the journal."

Owen handed back the page. "Shakespeare, is it?"

"It is," Lottie confirmed, both surprised and impressed. It had taken her longer to remember where she had read the quote than it had to decipher the text. "*Julius Caesar.*"

"Is he referring to us?" Gabriel asked. "Are we the blocks?"

"No, it's a clue, not a taunt. I rather doubt he imagined you would ever read it." She smiled a little. "Though I do imagine he would have enjoyed the unintentional insult."

"What stones, then? Statues?" Samuel guessed.

"Headstones?" Gabriel offered. "Where did the Globe Theatre stand? Could there be a graveyard near the site?"

"No," Lottie replied. "You're taking the quote out of context."

"How do you know he hasn't?" Gabriel inquired.

"Because I know my father." Only she didn't, really. "I know his puzzles. He liked to layer them, make you dig." Thoughtful, she tapped her fingers against the table. "In the play, Marullus is speaking with the cobbler. He's angry because people are celebrating Caesar's return. Hard-hearted men...senseless blocks..."

"Cheering for a man undeserving of praise and loyalty," Esther said.

"A ruler." Gabriel looked to his companions. "The queen? Is he referring to the queen?"

Lottie shook her head. "It isn't about Caesar; it's about the heartless men who followed him, cheered for him..."

"The House of Lords," Samuel guessed.

"Perhaps." Lottie looked to Esther. "Do you think he hid something in London? A message of some sort?"

"I don't know."

"No." Owen leaned over her to tap the journal. "This encryption was left for you. No one but you and Esther knew about the Tulip. If Will wanted to hide something *for* his children and *from* everyone else, he'd hide it in his own home, amongst his own things. And he'd hide it in an item he knew you valued. Something he could be certain you'd not toss out after his death."

"But what?" Lottie murmured. She'd already

looked through every volume of Shakespeare they owned in search of the quote. There was nothing in any of them. "The House of Lords," she muttered to herself. "The House of Commons."

Esther let out a small groan. "Oh, I should have *known*."

"What?"

She gave Lottie a wry smile. "Parliament."

"Parli…? Oh." Oh, *of course*.

As one, they rose from their chairs and hurried into the main hall.

Owen and his men were quick to follow. "What? What is it?"

"Esther's sketch," she shot over her shoulder. "In the hall."

They didn't have far to go. A small grouping of Esther's artwork hung just outside the foyer. At the top was a detailed sketch of Westminster, still under reconstruction.

Esther stretched up for it but only caught the bottom edge with her fingers.

Reaching over her head, Samuel retrieved the picture off the wall. He gave it a quick, appreciative glance before offering it to Esther. "You drew this?"

"Years ago." She motioned for him to give the picture to Lottie. "I must have been…"

"Thirteen," Lottie answered for her. "I took you there." She turned the picture over and studied the back. "Father had it framed shortly before he died." The one and only sketch of Esther's he had ever bothered to frame. Now they knew why.

Worried, she glanced at Esther, but her sister

merely shrugged. "I *really* should have known. Take off the back, then."

"I need a knife."

Her companions immediately produced a half-dozen blades.

Lottie took in the display of weaponry with a combination of amusement and horror. "Good Lord." She accepted one of Esther's daggers. "I don't require a scimitar, thank you, Samuel."

"It's a kukri," Samuel grumbled as they returned to the library. "A small one."

Ignoring him, Lottie sliced through the backing of the frame, tore off the pieces and revealed a large velvet pouch wedged against a second, hard backing. She drew the string loose, opened the bag, and poured a fortune in diamonds onto the table.

"Oh, *heavens*." With a hand that shook, Lottie brushed her fingers over the tangle of sparkling bracelets, necklace, earbobs, rings, brooch, combs, and what looked to be the broken pieces of a tiara.

With a soft curse, Gabriel picked up one of the rings for a closer inspection. "Appears real. My God, do you know what these are? The Strale diamonds."

"That isn't possible," Esther whispered in awe. "The Ferret took them."

That statement was met with stunned silence by the men, followed by a nervous sort of humming noise from Esther. She cast a sidelong glance at Lottie. "You haven't told Renderwell, then."

"I did." She looked to Owen, took in his shocked expression, and thought back to the scene in his bedroom. She'd been angry, and heartbroken, and not thinking with perfect clarity. Oh, dear. "Or perhaps not."

"Tell me that your father stole the Strale diamonds?" Owen's tone was cool and very, very annoyed. "No. You did not."

"Right. Well. It had been my intention." Like intending to call for him when she'd seen the stables on fire, she felt that ought to count for something.

"Why don't you tell me now," he suggested.

She didn't care for the layer of extreme patience he'd added to the annoyance, but she couldn't blame him for it. "Very well. Father—"

Esther laid a hand on her arm. "No. It's for me to tell." She looked at each of the men separately and then straightened her shoulders and said, "I helped our father steal the Strale diamonds." Her eyes flicked to the table and back again. "Evidently."

Over the next few minutes, Esther related her story in a flat, concise manner. She showed no emotion, offered no apologies, asked no philosophical questions about their father's love or motivations. By all appearances, she was a woman detached from the telling, rather as if it were a dull play she'd learned by rote.

But Lottie saw the way her sister's fingers dug into her skirts and the way she held herself so stiffly it seemed as if she might shatter at any moment. Esther wasn't detached. She was humiliated and doing everything she could to hide it.

"He must have made a switch," Esther said at length. "He must have had replicas made. He gave the fakes to the Ferret and kept the real ones for himself."

"You should have told us." Samuel didn't spit the words at Esther, but it was a near thing.

"She has," Lottie responded in a clipped tone. Silently, she recognized that Samuel was owed an apology. They were all owed an apology. But he would not obtain it by shaming Esther in front of everyone. "It's done. Now, you may stay here and help us figure out what is next to be done, or you may join Peter for a sulk."

Samuel's eyes narrowed, and he opened his mouth, but whether he meant to argue or simply snarl at her, Lottie would never know. He glanced at Esther, his gaze falling on her hands, and the anger seemed to drain out of him.

"Fair enough," he muttered, and then he turned to Owen. "I thought the diamonds were recovered with Lady Strale."

"They were."

"Did you see them for yourself?" Lottie asked.

"Not well." He reached for the velvet pouch. "They were in something like this. We glanced inside and then set it aside. They were delivered to Strale within a few hours."

Samuel nodded. "We had casualties. And prisoners. The diamonds weren't a priority."

"They must have been replicas," Gabriel mused and then shook his head. "It doesn't make sense. We may not have noticed, but someone would have, eventually."

"One would think," Owen agreed. "But the Strale diamonds haven't been on display since the night of that ball."

"Could Strale have known?" Lottie asked him. "But why keep it a secret? Embarrassment?"

"Perhaps. Or perhaps the diamonds were immediately put away after their recovery and not taken out since." Owen tossed the bag back onto the table. "Strale was exceedingly fond of his wife. He may not have cared for a reminder of her kidnapping."

"Strale died four months ago," Samuel said.

"True, but I doubt Lady Strale is eager to put the jewels on and make herself a target again. Kidnapping makes for a good story, but it's not an experience one wants to relive."

Esther ran a finger over a piece of the tiara. "Father would have needed help for this. Beyond Gage and his men. Someone who knew the diamonds well enough to commission a convincing set of fakes."

"Not necessarily," Gabriel replied. "The Strale family jewels have been famous for over a century. There have been countless descriptions, sketches, paintings. There's likely a photograph or two about. Copies could have been made from any one of them."

"And Father needed only to fool his accomplice for the time it took to pass off the jewels," Lottie murmured. "And run away."

"And run away," Esther agreed softly. She picked up the broken bit of tiara and frowned at it. "He did this so it would fit behind the narrow frame."

That was Lottie's suspicion, as well. "Yes."

"He would have broken them all eventually. He would have removed the stones and melted down the metal so he could sell it all in bits and pieces. The artistry meant nothing to him." She looked to Owen. "I'd like to have it repaired, if possible, before you return it to the family." She waited for his nod and then set the piece of tiara down with care and scrubbed her hand against her skirts as if to clean it off. "Thank you. If you will excuse me."

∽

Samuel and Gabriel made their own excuses shortly after Esther's departure, leaving Lottie and Owen to stare at the jewels in silence.

Lottie brushed her fingers over the elaborate necklace. "It isn't revenge the man in the woods wants." She took the necklace by the clasp and held it up. "It's these."

Owen's hand came to rest on her back. "Yes, I suspect he does."

Nodding, she set the necklace atop the velvet bag. "The attacks have been sporadic. A clumsy burglary attempt, random shootings, the fire. He doesn't seek to do us bodily harm, necessarily—"

"Samuel might take exception to that."

"No doubt," she agreed with a wince. "But Samuel was shot by chance. The drapes were closed. One cannot aim through closed drapes. Do you suppose his intention has been to threaten? To scare us away? That would make sense," she continued without waiting for a reply. "If he assumed we knew of the diamonds, then he would assume we would not leave the house without them. And it would be easier to overtake a carriage than invade a house, as you've said. Particularly if he has help watching the roads."

"A reasonable theory. It is also possible he believes you remain unaware of the diamonds, and he simply wants the house vacated so he might search for them himself."

"Or search for my father's journals. My father never lived in this house. The man in the woods might assume the diamonds are hidden elsewhere, and the clues to their location are hidden in the journals."

"Also a reasonable theory." He drew his hand down her back in a careless caress that felt like a balm against raw nerves. "We've no shortage of them, it seems."

"And now we've a new one," she murmured. "My father didn't go into Gage's building for the diamonds. Or for the reward. He had what he wanted right here." She rubbed a thumb over the smooth surface of the brooch. "He really did go in for Lady Strale."

Owen was quiet for a long moment. "It would appear he did."

"That is something. That counts for something."

"It does," he agreed, and he wrapped an arm around her shoulder. "More, I think, than I would have imagined possible. Perhaps some part of him wished for redemption after all."

"Maybe he wasn't all bad," she whispered.

Owen didn't reply, and she didn't expect him to. They would likely never know for certain what her father's intentions had been. She would never know if he had truly tried, or even wished, to be a better man. *Maybe* would have to be enough.

Slowly, she began to replace the jewels in their pouch and tried not to think of how much they had cost them, how much had been lost.

"Ouch."

"What's the matter?"

"It's nothing. Brooch pricked me, that's all." She

turned her hand over to reveal a small bead of blood on her thumb. "Only a scratch."

"Here." Owen held out a handkerchief, and she accepted it absently.

"A scratch," she mumbled to herself as a new idea began to form. "Kitten."

"Beg your pardon?"

"He used Tulip for me, Kitten for Esther. What if…" Suddenly excited, she jumped up from her seat. "Wait here. Wait right here."

In a thrice, Lottie had darted to her room, gathered the letters and her supplies, and brought them back to the library.

"What are you doing?" Owen inquired over her shoulder as she got to work at the table.

"With any luck, deciphering the rest of these blasted letters. If we operate under the assumption that Ferret used a code created by my father for the purpose of leading you, and by extension him, to the Walkers, then it stands to reason that the code he used is the very same they employed during the theft of the Strale diamonds." She double-checked a piece of her work before continuing. "The keyword Father used to encrypt the whereabouts of the diamonds was Tulip. Why? I had no connection to the theft." She stopped briefly to shake her pen at him. "But Esther did. Maybe he used my nickname to hide the diamonds, because he used Esther's to steal them."

"Kitten." Owen reached for one of her papers and scowled at her when she slapped his hand away. "It's a guess."

"It's a good one," she replied, and she went back to

work. "It's a simple keyword. Easy for Gage and Ferret to remember and put to use. And a less-than-subtle reminder of Esther's skills." She paused in her frantic scribbling and took in the initial results. "It works. I can't believe it. It really works. It's the keyword."

"What does it say?"

"Very little, so far." A few words, yet, nothing more. "Give me a few minutes."

He gave her twenty, pacing back and forth behind her chair, before impatience got the better of him. "Why use the original code to encrypt the body of the letter and another for the dates?"

"Hmm? Oh, to hedge his bet, I should think. Without the keyword, you could never decipher these letters. That was a real possibility. But you could still recognize it as my father's work, or wonder if it was his work, at the very least. He was a master of encryption, after all."

"And the dates were included to ensure I did more than wonder. They ensured my cooperation in leading him to Willowbend."

"Yes, threats will do that. Also"—she stopped to read through what she'd managed to decipher so far—"he is most assuredly mad."

"Why? What does it say?"

"It's just gibberish." She waved her hands over the paper in front of her. "Threats and insults and nonsensical ramblings. Listen to this… 'I will win by force what he took by deception. I am the fox and the snare. A man will forget more easily the death of his father than the loss of his patrimony.' It's nonsense."

"Let me see." He took the seat next to her, scooted close, and bent his head over her notes. "It's Machiavelli."

"Beg your pardon?"

"He's quoting, or mangling, rather, several quotes from Machiavelli. Taken them out of context and cobbled them together like patchwork."

"Has he?" She frowned at the letter. "I've never read anything by Machiavelli." She gave him an appraising look. "You're quite a man of literature, aren't you?"

"My father was an admirer. He made me read several of his works."

"Oh. Pity. I rather like the image of you sitting in an enormous library surrounded by a sea of books." She grinned at the mental picture. "All those little pages folded down at the corners so adorably."

"Yes, well"—his head jerked up—"adorably? You said you found it intriguing."

She shrugged, enjoying the moment of silliness. "One can be intrigued by adorableness."

He grumbled something unintelligible.

"A grown man pouting is somewhat less adorable," she informed him.

"Good."

She laughed softly and then stopped abruptly as a new realization dawned. "Oh, that's it! That is *it*."

"What is what?"

"Esther said Ferret had neither a sharp mind nor an education. How, then, did he write these letters? A man of little education is unlikely to quote, however inaccurately, a seventeenth-century Italian philosopher."

"Late fifteenth, early sixteenth."

"Only proves my point. But it's more than that." She pushed the paper closer to him. "Look at the deciphered text. You said the letters had been tidied by the person charged with creating the copies, but the code itself was wholly unchanged."

Owen scanned the contents. "It's madness, as you said." His eyes narrowed. "But rather well constructed."

"Yes." She beamed at him, delighted by how quickly he spotted the pattern. "There is but one spelling error, that I can find, in almost an entire page of encryption employed by a man of little sense and education."

Owen glanced up, and a look of understanding passed between them. "He didn't write them."

"No. They're from someone else."

Another enemy, she thought. Another threat to her family. Another threat to Owen. Suddenly, the excitement that came from finally deciphering the letters drained away, and the deep chill of fear settled in her bones.

Owen slid his hand over hers. "I'll catch them, Lottie." He drew her hand to his lips and pressed a kiss to her palm. "I'm close. I swear it."

Twenty-three

HE WAS CLOSE.

Owen stayed low and kept to the shadows afforded by the thick brush and dying light of day as he picked his way over twigs and fallen leaves.

He could see the man now, thirty yards due east. His face was turned up to the rapidly clearing sky. Rethinking his decision to remain so close to the house, no doubt. But it was too late. The mistake had been made.

Owen closed half the distance between them and then stopped and weighed his options. He was tempted, sorely tempted, to put his gun away and go in with fists. He longed to feel the bastard's nose break against his knuckles. But he was a man of the law, or at least a man only one or two degrees removed from the law. He wasn't a damned vigilante, in either case. He held himself, and his men, to a higher standard.

Also, they needed answers, and individuals with broken noses were invariably difficult to understand.

He waited until the man turned his back and crouched down in front of a small stack of wood and then he moved forward, quickly but quietly, and raised his gun.

"Good evening."

His prey jumped and then went dead still. "Hell."

"Soon enough," Owen promised. "Drop the wood. Stand up, hands out. Turn about slowly. Let's have a look at you, then."

Grumbling, the man obeyed. It was the Ferret, without question. The pinched face and beady eyes were just as Esther described, only they were weighted by exhaustion. His face was drawn, his eyes deeply shadowed. No simple matter, Owen thought, for a man of the city to survive in the woods.

"Had a rough time of it, have you?"

The man curled his lip. "Not half so rough as you, eh?"

Owen considered the man, the sneer, and all the events that had led up to this moment. Then let his fist fly.

❧

"Hello, Kitten. Bring your claws?"

Ferret grinned at Esther through a bloodied lip. He was, Lottie could not help but notice, rather cheerful for a man tied to a chair in her front parlor. His smile broadened at Esther's silence, exposing a set of rotting teeth. "What, has Walker's guard dog gone lame? Always figured you for a proper bitch without a proper bite."

Lottie tensed, ready to haul her sister back from responding to the insult with force, but it was Samuel who stepped forward and delivered a smart slap to the side of their captive's head. "Mind your tongue," he growled.

The Ferret shook off the blow with a chuckle. "Fair enough. Fair enough. Just a bit of fun between old friends."

"Old friends, is it?" Esther replied sweetly. "Well then, you won't mind reminding me of your name. I seem to have forgotten it."

The Ferret puckered his swollen lips and squinted in mock concentration. "Joseph. Aye, Joseph. Always did want a biblical name."

"The Ferret it is," Samuel decided.

The Ferret wrinkled his nose in distaste. "Here now. No need for that. We can be civilized, you and me."

"You *shot* me."

The man had the gall to laugh. "An accident. God's truth. I weren't aiming for you. I don't shoot a man what don't needs it. Generally speaking."

Lottie fought back a wave of revulsion. "But you would trap a helpless animal in a burning stable."

The Ferret shook his head. "Took no pleasure in it. No pleasure. Needed you to see reason, is all. Needed you to leave the bloody house." He shot an exasperated look at Owen. "What sort of gentleman don't see the ladies to safety, I ask you?"

"The sort who understands that a stone house is easier to protect than several carriages traveling over an open road or an easily tracked train," Owen replied.

The Ferret's beady eyes shifted back and forth as he worked through the logic.

"Ah," he said at last and began bobbing his head in understanding. "You thought I meant to follow." He shrugged in the limited fashion allowed by his bindings. "Weren't planning on it."

"That is of particular use to us now," Gabriel drawled. "Thank you."

The Ferret continued on as if he'd not heard. "I figured, if a pair of you took the ladies off, the boy would follow and most of the staff. That would leave a groom or two, maybe a footman, guarding the house. And just one of you. I could handle one of you."

"Do you think?" Gabriel asked softly.

Another abbreviated shrug. "It's what I figured."

"What's in the house?" Owen asked.

The Ferret's blackened smile spread. "Diamonds, milord. The Strale diamonds. Old Will Walker hid ' em." He winked at Esther. "Didn't know that, did you?"

"Perhaps I did."

"Ah, bollocks. Those jewels ain't been sold. I'd've known. Wouldn't be a man in London what wouldn't hear of something rich as that turning up for sale. And a Walker wouldn't sit on a prize pretty as that for eight years. Not if he knew they was there." He offered Owen a conspiratorial whisper. "Ain't the patient sort, a Walker." He looked back to Esther and shook his head. "No, either you didn't know old Will took 'em diamonds, or you don't know where he hid 'em."

"Will Walker never lived in this house," Gabriel pointed out.

"But his things are here, ain't they? He were always about, scratching in those books of his." He nodded knowingly. "That's where the secret is. There's a treasure map in 'em books, there is. Lead a man right to the Strale diamonds."

He had it more right than wrong, Lottie thought, and she exchanged a concerned glance with Owen. This was too easy. The Ferret was being cooperative, even friendly. They'd not had him a quarter hour and already he was offering everything but his name. It didn't make sense.

"You tracked us from London," Samuel said. "How did you know we were coming here? Who told you?"

"Not a soul."

Owen glanced down at his scraped knuckles. "It wasn't luck."

"It was work. I watched you for weeks."

"A man has to sleep," Samuel pointed out. "He has to eat."

Gabriel nodded in agreement. "Three of us and only one of you. You weren't watching all of us all the time."

"Had a bit of luck, I did."

"No," Owen said quietly. "You had a bit of help."

"Don't know as I'd call it help. Competition. That's what it were."

"How many competitors?" he asked.

"Six, to my count. But they didn't know what they was watching you for, did they? Didn't know about old Will and his journals, or they might've tried a bit harder." His tone turned boastful, his expression smug. "It were me watching when you left town."

Lottie stifled a shiver of fear at the thought of a half-dozen nefarious characters like the Ferret watching Owen and his men from the shadows. But at least he'd come alone. "Someone set you on them. Who?"

"Can't say as I know what you're talking about."

"You're working alone then, are you?" Gabriel inquired. "You wrote the letters? Stole the artwork? Hired your competitors?" He paused to inspect a nail. "You murdered Mrs. Popple?"

"*Murder?*" He wiggled about in his chair. "There'll be none of that talk. I was to follow you, that's all. I was to follow you to Will Walker's journals. Weren't expecting to find them *with* the Walkers themselves. Word is you lot left the country ages ago."

Esther shrugged and offered another cheerful smile. "Word now is you're going to hang for murder."

He shook his head rapidly. "There'll be none of that. None of it. Here's what we do, then. You give me Walker's journals, and I'll be on my way. When I'm clear of you, I'll see the boy released. No harm done."

"What boy? What…?" Lottie turned to Esther as her heart squeezed tight. *No, no, no, no.* "Where's Peter? Where is he?"

"In the study. He's been in there all day… Oh, God." Esther paled, spun, and bolted from the room.

Lottie rounded on the Ferret. "You don't have him."

"Fine bit of luck running into the boy on the empty road. Weren't no one around far as the eye could see. Couldn't pass up a chance such as that, could I? That were hours and hours ago. And you ain't noticed the boy gone all this time."

Because he wasn't gone, Lottie told herself. Peter had gone off to sulk and they had given him the solitude he needed.

Ferret was lying. He had to be lying.

Even as she prayed for the words to be true, she knew they weren't. His confidence, his willingness to talk, it all made sense now. He knew he wasn't truly caught, not so long as he could bargain Peter's safety for his own freedom. He could leave, and without giving them a name, without giving them any idea where he might go. They would never be able to track him.

But maybe, just maybe, it was a bluff. Maybe he…

The dagger flew across her line of sight a split second before it landed with a sick thud in Ferret's upper arm.

Esther's furious shout followed a heartbeat later. "*Where is he?*"

"Ahhhh!"

"Christ Almighty, Esther!" Samuel rushed forward, wrapped his uninjured arm around Esther's waist, and hauled her off her feet. Owen plucked a second dagger from her hand.

Esther twisted in Samuel's grasp. "Put me down!"

"You can't kill him," Owen snapped, handing the dagger to Lottie.

Samuel adjusted his hold, yanking Esther higher against his chest. "If anyone is going to kill him," he said in a voice cold and hard as ice, "it will be me. Understood?"

"I'm not going to kill him. Bloody imbecile." She jabbed a finger at the Ferret. "Tell me where he is!"

Where's the money? Tell me where the money's gone!

"Esther, stop." Lottie struggled to keep her calm. "Put her down, Samuel."

"If she tries—"

"I said put her down!" She tugged her sister free and pulled her aside before she could charge their prisoner. "This is not the way, Esther."

"He will talk," Esther hissed back. "I can make him talk."

"Not like this." They were better than this, better than people like Mr. Fensley.

"But—"

"My way first. We try my way. If it doesn't work"—she took Esther's hand and slapped the handle of the dagger into her palm—"you stab him, and I will twist the blade myself."

She wouldn't. She wouldn't let it come to that.

Esther's gaze shot to the Ferret and back before her fingers curled around the handle. "You have five minutes."

"I need ten. Owen?" She motioned the men over and kept her voice down to a whisper. "We need a plan. Right now. We need—Owen, are you listening to me?"

He didn't appear to be listening. He was watching the Ferret with a strange new intensity. "Lottie, look at him. Notice anything odd?"

She studied their hostage as he alternated between whimpering at his wound and snarling at Esther. "He looks dreadful."

"No, he doesn't. Well, apart from the stabbing, he doesn't," he clarified. "He looks run-down, but he doesn't look like a Londoner who has spent days in the woods, sleeping in the rain and mud, eating what he could find or hunt. He should be exhausted, hungry, and filthy. He should look far worse than he does."

"He's had access to food and shelter," Lottie said, catching on.

"At least some of the time. I'm sure of it. And wherever he's been—"

"Is likely where we'll find Peter," she finished for him.

"And possibly the Ferret's coconspirator."

"Someone in the village?" Gabriel suggested.

"No," Owen replied. "Too many people who might notice a stranger and recognize him as the man we've asked after."

"And it's too close," Lottie added. She glanced at the Ferret and studied his drawn face and muddy coat. "He hasn't had *regular* access to food and shelter."

"Close enough to reach but too far to be a convenient daily trip," Samuel said.

Lottie suppressed a groan of fear and frustration. Not too close, but not too far. That told them nothing. Depending on terrain, roads, weather, and condition of rider and mount, the location could be anywhere in a ten- to twenty-mile radius.

Panic began to grow and nip at her control. Peter had to be terrified. He might be hurt. Someone could be hurting him *right now*. And they didn't even know where to begin looking for him.

"He could be going into another village," Esther said.

"Again, too many people," Owen replied. "Too much talk between the villages."

Too many people like Mrs. McKinsey, Lottie translated. A woman who kept an ear out and her tongue wagging around the gossip of every village within a half day's travel. But a man accustomed to the anonymity afforded by London might not be aware of how quickly talk spread in places like Wayton.

There was one way they might find out for certain.

She stepped away from the group to stand before their captive. Bending down, she faced him eye to eye. "Have you been going to a village, Ferret?"

He took two hard breaths through his nose and shook his head. "Bitch *stabbed* me."

"She did, indeed. A cottage?"

He shook his head again. "Go to hell."

"Hunting box?"

He snarled this time and bobbed his head once. "To hell."

Her voice blended with Owen's. "Hunting box."

The Ferret's pain was momentarily forgotten. "Didn't say that. I never said that."

"You did." With that one nod, he'd said it. She returned to the group. "It makes sense. A gentleman who can afford a hunting box can afford to have it stocked regularly, even if the goods go to waste."

"Maybe. If he used the box with some regularity." Owen glanced at the Ferret. "The return of the owner would be a constant risk."

"Unless he knew the owner to be away," Gabriel replied. "Or he had permission."

"We know he has an accomplice," Lottie said, keeping her voice low. "Whoever wrote those letters." The madman who wrote those letters. The man who'd strangled Mrs. Popple. Peter could be in the hands of a murderer. They had to *hurry*.

Owen nodded in agreement. "It shouldn't be difficult to narrow down where he's been going. We start with every hunting box within a twenty-mile radius."

It was easier to compile a list than Lottie expected. She couldn't hope to name everyone who lived or owned property within a twenty-mile radius of Willowbend, but families who could afford the luxury of a hunting box were families of note. Everyone knew them.

There were only five, three of which could be immediately eliminated. The Earl of Fent was four years of age and had no adult male relatives to make use of his box. The widowed Mrs. Cuttingsworth and her three young daughters were also unlikely to either use or lend their box. Baron Vabrey was a notorious miser. He would neither stock his box nor offer it to someone who might.

"That leaves Lord Brock and Mr. Edwards."

"Did your father have dealings with either?" Gabriel asked.

Lottie shook her head and gave into the urge to twist her hands into her skirts. They were so close, and still it wasn't enough. "None of which I am aware."

Esther looked to Lottie. "Lord Brock was there that night. At the Strale ball."

"He is also a particular friend of the current Lord Strale," Owen added. "The late Lord Strale was quite fond of him."

Lottie worried her lip as she considered the connection. "Sufficiently fond to have been allowed to issue invitations of his own to the Strale ball?"

"Possibly."

"That would explain how Father and I gained entry," Esther said. "And he might have kept family and staff occupied, away from an increasingly drunk Lady Strale."

"They trusted him," Owen replied. "If he told them she was being watched and cared for, they would have believed him."

Lottie strode back to the Ferret. "Lord Brock's box. Is that where you've been hiding?" she demanded.

The Ferret may have been a poor liar, but in this instance, he was a quick study. He closed his eyes, sat still as death, and said nothing.

"Mr. Edwards?" When that produced no reaction, she rattled off the other names on the list, but he gave nothing away.

Damn it. Lottie was certain she could pry the truth from him eventually. The man couldn't remain a statue forever. But it would take time they didn't have. Then again, so would riding the fifteen miles to Lord Brock's box only to find it empty.

They had to make a decision. They had to hurry. And they had to be *right*.

She turned to Owen. "What do you think?"

"Brock's first. It's the most likely choice." Owen jerked his chin at Gabriel. "Ready the horses. Send Haden and Lemke here when you've done."

The two burly groomsmen to guard the prisoner, Lottie thought. "This could all be for nothing. We could be wrong."

Oh, God. What if they were wrong?

"Find out what you can from him." He jabbed a finger at Esther. "From a distance. And have one of the men remove that dagger—"

"I'm going with you," Esther declared.

It was Samuel who answered. "No."

"It is not your decision—"

"Neither of us ride well, Esther," Lottie cut in. "We would only slow them down."

"And he won't?" Esther gestured at Samuel and then scowled at him. "You're injured."

"If I slow down," Samuel replied, "I'll be left behind. If you slow down, we all fall behind."

Esther opened her mouth to argue and then wisely snapped it shut. "Damn it. I'll help with the horses."

Preparations were completed with dizzying speed. Within minutes, Lottie was following Owen to the front door, moving down the hall in a kind of daze. Everything seemed to be moving so fast, and still not fast enough.

Owen paused at the door to give her a brief kiss. Too brief. Without thought, she grabbed his arm. "Wait."

"What is it?"

She didn't know what she wanted to say, couldn't find a way to put what she feared into words.

Owen stroked her cheek with the back of his fingers. "Trust me. I'll bring him back to you."

"You don't know that," she whispered. "You can't promise that."

"I'll bring him back, or I'll die trying."

Her heart gave one painful jolt. "That is not a comfort."

"Trust me to do my best."

"I do. I do. I only…" She wrapped her arms around him and held tight. "Come back to me. I love you. Please come back."

For a moment, he went perfectly still. Then his arms tightened around her with bruising force. "Say it again." He buried his face in her hair, his voice a rough whisper. "Before I go. Say it again."

"I'll say it again when you come back to me." She would say it then, as she had wanted to say it, with joy and wonder and shared laughter. That was how she had imagined telling him for the first time. Not like this. But she couldn't let him go without him knowing he was loved. She couldn't let him go without the truth. "I need you. You have to come back."

"A bribe." He pulled back to grin at her. "And a damn fine one."

Twenty-four

I LOVE YOU.

Neither the words nor the woman were what Owen needed to concentrate on, but there was no shaking the thoughts of either.

I love you.

Bending low in the saddle, he ducked under a tree branch that stretched across the old drover's trail. It was dangerous using this route, despite the light provided by a full moon and clear sky. The trail was riddled with ruts and rocks. There were long stretches where moonlight cut through the surrounding woods, and he and his men could guide their mounts around hazards at a punishing speed. But where the trees hemmed in tight, casting dark shadows over the path, they had no choice but to slow to a near walk.

Owen gritted his teeth at every delay. The drover's trail would cut close to a half hour off their time, even with the slower pace, but it was hell to walk when every instinct screamed at him to charge ahead full tilt.

Come back to me.

She meant it.

Actually, what she'd meant was, *Come back to me—and bring Peter*. But he couldn't think about that. He couldn't stop to wonder what it would mean for all of them if he failed.

And he sure as hell didn't want to wonder if he might already be too late.

Couldn't pass up a chance such as that, could I?

It was the Ferret's words that echoed in his head now. The man had seen an opportunity to grab a hostage and he'd taken it, but Brock may not have appreciated the initiative. Peter was a bargaining chip, but he was also a liability, someone who could identify them. There was a very real chance Brock intended to rid himself of that threat at the earliest opportunity.

❧

Even with the shortcut, it took nearly two hours to reach Brock's hunting box.

Samuel was the first to catch the scent of wood smoke and signal the others. They dismounted quickly and crept through the dappled moonlight, following a thin path at first and then a dim light flickering through the trees until they reached the modest stone structure settled deep in the woods. They circled the building on foot, assessing dangers and weaknesses. There was a single man guarding the front door and one more in back. The interior of the house appeared dark and still except for the glow of candlelight visible in one upstairs room. That's where Brock would keep Peter, off the ground floor, away from the exits.

From the cover of the shadows, Owen considered his options. The room had a balcony. The smooth stone of the old walls would be difficult to climb, but it would be even harder for a man to scale the nearest tree and launch himself onto the balcony. An agile man could probably accomplish it, but he couldn't do it quietly.

It would have to be the wall.

"Take care of the guard in the back," he told Gabriel. "Move their mounts and then climb the wall to the balcony. Samuel and I will clear the front and inside. I'll keep whoever is in the room occupied. Distract and ambush."

"Aye."

As Gabriel headed around back, Owen and Samuel stole through the trees to reach the corner of the house, just out of sight of the front guard.

He was a big man, and a restless one, lumbering back and forth along the front of the building. He went from one corner to the other, coming within just a few feet of Owen and Samuel before turning back again. In his right hand, he carried a holy water sprinkler—a large club spiked with nails. One hit and a body bled from half a dozen holes.

Owen reached for his gun, intending to threaten the man into submission, but he paused when Samuel sent him a pleading look.

Let me.

Owen considered it and then put his gun away.

It wouldn't hurt to have the guard put out of commission without a fuss.

The next time the guard reached their side of the house, Samuel stepped out from around the corner. Shock flashed across the guard's broad features a split second before he began to lift his weapon. Samuel simply grabbed him by the lapels, jerked him forward, and then delivered a brutal head butt that sent the man crumpling to the ground like a sack of flour.

"Feel better?" Owen whispered, pulling out a length of rope.

"A bit."

They left the man bound and gagged in the bushes and then slipped through a side door. Inside, the house was silent but for the shuffling of footsteps upstairs. Most of the furniture was draped in sheets and covered in a fine layer of dust.

They searched the downstairs quickly and efficiently. When every room was cleared, Samuel stepped back into the shadows at the base of the stairs to assume his position as rear guard. The last thing they needed was to be surprised by a new arrival.

Owen crept up the back steps as Peter's muffled voice floated down the hall. Relief flooded him. It took everything he had not to rush toward the sound. He willed his body to be calm, his mind clear and focused. Every decision, every move, had to be careful and deliberate. For Peter's sake, there could be no mistakes.

He checked the upstairs quickly and then stood outside the only occupied room and listened, counting voices and footsteps. The plan was to distract and ambush, and he would provide the distraction. He would make himself a target. But it was always nice to know how many armed individuals would be aiming in one's direction before one walked through the door.

There were at least two other men in the room with Peter.

Could be worse, Owen thought, and he took a steadying breath. Gun in hand, he pushed through the door and quickly took stock of his surroundings—a small bedroom, plenty of light, limited furniture. And standing near the balcony doors behind Peter was not Lord Brock as expected but the young Lord Strale. Next to him was another large guard.

All three occupants jumped at the intrusion. The guard pulled a large blade from under his coat. Strale positioned himself squarely behind Peter, lifted a gun already in his hand, and held it to the boy's head. "Stay where you are." He held back his man with a subtle gesture. "Everyone stay where you are."

Owen sized up his opponents. Strale wasn't tall—his blond head barely topped Peter's—but he was large boned, and years of excess had given him a wide build that left him exposed on either side of his makeshift shield. A sallow countenance and furtive, bloodshot eyes gave credence to the rumor of an opium habit. He was sneering, appearing more amused than afraid at the sudden turn of events. But the confident demeanor was an act. The hand holding the gun trembled, and there was a visible twitch in his left eye. This was a man hanging on to sanity by a thread and doing a poor job of hiding it.

His silent companion looked quick, mean, and in complete possession of his wits. Tall and lean, with a thin scar down his left cheek, he had the hollow-eyed stare of a man who had long ago unburdened himself of a conscience.

"I'm not moving, Strale," Owen replied calmly. "Are you injured, Peter?"

The young man shook his head. His face was pale, his clothes showed the wear of a long, hard ride, and he was bound at the hands and feet, but he looked otherwise uninjured.

"Peter, is it?" Strale asked with great interest. "Do you know, he wouldn't say. He's Walker's boy, isn't he? I thought perhaps a grandson or nephew. But, no." He leaned forward just a hair and snarled in Peter's ear. "You've your father's look about you." His lip curled in disgust. "And his stench."

"Why don't you let go of the boy?" Owen suggested. "Let us settle this as gentlemen."

Strale straightened again and cocked his head. "You want the boy? I want Will Walker's journals."

"I have them." Owen reached inside his coat and pulled out a leather journal. "But it's the diamonds you really want, isn't it?"

The eye twitch intensified. "You found them?"

"Maybe. You'll never know if you shoot me or Peter."

Strale seemed to consider the possibility and then shook his head. "You don't know where they are," he decided, but he didn't move the gun. Clearly, he wasn't ready to completely dismiss the idea that Owen had information he might need. "Slide the journal across the floor."

"Let Peter go."

"The journal first."

Owen slipped the book back into his pocket. "It would appear we are at an impasse."

Strale jerked his chin at the guard. "Take it off him."

Owen raised his own gun and leveled it at the second man. "I don't think so."

"If you shoot him," Strale warned with mock regret, "I'll be forced to shoot the boy."

"Then you won't get your diamonds."

"Yes, my diamonds. They are *my* diamonds," Strale replied impatiently, as if explaining something to a dim-witted child. "You've no claim to them. So, why don't you give me what's mine, and in exchange, I'll not put a bullet hole through what's yours, and there is an end to the matter."

"They are yours," Owen agreed easily, as if they were holding a perfectly polite, perfectly ordinary conversation. He needed to keep that conversation going, find a way to pull the man away from Peter, and give Gabriel time to reach the balcony. "Which leads me to wonder why you went to such lengths to steal them eight years ago. Debt, was it?"

"I can't see how that's any of your concern. But yes." He rolled his eyes and sighed. "If you *must* know, it was debt."

And just like that, the very thin hope Owen had retained that he might be able to safely exchange Peter for the journals was gone. Strale was already in over his head. He wouldn't admit to the crime of his stepmother's kidnapping if he had any intention of leaving his enemies alive to tell the tale.

"Didn't your father provide for you?" he asked. "By all accounts, he was a generous man."

Owen wasn't aware of a single account that marked the late Lord Strale as either generous or miserly, but the lie succeeded in further loosening Strale's tongue.

"Generous?" Strale forced out a bark of laughter. "Miserly goat gave me a thousand pounds a year." He used his free hand to smooth the front of his coat with dramatic flair. "And there are appearances to maintain."

"So you hired Walker to steal the diamonds."

"I hired Gage. He sent me Walker and his daughter. They could blend in at the ball."

"Gage betrayed you. He made a fool of you."

Strale snorted and, as Owen suspected, denied the insult. "Gage did as he was told."

"It was your idea to kidnap your stepmother?"

"I could get more for her than I could the diamonds," he replied without a hint of shame. "Even more for both."

"Didn't work out quite as you had hoped, though, did it?"

The twitch returned as Strale became more agitated. "Paste," he spat, and he snarled against Peter's cheek. "Your whoreson of a father left me with *paste*."

"And no one noticed? All these years, and no one but you knew the diamonds were fakes?"

Strale said nothing, but his face flushed with the heat of old anger and humiliation.

"Ah." Owen drew the word out, just a little. "Your father figured it out. Because it was you who issued the invitations to the ball. You who promised Lady Strale was being cared for that night. What did he do when he discovered his son was a common thief and kidnapper? Not a proud moment for any father."

The confident facade slipped a little further, and Strale finally turned the gun on Owen. "Shut up."

"He paid your debts, didn't he? Then he put the paste jewels away for good, so no one else would know what you'd done. Just the two of you. I wager he wielded that knife often and well."

No doubt, he'd used that knife to keep his son in line. Strale hadn't been imprisoned nor pushed to desperate measures after years of failing to find the Walkers. He'd come for the diamonds now because, for the first time in years, he no longer had a mistrustful and powerful father watching over him like a hawk.

Eight years, Owen thought. Eight years of being trapped under the thumb of a father he detested. And all because he'd been outsmarted by Will Walker, a common man. A lowly criminal.

That was a long time for humiliation and bitterness to fester. Plenty of time for it to grow into something sinister, something deadly. The recent opium habit had likely pushed him over the edge.

"Did you kill him?" Owen asked. "The way you killed Mrs. Popple?"

Strale's angry expression softened, and his mouth curved into a sly smile. "My father died in his sleep. *Everyone* knows that. He simply…stopped breathing."

"A pillow to the face will do that."

"Well"—Strale returned his aim to Peter and pointedly tapped the muzzle of the gun against the boy's head—"one does grow weary of waiting."

Owen tensed as Peter squeezed his eyes shut. He had to divert Strale's attention, keep him focused on something other than his captive. And he needed to push him into making a mistake. But it was a fine line between antagonizing a madman into switching targets and antagonizing a madman into shooting.

"And Mrs. Popple? Did you grow weary of her?"

"No, not at all," Strale drawled with affected feeling. "*Lovely* woman, our Mrs. Popple. Poor dear fell and hit her head... I'm not a monster," he offered almost as an afterthought, and then he proceeded to wag the gun back and forth as if it was an extension of his hand. "I don't go about murdering people *willy-nilly*."

"You strangled her."

"Only a little. I wanted answers. She knew where to find the Walkers. And the Walkers knew where to find the journals."

Only a little. Christ. "She didn't know."

"No? Ah, well, you did." Strale's face lit with giddy humor. "Oh, Walker *did* like bragging to the son of a duke. He was ever so eager to tell me how he was keeping Scotland Yard out of our hair. Pretending to help Detective Inspector Renderwell with those tricky ciphers. That's how I knew my letters—after I caught your attention—would force you to lead me to Will Walker's journals. They were written in a cipher of his own making, with my own clever twist, of course—"

Strale and his man both flinched and whipped their heads around at the sound of the balcony doors lightly rattling.

Gabriel. Finally.

Strale's gaze flew back to Owen. "Your men, I suppose?" He jerked his chin at the quiet man. "Get rid of them."

The guard adjusted his grip on his blade as he strode to the balcony and pushed open the doors.

Owen shifted, ready to charge when Gabriel came rushing inside.

But only the wind blew in.

The guard stepped outside, looked about, and stepped back in again. "Nothing there."

Owen swore silently and viciously. Gabriel must have run into trouble, been delayed somehow. A surprise ambush was no longer possible. With the balcony doors left cracked open, there was no way for Gabriel to sneak up without being heard. He'd have to climb up the damned tree.

Strale turned suspicious eyes on Owen. "You came without your men?"

"You shot one of my men."

"That wasn't me. Where is the other one? Sir Gabriel."

"I couldn't leave two women and a wounded man unguarded, could I? Not with your man still lurking in the woods."

"Slippery fellow, isn't he?" Strale teased. "Extraordinarily useful chap."

"Did you use him to kill Walker and pin the murder on Gage?" Owen asked. He had to keep stalling, keep pushing. "Or did you take care of the matter yourself?"

"Regrettably, it was Gage who had the pleasure of pulling the trigger. Shot Walker in the back as he ran." His eyes danced with unholy glee. "I heard the bastard made it four blocks carrying the duchess before he fell."

"Four and a half. How did he get in?"

For the first time, Strale laughed with real humor. The unnatural sound sent a chill down Owen's back. "The front door," Strale chortled. "Idiot talked his way in the *front door*. He said he'd hidden the diamonds. Left their location in an encrypted letter and left the letter with someone he could trust. If we let the duchess go, he'd send us the letter."

"You didn't like the deal?"

"I agreed to it. Gage did as well, until Walker made it to the street, and then he changed his mind."

Gage hadn't changed his mind. It had been a lesson and a message. No one crossed Horatio Gage. "He didn't expect Walker to keep moving."

"I don't know. Frankly, I don't *care*. My only regret is that I didn't follow Walker and watch him bleed to death on the sidewalk like a dog. Happily, I can still relive the experience through his son." He turned the gun on Owen once more. "The journals. Now. Or I kill you first and let Jim here pluck the journals from your corpse."

"Grown weary of me, have you?"

"Oh, quite."

They were out of time. Talking had nudged Strale a little closer to losing control—remembering Walker's betrayal and his father's crushing dominance had brought him to the brink. But he wasn't quite where Owen needed him. He needed one more push. He needed Strale to make just one mistake. And he needed Gabriel to be in position.

"Well, as I said, it's not the journals you want." He pulled a single diamond earring from his pocket and held it up. "It's the diamonds."

Strale's eyes grew as round as saucers. The twitch grew into a full-blown spasm, and his cheeks turned scarlet as he gazed at the glittering diamonds with wild desire. And no small amount of loathing.

They weren't just jewels to him, Owen thought.

They were the symbol of betrayal. A reminder of his humiliation. He hated them every bit as much as he craved them.

"You do have them." Strale licked his lips. "You found them."

"I found them. I have some of them with me. If you want to know where to find the rest, you'll let Peter go."

"Give me your knife," Strale snapped at Jim. "Bring it to me!" He snatched the blade out of Jim's hand and shoved the gun at him. "Now," he barked at Owen, and he brought the point of the blade to Peter's ear. "You give me what you have, or I start giving you the boy in bits and pieces."

And there it was. The mistake. No man in his right mind traded a gun for a knife.

"All right." Owen held up both hands. "All right. You can have them"

"See what he has," Strale ordered Jim. "Search him. I have waited years for this. *Years*." He tapped the flat of the blade against Peter's cheek. "Your father loses after all."

Jim aimed his gun at Owen. "Gun on the floor. Kick it 'ere."

Owen crouched, set down his gun, and then rose smoothly and kicked the weapon across the room. It slid across the floor and under the bed, out of his opponent's reach.

"No matter to me," Jim commented with a shrug. "What I need two for? Keep your 'ands where I can see 'em." He made a prompting motion with his left hand as he approached. "Give me the bauble, then."

Owen held up the earring as Jim stepped closer.

It was now or never.

The moment Jim reached for the piece of jewelry, Owen dropped it, caught the man by the wrist, and yanked him forward. He sidestepped Jim's lurching form, threw a kidney punch to his exposed back, and then knocked Jim's legs out from under him with a hard kick to the back of the knee. Jim twisted as he fell, bringing the gun around, but Owen caught his wrist again and twisted with enough force to break bone. The man relinquished the weapon with a howl of pain. The noise blended with the sound of Samuel charging down the hall and Strale's bellow of fury.

"No! Stop it! Stop!"

Jim leaped back to his feet and swung wide with his good arm. Owen dodged, balled his fist, and sent him to the ground again just as Samuel stepped inside.

Leaving Samuel to keep Jim on the floor, he turned his attention to Strale.

"Stop!" Strale pressed the knife to Peter's throat. "Stop or I kill the boy!"

Owen aimed the gun at Strale, but he didn't have a clear shot and couldn't risk hitting Peter. "Let him go, Strale. You're surrounded. Your men can't help you, and your mounts are gone. There's no way out of this."

"No. *No.* You think I'll let a Walker have the diamonds again?"

"The diamonds will be returned to your family."

"He still wins," Strale all but bellowed. "If I lose, he wins. You think I'll let that happen *again*?"

He didn't have a choice. All he had was a knife.

Even if he managed to make it out of the house using Peter as a shield, there was nowhere for him to go, no way for him to escape the area. He had lost, and he knew it. Owen saw the moment Strale accepted it. Accepted that he had been bested. A dark and terrifying resolve settled over his features.

Owen took a cautious step forward. "Walker is dead. You can't best a dead man, and there is nothing to be gained by the attempt."

"Oh, but I *can*, and there is," Strale hissed. "If I can't have what's mine," he lifted the knife over Peter's head, the lethal blade glinting in the candlelight, "I'll have something of his."

He swung the knife down just as a shot rang out from the balcony. Strale jerked, released Peter, and stumbled back with a scream. Red bloomed through the side of his coat.

Gabriel had taken his shot. Astonishingly, he'd spotted his target between the crack in the balcony doors and hit the only mark that would disable Strale without injuring Peter. Owen rushed forward as Peter dove out of the way.

Strengthened by madness and fury, Strale was still standing and still gripping the knife. Owen didn't give him the chance to use it. Catching Strale around the middle, he used momentum to bring them both to the ground. Strale landed hard on his back, but he managed to turn the knife in his hand and plunge the blade toward Owen's chest.

Rearing back, Owen caught Strale's arm at the last second and slammed it to the floor.

There was a crash on the balcony, and Gabriel came

rushing inside. He reached them just as Owen snatched the knife from Strale's hand and tossed it aside.

"Have him?" Samuel called out from where he was standing with his foot on Jim's neck.

"Almost." Owen pinned down Strale's other flailing arm. Gabriel yelped and yanked his hand away from Strale's snapping teeth.

"Damn it, he's a biter." Gabriel reared back and delivered a powerful blow to Strale's jaw, stunning the man just long enough for them to roll him over and secure the manacles.

Owen took a seat on Strale's back, effectively subduing the man's renewed struggles. He threw Gabriel a hard look. "You climbed the damned tree, didn't you? What happened to the plan?"

"The wall's crumbling. I had to improvise." Gabriel shook his hand, hissing through his teeth, and then stared down at the mild injury with utter disgust. "I *hate* it when they bite."

"Number six, my friend," Samuel noted with conspicuous pleasure. "You just need a few more."

"Would you like to come over here and try for number seven? I'd be happy to give you that fifth bullet."

Owen listened to his men trade threats and insults while Strale howled and cursed and bucked beneath him. He would miss this, he thought with a grin. He no longer wanted the rest of it. He was done with the danger, the violence, the constant need to be on guard.

But he would miss *this*.

"Come on, then, Peter." He jerked his chin at Gabriel, signaling him to take charge of their prisoner. "Let's get you home."

Twenty-five

PETER WAS THE FIRST THROUGH THE FRONT DOOR AT Willowbend and the first into Lottie's arms. She hugged him close and let the healthy warmth of him seep in to chase away the chill of terror that had settled in her bones. "You're not hurt? You're not injured?"

"Not a scratch between us," Owen assured her.

With a small cry of relief, she relinquished her brother to Esther and flew into Owen's waiting arms. Uncaring of their audience, she buried her face in the fabric of his coat and breathed in the familiar scent of him while her trembling hands moved over his back, down his arms, across his chest. She needed to touch him, needed to feel him whole and hale.

"Your men?" She heard Esther ask. "…Samuel? He was injured, and…"

"Safe."

"I'm sorry." Peter's voice was thick with remorse and swallowed tears. "I'm so sorry. For everything. I'm sorry. I—"

Lottie turned her head in time to see Esther cut off the next apology with her own enveloping embrace and then follow it up with a sound slap to his arm. "What were you thinking, trying to capture a murderer on your own?"

"Ow." Peter rubbed his shoulder and then shook his head vehemently. "I wasn't. God's truth, I wasn't. I thought to ride to Wayton and send a wire to Michael's father."

"Your friend at school?"

Owen explained for him. "Michael's father is Inspector Ernswot of Scotland Yard."

"I thought he could help," Peter whispered. "I thought, if he sent more men, we could catch the man in the woods. I thought…"

"You thought to protect your sisters," Owen finished for him. His hand moved over Lottie's back in soothing circles. "Esther, would you mind…?"

Esther wrapped an arm around Peter's shoulder. "Let's get something warm in you. We can sort everything out later."

Lottie didn't watch them go. She squeezed her eyes shut and tried to will away the shivers that raced over her skin. "I might have lost you," she whispered as every dark possibility of what might happen, every horrible, worst-case scenario she'd managed to hold at bay for hours flooded her mind all at once. She'd been so careful not to think of them, so careful to focus on drawing information out of the silent Ferret. But there was no holding back the fear now. "I could have lost both of you."

Owen caught her hands and held them against his chest. "You didn't. I'm here, Lottie. Look at me, now. I'm here."

"You're here." And Peter was with Esther. And she was here too, standing in her foyer with the man she loved. She freed one of her hands to dash away an errant tear. "We're here."

The dark images faded. For once, she thought, everything really was all right. Probably. "Where are your men?"

"With Strale and his men. They'll wire London and wait—"

"Strale? Lord Strale?"

Keeping a firm arm around her waist, Owen led her into the front parlor and took a seat next to her on the settee.

Exhausted to the very core, she rested her head against his shoulder while he related the events of the night. He explained Lord Strale's involvement and then his own plan to see justice served without endangering the Walker family.

"Strale and his men are entitled to a trial," Owen told her, "but Strale is unlikely to insist upon it. England is not in the habit of hanging its peers, but even the unlikely chance of a death sentence is a possibility he'll want to avoid. He'll accept incarceration out of the country, as will the men he hired."

"And if they won't?"

He hitched up one shoulder. "I doubt her majesty will concern herself with their whinging."

"You're certain?"

"The queen doesn't care for scandals. The quiet removal of a disgraced duke and his cohorts is more to her taste. Also, I can offer her a boon."

"What boon?"

"My retirement. She doesn't care for scandals, as I said, and a viscount employed as a private investigator does raise eyebrows."

She sat up to look at him. "You mean to retire?"

"I do. I have for some time. I've sufficient funds to keep my family comfortable, and I'd like to see what the idle life has to offer. Peace, I should hope."

"Oh. I see." It seemed as if she should add something of substance to that remark, but all she could think to say was, "Now what?"

"Well, there are a few details left. I imagine we'll find the missing artwork in the hunting box or in one of Strale's holdings. We'll need to find out if Brock was involved in any way; though, at this point, he doesn't appear to have been. Gabriel can track down the other men hired to follow us in London and make certain the Ferret's claims of their ignorance holds true. And I'll send Samuel to speak with Mrs. Popple's sister. He's good at that sort of thing."

"No, I meant…" She forced herself to meet his eyes. "What do *we* do now? Us."

"Ah." Cocking his head, he studied her. "What would you like for us?"

"I should like…very much…" For a fair bit more courage, just now. "To see you again."

He smiled at that and, reaching up, stroked her cheek with the back of his fingers. "You could see me every day, if you agreed to become my wife."

"Your *wife*?"

"Hmm." He gave her a teasing half smile. "But you have to ask me first."

"You're not serious."

"I am. I want to be wooed."

"That is not what I meant. Owen..." She shook her head at him. "You can't have a viscountess like me."

"I can. If you'll let me."

"You would be living a lie." It was little trouble for her to do so. She was accustomed to leading a fictitious life. He was not. "Married to a woman with a false name and a fabricated past."

"I would be married to *you*. And we would be the reclusive Lord and Lady Renderwell of Greenly House—or we can make our home on the Continent, if it suits us. Whatever we need. Whatever you like. But first..." Leaning close, he cupped her face in his hands. "You promised me something."

"I did?"

"You did." He kissed her softly and then whispered against her lips, "Say the words. I came back. Say them."

She closed her eyes and covered his hands with her own. "I love you," she whispered back, and when she felt his mouth curve into a smile, she said them again, just for the pleasure of it, just for the pleasure of feeling his smile. "I love you. I think I have always loved you." She smiled back. "Even when I wanted your head on a pike."

He laughed at that, and she thought, *Yes. Oh, yes.* Here was the laughter and the joy she had wanted, and it was every bit as wonderful as she had imagined.

"And I, you," Owen said. "Without the pike bit." He pulled back and dipped his head to catch and hold her gaze. "I don't love everything you have done, and I can't promise to love everything you will do, or that you will love everything I do. But I love the person you are, the person I have always known, and the person you will be. I can promise that."

"I can promise that too."

"Then trust us. Trust us to make this work. To make each other happy. To keep each other safe. Trust love."

Love. A life with Owen. No secrets, no fear, no lies. Just love. It was a dream she'd never dared to hope for, a life she'd always imagined outside her grasp. But here it was, hers to have, to cherish, to keep. All she needed was the courage to grab hold.

"I do. I do trust us." This time, it was she who reached out and took his face in her hands. "Owen Renderwell, will you marry me?"

"I don't know." He brought her hands down and made a face at her empty palms. "I believe a ring is the fashion. You don't appear to have one."

"True," she replied with laughter of her own. "But if you say yes, I'll let you buy me something quite nice." She considered that a moment. "But not a diamond."

"Not diamonds," he agreed. He pressed a kiss to her fingers. "Yes, I will marry you, Charlotte Walker-Bales, if you'll have me."

"I will. I absolutely will. And you'll have me. Always."

Read on for a sneak peek from

A Gift for Guile

1872

"HELLO."

Hello. Quite possibly the single most innocuous comment in the whole of the English language. Under nearly any circumstance, it was difficult to take exception to the word *hello*. Unless, of course, it happened to be uttered in the wrong place, at the wrong time, by the wrong man. In which case, that one simple word spelled disaster.

Esther Walker-Bales stood amid the bustling crowd of Paddington station and, for several long seconds, did nothing but stare through the thick crepe of her weeping veil at the man who had greeted her so unexpectedly. Sir Samuel Brass. All six feet and three and a half enormous inches of him.

"I said…" Samuel leaned forward to tower over her, his deep voice edging toward a growl. "Hello, Esther."

His misguided attempt at intimidation goaded her into action. "What are you *doing* here?" she demanded, then shook her head once. "No, never

mind. It doesn't matter. You have to go. Right now."
She gave him a discreet push. "Go."

He didn't budge an inch.

"No." Straightening, he flicked the edge of her veil
with his fingers. "Who died? A husband? A father?"

No one had died, and he damn well knew it.
"An interfering acquaintance of mine. A woman
threw him on the tracks at"—she looked pointedly
at the station clock behind him—"eight minutes
past six."

"You've taken the death to heart, I see. I'm touched."

She was tempted to touch him with the dagger she
had strapped to her ankle. "You have to leave."

"No. What are you doing in London?"

"Standing on platform number one in Paddington
station."

His smile grew a little more strained. "Why are you
standing in Paddington station?"

"I like trains." As if on cue, a locomotive began its
laboring journey out of the station, sending a billow of
smoke and steam to the ornate ironwork above. Just
the sight of it made her throat itch and eyes water. She
didn't like trains especially.

"Right." Samuel threw a quick look over his shoulder at a noisy group of passengers. "We're leaving."

"No, I can't."

"Why not?"

She gathered her own meager supply of patience.
"Samuel, listen to me. I will tell you everything you
wish to know." Some of it, anyway. "But not right
now. Please, if you won't leave entirely, then at least
go…" She waved her hand in the direction of an

empty, and distant, alcove. "Stand over there. Pretend you don't know me."

"God, if only," he muttered. "Esther, you will tell me what is going on, or I will haul you out of here. Over my shoulder if necessary."

He could probably get away with it. Samuel had been a police officer once. He'd since left the police with his friends to become a private investigator to the wealthy and well connected, but he retained some notoriety. If the crowd in the station recognized him, no one would move to stop his departure, however unorthodox, with an unknown woman.

Still, Esther didn't think he would risk the attention for the same reason she wouldn't risk leaving her hotel without the veil. She couldn't afford to be seen. "You'll not make a scene."

"I will take a thirty-second scene over arguing with you indefinitely." He cocked his head at her. "Do you doubt me?"

Yes. Or maybe no. Damn it, she couldn't tell if he was bluffing. "I'm waiting for someone."

"Who?"

"It is not your concern." She half turned away, giving him her shoulder and, hopefully, giving the impression to passing travelers that the two of them were not together. As Samuel was staring right at her, however, she feared it was a futile gesture. "*Please.* Go away."

"Are you waiting on a mark?" he guessed. "An accomplice?"

"What? No. I'm not a criminal." Not anymore. Not for a long time.

"Then you've no reason for secrecy. For whom are you waiting?"

"My lover."

"Try again."

She honestly didn't know if she was pleased or insulted by how quickly he dismissed the idea. "I don't know. And I'll not find out if you stay here. *Go. Away.*"

This last she punctuated by turning her back on him completely.

And that was when she saw him—a scrawny young man of maybe sixteen, with a long face, sallow complexion, sharp chin, and filthy blond hair peeking out from under a ragged cap. He stood ten yards away and was staring at her as if he'd known her all his life. Only he didn't. Esther had never seen him before. And he couldn't possibly see her clearly behind the veil.

She sensed Samuel tense behind her. "Is that him?" he asked.

"I don't know."

The boy's gaze flew to Samuel, then he spun about and bolted in the opposite direction.

"Damn it," Esther hissed.

Samuel brushed past her with a curt, "Stay here."

The ensuing chase was oddly subdued, with the young man's escape hampered by the crowd and Samuel slowed by his apparent unwillingness to draw attention to himself. Esther knew him to be quick and agile, particularly for such a large man. He would have no trouble running the boy down under normal circumstances, but today he strode after his prey in long, unhurried strides, neatly sidestepping people and luggage alike.

Grab him, she thought, heart racing. *Grab him!*

Samuel stretched out an arm, but the young man dodged left, dashed to the edge of the platform, and leaped into the path of an oncoming engine. Nearby onlookers sent up a cry of alarm, but the young man was over the tracks and out of danger in the blink of an eye. Samuel, on the other hand, was trapped on her side of the station, his path blocked by the long line of passenger carriages behind the engine.

For a moment, Esther thought he might hop on one of the moving carriages and pass through the other side to continue the pursuit. In fact, she rather hoped he would. She'd not wanted him there, but since he'd been the one to scare the young man off, the least he could do was bring him back.

But Samuel casually turned away from the platform edge as if he'd merely been a curious bystander, and began a leisurely stroll back to her.

The young man was gone.

Esther balled her hands at her sides. Oh, this was awful. This was a dreadful, dreadful mess. Seething, she waited for Samuel's return and wholeheartedly wished he could see her look of derision through the veil. "I *knew* you wouldn't make a scene." And because of it, the young man had been able to dash away.

His gray eyes narrowed dangerously, but he didn't respond other than to say, in the stiffest manner possible, "Shall we, Miss Bales?"

He offered his arm.

She glowered at it. Then she headed for the exit on her own.

Samuel fell into step beside her, and to her chagrin, his large hand came up to settle lightly at the small of her back, herding her out of the station and to a public hackney.

"I've rooms at the Anthem Hotel," she told him.

He didn't comment. Instead, he simply assisted her inside the carriage, spoke to the driver briefly, then climbed in after her.

The instant the door was closed and the curtains drawn, Esther lifted the stifling crepe veil and scowled at him. "How the devil did you find me?"

"I followed you."

"What? All the way from Derbyshire?"

"No, I tracked you from Derbyshire." The carriage started with a soft jolt and he pulled back the edge of a curtain for a glimpse outside. "I followed you from your hotel."

"How did you know where I was staying?" It might have been easy to find out that she'd boarded a train headed for London the day before yesterday, but he couldn't have known where she'd gone after that.

"London has a finite number of hotels."

As *finite* didn't necessarily mean *small*, she decided not to ask how long he'd been looking. "You shouldn't have come after me."

"I had no choice." He let the curtain fall back into place. "You snuck away in the dead of night."

"What rot. I departed from my own home at half past five in the morning in full view of my staff." That wasn't anywhere near the same thing as sneaking.

"You sent no word to your family."

"Nor was I obligated to do so." Her brother, Peter, was sixteen years old and away at school, and her older sister, Lottie, was traveling with her husband, Viscount Renderwell, in Scotland. It wasn't as if they might pay an unexpected call upon her little cottage and be shocked to find her missing.

"They'll worry," Samuel said. "London isn't safe for you."

She didn't need him to point that out. "Of course they'll worry. That's why I didn't send word. And neither will you. You'll keep this to yourself."

"Lottie has a right to know."

"She does not. Lottie is my sister, not my mother. I am twenty-eight years of age. I keep my own house and I may take leave of it anytime I please." She gave him a taunting smile. "I may even sneak out of it if I like."

❧

Samuel studied the small woman sitting across from him. She wasn't beautiful by traditional standards, but the flaxen hair, heart-shaped face, ivory skin, and wide blue eyes lent her an air of angelic innocence. An impression that was otherwise wholly undeserved.

Miss Esther Bales, formally Walker, was the youngest daughter of the late William Walker, one of England's most infamous criminals until Scotland Yard had tracked him down thirteen years ago. Confronted with evidence of his crimes, Walker had agreed to turn informant in exchange for his freedom and a chance at redemption.

Only he'd not given up his old life. Will Walker

had kept up his criminal activities in secret, and Esther had helped him.

Though he suspected she'd be surprised to hear it, Samuel didn't hold it against her. She'd been hardly more than a girl at the time. He didn't fault her for foolishly trying to help her bastard of a father. Moreover, he believed she regretted it.

No, it wasn't Esther's past as Will Walker's daughter that drew his ire. It was her stubborn refusal to become anything more, anything better, anything *other* than Will Walker's daughter.

Esther cocked her head at him. "If you think to unnerve me by staring at me for the whole of our trip, you are bound for disappointment."

He rather doubted she'd have mentioned his staring if it didn't unnerve her. To test his theory, he sat back against the thin cushions of the bench and went right on staring.

She folded her arms across her chest and stared right back.

She had spine, he'd give her that.

It was tempting to see how long she could hold out, but a battle of wills fought in silence wasn't in his best interest. He wanted answers. "Who was the man at the station?"

She matched his clipped tone. "I honestly do not know."

"Why did you come to London?"

"I've already answered that."

"No, you refused to answer."

"No, my answer did not meet with your satisfaction, but that is your misfortune, not mine."

Samuel was not a man given to speeches, even small ones. He preferred an economy of words over lengthy discourse. In fact, sometimes a simple grunt was sufficient to get one's point across. But there were times when nothing short of a lecture would do.

"You wish to speak of misfortune, Esther? Then let us speak of the misfortunes you court in coming to London. Nine years ago, your family was forced to leave town under assumed names in order to hide from men who might strike at you in revenge against your father. Last year, one of those men found you, nearly killed you and your sister in a stable fire, shot me in the shoulder, and kidnapped your brother."

Esther did not appear to appreciate his oratory efforts.

"Heavens, I'd quite forgotten," she drawled in a voice that could only be described as sweetly caustic. "Thank *goodness* you are here to remind me of all the little details of my life."

God, she was infuriating. "If you don't wish to be spoken to like a fool, don't act like one."

She rolled her eyes at that and half stood in the carriage as if to knock on the ceiling. "Oh, this is all quite pointless. I'm leaving."

Leaning forward, he caught her fist before it could connect. "Sit down."

She went utterly still but for a gentle sway in time with the rolling carriage. She didn't struggle or shout or try to pull her hand away. She didn't so much as bat an eyelash. She simply remained as she was, so close he could smell the rose-scented soap on her skin, and regarded him through cool blue eyes.

"Let go of me."

There wasn't a trace of anger or fear in her voice. It was low and steady and, like the rest of her, perfectly calm. Unnaturally calm. Like the eerie quiet before a storm.

Samuel risked a quick glance at the hem of her skirts. She likely had at least one dagger strapped to her ankle. Her father's favorite role for her had been that of henchman.

When she didn't immediately reach for her weapons, he looked up again and discovered that, although her expression remained devoid of any emotion, an unsettling shadow had fallen over her pretty blue eyes.

"I am not going to stab you," she said quietly.

He wasn't sure why he felt like a brute all of a sudden, as if he'd bruised her somehow.

He released her hand with more care than was probably necessary. "Take your seat. We're almost there."

She sat down slowly, and with a subdued air about her that he found as unsettling as the shadow. "My hotel is at least another ten minutes away. I would prefer to procure my own transport."

"We're not going to your hotel."

That announcement had her perking up a little. "You cannot mean to take me all the way to Derbyshire in a public hackney."

"We're not going to Derbyshire. My house is in Belgravia." On the very, very, uttermost edge of it, which was the only slice of Belgravia he could afford without begrudging the cost. He'd just as soon live elsewhere, but his work sometimes required he entertain clientele at his home, and his clientele were the sort of men and women who expected to be entertained in homes with fashionable addresses.

"Why are we going to your house?"

"I imagine you can figure that out. I'll send someone to the hotel for your things."

Now she looked quite like her bristly self again. "No. Absolutely not. I am not staying with you. It isn't decent."

"Isn't *decent*?" Of all the arguments a woman like Esther might produce, *it isn't decent*, had to be among the most absurd. "You cannot be serious."

"I'll not be a source of gossip for your staff."

"We'll tell them you're my cousin."

"People marry their cousins."

"Then we'll tell them you're a client." She wouldn't be the first individual with an assumed name to spend time under his roof. Granted, she'd be the first woman to do so, but his servants were accustomed to the peculiar necessities of his work. Not one of them would bat an eye at her presence, nor breathe a word of it outside of the house. He had chosen each member of his staff with extraordinary care.

"Do your female clients often spend the night?"

He almost told her yes, just to put an end to the argument. And he very much wanted this argument to end. The carriage was already rolling to a stop in front of his house. But the lie would probably bring him more grief than it was worth.

"What does it matter what my staff thinks?" he asked. "You'll never see them again."

"It isn't just your staff. Lottie will find out. And so will Peter. Lord knows you'll tell Renderwell and

Gabriel. And Renderwell's sisters might hear of it, which means his mother certainly will, and she'll tell everyone in the village and—"

"All right. All right." Bloody hell. "I'll take you to the hotel after I'm done here."

He imagined that, given the circumstances, Esther's immediate family wouldn't much care that she'd spent the night under his roof, but he couldn't be absolutely certain of it. And damned if he had to haul the dratted woman all the way back to Derbyshire, only to be subjected to a lecture on decorum from the Walkers, of all people, for his troubles.

Resigned, he threw open the carriage door, hopped down, and offered Esther his hand.

She wouldn't take it. "I am not going in with you."

"Fine. Keep the doors shut and the curtains drawn. If you attempt to run off, I will return you to your family trussed up like a duck."

She gave him a pretty smile. "What if I've a mind to run off to Derbyshire?"

He growled at her, because sometimes a grunt wouldn't suffice.

She reached out, grabbed the handle, and closed the door in his face.

He wasn't particularly worried that Esther might try to run away. If she wanted to escape, she'd have tried at the station. Still, he thought it prudent to flip the driver an extra coin.

"Wait here." He thought about it, then added another coin. "Ignore everything the lady tells you."

Two

THERE HAD BEEN A TIME, NOT SO VERY LONG AGO, when Samuel could expect to be greeted at his door by one of his maids. She would take his coat and hat, make polite inquiries after his day, and inform him that all was well in the house. Then he'd been left alone to go about his business in peace.

Oh, how he missed those times.

There was no one waiting for him in the foyer that evening. He tossed his hat and gloves on a side table and winced when a great crash arose from the other end of the house. It was followed by a feminine shriek, another crash, and then a cacophony of angry voices, slamming doors, and pounding footsteps.

Within seconds, a shaggy gray beast with gleaming white teeth tore into the foyer. It reared up and planted two hulking paws on Samuel's chest, knocking him back a solid foot. Samuel stumbled to the left, the beast slipped, stumbled to the right, and slammed into the side table, sending the hat and gloves toppling to the floor, along with an expensive vase that shattered against the tiles.

Undeterred, the beast gathered itself and launched a second attack.

"Off, you sodding beast! Off—" Samuel was forced to snap his mouth shut when a great, wet plank of a tongue lapped at his face.

Swearing silently, he threw an arm around the animal's shoulders and managed to wrestle it to the ground just as a young maid came hurrying into the room carrying a lead. "I'm sorry, sir. I'm sorry. He got away from me."

Samuel scrubbed his sleeve over his face as the girl struggled to slip the lead around what was, at best guess, an ill-advised cross between your average Irish wolfhound and an exuberant hippopotamus. "Quite all right, Sarah."

Sarah dodged a series of desperately happy tongue laps. "Gor, it's like wrestling a ship of the line." She dipped her hand in her apron pocket and pulled out a sizable chunk of bread. "Here now, beastie. Look what I have. Look. Wouldn't you like a taste of this?"

The beastie would, indeed. He ceased his squirming and gobbled up the treat while Sarah attached the lead. "There we are, nothing to it."

Brushing off his trousers, Samuel gained his feet and discovered his stout, silvered-haired housekeeper, Mrs. Lanchor, glaring at him from the across the foyer. "Sir Samuel, this animal is out of control."

He spat out a piece of dog hair as discreetly as possible. "He's just excitable."

"A Pekingese is excitable. This dog is deranged."

Samuel glanced down at the wild, gleeful amber eyes and lolling tongue. A thick glob of food-laden slobber gathered at the edge of the dog's mouth, then made a slow but steady descent toward the floor. Mrs. Lanchor could be right. "He's young, and this is all new to him yet."

"He has been here two weeks."

Was that all? He looked at the jagged remains of the vase. The second in four days. "He'll calm with age. Take him into the garden."

"With age?" Mrs. Lanchor planted her hands on her hips. "We cannot have this sort of nonsense going on for years. What if you'd had a guest with you? What if he leaps upon a young lady? What if—?"

"I'll continue to work with him. The garden, please, Mrs. Lanchor," he repeated as he headed for the stairs. "I'm in a hurry."

He pretended not to hear Mrs. Lanchor's final, dire warnings on the perils of keeping dangerous animals in one's home.

The dog was undisciplined, not a danger. Well, not the sort of danger she was implying. Besides, this wasn't his home. It was merely a house Renderwell had insisted he buy. It was where he ate, slept, and sometimes worked, but it was not his home.

He had a modest country house in Cheshire decorated in the comfortable style he preferred—lots of dark colors and solid furniture. It had a generous garden and plenty of land on which to roam. That was where he felt most at home, and where he had been spending more and more of his time lately. Particularly since Renderwell had taken up permanent residence at Greenly House in Derbyshire, a mere twenty miles away.

Maybe he'd retire, as Renderwell had last year. He had more than enough funds to live on comfortably for the rest of his life. Gabriel could buy out his portion of the business, if he liked.

He could take his staff to Cheshire permanently. Mrs. Lanchor was fond of the area. She'd grown up in nearby village. And the beast would enjoy the space, the freedom. It wasn't fair to confine a dog of that size to a garden with the diameter of a dinner plate.

Yes, maybe he would retire.

Maybe…if he survived the next twelve hours with Esther Walker-Bales.

୨ଚ

Five minutes later, Samuel tossed a valise onto the carriage floor and took his seat across from Esther.

Eleven hours, fifty-five minutes to go.

She scowled at the bag at her feet. "What is that?"

Assuming the question was rhetorical—anyone could see it was a valise—he didn't bother with an answer.

She rolled her eyes and huffed. "Where are you going, Samuel?"

"To your hotel."

"To…? No. You cannot stay with me. That is worse than me staying with you."

"I'll obtain my own rooms." Next to hers, if he could manage it. He wondered if he should try for adjoining rooms, or if that would be *indecent*.

"People will see if you come knocking on my door."

He shrugged. "People will assume I desire a word with my sister."

"You cannot tell the hotel I'm your sister. You don't have a sister."

"I do tonight."

She cast her gaze up as if to beg for patience. "Samuel, be reasonable. Everyone in London knows who you are, and everyone knows you do not have a sister."

"I'm not as famous as you seem to think."

"Yes, you are. Lottie said you and Gabriel and Renderwell became tremendous sensations for rescuing Lady Strale."

"It was a decade ago," he said. In truth, it had scarcely been more than nine years, but a decade sounded better.

Esther seemed to think so, as well. "People still recognize you, I'm sure."

"I'm not being stopped in the street by strangers." Not anymore. Thank God.

"The concierge will recognize your name at the very least."

"I'll use an alias."

"And if he recognizes you on sight?" she asked. "He'll know you're lying."

"He will assume I've either taken on a widow as a client who prefers to conduct business in secrecy, or…"

"Or what?" she asked warily.

He probably shouldn't have mentioned the *or*. "Or he will assume I have taken on a widow who prefers to conduct a different sort of business in secrecy."

"Oh *God*."

"It's a hotel. It won't shock him. And your family will be satisfied if we have separate rooms." They had damned well better be.

"It will draw attention to me."

"You drew attention to yourself in coming to London."

"I am aware of the risks," she snapped. "I have taken every precaution—"

"The best precaution would have been to stay out of London."

She pressed her lips together in frustration. "We will not agree on this."

"No."

He didn't expect that to stop her. Esther struck him as the kind of woman who would argue with an empty room until she was blue in the face. He was a little surprised, then, when she sat back against the bench cushions, crossed her arms over her chest, and flatly refused to say another word.

Very well, if she wanted to pout for the duration of their carriage ride, she could pout. They'd discuss her trip to London, and her immediate return to Derbyshire, once they reached the hotel.

❧

Esther wasn't pouting. She was thinking. And also ignoring Samuel, but only because that made it easier to think.

More than anything right now, she needed to be sensible. She had planned the trip to London with extraordinary care, paying meticulous attention to every detail. If she let her temper get the better of her now, all that hard work and preparation might come to nothing.

Yes, Samuel was a presumptuous, maddening, dictatorial arse.

No, she would not boot him from a moving carriage. Or, more realistically, give him the slip when they reached the hotel.

It would be tantamount to cutting off her nose to spite her face. Because, despite all that careful planning, things had spiraled out of control rather quickly in London. And Samuel might be just the presumptuous arse she needed to set things right again.

For all his many, many unfavorable qualities, he remained a clever, well-connected gentleman accustomed to working in secrecy. And he was a man she could trust. Not unequivocally—she didn't trust any man unequivocally—but she was fairly confident that he was, in a general sense, a reasonably decent human being. It was more than could be said of most people.

Furthermore, she was stuck with him. She simply didn't have the time or resources to engage in a game of cat and mouse with the man. Trustworthy or not, welcomed or not, Samuel was staying. That being the case, he might as well be of some use.

She was putting the finishing touches on her plans of how best to utilize his presence when they reached the hotel. Esther allowed Samuel to assist her from the carriage but left him to secure rooms on his own. She had no interest in being subjected to the staff's knowing smirks.

Inside her own rooms, she yanked off the loathsome mourning bonnet and tossed it aside. She wished she could change out of the itchy crepe dress, as well, and into her soft cotton nightgown. It wasn't quite seven, but she would have given nearly anything just then to crawl into bed and sleep for a week.

Instead, she used the few moments of solitude to practice what she wanted to say to Samuel, then took a series of deep, steadying breaths to settle what remained of her temper.

When Samuel knocked softly on her door a few minutes later, she was ready to have a civil, rational conversation with the man.

"It's open," she called out.

Samuel locked the door behind him and gave her a look of reproof. "It shouldn't have been open."

"I knew you were coming."

He removed his hat and tossed it on a chair. "So you're talking to me now?"

"I wasn't being quiet to punish you." That had merely been a happy coincidence. "I needed to think."

"Fine. Now I need you to talk."

"Very well," she said but offered no other response. She would let him talk first. It would give him a sense of control, which every man desired, and it would give her a sense of what cards he might be holding.

He gestured toward the door. "I've ordered a meal for us."

Not a promising hand, Sir Samuel. "Thank you."

Then he gestured toward a set of armchairs. "Will you sit?"

"Thank you, no." If she sat and he didn't, it would put him in a position of power. He already towered over her by a solid foot, no point in making it three. "But you may sit, if you like."

"No." He caught his hands behind his back, the dark fabric of his coat pulling across broad, muscular shoulders, "To business, then. I've a compromise to offer, Esther."

Well, it appeared he had been making plans of his own. "I am all ears."

"If you will agree to leave London first thing tomorrow, I will promise to keep this little excursion a secret from your family."

And that, she thought, was why she trusted Samuel, and even liked him on occasion. Another man would continue to demand to know, first and foremost, what she was doing in London. Samuel sought first to secure her safety, and through compromise no less. Unfortunately, his approach did not meet her needs, but she appreciated his choice of priorities nonetheless.

"That is a reasonable offer," she returned, "but I'm afraid there is no benefit in it for me. I have every intention of informing Lottie of my trip upon my return."

"Have you?"

"Of course. The purpose of my secrecy is not to deceive my family. It is to keep them from worry, which they'll not do once I am safely back in Derbyshire." She held up a hand when it looked as if he might argue. "I have another suggestion." One she had worked out during the long, silent carriage ride. "I will allow you to aid me in my purpose in coming to London, thereby speeding its conclusion. In exchange, you will promise not to send word to my family or Sir Gabriel or Lord Renderwell that I am currently in London."

"Gabriel will be back in town in a little over two days."

"Well, with any luck, my business will be done by

then." Oh, she hoped she would be that lucky. She liked Samuel's fellow private investigator, Gabriel, even more than she liked Samuel, but she trusted him far less.

"What is your business?"

"Promise first."

He shook his head. "Tell me what you are doing in London and who the young man we saw today is, and I will consider keeping your confidence while you're here."

"That is not—"

"I'll make no promises until I know what sort of danger you're facing."

Damn it, she would have to compromise on the compromise. "I don't know who he is. I don't," she insisted when he growled at her. Again. "I've no idea. I... Here. Look." She retrieved her chatelaine bag from the bed and pulled out a small, torn piece of paper which she handed to Samuel.

He read the short note in silence.

I know who you are. Meet Wed. Pddy Sta. 6pm. Come alone. Bring 10p.

It was rather funny to watch his expression jump from grim to befuddled. "Ten pence? Ten *pence*?"

"It is most odd," she agreed.

"What sort of blackmail is ten pence?"

"Perhaps he meant pounds," she ventured, then shrugged when he gave her a dubious look. "It is as good a theory as any you've offered."

He held up the note. "Was this sent to your rooms?"

"No, it was handed to me by a young boy in Spitalfields."

"Spitalfields?" He dropped his hand. "You went to *Spitalfields*? You idiot."

Oh, he *did* make it hard to be civil. "I am not an idiot."

"You went to Spitalfields," he repeated, very slowly, as if she was, perhaps, too much of an idiot to understand why he thought her an idiot. "Realm of rookeries and flash houses. Home to footpads and cutthroats and—"

"And people like me," she finished for him.

"You are not—"

"I was born in Spitalfields."

That seemed to bring him up short, but only briefly. "You may have been born there, but—"

"But I grew up in boardinghouses in places like Bethnal Green. Quite an improvement over the common lodging house of my infancy, I'm sure. We had a room, sometimes two to ourselves. Such luxury."

"I don't—"

"And when I was six, my father took us to Bath, where he swindled a small fortune from a young woman and used those ill-gotten gains to rent an entire house. We lived there for three months, until the young woman's brother came home from abroad, broke into our house, beat my father senseless, shot him in the leg, and gave Lottie three pounds to see the lot of us out of town. We came back to Spitalfields."

She paused, but he didn't try to speak, which was a little disappointing. She rather liked interrupting him. "It was several more years before my father became a proficient criminal. I was ten the last time we paid for lodgings in the East End."

And she'd been nineteen the last time she'd worked there with her father, but she didn't mention it.

She gave him a look of reproach. "How quick you are to remind me of my filthy origins when it suits your purpose, and how easily you forget when it does not."

"I didn't mention your origins. You did."

"I…" Oh. Right. She had. She was, perhaps, a mite touchy about her sordid past. Particularly in the company of someone like Samuel, whose pristine beginnings made her own seem even shabbier by comparison. But Samuel was not wholly without blame.

"You assumed I was waiting for a mark or an accomplice at the station," she pointed out. And he'd been worried she might stab him in the carriage. That had cut to the quick. Years ago, she had flashed her blades at a few of her father's more unpredictable cohorts because he had asked it of her. She'd been a foolish young woman then. She wasn't a monster now.

"I didn't assume," Samuel retorted. "I merely asked. And for what it's worth, I didn't know of your origins."

Frowning, she retrieved the note from his hand. "How could you not?"

"Your father's early career and whereabouts were always a mystery."

"Renderwell must know by now." As far as Esther could tell, Lottie told her husband every damned thing.

"Probably. He's never mentioned it." He studied her a moment, his expression one of idle curiosity. "You have the speech and manners of a lady of breeding."

She didn't mind curiosity, so long as it wasn't a

precursor for judgment and disdain. "My father's doing. It is difficult to swindle a class of people with whom you can't converse. Father was a great mimic, and he taught us well. He wouldn't allow anything but fine manners and speech under his roof. When we had one."

"It's an act?"

"No. I suppose it must have been, once," she admitted. "But by the time we went to Bath, the fine accent and manners were natural to me."

"Didn't your friends wonder at both?"

"I didn't have friends," she replied, a little surprised at the question. "Father kept us isolated regardless of our neighborhood. He had too many enemies. When interaction could not be avoided, we used an alias." And had learned early how to remember a fabricated family history. They had been the Oxleys, the Farrows, the Gutierrez family. Her father had quite enjoyed being Hernando Gutierrez, the dashing Spaniard who'd taken in his orphaned nieces and infant nephew. Lottie and Esther had been forced to call him Uncle Hernan for months. "I thought you knew all this as well."

"I knew that to be the case when your father worked for us." He tipped his head at her. "I didn't know you'd always been alone."

"I wasn't alone. I had Lottie. And later Peter." And she didn't like the way he was looking at her. As if he pitied her. What was that, but another kind of insult? "We are quite off topic. I am not an idiot for having gone to Spitalfields."

"Anyone who goes into places like Spitalfields when they have a choice otherwise, is an idiot."

"That is unfair. There are decent, honest, hard-working people who live there."

"A great many. But their combined innocence does not render the cutthroats less vicious. What were you doing there?"

She shook her head. A compromise went both ways. "I'll have your promise first."

Samuel rubbed his chin with the back of his hand in a thoughtful manner. "If I agree to help you with your business, then you must agree that I am in charge of that business, and you, for as long as you are in London."

"No." *Good Lord, no.* She couldn't believe he'd even suggest such a thing. Either he was jesting, or he was testing her, or she had significantly overestimated his intelligence.

"Esther—"

"I'll not take orders from you." She didn't take orders from anyone. "You may give orders, if you like, but I'll not promise to follow them."

"Orders that don't have to be followed are called suggestions," he replied in a bland tone.

"Then I shall agree to take your suggestions under advisement."

About the Author

Alissa Johnson is a RITA-nominated author of historical romance. She grew up on air force bases and attended St. Olaf College in Minnesota. She currently resides in the Arkansan Ozarks, where she spends her free time keeping her Aussie dog busy, visiting with family, and dabbling in archery. Visit her at www.alissajohnson.com.